P9-CAA-152

Praise for the novels of Anne Gracie

An Honorable Thief

"She's turned out another wonderful story!"
— *All About Romance*

"A true find and definitely a keeper." — *A Romance Review*

"A thoroughly marvelous heroine." — *The Best Reviews*

"Dazzling characterizations . . . provocative, tantalizing, and wonderfully witty romantic fiction . . . Unexpected plot twists, tongue-in-cheek humor, and a sensually fraught battle of wits between hero and heroine . . . embraces the romance genre's truest heart." — *Heartstrings*

How the Sheriff Was Won

"Anne Gracie provide[s] pleasant diversions."
— *Midwest Book Review*

continued . . .

Tallie's Knight

"Gracie combines an impeccable knowledge of history, an ability to create vibrant and attractive characters, and an excellent storytelling ability. *Tallie's Knight* is far and away the best Regency romance I have read in a long time."
— *The Romance Reader*

"Gracie's writing style is charming and wonderful and the love scenes are very sensual . . . a special book with excellent writing and characters that touch the heart."
— *All About Romance*

Gallant Waif

"A great heroine . . . This is as polished a piece of romance writing as anyone could want." — *The Romance Reader*

"I loved everything about it." — *All About Romance*

The Virtuous Widow

"A wonderful, warm, emotionally stirring Christmas story of love found, wishes fulfilled, and promises kept."
— *Romantic Times*

THE
Perfect
Rake

Anne Gracie

BERKLEY SENSATION, NEW YORK

THE BERKLEY PUBLISHING GROUP
Published by the Penguin Group
Penguin Group (USA) Inc.
375 Hudson Street, New York, New York, 10014, USA
Penguin Group (Canada), 90 Eglinton Avenue East, Suite 700, Toronto, Ontario M4P 2Y3, Canada
(a division of Pearson Penguin Canada Inc.)
Penguin Books Ltd., 80 Strand, London WC2R 0RL, England
Penguin Group Ireland, 25 St. Stephen's Green, Dublin 2, Ireland (a division of Penguin Books Ltd.)
Penguin Group (Australia), 250 Camberwell Road, Camberwell, Victoria 3124, Australia
(a division of Pearson Australia Group Pty. Ltd.)
Penguin Books India Pvt. Ltd., 11 Community Centre, Panchsheel Park, New Delhi—110 017, India
Penguin Group (NZ), Cnr. Airborne and Rosedale Roads, Albany, Auckland 1310, New Zealand
(a division of Pearson New Zealand Ltd.)
Penguin Books (South Africa) (Pty.) Ltd., 24 Sturdee Avenue, Rosebank, Johannesburg 2196,
South Africa

Penguin Books Ltd., Registered Offices: 80 Strand, London WC2R 0RL, England

This is a work of fiction. Names, characters, places, and incidents either are the product of the author's
imagination or are used fictitiously, and any resemblance to actual persons, living or dead, business
establishments, events, or locales is entirely coincidental. The publisher does not have any control
over and does not assume any responsibility for author or third-party websites or their content.

THE PERFECT RAKE

A Berkley Sensation Book / published by arrangement with the author

PRINTING HISTORY
Berkley Sensation edition / July 2005

Copyright © 2005 by Anne Gracie.
Cover art by Tim Barrall.
Cover design by George Long.
Interior text design by Kristin del Rosario.

All rights reserved.
No part of this book may be reproduced, scanned, or distributed in any printed or electronic form
without permission. Please do not participate in or encourage piracy of copyrighted materials in
violation of the author's rights. Purchase only authorized editions.
For information address: The Berkley Publishing Group,
a division of Penguin Group (USA), Inc.,
375 Hudson Street, New York, New York 10014.

ISBN: 978-0-425-20395-8

BERKLEY® SENSATION
Berkley Sensation Books are published by The Berkley Publishing Group,
a division of Penguin Group (USA) Inc.,
375 Hudson Street, New York, New York 10014.
BERKLEY SENSATION and the "B" design are trademarks belonging to Penguin Group (USA)
Inc.

PRINTED IN THE UNITED STATES OF AMERICA

10

If you purchased this book without a cover, you should be aware that this book is stolen property. It was
reported as "unsold and destroyed" to the publisher, and neither the author nor the publisher has
received any payment for this "stripped book."

This book is dedicated to
Marion Lenox, Sophie Weston, and Alison Reynolds—
wonderful writers and generous friends—
with my heartfelt thanks.

And for all those who've waited patiently
for "B.G." to arrive.

Chapter One

∞

"It is not in the stars to hold our destiny but in ourselves."
WILLIAM SHAKESPEARE

"PRUE! PRUE! COME QUICKLY. HE IS BEATING GRACE IN THE ATTIC!" Seventeen-year-old Hope burst furiously into the room. Her twin, Faith, followed, her eyes huge with distress.

Prudence Merridew leaped up from the household accounts, her dropped pen scattering blobs of ink unheeded across the page. She dashed from the room, her sisters at her heels.

"What set him off this time?" Prudence flung over her shoulder.

"I don't know. Charity said he found her in the attic making a gift for your birthday," Hope panted.

"Charity tried to stop him," Faith interjected. "But he hit her."

Her twin added, "I wanted to go up and try, too, but I could not get this undone in time." She gestured to her left wrist. It still bore rope marks. "Besides, he's locked the door. Charity said to fetch you and the keys."

"Yes, I have them. James! James!" Prudence called for their stalwart young footman. She raced upstairs, taking the steps two at a time, knowing he would follow. By the second flight he caught up with the two girls.

"Lord Dereham is beating Grace in the attic. Hurry!" Prudence urged. They reached the third landing and turned to the narrower flight that led to the servants' quarters and, beyond that, the attic. Nineteen-year-old Charity sat on the stairs, sobbing, one hand cupped against her cheek.

"Oh, Prue, I tried . . ."

Prudence gently lifted her sister's hand. Two livid red weals marred the purity of Charity's pale complexion. Prudence bit her lip. Charity was the gentlest creature!

"It was very brave of you to try, love."

She glanced at Faith, the timid sister. She was shaking like a leaf but she'd still come prepared to brave Grandpapa in a rage. "Faith, take Charity to my bedchamber. Get salve and liniment from Mrs. Burton. Charity, off you go and get that cheek seen to. And make things ready for Grace."

The two girls crept back down the stairs. Prudence called after them, "As soon as Grace and Hope arrive, lock the door. Don't open it to anyone except me."

Prudence resumed the race up the stairs. As they reached the last landing, she paused. "We shall enter silently, then I will rush at him. At the same time James will snatch Miss Grace and take her to safety."

"You can count on me, Miss Prue," the tall young footman responded grimly.

Prue nodded. "I know. I do not know what will come of this day's work, but I'll see you right, James, I promise."

"But Prue, he's mad with rage!" Hope exclaimed. "He'll beat you, too."

"Aye, Miss Prue, better I tackle him." James had a militant light in his eye. "I'm bigger 'n you."

"No, he'd have you transported or hanged! If he hits me, I'll hit him back!" Prue fiercely responded. "I've had enough of his vile rages and his bullying ways. I am almost one and twenty, and when I come of age—" She broke off. They had reached the attic door. She lowered her voice to a whisper.

"Hope, you must go with Grace to Faith's room. And stay there."

"No! I want to help. I hate him, Pru—"

"I know, love, but you can help more by taking Grace to safety and comforting her."

Hope opened her mouth to argue, but Prudence held up her hand for silence. She inserted the key, turned it, and opened the narrow, cupboard-like door to the attic. There was no need for stealth. Her grandfather was roaring, beyond any distraction of creaking hinges and the like. He was bent over a small, huddled shape.

"You filthy little heathen!" *Thwack!* "Rank obscenity!" *Thwack!* "Idolatrous blasphemy!" *Thwack!*

With each epithet, his sinewy old arm brought down his riding crop with as much force as he could muster. The crop whistled with each downward slice. Ten-year-old Grace was coiled into a tight ball on the floor, her hands clasped protectively over her head, making herself as small as possible.

Prudence shot across the room like a small, furious cannonball. "Leave my sister alone, you great filthy bully!" She hurled herself against him, shoving with all her might, for she was not a large person. Her grandfather might be well past sixty, but he was six feet tall, his body strong and lean from hunting, shooting, and fishing.

And from beating little girls.

He staggered, caught off balance. Prudence took advantage of his momentary unsteadiness and pushed him again, hard. He tripped over a trunk from which old clothes spilled—Grace and the twins' dress-up clothes—and lay for a moment, gasping, sprawled among faded brocade and moth-eaten lace.

Obedient to his orders, James scooped Grace up and strode from the room. Hope hesitated.

"Go!" Prudence hissed at her. "Quickly!" She went.

In a surge of old gowns, her grandfather staggered to his feet. His face was purple with rage. Veins stood out at his neck and temple. Spittle foamed at his mouth. "Brazen-faced little bitch! I'll teach you!" Grasping his riding crop he strode toward Prudence.

She flung him a contemptuous look. "How dare you use that disgusting weapon on a child!" she spat.

"That little hellcat was engaged in filthy, idolatrous evil, and I'll scourge her of it if it's the last thing I do!"

Filthy, idolatrous evil? Prudence glanced at the three-legged table where Grace had been working in secret. On it lay a pasteboard reticule and several of the old magazines passed on in secret to the girls by their neighbor, Mrs. Otterbury. At the time, they had all exclaimed over the Egyptian designs in one of the magazines—strange and fanciful creatures like the Sphinx and others, half animal and half human.

A shard of guilt pierced Prudence as she recalled how she'd admired the Egyptian designs. Grace had used them to decorate the pasteboard reticule, these "idolatrous and evil" pictures. Her little sister had been beaten for making Prudence a gift for her birthday.

"It is *not* filthy idolatry—it is merely a whimsy of fashion. Grace is just a child. Those designs are simply attractive curiosities to her!"

"They are blasphemous and that . . . that *thing* she created bears the taint of the Devil. It must be burned, and she must be cleansed. I'll thrash the evil out of her if it's the last thing I do!" He knocked the magazines and reticule to the floor.

Prudence darted in and snatched the battered reticule to her breast. "There is not a *shred* of evil in Grace. She is a dear sweet child and—"

"She bears the stamp of Jezebel! As do you!"

Prudence dashed her fiery curls from her eyes. "It is not the stamp of Jezebel! It is simply *hair,* Grandpapa! Grace and I cannot help its color! Our mother had red hair."

The old man let out a growl of rage and sliced at Prudence with his whip. "I forbade you to mention that harlot under my roof! She was a shameless Jezebel who enticed my son away from me, and you and that other she-cub bear her mark! I may not have beaten the evil out of you, yet, but I'll make sure—"

Prudence interrupted. "If you lay so much as a finger on Grace or Hope—or any of my sisters—ever again . . . I'll, I'll *kill* you! Hope cannot help being left-handed and Grace's and my hair is just an excuse! You are nothing but a despicable bully and I'll have no more of it, do you hear?"

"Insolent baggage!" roared the old man. "I am your legal

guardian and I'll have respect and obedience from you—the way your sisters respect me—if I have to thrash you within an inch of your life!"

"Hah!" Prudence's voice was filled with scorn. "Respect does not come from beatings, Grandpapa; it must be earned! You see my sisters' meek obedience as respect, but you command only fear and hatred in them. In me you command *nothing!*"

He lunged and caught her a vicious blow across the face. Prudence reeled back, clutching her cheek. Blood stained her fingers. He eyed the blood with satisfaction. "We'll see if you sing the same tune when I've finished with you. A disobedient bitch always cowers after a good thrashing."

"I'm not a setter or a beagle, Grandpapa! You can't make me cower the way you did when I was a child. And I'll tell you to your face, the thrashings have come to an end. In eight weeks' time I shall turn one and twenty, and then *I* shall have the legal guardianship of my sisters. You cannot prevent it. Papa's will made it so."

He leaned briefly against a broken table, huffing and puffing from his recent exertion. The purple color faded slowly from his face. "Oh, can I not?" he said. "You may have the legal guardianship, girlie, but I still control the purse strings until you marry." He chuckled, a dry, rasping wheeze. "You'll none of you get a penny unless you wed, and I'll ensure you will not wed!" His thin lips curled in a sneer. "You may cherish your sisters to your heart's content, missy, but you'll starve without a penny to your name!"

"Maybe I don't have a penny at the moment, but I have resources you know nothing about. Once I am of age, we will leave this place, and you will not be able to stop us."

Prudence felt a small surge of satisfaction. He'd taken most of her mother's jewelry years ago, when they'd first come to Dereham Court, but the eleven-year-old, newly orphaned Prudence had been too sentimental to hand her Mama's favorite pieces over to the grim old man who demanded them. She'd held a few precious pieces back, and kept them hidden all these years. The jewels would be the saving of them now.

"Harlot! Sell your body, would you? It does not surprise

me! But you will not escape to shame this family so!" He came storming forward in a fresh surge of rage. Prudence ran for the door and hurried down the steep, narrow stairs as fast as she could.

Behind her came Grandpapa, crashing and cursing her, swiping at her with every step. The whip lashed her more than once, and as she reached the narrow landing, she tripped on her skirt and fell to her knees.

He came roaring down the last steps in triumph, but in his haste he stumbled, lurching forward in an avalanche of curses, his whip flailing. Prudence ducked aside as, carried forward by the momentum of his rush, her grandfather careered down the steps past her, tripping and rolling and crashing.

His fall was broken, eventually, by the curve of the rails where the stairs turned.

The house was suddenly, shockingly silent.

Prudence hurried upstairs to her bedchamber. "It's me, Hope. Open the door."

The door creaked open. Hope peered out. "Prudence! Your face! Did he do that?"

Prudence touched a tentative finger to her face. In all the drama she'd forgotten the cut on her cheek. "Don't worry, it probably looks worse than it is. How is Grace?"

Hope gestured to the bed, where Charity and Faith were sitting, their arms around Grace, who was huddled in a hard little knot, hugging her knees, her face quite hidden. The arms wrapped around the knees were covered in ugly red welts. Sobs shook her thin body.

Prudence slipped onto the bed and put an arm around the tense, hunched body. "Graciela?" It was their mother's pet name for her.

Grace looked up and her pale, tear-streaked face crumpled anew as she saw her oldest sister's injured face and worried eyes. She hurled herself into Prudence's arms. "Oh, Prue, Prue, he hurt you, too. I'm sorry, I'm sorry."

Prudence felt a surge of anger at the man who had saturated a young girl's life with such guilt that Grace would blame herself for Prudence's injury. She forced herself to speak lightly. "Don't be sorry, love. It doesn't hurt a bit, I promise you. Grandpapa got much the worst of it. He's in no state to hurt any of us now."

That caused them all to sit up. "What do you mean?" asked Faith.

"He tripped and fell down the stairs." She shivered. Her mind still held the sound of flesh and bone crashing down the stairs, against the wall. And that sudden silence . . .

Hope was the first to speak. "Is he dead?"

"No, though I thought—we all thought—for a moment that he was. He lay there, not moving, for the longest time. Everyone just stared, for all the servants had come running." She took a deep, shaky breath. "But he was not, of course. You know what a hard head Grandpapa has."

"Pity," Hope muttered.

"He's been carried to his bedchamber, and Dr. Gibson is with him now. He won't touch any of us again, I promise."

There was a long silence in the room. None of her sisters believed Prudence could keep such a promise. They knew empty comfort when they heard it. Grace's face crumpled afresh and she turned back to her big sister's arms. "Oh, Prue, why does he hate me so?" she sobbed.

Prudence hugged her little sister to her. "Oh, darling, he confuses you and me with our mother. Because we have the same red hair that she did. "

"Was Mama so very bad, then?"

"No! She wasn't bad *at all!* It's just that when Papa fell in love with her, he left the Court and he never came back, so Grandpapa never forgave her."

"Tell us about Mama and Papa again, Prue," Grace said, leaning into her.

Their parents had died when Grace was just a baby. The twins, too, had been very small. Charity had been nine when Mama had died, Prudence, eleven. The young ones had few memories of their parents and it comforted them to hear the tales, over and over.

"Mama was very beautiful. You all take after her. Charity is her image, except for the golden hair. And you twins and Grace look so much like her, too. You all take after Mama's side of the family—the beautiful Ainsleys." She pulled a wry face. "I was the poor unfortunate to be saddled with the horrid Merridew nose and the horrid Merridew eyes. I just wish I had the Merridew height and thinness, too."

"Your nose isn't horrid, exactly, it's just . . . a little long," Faith said.

"It's a very nice nose," Grace defended her hotly, "and your eyes are lovely and gray and kind and—"

"Oh hush," Prudence said, laughing a little. She gathered her sisters around her on the bed. "I don't care about my silly old nose. We were speaking of Mama, anyway."

Her voice adopted the singsong quality of a beloved tale, oft repeated. "Mama was a great beauty, though her family was in trade, and Papa took one look at her and fell instantly in love. And although she had hundreds of admirers, and he was by no means the handsomest, nor the richest, nor the one with the grandest title, Mama fell instantly in love with him, too." All five girls sighed, blissfully.

"But both the Ainsleys and the Merridews opposed the match," prompted Grace, "and that is why Mama and Papa ran away to Italy and got married and had us. Keep going, Prue. Tell us about Mama's hair."

Prue wriggled back against the pillows. Her sisters drew closer; Grace snuggled like a kitten at her side. "Mama was golden, all golden," she said. "Her hair was red, but it was like it had just come out of the smithy's furnace—all red and gold and full of life—like yours, Grace. And Papa loved Mama's hair—I want you to remember that, Grace, whenever you think your hair is bad or ugly! Papa was always playing with Mama's hair, stroking it, loving the way it would curl around his fingers. He used to joke that Mama wound him 'round her little finger, just the same way. And one day you will find a man who loves you, and your hair, the same way Papa loved Mama."

Grace sighed. "The way Phillip loves you?"

Prudence smiled and smoothed back her little sister's curls. "Maybe." She continued, "It wasn't only Mama's looks that were golden—she had the most wonderful, soft voice, like honey, like Faith's voice. She would sing to us all for hours. And when she laughed it was like the music of sunlight—"

"I remember her laugh," said Charity suddenly. "So happy. It made me want to laugh with her."

"You did, too," agreed Prudence. "We all did. Mama and Papa adored each other. They were always touching each other, holding hands, kissing, hugging, laughing . . ."

All the sisters sighed. It was a far cry from the cold and loveless regime they'd grown up under.

"And they loved us all, too, so very much. Papa was always picking us up for a cuddle and a kiss and he never cared about sticky fingers or grubby faces. Mama always carried the baby—that was you, Grace—with us when we went walking along the beach or through the village, even though Concetta—she was your nursemaid—said it was bad for a baby to be outside. Mama said she wanted all her little sunbeams with her . . ."

She looked at her sisters squeezed together on the big, old bed. They didn't look much like sunbeams in the chill gray light, their faces pinched and pale and their beautiful eyes still red-rimmed from weeping. Love was their birthright. Mama had promised. Prudence had to make them believe it, she just had to!

"Never, ever forget that we do not belong in Grandpapa's grim and loveless world," she said. "We were all born in Italy, in a house filled with sunshine and laughter and love and happiness, and I *promise* you, no matter how bad it seems, one day we shall all live like that again. With sunshine and laughter and love and happiness. *I promise!*"

Outside, the bitter wind whistled around the eaves, as if mocking her words. Prudence ignored it. She had a plan.

Dr. Gibson placed his bag on the side table and sat down. "Lord Dereham has a severe concussion, and his ankle is broken in several places."

Prudence poured him a cup of tea. "But he will recover?" She might despise her grandfather, but she didn't want to be the cause of his death.

Dr. Gibson sipped the hot tea cautiously, then said, "His injuries are quite severe, but I believe his faculties to be intact. I feel certain he will recover, though it may not be speedy."

"How long will it take?" Prudence leaned forward and passed him a plate of buttered scones. She had a particular reason for asking.

It was wild. It was audacious. It was risky. But it might work.

It was the only solution she could think of to their problems.

The doctor munched on a gingernut. "The head injury will take a few days, possibly a week. He will need to lie in a darkened room, in absolute silence." He sipped at his tea and added, "The ankle will take longer to heal, however. It is broken in several places. He will have to keep his leg immobilized for six or seven weeks at the very least."

Six or seven weeks! Prudence hugged the knowledge to her breast. Six weeks or more would make all the difference in the world to her plan. But she would need the doctor's help. She set her cup aside, took a deep breath, and said, "Dr. Gibson, do you know how Grandpapa's accident came about?"

He sniffed and reached for another gingernut. "The groom who fetched me told me some wild tale but you know how servants are apt to exaggerate."

"I doubt he exaggerated. Have you not heard how severe my grandfather's rages—"

The doctor waved his hand. "Bah! I hope I know better than to listen to village gossip."

"The tales are true," Prue said vehemently, "and we cannot go on like this. Can you not see for yourself how very . . . *extreme* Grandpapa has become?"

"He has never been one to spare the rod, I grant you, but a man must be strict—"

"Strict! It is more than that, I promise you. Poor Hope has spent most of her life with her left hand tied behind her back to prevent her using it—he says it is the devil's hand. Faith lives in fear of inadvertently humming under her breath, for that would merit a beating. And you should see how he regards my little sister Grace. He is convinced she bears the stamp of Jezebel, all because of the color of her hair."

The doctor's gaze strayed to Prudence's own fiery locks, and she nodded. "Yes, me too. He has tried to thrash the evil out of me since I was eleven." Prudence's voice shook with distress and anger. "And I will *not* have it—do you understand? He shall *not* thrash my little sister the way he thrashed me."

The doctor shifted uneasily in his chair. "Hope's left-handedness needs to be corrected, though I can see it distresses you. But Faith and Grace are such quiet, good little souls."

"Grace made this." She thrust the Egyptian-style reticule toward him.

Bemused, the doctor took the decorated reticule. "This Egyptian stuff was all the rage in London some years ago. I know, for my wife was mad for it, too."

"Is your wife a filthy heathen?" asked Prudence bluntly. "Given to idolatry? Blasphemy? Filth? Rank obscenity?"

The doctor looked taken aback. "What the—"

"Because that's what Grandpapa called Grace for making this—a *filthy little heathen*. And he beat her unmercifully with his whip until I stopped him. That's how the accident happened. He was chasing me down the stairs. With his whip. Luckily for me, he tripped."

The doctor put the reticule down, his composure shaken. "He beat her for making this?"

"Severely. He seizes on any excuse. I want you to help us leave here."

The doctor sighed heavily. "Prudence, you know I cannot. He's not an easy man, I grant you, but I'm his doctor, girl! Do you expect me to look him in the eye and lie to him? Deceive him—"

"Little Grace's body is covered with red welts simply because she made that reticule," Prudence said with quiet emphasis. She was determined to stir his conscience to action and force him to face the truth now. Grace had always been his favorite. "It is not the first time Grace has been severely beaten for no good reason. He beats all of us. We have never been allowed to call you when he has injured one of us before, but I want you to come up to her bedchamber and see for yourself."

With a heavy sigh, he put down his cup. "Very well, I'll take a look, but I make you no promises."

The doctor examined Grace in grim silence. He noted the weals on Charity's face, and those on Prudence's. Afterward, in the room downstairs, he sat heavily in his chair, clearly shaken. "I'm sorry. I had no idea. And you say this is not the first time?"

Prudence nodded. There was no point in dwelling on the past. She had her eyes firmly fixed on the future. "When I turn one and twenty, in eight weeks' time, by my father's will I shall become my sisters' legal guardian."

"Well then—"

"However, we can only gain access to the money our mother left us when we marry. We have no money. Only enough for a few months. After that, unless Grandpapa gives us our inheritance, we will starve." She fixed the doctor with a look. "He will not give us the money. He says he will *never* let any of us marry. On that point he is adamant.

"We go nowhere, not even to church anymore. We see no one. And no one sees us. How can any of us marry? Yet, you know how beautiful my sisters are, what a crime it is to shut them away from society." Prudence scanned his face, trying to gauge whether his conscience was well and truly stirred. She took his hand and said, "Dr. Gibson, we *must* escape. We have been given this small piece of time, while he is confined to his bedchamber, as if it is meant to be. But if Grandpapa is not to discover it immediately, you *have* to help us."

The doctor sighed heavily. "What do you want me to do?" It was capitulation.

Prue frowned over the words she had penned with a critical eye. The crabbed copperplate script looked just right. Perhaps a shade less flamboyance in the loops and a more precise dotting of the *i*. Grandpapa always dotted each *i* very precisely.

"Has the doctor gone? What did he say?" Prudence's sisters entered the room.

Charity peered over her shoulder. "Who are you writing to? Phillip, again?"

"No, not Phill—"

"Oh, who cares about Phillip?" interrupted Hope.

"You're always writing to him. What did Dr. Gibson say about Grandpapa?"

"The letter is not to Phillip." Prudence blotted the ink carefully. "It's to Great-uncle Oswald."

"Great-uncle Oswald?" Hope exclaimed in amazement. "Grandpapa's wicked brother?" She frowned. "Is Grandpapa going to die, after all?"

"No, he should recover in about six or seven weeks."

"Then why are you writing to Great-uncle Oswald?" Charity asked. "He won't want to comfort Grandpapa on his sickbed. There is no brotherly love between them at all."

"I am counting on it," said Prue. "As for why *I* am writing to him, *I* am not. This letter is from Grandpapa."

"Whaaat?" came a chorus of voices.

She read,

> *"My Dear Oswald,*
> *I know we have not always seen eye to eye, as broth-*
> *ers surely should, however I am willing to let Bygones be*
> *Bygones for the sake of the Girls."*

In the stunned silence that followed, she lifted the letter between two fingers, waving it in the air to dry the ink. "In short, Grandpapa is asking his brother to give us a season in London. And find us husbands." She laid the letter down carefully. "We're escaping. We're never coming back to the Court!"

"Prudence!" Charity exclaimed. "That letter is worse than a fib. It's forgery!"

Prudence shrugged. "Yes, but what choice do we have? I am resolved that Grandpapa shall never lay a finger on any of us again."

"It's wicked, Prue," Faith whispered.

Prudence tossed her head. "Well, Grandpapa has always said I'm wicked, so at last I shall prove him right! We are all going to London. And we are taking Lily and James with us; Lily because Great-uncle Oswald is a widower and may have no maidservants, and James because Grandpapa will never forgive him his part in this day's work."

Her sisters glanced at each other, stunned by the audacity

of the plan. Prudence carefully scribed Great-uncle Oswald's London address in a crabbed-looking copperplate.

"Grandpapa will never let us go," Hope said.

"He won't know. He'll think we've moved to the dower house—"

"That moldy old place! Why would—"

"Because by the time his headaches have subsided, Grace will have contracted scarlet fever and we shall all be in quarantine. Dr. Gibson is going to aid in the deception. You know what a horror Grandpapa has of infection. He won't come near us. Mrs. Burton said as housekeeper she could vouch for the cooperation of the other servants, and she and the doctor will give regular, albeit false, reports to Grandpapa of our progress."

Her sisters gaped.

"And in the meantime, we will stay with our great-uncle, see all the grand sights of the capital, go to parties, wear pretty dresses, and go to—oh, I don't know, Venetian breakfasts and things. Even attend the opera! And with any luck, by the time Grandpapa has recovered, one of us will have found a husband, and I shall have turned one and twenty, and you can all legally live with me."

"Parties and pretty dresses!" whispered Charity.

"What is a Venetian breakfast?" Grace asked.

"Who cares?" Hope said, shrugging. "It will not be a bowl of oatmeal, that's certain."

Faith sighed rapturously. "Oh how I would love to hear an opera."

"But how can we? We have no money, Prue," Hope, ever the practical one, said. "We have not even enough between us to get one of us to London."

"Mama's jewelery," Prudence explained. "Her garnet bracelet will fetch us enough to pay for tickets on the stage." She regarded her sisters a little guiltily. "In fact, I sold it months ago, for just such an eventuality."

"So we can go to London," breathed Charity.

"Yes indeed." Prudence smiled. "And if one of you can find herself a splendidly rich, handsome, kind, and loving husband, she wouldn't mind handing over her inheritance from Mama to support the rest of us, would she?"

"Oh, of course we would! It sounds heavenly, Prue. You might even find a handsome husband yourself," Hope added.

"Hope! Have you forgotten Phillip?" Charity looked shocked.

"Oh, yes, Phillip," Hope amended hastily. "To be sure, Phillip. How long is it since he last wrote, Prue?"

"Six months," Prudence said with dignity, "but you know how slow and unreliable the mails are from India. The voyage alone takes months and if a ship should founder and sink, bearing Phillip's letter . . ."

"Yes, yes. The mails are slow and very unreliable," Charity agreed. "But when he does reply—"

"I am sure he will come. And then he and I shall be married, and we shall all be safe at last." There was a short silence.

"Well, I shall not depend on Phillip," Hope announced. "I'm going to do my best to find a husband for myself in London. I want to go to a grand ball and wear a pretty dress instead of these horrid homemade ones. And I'm going to dance the waltz in the arms of a handsome man! I'm going to fall madly in love, just like Mama and Papa."

There was a small silence as the sisters considered the enormity of her aspirations.

Prudence was the first to recover. "Dance the *waltz,* Hope? Since none of us even know how to dance *at all,* we cannot be worrying about waltzes."

"I don't care. I don't know how it will happen, but somehow, some way, I *will* dance the waltz!" Hope declared mutinously.

"Perhaps you should put that in the letter, Prue—ask Great-uncle Oswald to get us a dancing instructor," Faith suggested.

Grace grimaced. "Then, silly, he would *really* know that this letter is a forgery. Can you imagine Grandpapa suggesting any such thing?"

Prudence grinned. "Grandpapa certainly won't ask Great-uncle Oswald to have us taught to dance, Faith. Listen to this:

"And, Brother, since Musick and Dancing are Abominations and the Work of the Devil, I must remind you to ensure the Girls are not Corrupted by exposure to such Evils while in Town. I have brought the girls up according to the most Stringently Correct Principles, and since they are Female and thus Foolish, Frivolous and Easily Led you must watch them carefully and not allow them to Stray."

"What!" gasped Hope. "Are you mad?"
Prudence winked and continued,

"Therefore, Brother, as Head of the Family, I utterly Forbid you to take my Granddaughters to Any form of Ball, Rout, Musickal evening or similar Wickedness. I merely wish you to ensure they find decent, Sober husbands of an Appropriate Station in Life with Solid Principles and a Good Fortune. Older heads would be most suitable—no young gadabouts."

"But that is terrible!" wailed Hope. "I don't want a stuffy old husband with solid principles—a young gadabout sounds lovely. One that's handsome and nice and young!"

"Me, too!" agreed Faith. "If you send that letter, Prue, you might as well just leave us here, to molder and be miserable with Grandpapa."

"And be beaten and tied up," Grace added dolefully.

"Stop talking like that, Grace," Prudence ordered. "I told you, no one will beat you again! And nobody is ever going to tie Hope's hand behind her back again! Now, trust me, all of you, and consider these points: Firstly"—she ticked the point off on her finger—"Great-uncle Oswald has lived in London for years, so he must like it there. And he hasn't been to Dereham Court since we've lived here, so obviously he doesn't like it here."

"Who does?" Hope muttered.

Prudence grinned and continued her list. "Secondly, we know from Phillip's mother that Great-uncle Oswald goes to the opera, is terribly fashionable, and goes to a great many parties. Thirdly, we also know that he had a great falling-out with Grandpapa and that Grandpapa calls him an irreligious dog and a frivolous fop and a great many other such insulting epithets."

"Old Cook says the young Master Oswald she remembers was kind and nice and good for a laugh," Charity objected.

"Exactly," Prudence said triumphantly. "If Great-uncle Oswald is half the man I think he is, he'll be so incensed at Grandpapa's instructions that he will positively hurl us into a sea of balls and parties and all kinds of frivolous wickedness, and let us meet lots of delightful young men—just to spite Grandpapa!"

All five sisters contemplated the notion. "If you are right, Prue, it would be wonderful," Charity whispered.

"It is bound to go wrong," Grace predicted gloomily. "Everything always does."

"Nonsense!" Prudence hugged her little sister. "Try to be positive, my love. I am certain I have thought of everything."

Chapter Two

∞

*"Oh what a tangled web we weave
When first we practice to deceive."*
Sir Walter Scott

"You said when we came to London we would be able go to parties, Prue!" Hope said in an aggrieved voice. "And to balls and routs and Venetian breakfasts!"

"And the opera!" added Faith plaintively.

"I know." Prudence winced. "But—"

"And you said I could dance the waltz with a handsome young man—"

Prudence winced again.

"At least we all have had dancing lessons—" Charity began.

"Pooh! Who cares for dancing lessons! Next you shall say Monsieur Lefarge is a handsome young man!" Hope declared scornfully.

All the sisters giggled, thinking of the fussy, mincing, middle-aged Frenchman whom Great-uncle Oswald had engaged to teach the Merridew girls their steps. But Hope was not to be distracted. "In five or six weeks, Grandpapa's ankle will have healed enough for him to leave his bedchamber, and then how long after that do you think it will take him to discover we have run away? One of us *must* find a husband before then, Prue, and so far the only person who has met a man—an eligible man—is you! And what good is an eligible man to you?"

"You said nothing would go wrong," Grace said, "but it has." She heaved a lugubrious sigh. "I said it would. It always does."

Silence fell in the back parlor that had been set aside for the young ladies' use while in London. Prudence slumped in her chair. It *had* gone wrong—and it was all her fault.

Great-uncle Oswald had lived up to every one of Prudence's hopeful expectations and more. He had been everything that was kind and avuncular. Far from expressing any reluctance to receive the five young females foisted on him with no warning, the elderly widower had welcomed his great-nieces into his large, elegant London home with every evidence of pleasure.

In some ways he had exceeded their most optimistic expectations. A man who even the most countrified and ignorant young ladies could see at a glance was a veritable pink of the ton, though rather elderly, he had taken one comprehensive and horrified glance at their plain, gray, homemade gowns and declared they must instantly have complete new wardrobes.

"For whilst I have not the slightest objection in the world to housin' you and takin' you about, I cannot and will not have my great-nieces—and such dashed pretty creatures you are!—goin' about dressed in such atrocious garments!" He shook his head. "Tomorrow I shall take you to visit mantua makers and milliners and glovers and haberdashers and the rest."

The girls' mouths had dropped open in amazement, accustomed as they were to Grandpapa's nip-farthing ways.

He had examined each astounded girl with the eye of an experienced man of fashion. "Such coloring, such exquisite complexions as you all have, and such bearin'—Charity, my dear, you are a diamond, positively celestial! That golden hair, those eyes. And the twins—divine, the pair of you—I daresay I will learn which of you is which, but really it doesn't matter, so stunnin' as you are! And even little Grace, buddin' fair to outshine your sisters, even yet. Oh, it will be a pleasure to see you all dressed as your beauty demands."

He'd rubbed his hands in satisfaction. "There'll be no trouble findin' husbands for you gels—I don't think it's exaggeratin' to expect some ducal interest . . . yes, a duke at least, to be sure, with such visions as you are." He'd beamed around at them. "I do not remember when four such lovely gels have ever come to London at the same time. And all in the same family—my family!" He clapped his hands in excitement. "It will be a sensation! The ton will not know what hit 'em!"

And then his eyes had come to rest on Prudence, and his smile had slowly faded. He'd pursed his lips and frowned as he examined her thoughtfully. And the longer he looked her over with that troubled expression, the more Prudence felt it: she didn't compare well.

Her hair might be the same color as Grace's, but it had an unfortunate tendency to frizz in damp weather. It didn't compare to shining, silky, golden curls, like her other sisters'. Her complexion might be smooth and soft, like theirs, but there were five or six tiny freckles that marred it, for she was often careless about wearing a hat in the sunshine. And her eyes were a dreary gray when everyone else in the family had eyes of varying shades of glorious blue.

She felt Great-uncle Oswald's bright blue eyes dwell on her Merridew nose and saw his mouth purse in an even tighter line. He had the same nose, she thought defiantly, and hers was a lot smaller than his, though it probably looked better on a man, she had to admit.

There were very few looking glasses at Dereham Court, because vanity was a terrible sin. And since they almost never had visitors, and were not allowed out, and since Phillip had been gone for some years, Prudence had never given much thought to her looks.

To tell the truth, it was a bit of a shock to read in the eyes of her doting great-uncle that she was the plain one in a flock of beauties. But there were more important things to worry about, Prudence told herself firmly.

"If you truly believe one of my sisters could be happily married by the end of the season—oh, that would be so wonderful, Great-uncle Oswald. It is—" Prudence looked around at her sisters in relief, "It is exactly what we had hoped for!"

So excited was she at the prospect of the success of her bold plan that she quite forgot herself, jumped out of her chair, and hugged him. "Oh, thank you, *thank you,* dear Uncle Oswald! You are so very kind, so very generous." Her voice choked a little. "I cannot tell you how happy you have made us." She kissed his cheek.

He'd blushed and beamed and pooh-poohed her nonsense about generosity and kindness, and said they'd made a lonely old man very happy! What were uncles for, after all?

Her sisters, having recovered from their astonishment at Great-uncle Oswald not only allowing Prudence to hug and kiss him without retaliation, but even seeming to welcome such shocking forwardness, also crowded forward to hug the old gentleman and plant shy kisses on his cheek and balding dome.

But when the girls resumed their seats and addressed themselves tentatively to the herbal tea and seed cakes Great-uncle Oswald had ordered for their refreshment, he'd regarded Prudence for a long moment, frowning.

Prudence, foolish female that she was, hadn't realized that *she* was the fly in the ointment.

It was the mantua maker who put it most succinctly. Measuring her sisters for their new apparel, the elegant Frenchwoman had gushed, "Such beautiful figures *ze mademoiselles* have, so graceful, of an elegance, like young gazelles, veritably!" And then her eyes had fallen on Prudence and her mouth got that familiar pursed look. She frowned for a moment and then said with brutal Gallic frankness, "You, *mademoiselle*, will be a leetle more *difficile*. You are no gazelle; you are more of ze leetle pony. But I do not despair, I do not despair. Me, I can make anyone elegant!"

Prudence was inclined to be indignant. She ate as much as her sisters—in fact, generally a lot less than the twins—so it really wasn't fair that they should all be slender and sylphlike and she should be . . . a round, little pony.

Vanity was a sin, Prudence told herself firmly at the end of the day as she climbed into bed feeling crushed and clumsy. It was shallow to think her looks mattered. What mattered was that one of her sisters would soon find a husband and then they would all, especially Grace, be safe from Grandpapa.

But her looks mattered more than she realized.

The fourth morning at breakfast, Great-uncle Oswald made the fatal announcement. He brought Grandpapa's supposed letter to the breakfast table and read one part aloud:

> *"I have other plans for Prudence, the eldest, so there is no need for her to make her coming-out. She can chaperone her sisters and take care of most matters, so that the girls' Female Chatter will not bother you unduly."*

He'd glanced at Prudence across the table and asked, "You know what your grandpapa intends, don't you? Always was a selfish one, my brother. Just like him to keep you back to care for him in his old age." He snorted and put the letter aside. "I've watched you with your sisters, missy. You take excellent care of 'em, don't you?"

Prudence had blinked at the unexpected praise. She could not remember when anyone had said anything so kind to her.

Great-uncle Oswald nodded emphatically. "Yes, you're a good, sweet girl, Prudence Merridew, and—dash it all!— you *shall* have your chance! You may lack your sisters' dazzlin' looks, but I'm confident we can fire you off well enough. There are plenty of sensible fellows who look for more than beauty in a wife. We'll find a husband for you yet, little missy, don't you fret! You'll not waste your life away runnin' around after other people and lookin' after selfish old men."

"Oh but she alrea—" began Charity, and then stopped, flustered, at Prudence's urgent look.

"It is all right, Great-uncle Oswald," Prudence assured him hastily. "Please don't worry about me. I am very happy as it is. I very much look forward to being my sisters' chaperone and going about with them. It will be such fun."

Great-uncle Oswald smiled at her gently, and with pity. "Dear, noble little creature. You lack your sisters' looks, but you have a truly beautiful soul."

Prudence gritted her teeth and forced herself to smile. His next pronouncement wiped the smile off her face.

"I'll fire you off first, without your sisters. Once the ton claps eyes on that bevy of beauties, you won't stand a chance." He nodded and beheaded a boiled egg with gusto. "Then, once you're safely buckled, we can let loose these diamonds to dazzle the world." He beamed around the table at her sisters, and before Prudence could think of some way to change his mind, the carriage arrived to take them shopping.

But now, after a week in London, it was very clear that Great-uncle Oswald meant exactly what he had said. He wasn't going to allow Charity, Hope, or Faith to be presented to the ton until Prudence was married! And nothing Prudence could say or do would budge him from that position.

"I am sorry," she explained to her sisters in a despairing voice one night in the upstairs parlor, "but though Great-uncle Oswald is so very kind and generous, in his own way he is *just* as stubborn and impervious to reason as Grand-papa is!"

"You *have* to tell him about Phillip," Hope said. "It is the only thing. Once he realizes you are already betrothed, there is no reason to keep the rest of us in seclusion."

"I *cannot* tell him about Phillip," explained Prudence wearily. "I *promised* Phillip that I would not announce anything until he gave me permission, and you know I never break my promises."

"Could we not explain Phillip to Great-uncle Oswald?" asked Faith.

Prudence bit her lip. "I daren't risk it. He might defy Grandpapa in small matters, such as dancing and parties, but marriage is a different thing altogether. Besides, he would probably think Phillip unsuitable, too—a younger son of undistinguished family and no fortune!" She sighed. "And since the Otterburys live so close to Dereham Court, he might contact Grandpapa about it . . ." She shook her head. "We would all be in the suds then. And for harboring us, Grandpapa would probably cut Great-uncle Oswald off without a penny—you know how he complains incessantly of his extravagance."

"I *love* Great-uncle Oswald's extravagance!" Hope declared, twirling around in her pretty new dress.

Charity nodded. "Yes, but let us hope he doesn't send Grandpapa the bills from the mantua maker. He would know then that something was amiss. But, Prue dearest, Great-uncle Oswald seems very romantical. Would he not rejoice that you have found a man to marry you?"

Prudence pulled a wry face. "Perhaps, but he is also ambitious and something of a snob—recall those dukes you diamonds are to dazzle! In any case, even aside from my promise, have you forgotten that Phillip works for Grandpapa's Oriental Trade Company, and that Great-uncle Oswald is also connected with it? Do you really think he'd be delighted by the news that an employee of his, a penniless younger son currently residing in India, contracted a secret betrothal more than four years ago to his eldest great-niece? I think not!"

The sisters sighed gloomily.

"Exactly! Phillip would lose his position and be unable to afford a wife, I would be in disgrace, and we should all be sent back to live with Grandpapa again."

"Yes, but Great-uncle Oswald is not mean-spirited and nasty, like Grandpapa. Surely he would—" began Hope.

"No, Hope." Prudence shook her head. "I'm sorry, but the risks are too great. Great-uncle Oswald is a dear, sweet man, but we cannot expect him to put our welfare before his own. You know what it took to convince even Dr. Gibson, and he's seen the bruises! But I promise you, I shall think of something. And soon."

Hope sniffed. "You always make these promises."

"And I keep them," responded Prudence quietly.

"Should you object if I try to talk the old gentleman around? Because I will *die* rather than be returned to the Court," declared Hope passionately.

"Of course not, Hope darling. As long as you respect my secret, I am more than happy for you to try." Prudence rolled her eyes comically. "The more I argue in favor of letting you make your coming-out, the more noble he tells me I am."

• • • •

"No! I've said it once, and I don't intend to waste my breath on repetitions!" Great-uncle Oswald glared at the exquisite matching female faces turned imploringly to him.

"But we are only allowed to stay in London for this one season," argued Hope. "Grandpapa will surely not allow us to stay any longer. He has given us only a handful of weeks in which to find husbands. And Prudence is already almost on the shelf—"

"She is almost one and twenty, you know," interpolated her twin.

"—and so is not likely to attract a husband at this late stage—even with her *very* beautiful soul," Hope added hastily, aware of the narrow look Prudence was casting her. "If we are forced to wait much longer, we are all likely to remain on the shelf."

"Fustian!" Great-uncle Oswald snapped from behind his paper. "Beauties like you two will be snapped up the moment you make your bow to society. Don't be selfish. Give your sister her moment of glory."

"But if we all came out—"

"No! Not until your sister has found herself a husband. Our Prudence is a dear, good girl, and one day a man will come along and take one look at her and snap her up—but not if the rest of you are there dazzlin' the poor fellow instead!"

"I, for one, do not care if Prudence never gets a husband," announced Grace loyally. "I doubt I shall ever marry. I shall be like Great-aunt Hermione—a sad and lonely spinster, jilted by my one true love. I shall keep cats and live off my memories."

Great-uncle Oswald snorted. "You'll marry, my girl, and I'll hear no more of such nonsense from you. Keepin' cats indeed! Hermione was always peculiar!"

There was a short silence while each of the girls contemplated a bleak future.

"Does Prudence actually have to *marry* before Charity can make her coming-out?" asked Hope suddenly.

Great-uncle Oswald plonked down his newspaper in an irritated gesture. "I told you, missy—"

"I mean what if she were *betrothed?*" Hope explained

hurriedly. "And, and what if her betrothed wished to wait for some time until they were wed. If Prudence were betrothed, then could the rest of us, Charity and Faith and me, make our debuts?"

Great-uncle Oswald shrugged. "If Prudence were betrothed, I see no reason why not, but Prudence ain't betrothed, missy, so cease plaguing me until she is."

Hope shot a look of triumph at Prudence. "See! We *could* make our come out. Tell him, Prue," Hope said fiercely.

If looks could kill, Hope would have been fried where she sat, but Prudence said not a word. How could she when her betrothed's reputation, livelihood, and future prospects depended on her silence? And besides, she had promised to keep it secret from all except her sisters.

Great-uncle Oswald frowned in sudden suspicion. "Somethin' you ought to be tellin' me, girlie?"

"No, Uncle, nothing at all." Prudence threaded a length of scarlet silk with shaking hands.

"If you do not tell him, I shall," Hope said vehemently. "It is not fair that we should all be at risk simply because Phil—"

"Be quiet, Hope!" Prudence jumped to her feet. "You have no right—"

"Silence!" Great-uncle Oswald roared. He glared at his great-nieces, his face suffused with anger. "So, deceit and deception under my own roof, is there? You two—out!" He stabbed a finger at Faith and Grace. "Now!" he bellowed. They fled.

Prudence tried to think. Any moment now Hope or Charity would be made to confess that Prudence had entered into a clandestine betrothal, and then he would demand to know the name of her betrothed. And Prudence, knowing the damage it could bring him, had sworn never to reveal it without Phillip's permission. She had to do something. But what?

"Well, gels?" Great-uncle Oswald stared at each of them in turn. They said nothing. He addressed Hope. "Come, Miss Hope, out with it! Has your sister secretly promised herself?"

Hope nodded and burst into noisy tears. Charity joined her.

"God deliver me! Must females always cry?" grumbled Great-uncle Oswald. "Stop that dratted caterwaulin', will you?" He waited until the worst of the sobbing had died down, then turned to Prudence. "Now, missy, you have some explaining to do. Who is this blackguard who has cozened you into deceiving your legal guardian?"

Prudence thought frantically. She could not tell him the truth. She had promised Phillip she would protect his position. "Er, he is a perfectly respectable gentleman, I promise you, sir."

Great-uncle Oswald sniffed. "Perfectly respectable gentlemen don't enter into havey-cavey betrothals behind people's backs."

"Oh, but he is a very private gentleman, er, and does not enjoy the fuss and botheration of a public celebration."

Great-uncle Oswald snorted. "There's a big difference between a private arrangement and a clandestine one. Now stop beatin' around the bush, gel; name the blackguard at once!"

Prudence's mind raced. "It is . . . it is . . ." She could not betray Phillip. She could not!

"Spit it out, gel!"

"It is—" From the ether, Prudence plucked a name. The previous evening she'd overheard two ladies discussing a man who was a famous recluse, an unmarried man who apparently never came to London. "He is the Duke of Dinstable!"

There was a short, stunned silence in the room. Hope and Charity regarded her through astonished, drenched, beautiful eyes.

"The Duke of Dinstable?" repeated Great-uncle Oswald, stunned. "You've entered into a secret betrothal to the *Duke of Dinstable?"*

"Yes." Prudence attempted a bright smile, desperately attempting to recall everything she'd heard the ladies say about him.

"That fellow they call Hermit Ned?"

She nodded.

"Dinstable? Fellow who hates cities? Hasn't been seen in

London for years? Lives in some godforsaken corner of Scotland?"

Prudence nodded again. She was starting to feeling quite pleased with herself. The Duke of Dinstable. It was positively inspirational. The Duke of Dinstable might be odd, even peculiar, but he was reputed to be extremely rich. And if he never came to London, Great-uncle Oswald couldn't ask him to explain a secret betrothal. Of course he could always write, but letters took a long time and perhaps the reclusive duke would not answer. It was a reprieve, if only a temporary one.

"The Duke of *Dinstable?*" Great-uncle Oswald repeated, shaking his head in amazement.

Prudence, tired of nodding, inclined her head.

"How did you meet him, this Dinstable fellow, if he never comes to London? Imagine not liking London!"

"He may not come to London, but there is no reason why he would not come to Norfolk," she said, careful not to compound her sins by uttering any more actual lies.

Her great-uncle frowned. "How old were you when you agreed to this demmed irregular arrangement?"

"Nearly seventeen," Prudence said. It wasn't a lie either, not precisely. Not that she had even met the Duke of Dinstable, but she *had* become betrothed at sixteen—to Phillip Otterbury, whom she had known all her life. Phillip, who had sworn her to secrecy and gone away to India, promising to return a nabob.

"You were only sixteen?" Great-uncle Oswald exploded wrathfully. "And you have waited more than *four years* for this blasted duke to come to the point and wed you?"

Prudence nodded. Was it really that long?

"No wonder your sisters have been chafin' at the bit! Can't blame 'em, now I come to think of it. Dashed casual attitude to take to m'great-niece. Four years! Why the devil didn't you tell me?"

Prudence didn't reply. She could hardly meet his eye as it was, he'd been so kind and generous. But as soon as they were safe, she would confess it all. And she vowed she would make it up to him.

"Dinstable, eh?" Great-uncle Oswald walked over to the

fireplace, frowning. "Dukes, even rackety hermitish dukes, don't just up and propose to chits of sixteen. You didn't let him do anything to you, did you? Anything you shouldn't have let him do." He peered at her shrewdly. "You know what I mean, missy?"

Prudence flushed rosily. "He never touched me," she declared with complete truth

"Hmm. And it was four years ago." He frowned thoughtfully. "And why so secretive, eh? Not as if he were the younger son of a farmer, after all."

Prudence flushed. It was a perfect description of Phillip. "Grandpapa wouldn't allow us any visitors at all, let alone suitors."

Great-uncle Oswald snorted. "Always was short-sighted in matters of business, Theodore. I don't suppose this duke put anything in writing?"

Prudence shook her head. "Grandpapa would never allow us any correspondence."

"Not even clandestine letters? Never knew the gel yet who didn't manage a bit of illicit correspondence in matters of the heart."

She flushed and glanced at the fire.

"Ah. Burned 'em, did you? Pity. Letters might have clinched the deal. I don't suppose he gave you any love token? Nothing with a crest or anything?"

Prudence hesitated, then pulled Phillip's grandmother's ring from her bodice. She'd worn it on a chain for four years.

"Aha!" Great-uncle Oswald leaped forward and examined it. "A trumpery thing and no ducal crest to nail him down, but it's old. Probably some family thing. It might do the trick." He nodded resolutely. "Not so bad as I thought then, if he's given you a ring. Might be draggin' his feet, but dash it, if the fellow didn't wish to become a tenant-for-life, he should never have handed over the evidence. Now don't you fret any longer, m'dear, I'll fix it, make it all legal. Hah! Thirty thousand a year, I'm told."

Prudence nodded dazedly, hoping that the weather on the roads to Scotland would be foul and the mail delayed for weeks, preferably swept away in a flood.

Hope, recovering from her bout of guilt with remarkable speed, asked tentatively. "So may Charity and Faith and I make our coming-outs?"

"Eh? What's that? Charity and you twins, eh? Well, if your sister's betrothed—even in such a dashed, hole-in-the-corner fashion—I see no reason why the Merridew diamonds may not begin to dazzle society." Hope uttered a squeak of excitement, so he added witheringly, "Startin' with Miss Charity. We shall see about you and your twin after that. Mistress Prudence, you'll wait not a month longer. You may begin preparations for your bridal at once. I'll call on the fellow first thing in the morning and make the arrangements."

Prudence felt the pit of her stomach drop in horrid antic-ipation of disaster. "Wh-what did you say, Great-uncle Os-wald? Call on whom, first thing in the morning?"

"Dinstable, of course," Great-uncle Oswald replied. "Make the arrangements for the weddin'—St. George's, Hanover Square, I think. And all the usual fuss and nonsense you ladies enjoy. Fellow may have botched the betrothal, but we'll fire you off in style, m'dear, don't you worry."

Prudence, Hope, and Charity stared. Prudence gathered her wits first. "But the Duke of Dinstable resides in the far north of Scotland, Uncle. How on earth can you make a morning call on him?"

Great-uncle Oswald grinned and patted the side of his nose knowingly. "Hah! You didn't know, did you, missy? No doubt I've spoiled the fellow's romantical surprise. But this probably explains why he's broken his rule after all these years. All the tabbies have been buzzing about him, won-dering what's brought about his unexpected arrival in the metropolis. And even if he didn't intend a romantical sur-prise, I'll give him one! He'll not out-jockey Sir Oswald Merridew!" He rubbed his hands in glee. "Won't the match-making mamas be green when they hear! My plain little Pru-dence—a duchess, eh! We might yet snag a brace o' dukes yet, stap me if we don't!" He left the room, chuckling with pleased anticipation.

The three girls stared at each other in shocked silence.

"Whatever made you say such a thing, Prue?" Charity shook her head. "Now we are more than ever in the suds."

Prudence subsided onto a chair and shook her head. "I don't know. I was clutching at straws. I didn't want Phillip to lose his position and when Great-uncle Oswald was roaring at us, so very like Grandpapa, the name came to me and just popped out."

"Can he really be going to call on the Duke of Dinstable tomorrow?" said Charity at last.

Prudence shook her head in despair. "But people the other night said the duke of Dinstable *never* comes to London —that's why I picked him. They said that he hasn't been here for *years*."

"I must say, Prue, it was frightfully clever of you—" began Hope.

"Don't you *dare* say a word, you horrid little snake in the grass!" snapped her loving older sister. "If it hadn't been for you—"

"Yes, and I'm sorry, but I was desperate, Prue. I so want to go to balls and parties. I want to dance the waltz with a handsome man and fall madly in love. I would rather *die* than go back to live with Grandpapa. But Phillip's tardiness has ruined things for all of us—I don't blame you—I would have grabbed at him, too, if it was the only chance I was likely to get—"

"I did not *grab at* Phillip!" interrupted Prudence indignantly. "Nor was it the only chance I was likely to get! It was the most romantic moment of my life—"

"It was the only romantic moment of your life," Hope interrupted crushingly. "And it was more than four years ago."

"I still do not understand how Great-uncle Oswald can call on the Duke of Dinstable first thing in the morning if he lives in the North of Scotland," Charity said plaintively, ignoring the sisterly squabbling.

Prudence and Hope, reminded of the disaster that faced them, instantly forgot their differences.

"When he said the duke might be planning a romantical surprise, he glanced at the newspaper," Prudence said slowly. "Perhaps . . ." The sisters fell on the newspaper, divided it between them, and began to scan the sheets avidly.

"Here it is!" Charity announced after a few moments. In a hollow voice she read,

> *"This metropolis has been graced by the rare presence of the D— of D—, who has left his Northern Hermitage and come to Town. Rumor has it that the D— is considering Matrimony."*

She stared at Prudence in dismay and passed her the dreaded passage.

"The Duke of Dinstable in town? He hasn't been to London in more than ten years!" Prudence stared in disbelief at the paper and crushed it slowly in her hands. "Oh, how wretchedly inconvenient! He has been perfectly happy in the wilds of Scotland for years. Why come to town now?"

She considered the disaster for a moment and with a groan added, "And whatever will he think when Great-uncle Oswald calls on him and tries to force him to marry me?"

There was a long silence in the room.

"What are you going to do, Prue?"

Prudence considered the problem from all angles. "No matter how I look at it, I can see no alternative . . ."

Charity nodded. "I know. Oh dear, oh dear." Tears began to roll down her damask cheeks.

Hope, too, began to sob. "He'll send us all back to Grandpapa, now. Oh, Prue, I am so sorry I said anything, now. I did not think." She snuffled and groped for her handkerchief.

Prudence sat up and regarded her sisters with astonishment. "Whatever are you carrying on about? We are *not* going back to Dereham Court!"

Charity blinked through her tears. "But when you confess to Great-uncle Oswald, he—"

"Confess to Great-uncle Oswald?" Prudence exclaimed. "I have no intention of confessing to Great-uncle Oswald. "

"But what else can you do?"

"I'll speak to the Duke of Dinstable, of course. There's no other solution."

After an astonished pause, her sisters finally found their tongues. "But where—how will you meet him? And when?

Great-uncle Oswald plans to call on him tomorrow morning!"

Prudence smiled grimly. "Well then, Prudence Merridew will just have to call on the duke a little bit earlier, won't she?"

Charity was horrified. "Call on a man! In his own home! Unannounced and without a proper introduction? Prudence, you cannot!"

Prudence squared her shoulders. "Just watch me!"

Chapter Three

∞

"A girl, no virgin either, I should guess——a baggage
Thrust on me like a cargo on a ship
To wreck my peace of mind."
SOPHOCLES

"MISS MERRIDEW TO SEE HIS GRACE, THE DUKE OF DINSTABLE."

A butler looked down his nose at her in faint, superior disapproval. Prudence drew herself up to her full height and stared him straight in the livery, attempting to look assured and unconcerned, as if she called on strange gentlemen at their homes every day. Strange ducal gentlemen. Strange ducal hermits.

The butler's gaze shifted to Prudence's nervous maidservant, Lily, who blushed and stared at the white steps of the London mansion of the Duke of Dinstable. The butler returned his attention to Prudence.

"And is His Grace expecting you, miss?" said the butler in a tremendously bored voice.

Prudence attempted to look tremendously bored in return. It was a difficult task when her pulse was rattling along like Herr Maelzel's metronome, but necessary; boredom, she had learned since coming to London, was a sophisticated acquirement. The more bored she looked, the more sophisticated she would seem and she could tell that only the most terribly soignée of misses would gain entry from this butler.

And besides, he smelled of musk. She refused to be intimidated by a butler who smelled of musk. She raised her eyebrow in faint, sophisticated surprise. "I believe His Grace will be most put out if he misses me."

The butler hesitated.

"Come now," Prudence said in a firm voice. "It is raining and my maid is getting cold."

The butler glanced at Lily, who, discreetly nudged by Prudence, shivered obediently.

"Very well then, miss, if you would care to wait in the green drawing room, I shall inform His Grace." He held open the door, and with a sigh of relief Prudence entered.

Silently indicating that Lily should remain on a seat in the hallway, he took Prudence's hat, umbrella, and damp cloak and ushered her into a large room, furnished in the Egyptian style.

"If you would care to wait, miss." The butler bowed and left the room.

Prudence glanced around the room, deciding where to sit. The choice was not a simple one. The main item of seating was a green and gilt settee, shaped for all the world like Cleopatra's barge, with a carved headboard depicting a river scene with water lilies and dolphins surrounded by writhing asps. The other end looped up in a gilt and ebony curve, rather like a sultan's slipper. And the feet looked horridly like crocodile's feet.

It was not the sort of settee on which one could sit correctly: It was the sort of seat that invited one to loll. She could not greet an unknown duke lolling. She needed every shred of dignity and poise she could muster.

Gingerly seating herself on a carved ebony chair with snarling one-legged gilt lion armrests, Prudence waited.

She sat in her most ladylike pose, smoothing her dress and gloves, willing her heart to slow. The jackal-headed Anubis and the hawk-headed Horus stared impassively down from a sideboard. Nearby, a footstool sported four lions' feet that mysteriously became the top half of very immodestly dressed ladies. She tried to imagine Grandpapa in this room. He would have an apoplexy, she decided. The thought cheered her.

She had never done anything so bold in her life. Apart from becoming secretly betrothed to Phillip, that is. But for an unmarried lady to call uninvited on a strange gentleman in his home—that was truly shocking. Great-uncle Oswald's coachman had even been shocked when she'd inquired about the duke's direction. It was a thing, apparently, that unmarried ladies did not even ask.

A sphinx stared silently at her from the wall. Her fingers tapped an impatient, anxious tattoo on her reticule. It was the pasteboard reticule, slightly lopsided from where Grandpapa had damaged it in his rage, and very dear to Prudence's heart. It matched the room, being shaped like an Egyptian sarcophagus and carefully painted in blue, green, black, and gold.

Grace would be thrilled to see this room. Her little sister would see that not all the world thought the Egyptian taste to be wicked, heathenish vileness. Her fingers were clenched around the reticule, she realized. She forced them to relax.

If she handled things properly, Grace would never again be beaten for an innocent mistake. It all depended on how well she handled this duke. And Great-uncle Oswald.

An ormolu clock mounted on gilt gryphons ticked noisily on the overmantel. It was well after nine o'clock. Great-uncle Oswald would have finished his hot water and apple-cider vinegar drink by now and be beginning on his shirred eggs. She had, perhaps, twenty minutes. If Great-uncle Oswald was not early. He was a man of regular habits.

Prudence smoothed her skirts for the hundredth time. She'd thought it would be quite exciting to be bold and adventurous instead of always trying to be invisible, so as not to attract Grandpapa's attention. But the longer she waited, the more anxious and the less bold she felt.

She told herself to be calm. Nothing dreadful could happen with Lily so close outside. Besides, she had no choice.

The clock ticked remorselessly on. The Sphinx stared. The lion heads snarled in frozen gilt fury.

Oh, where was this wretched Duke? Great-uncle Oswald would be here any minute!

"What have we here, Bartlett?"

Prudence jumped. In the doorway stood a tall, dark, rather raffish-looking gentleman. Prudence blinked. She had seen several dukes since arriving in London. This one did not look as a duke ought to look. Though his clothing was of the finest quality, it was rumpled and crumpled. His coat was unbuttoned and carelessly worn. His neckcloth was a little skewed and knotted negligently beneath quite moderate shirt points. And he seemed not to have shaved, for his chin, though attractively shaped, was decidedly dark and rough-looking.

She had expected a duke, even a hermit duke, to be a little more dapper in appearance. Only royal dukes looked this disheveled. But perhaps this was why he was a hermit. Or perhaps she had got him out of his bed. For some reason the thought made her blush.

Had she not known who he was, she might have been concerned at being alone with such a man, for he looked decidedly dark and dangerous. And the gleam in his eye as he looked at her was certainly not one a girl should trust, Prudence decided, duke or no! His eyes were dark and narrow and seemed to be laughing at her for no reason she could imagine.

She sat a little straighter on the hard chair and clutched her reticule beneath her bosom.

"Bartlett?" he repeated to the butler standing just outside the door. He sauntered in, not taking his eyes off Prudence. "Who is our charming visitor?"

The butler followed him into the room, bringing with him the faint scent of musk. "This young person, sir, arrived intemperently this morning, announcing her determination to converse with the Duke of Dinstable. There is another female outside, who accompanied the young person."

Prudence jumped up indignantly. "How dare you speak of me in that tone! I am not a young person at all—I am a young lady! And I did not arrive intemperently. It is a perfectly reasonable hour—"

The tall gentleman's brow quirked skeptically, and she flushed and corrected herself with dignity, recalling that she had probably got him out of his bed. And that she was supposed to be a bored and soignée young lady, quite accustomed to calling on gentlemen.

"Perhaps it is a little early for some people, but when you hear what I have to say, Your Grace, I am sure you will understand."

"Oh but—" began the butler.

"That will be all, Bartlett," the tall gentleman said suavely.

The butler hesitated a moment, looking doubtfully from the duke to Prudence.

Prudence bridled at his expression. "Your master will be quite safe with me," she snapped. "I mean him no harm!"

The tall gentleman chuckled softly. "You heard the lady, Bartlett. I am quite safe with her. You may go."

The butler left.

"What a perfectly detestable man!" Prudence declared. "Although I suppose you pay him to be detestable."

"Not at all—it comes naturally to him," the duke said, "Though I must confess I find his, er, repellent skills useful at times." He sat down on Cleopatra's barge, crossed one long leg over another, and regarded her with a faint look of amusement on his face. "Now, what can I do for you, Miss, er . . . ?"

She watched him critically, noting that he quite definitely lolled. "Miss Merridew. Miss Prudence Merridew," she explained in as composed a voice as she could manage. The way he was looking at her was quite disconcerting. "I have four siblings—all sisters. I am the eldest."

"Indeed?" he asked politely.

"Yes, and that is the heart of the problem," she said. "For one of us must marry." She frowned, realizing she had started her speech wrongly. She had rehearsed and rehearsed it last night, until she had it perfectly off by heart. But something in the way this dark-eyed man watched her had the effect of scrambling the words in her mind.

"I see. And you imagine this has something to do with the Duke of Dinstable?" His words were perfectly polite, but a certain harsh quality had entered his tone. His dark eyes regarded her intently, and Prudence felt her nervousness increase.

"Yes. Well, no. Not directly. It was a mistake on my part." She stopped, realizing she wasn't making sense. It was most unlike her. "I am sorry. I am making a shocking mull of this. It is extremely awkward, you see."

She stood up and took a few paces around the room to cool her suddenly heated cheeks. The way he looked at her was most unsettling. She took several deep, calming breaths and considered how best to explain. He was right to be suspicious of her motives. She had claimed to be betrothed to him. He was about to be confronted by an angry great-uncle. She gripped her reticule a little tighter, glanced at the clock, and forced herself to go on.

"I must apologize, Your Grace, for it is all my fault. I truly *never* meant to drag you into it, only . . ." She sighed. "It is a complicated tale, but I shall try to cut it to the bare essentials."

He smiled. "Good. I always prefer essentials bared."

Somehow, he made it sound . . . wicked. Prudence blinked hurriedly and wished she'd brought a fan. It really was very warm in there all of a sudden. "You see, one of us must find a husband quickly, only it cannot be me."

One dark, winged eyebrow arched in a sardonic query.

She hurried on. "It must be one of my sisters. Only my great-uncle thinks that we should not come out together, that I should come out first."

"I see."

She flushed and for some reason found that she could not bring herself to explain the reason to him. "Yes. So I told him a lie and, and, your name came up, and I'm sorry, I truly am. I thought it would help my sisters to come out, only it has all come awry. I did not think it would cause such a problem because I thought you safe in the wilds of Scotland! I had counted on the delay, you see. And letters go astray, all the time."

The mobile mouth twitched a little and the hard expression in his eyes was replaced by an amused gleam. "It was thoughtless of me to come to London, I see. So inconvenient." He smiled a slow smile, and for a moment it drove all rational thought from her head.

She stammered, "Oh, n-no. You could not know. But I

was shocked to find you here. For you almost never mix in society, do you?"

"No," he said apologetically. "I do not care for many of the people, you see."

The clock struck half past the hour, chiming once in a somber, fatalistic fashion. Prudence jumped. "Oh no—half-past nine. Already!" She resumed her pacing.

"Yes, a ridiculous hour, I agree." He yawned.

Ridiculous? Prudence stared at him in amazement. He clearly had not grasped the urgency of the situation. If only he would stop looking at her like—like an amused satyr, she might be able to manage a clear and rational explanation! "The thing is, Your Grace, Great-uncle Oswald is coming to see you. Any minute now. To demand an explanation."

"Oh, Great-uncle Oswald is also vexed with me for not staying in Scotland, is he?"

"Oh no," said Prudence, distractedly. "He is delighted you are here, of course." She flushed and swallowed and tried to gather her composure. "For . . . for reasons that are rather complicated—but altruistic—I allowed my great-uncle to come to a certain conclusion about you. And me." She felt her face heat further. It was not like her to dither, but the situation was truly fantastical, and the way this man's gaze kept slipping over her was very disconcerting. He flustered her.

"A certain conclusion?"

She cast him a look of entreaty, putting off the horrid moment of truth yet again. "You must believe me, Your Grace. I never meant to land anyone in a pickle."

"No, of course not." His eyes were dancing now, she noticed. How could he be amused at a time like this!

He stood up, strolled across the room, and pulled at the cord hanging by the fireplace. In a moment the door opened and the butler stood there.

"A brandy, if you please, Bartlett. And something for the lady. Ratafia? Tea?"

Prudence was appalled. "You cannot possibly mean to be drinking spirituous liquor at this time of the morning!"

The duke nodded at Bartlett. "Tea for Miss Merridew, then, and brandy for me. And Bartlett, bring the decanter."

"But you cannot greet Great-uncle Oswald with a glass of brandy in your hand!"

My dear girl, I am afraid I cannot greet him any other way. It is not morning for me, you see, but the end of a particularly long and tedious night. And if I am to be thrust into a pickle without the fortification of a brandy, I cannot answer for the consequences."

Guilt stabbed Prudence at his words. She rallied. The situation was difficult enough to explain without the duke getting drunk. "But Great-uncle Oswald abhors the evils of liquor!"

"He can have tea, then."

"Oh, will you please be serious! You cannot imagine what is about to happen!"

He laughed at that, a deep-throated chuckle that filled the room. "I have not the faintest notion what *any* of this is about."

Just then Bartlett arrived with a tea tray on which stood a pot of tea, a plate of cakes, a cup and saucer, a fat crystal glass, and a tall crystal decanter containing a mellow golden liquid. As he placed it on a side table, the front-door knocker sounded thunderously. Prudence squeaked. "Oh no! He is here! Great-uncle Oswald!"

"I believe it is the lady's great-uncle at the door, Bartlett," the duke said. "Show him in, if you please."

Bartlett bowed, thin-lipped, then left the room in a stately manner to answer the summons.

"The thing is," Prudence gabbled, "for reasons I have no time to explain just now, I told him that you and I were secretly betrothed—"

The smile on his face froze. *"Betrothed!"*

"Yes, I am sorry. It was all I could think of to make him see reason about Charity and the twins making their coming-out—for which the need is urgent, though I cannot explain why. But Great-uncle Oswald will not let them come out with me—"

"I imagine he has good reason—" the duke said ironically.

"Well, yes, because—" She flushed. "The reason does not matter. What matters is that they cannot enter society until I am out of the way and I thought you would suit my purposes perfectly, being a famous hermit—"

"Are you really?" he interjected interestedly.

"Am I what?" demanded Prudence, confused.

"A famous hermit."

"Not me, lack-wit—you!" she snapped. "Oh, I do beg your pardon—my nerves are shredded! But *you* are the famous hermit! Except you've emerged from your hermitage, and some wretched busybody put it in the paper, and now here is Great-uncle Oswald come to demand that you marry me! Immediately!"

"What!"

That wiped the smile from his face, she noted with satisfaction. "I *told* you it was serious, Your Grace."

An expression of unholy glee flashed across the dark-visaged face. "I can see it is." He chuckled. "And I definitely need that brandy." He strolled across the room to the tray with the decanter. "Would you care to pour your tea, Miss Merridew?"

Outside, Prudence could hear Great-uncle Oswald noisily demanding to see the Duke of Dinstable. She hurried across to where the duke was standing and laid a reassuring hand on his arm. "Do not fear," she whispered hastily. "It may be a tangle, but it is *not* a trap. If you will only allow my uncle to believe we did have an understanding, I promise you most faithfully I will sever the engagement immediately. Please, I beg of you, just follow my lead. Trust me, Your Grace. I mean you no harm."

He glanced down at her hand patting his arm soothingly. "Trust you?" His eyes caught hers and held them for a long, long moment, and for a second Prudence felt as if something important had happened. But then he shifted, and his eyes laughed down at her again as if that moment of connection had never been. "Then bring on your dragons, fair maiden," he said, and lifted his glass to his lips.

Prudence scanned his face worriedly. He was very hard to read. For a second there she'd felt so . . . so heartened by that long look, as if she could depend on him in some way. Yet a moment later he seemed to find the whole thing hugely entertaining and was quite unworried by the prospect of

Great-uncle Oswald's imminent arrival. Was that because as
a duke, he thought himself perfectly safe?

She took a deep breath and braced herself for the coming
scene.

Gideon watched her interestedly out of the corner of his
eye. She was an attractive little thing, he decided, not con-
ventionally beautiful, but with a decided air of determination and a most appealing way of looking at him. Her
simple, pale green gown set off her thick, glorious hair, pale
skin, and wide gray eyes. The simple style, the direct gray
gaze was refreshing, in a Quakerish sort of fashion.

Not that her behavior was Quakerish in the least—but
then nor was his interest, he had to admit. That small, stubborn chin was braced for trouble, prepared to meet it head-
on. It seemed as though, having imagined she had got him
into hot water, she was now prepared to defend him.

He found it rather refreshing. He sipped the cognac and
made a small wager with himself as to how far she would let
the joke go before she confessed all. Of course she might be
a blackmailing harpy, but he didn't think so. He was all too
well acquainted with females of that variety.

"So, you will defend me from your great-uncle?" he
asked softly.

She turned back to him with wide, sincere eyes. "Of
course I will."

It was more than refreshing; it was irresistible, and
Gideon couldn't help himself. Without thinking, he put
down his glass, pulled her into his arms, and kissed her.
He'd meant it to be a swift, light kiss, something of a thanks
with a touch of mischievous provocation, but instead found
himself plunged into unexpected depths. She tasted of surprise and sweetness and innocence, but she could not disguise her instinctive response to him. No Quakerishness
there, he thought raggedly and took the kiss deeper.

The taste of her was intoxicating. He let his own instincts
rule him and drew her more firmly against his body, enjoying the way her soft curves molded against him. Her stiffness slowly dissolved and when he felt the first tentative
response from her, it sent a thread of pure possessiveness
arching through him.

A clatter outside the door brought him to his senses. Reluctantly he released her, and she moved back an inch or two, blinking up at him, looking adorably confused. He was very tempted to kiss her again.

She eyed him with a mixture of disapproval and shocked awareness. "You should not have done that."

He took a moment to respond. "I'll do it again in a moment if you don't stop looking at me like that."

"Don't you dare!" She gave him a haughty little warning glare.

He fought the urge to smile. Even her disapproval was appealing. Mastering the urge to kiss her again, he picked up his cognac and sipped. The door was thrown open. Prudence jumped visibly and clutched Gideon's arm. He was certain she had no idea of it.

"Good God!" A fussily dressed elderly man came into the room and stood stock-still on the threshold, staring at the occupants in stupefaction. "Prudence! How come you to be here?"

This was, no doubt, Great-uncle Oswald. In a leisurely manner, Gideon finished his cognac, well aware that the elderly man was snorting and snuffing in outrage, but forced by good manners to wait for his host to acknowledge his presence. Gideon let him wait. Miss Merridew was still clutching his arm—unconsciously, he suspected, though he couldn't be sure. He waited for Great-uncle Oswald to become aware of it. It did not take long.

"What shamelessness is this?" The old man's face darkened, and his white brows gnashed fiercely together.

Never one to overlook an opportunity, Gideon wrapped his arm around her waist. It was a delightful waist, he decided, soft and inviting, with the most appealing curves above and below. She stiffened under his clasp.

"Unhand my great-niece, you unshaven lout!" roared Great-uncle Oswald.

The unshaven lout ignored him and hugged the great-niece a little tighter around the waist. He leered down at her.

Great-uncle Oswald gobbled like an enraged turkey. Flushing, Prudence wriggled out of Gideon's grip, pushed his hands away, and stammered an introduction.

"Great-uncle Oswald, I'd like to present you to the Duke of Dinstable." She cast Gideon a minatory glance. "Your Grace, this is my great-uncle, Sir Oswald Merridew."

Abandoning his pose as vile seducer, Gideon bowed correctly. "Your servant, Sir Oswald."

Sir Oswald gibbered silently, shocked. "You—Your Grace. So it was true, then. But . . . you surely cannot be the blackguard who has cozened my niece in such a havey-cavey way!"

"I expect I must be," Gideon said meekly. "Does it seem havey-cavey to you? I confess, it never occurred to me. Although blackguard does seem a trifle harsh. Rascal, I might accept, even scallywag, and unshaven lout, certainly, since I have been out all night." He passed a rueful hand across his roughened jaw. "But blackguard? Surely not."

In the face of this barefaced provocation, Sir Oswald resumed his gobbling. "What the devil does my great-niece mean to you, sir?" he demanded.

Aware that Miss Merridew was holding her breath anxiously, Gideon hesitated, then cast her a soulful look. "I cannot say," he replied truthfully. After all, he knew almost nothing about her, except that her lips tasted delicious. He heard her exhale in relief and smiled to himself. Did the girl really think he would denounce her? When he was having so much fun?

"Do you deny that you have extracted from her a promise?"

"I could deny it, I suppose, but I doubt you would believe me." He sighed plaintively.

"Disgraceful! Especially for a man of your position. Y'must have known the girl was too young to be allowed to make a promise like that without the knowledge of her guardian!"

Gideon glanced at Prudence and shrugged. "She does not seem too young to me."

"Blast it, man—sixteen is far too young!"

Gideon stared at Prudence in shock. "You cannot be only sixteen! I do not believe it! You look, er, much more mature—" His eyes dropped to the evidence of her maturity.

"Do not prevaricate with me, man! I am talkin' about four and a half years ago, as you very well know!"

"Four and a half years ago?" Gideon repeated blankly.

Prudence, observing his hesitation, stepped into the breach. "When we became betrothed, of course. You must have known I was sixteen *at the time*."

"Must I?" He grinned. "How?"

"We discussed it *at the time*," she replied with composure. "You have forgotten."

"Ah yes, I must have been thinking of other things *at the time*," he agreed, adding softly. "So, that means you must be, what?—add four and a half to sixteen—more than twenty now? Such a great age. No wonder Great-uncle Oswald is desperate to fire you off! Almost on the shelf, as you are."

She narrowed her eyes at him and her fists clenched as if she itched to box his ears. She was utterly delightful, thought Gideon, enjoying himself hugely.

"But you are a duke!" Sir Oswald thundered. "Why wait four years if you wanted the girl?"

"Why, indeed?" Gideon poured himself another cognac. "Brandy, Sir Oswald?"

"Poisonin' your innards with brandy? At this hour of the morning? Disgraceful!" Sir Oswald turned puce.

"Ah yes, Miss Merridew did warn me. Tea for you, then," agreed Gideon gently and waved a hand toward the teapot. "Or shall I ring for a fresh pot?"

With visible difficulty, Sir Oswald harnessed his outrage and moderated his tone. "No, no. Nothin' to drink, I thank you. What I am tryin' to understand," he said, "is why all the secrecy and creepin' around?"

Gideon raised his eyebrows. "Have I been creepin' around?" he asked Prudence in a tone of dread. "How very peculiar of me."

Though she primmed her mouth at him, a dimple betrayed her. She was enchanting, caught like this between amusement and outrage.

Sir Oswald persisted. "You know what I mean, blast it! If you wanted the gel, you must have known your suit would be looked on favorably—dammit, you are a duke, after all, even if you do dress like a shag bag!"

Gideon looked affronted. "A *shag bag?*" He glanced rue-fully down at his disheveled clothing, sighed, and turned a pair of mournful eyes on Prudence. "I creep about, and I dress like a shag bag. Are you sure you still wish to be be-trothed to me, my dear?"

"No! Not at all," Prudence snapped in exasperation. The interview was not going at all as she had planned it. She should have taken control of the conversation much earlier, only her brain seemed to have seized up for a moment after that kiss. Several moments, in fact. Instead of concentrating on the matter at hand, her wretched mind kept sliding back to relive that scandalous kiss. Even her lips still seemed to tingle from it.

She was in command of herself now, but in the meantime the situation had galloped out of control. If only this wretched duke would stop his nonsense and let her enact the role she had spent half the night rehearsing, it would all be sorted out by now. Instead he seemed to be having a high old time of it.

"Enough of this shilly-shallyin' around!" snapped Great-uncle Oswald. "I want an answer—now! Why did you not come to speak to her guardian, like an honest man?"

Prudence opened her mouth to explain.

"Be silent, gel! I want to hear it from him, dammit! He has spent long enough avoidin' the question!" He turned to the duke. "Come, sirrah! Explain! Why did you not ask for her hand—openly —like a man?"

There was a short silence as the duke considered the question. Prudence held her breath.

"I was shy," said six-foot-one of bashful male. He grunted as a sharp, feminine elbow thudded inconspicuously into his side.

Prudence stepped forward resolutely. "Great-uncle Os-wald, my eyes have been opened. I no longer wish to be be-trothed to this . . . this . . ."

"Cad," the duke supplied, sotto voce.

"Cad," she declared, mastering the faint quaver in her voice. "I find I was mistaken in his character. I was foolish at sixteen, but now I am, er, a woman grown—"

"Beautifully grown," murmured a deep voice in her ear.

"And I could not possibly marry a man who did not have the courage to face you or Grandpapa like a ma—"

"Not Grandpapa as well!" The cad beside her groaned theatrically. "What a miserable coward I have been!"

"Yes," she agreed severely. "And now it is too late for that, since poor Grandpapa lies—"

"God rest his soul," the wretch intoned piously.

"Poor Grandpapa lies on his *sickbed!*" Prudence corrected him. "And he is therefore unable to be spoken to." She faced Great-uncle Oswald resolutely. "In any case, I find my eyes have been opened to His Grace's true defects of character—"

"After all this time, I thought you must be willing to overlook the defects," murmured the duke irrepressibly. "Don't tell me you didn't even notice them? I am mortified, simply mortified!"

Prudence pressed her lips together a moment, forced a bubble of laughter back down, and continued, "I cannot marry a man who is such a miserable coward—"

"Not miserable, surely. Quite cheerful at—"

"And who, moreover"—she flung him a quelling glance—"displays a deeply flippant attitude to the serious things in life."

"One of those being Great-uncle Oswald," the dreadful man beside her murmured. "He is frightfully serious, is he not? Could do with a bit of cheering up, in my opinion."

Prudence spluttered as the mirth bubbled up inside her again. "Great-uncle Oswald, I find, on reflection, this man is quite unsuitable, not to mention that fact that, he, er—" She tried desperately to think of a final, clinching reason to sever her betrothal.

"Dresses like a shag bag? Is an unshaven lout?" the duke offered, under his breath.

She ignored him.

"Brandy in the morning?" he muttered.

Prudence seized on it, "A man who drinks brandy at this hour of the morning could never be the right man for me!"

Great-uncle Oswald frowned and considered her statement. "Yes, that is all very well, and I take your point." He glared at the duke, who immediately looked crushed. So pathetically crushed, in fact, that Prudence found giggles welling up in her again. She glared severely at the wretch. The wretch winked at her.

"Don't you dare wink at my great-niece like that, you blasted scoundrel!" snapped Great-uncle Oswald. "She is not some loose woman to be winked at by the likes of you . . ." He seemed suddenly to recall that this unshaven, carelessly dressed lout was a duke and added, "Er, duke or not."

"I beg your pardon?" a soft voice said from the doorway.

Prudence and Great-uncle Oswald glanced around in surprise. In the doorway was a neatly dressed man of medium height. In many ways he was the opposite of the duke, Prudence thought. Where the duke was tall and loose-limbed and disheveled, this man was plump and square and compact. Where the duke was dark and unshaven and casually dressed to the point of carelessness, this gentleman was as neat as wax, freshly shaved, his hair perfectly coiffed, and his clothing crisp and fresh. He looked to be about thirty.

"Morning, Edward," the duke said, grinning.

"Good morning, Gideon," the gentleman responded. "There seems to have been a great deal of noise coming from this room. Could I prevail on you to explain it to me?"

"This is private business, sir," Great-uncle Oswald began. "And I'll thank you to—"

The gentleman ignored him. "Gideon?" he repeated.

"Hang it, sir," Great-uncle Oswald blustered. "Who the devil do you think you are to be demandin' explanations when I just told you it was our private business!"

The gentleman turned haughtily. "Who the devil am *I*?" he said in a cold voice. "I, sir, am Edward Penteith, the Duke of Dinstable, and this is my house. And who might *you* be?"

Chapter Four

∞

"She's as headstrong as an Allegory on the banks of the Nile."
R. B. SHERIDAN

THE QUIETLY UTTERED WORDS SEEMED TO ECHO AROUND THE ROOM.

Great-uncle Oswald gaped for a moment, then spluttered, "Wha—! What the devil d'ye mean *you* are the Duke of Dinstable?"

The neatly dressed man merely raised an eyebrow, but it was the sort of gesture one could only inherit from generations of haughty-browed ducal ancestors. Great-uncle Oswald needed no further convincing. "Then who the deuce is this smoky knave?" he demanded angrily.

The duke raised his eyebrow again. "Allow me to present my cousin, Lord Carradice. And you are . . .?"

"Lord Carradice!" exclaimed Great-uncle Oswald, goggling in horror. "Lord *Carradice?* Why, I—I've *heard* of you!"

Lord Carradice bowed. It was a perfectly correct bow, thought Prudence, annoyed, yet it conveyed all sorts of other things—mockery, indifference, amusement. How dare he bow at her great-uncle like that. How dare he trick her! She frowned at him.

"Delighted to meet—"

Great-uncle Oswald cut him off. "Delighted, nothing, sir-rall! I've heard all about *you*—you're nothing but a rake! A scoundrel! A blackguard of the worst sort!"

"You *have* heard of me," murmured Lord Carradice, with every evidence of delight, and he bowed again.

Prudence squashed an impulse to giggle at such disgraceful behavior. She glared at him again.

"How dare you deceive me as to your true identity!" Great-uncle Oswald turned to the duke. "Do you realize, Your Grace, that this—this—"

"Scoundrel," offered Lord Carradice helpfully. "Shag bag. Unshaven lout. Cad. Smoky knave."

"This unmitigated reprobate," continued Great-uncle Oswald, undeterred, "had the temerity to introduce himself to me—here in this very room!—by your own title."

The duke glanced at his cousin in inquiry.

"Actually, I didn't," Lord Carradice said gently.

"But—" began Great-uncle Oswald.

Lord Carradice held up a hand. "Ungentlemanly as it may be, I must point out that it was your great-niece who introduced us." He turned to Prudence. "Miss Merridew? You have the floor, I think." His eyes met hers with wicked amusement, belying the earnest, reproachful manner he had adopted.

The wretch! Prudence gripped her reticule hard. He was positively delighting in embarrassing her. He had led her most cunningly down the garden path, and was taking quite obvious delight in watching her flounder in her tangled web. That fact that she deserved it didn't make her any less annoyed. She longed to throw something at his handsome face.

No wonder he had been not the slightest bit perturbed when she explained the false betrothal ruse to him. He'd known all along he couldn't possibly be implicated—not as the Duke of Dinstable. He'd *known* that she'd be made to look the veriest simpleton, the most complete nincompoop! Oh, what a fiend! He could have warned her, could have explained, but no! He'd only compounded her errors with his silence.

Two can play at that game, my lord. What had the duke called him? Gideon, yes, that was it. His first name was Gideon.

She blinked innocently back at Lord Carradice and said in a soft, puzzled voice, "But Gideon, dear, I do not understand." She allowed her voice to falter. "You mean you are not really the duke? And this gentleman is?" She gave the real duke a brave little smile of piteous bewilderment. "But why would you—" She broke off artistically.

There was another short silence in the room as its occupants absorbed the implications of this speech. Too late, Prudence realized that her temper had led her into a worse case than before.

"Oh, vile deceiver!" Great-uncle Oswald leaped to his feet. "How dare you dupe an innocent gel in such an appallin' manner! Flyin' under false colors, you cowardly impostor! What a shockin' humbug! To try to dazzle an unworldly child by laying claim to a rank not your own—"

"Child?" interrupted the Duke of Dinstable.

"Sixteen, she was, when this blackguard first tried his bamboozlin' ways upon her! Sixteen!"

The duke looked at Gideon.

Unconcerned, Gideon pulled out a slender sheaf of papers from his coat pocket. He broke the seals and thumbed quickly through them, feigning complete indifference to the discussion at hand. He was enjoying the role of the callous heartbreaker. For once, he was innocent of all accusations. Not that he ever dallied with innocents; it was one of his rules. And he doubted he had ever broken anyone's heart. The ladies he dallied with bore little evidence of a heart.

He darted a quick look at Miss Merridew, and his amusement deepened. A most unusual female. Gently bred and, he thought, a true innocent, despite her brazenness in entering a strange gentleman's house and claiming a secret betrothal with him. Or perhaps because of it. No truly worldly female would have the temerity to try such a simple ruse. He had no idea what bizarre game she was playing, but there was no denying it, the whole thing was vastly amusing.

Sir Oswald shook a furious finger at him. "Use another man's title to steal the innocent heart from a maiden's tender breast, would you?"

Gideon tossed the papers carelessly into the coal scuttle and regarded the maiden's tender breasts with interest, examining their shape and fullness with great pleasure. They were hastily covered with a pair of militantly crossed arms. He lifted his gaze and met a maiden's glaring eyeballs. Her smooth cheeks were flushed and the tender breasts were now heaving in indignation beneath their green muslin armor. A small, slippered foot tapped angrily on the parquetry floor. Gideon chuckled.

Prudence had had enough. How dare he—he—look at her in such a manner. She felt hot, breathless, excited—furious! It was time to end this disastrous charade.

"So!" she declared. "You have been deceiving me!" Unable to muster a convincing sob, she whipped out a lace handkerchief from her reticule and applied it to her eyes. "All of this time, you have been filling my ears with lies!" She drew herself up and said with immense dignity, "I cannot bear it a moment longer! You are without shame! I could not possibly wed a man of such unsteady character!"

Lord Carradice, more than her equal in the dramatic arts, slapped a tragic hand across his heart and staggered back a pace, and demonstrated wounded to the quick, in silence.

Great-uncle Oswald watched, frowning. He looked unconvinced. Prudence cast around for some way to end the matter definitively. An idea flew into her mind.

She snatched up the papers he had tossed aside so carelessly. "My letters," she explained to her great-uncle. She turned and brandished them in Lord Carradice's face. "You are heartless to flaunt these in my face, to treat them with such cavalier disdain. It is over, Lord Carradice! I want never to see you again!" She ripped them up and dashed them into the fire with great panache. "Oh, that I was ever foolish enough to give my heart to a rake." The fire smoldered, then flared eagerly as the papers caught.

"Oh, no, not the *billets doux*. My love letters!" cried Lord Carradice in a choked voice. He leaped toward the fire and snatched in vain at the burning papers. He burned his fingers on one and dropped it with a mild curse.

Stunned, Prudence watched him. The shredded sheets of paper curled into twists of flame and ash. He couldn't be serious. Surely they could not be *real* love letters she had burned? He'd just glanced at them and cast them into a coal scuttle with a complete lack of interest. Anything thrown into a coal scuttle was meant for burning! Wasn't it?

And yet he looked so distraught. The hollow feeling in her chest grew.

What if they were love letters? Had he tossed them in the coal scuttle as a blind, meaning to collect them later? She'd used all sorts of devious methods of hiding Phillip's rare letters from prying eyes. Apart from one special letter that she treasured, his letters weren't romantic: Phillip was a prosaic writer and his letters were usually a short recital of his daily activities. Even so, she'd never tossed even the dullest one into a coal scuttle.

Prudence bit her lip. Lord Carradice was staring into the fire, watching his letters burn. He looked desolated, completely crushed. Even his giveaway eyes were no longer laughing.

She groaned inwardly. Why had she ever considered this mad idea? It had seemed quite simple at the time. There must be insanity in her family. Certainly Grandpapa was . . . eccentric. But even he had never burst into a strange ducal residence, claimed betrothal to the duke—who was really a lord and apparently a notorious rake as well—and then burned the rake's love letters.

Who knew, but the writer of those letters might have reformed him of his rakish behavior. Love could reform a rake, she had heard.

She thought of the one special letter Phillip had sent her. *"You are the sole dream that keeps me going in this hellhole on earth."*

Any moment now, Lord Carradice would turn on her in rage, abandon his inexplicable charade, and explain her outrageous folly to her Great-uncle Oswald and the duke. And then she would have to confess all, and she knew well what would happen then: she would be sent back to Norfolk in disgrace. And then her sisters and she would never escape.

Prudence felt sick. She thought she'd come up with such a clever plan, but in fact, she had ruined everything.

Lord Carradice heaved a huge sigh. It had the effect of drawing everyone's attention back to him. "Oh well, it was worth a try," he said in a regretful tone.

Prudence guiltily recalled his burned fingers. Even a charred shred of love letter was better than no love letter at all.

"I suppose such an imposture was bound to be exposed in the end," he added. "Imposture always does come out." He looked at Prudence sadly.

Imposture! He was about to expose her. Prudence took a deep breath and braced herself.

"I apologize for deceiving you, Miss Merridew."

Prudence blinked.

"You cannot mean you *did* deceive this young lady as to your identity, Gideon?" The duke looked mildly shocked.

Lord Carradice shrugged sheepishly. "I am such a worthless fribble, you know, Edward. Girls are so much more impressed with your title than mine."

The duke's eyes narrowed, but he said nothing.

Prudence held her breath.

Great-uncle Oswald finally spoke. "You, sirrah, are a disgrace to your name and your class! Tellin' a filly a few Banbury tales to impress her is one thing; masqueradin' as a duke and enterin' into a secret betrothal is quite another! And this poor, trustin' little creature has waited for you to speak to her grandpapa or me—as a man should—for nigh on four and a half years!"

"Four and a half years, four and a half months, four and a half minutes . . ." Lord Carradice gazed at Prudence soulfully. "Time means nothing, when one is in love."

The duke frowned, sent a piercing look toward his cousin, then turned his gaze on Prudence.

Prudence didn't know whether to kiss Lord Carradice or to strangle him! She was grateful that he had not exposed her, of course she was! But his talk of love was making things worse again. She had severed the false betrothal, and he was off the hook. If he would only be quiet, she could leave now, and though Great-uncle Oswald would be angry, it might not be the complete disaster she had feared a few moments before.

"Come, Great-uncle Oswald, let us leave," she said in a low voice. "I have no desire to have my folly any further discussed. My betrothal is at an end, no harm has been done, and I would be grateful if we could depart at once." She took the old man's arm and tried to steer him toward the door, but Great-uncle Oswald refused to budge. He glared from Lord Carradice to the duke and back.

"So that's it, then, is it?"

Nobody responded. Prudence tugged at his arm, in vain.

"You engage yourself to my great-niece in a dashed havey-cavey manner, under a false title, you keep the gel danglin' for four years, then I find you meetin' her in secret, alone and unchaperoned—"

"No, no! I brought Lily with me."

Great-uncle Oswald dismissed her maid with a wave of his hand. "In the hallway—doesn't count!"

"And there was the butler. He was with us almost all the time," Prudence added desperately.

"Pah! Butlers can be bought!"

An affronted snort came from outside the door.

Lord Carradice grinned. "Bribe Bartlett? But he's so expensive!"

"Be that as it may," said Great-uncle Oswald, "the gel has been compromised enough by—"

"No, no," cried Prudence, realizing Great-uncle Oswald was about to insist on marriage. "There is no question of compromise. I utterly refuse. The betrothal is off. I cannot marry a man such as, such as . . . this!" Unable to think of any sufficiently damning epithet, she gestured at Lord Carradice in disgust. She looked at him hard, willing him to take up her lead. Surely he would.

Lord Carradice opened his mouth to speak. Prudence relaxed a little.

"What if I shave?" he said. "I look much better when I'm shaved. My cousin will vouch for that—do I not look almost handsome when I shave, Edward? " He didn't wait for the duke's reply but turned earnestly back to Prudence. "Do you think you could marry me if I shaved?" The duke frowned and stared at Lord Carradice intently. Lord Carradice ignored him.

The man was impossible! Prudence glared at him. "No," she snapped. "I would not marry you if you were the last man left alive in the world! You are a complete—an utter—"

She waved her hands in frustration, but the words would not come. All she could think of was *shag bag,* or *scoundrel,* or *unshaven lout,* or *smoky knave,* and if she uttered those words, she knew she would be completely undone.

It was impossible. The whole thing had got completely out of control. She had tried everything she could think of and now she could see only one way out of her current predicament.

So she fainted.

It was quite a good faint, she thought, being unplanned and the first she had ever attempted. It certainly put an end to the ridiculous conversation about her betrothal to Lord Carradice. The only trouble was that she should perhaps have signaled her imminent collapse to Great-uncle Oswald—a sigh or a small gasp of feminine distress perhaps. Elderly men clearly found it not to their liking to be the recipient of an unexpectedly falling female.

Great-uncle Oswald staggered and gasped under her weight. He seemed in imminent danger of dropping her to the floor. It may have been a miscalculation on her part to fall toward him instead of collapsing gracefully into insensibility onto Cleopatra's barge. It took all her control to maintain the illusion of insensibility as she felt herself slipping.

And then, with shocking suddenness, she was snatched from disaster by a pair of muscular arms. She was only just able to prevent herself from squeaking as she was lifted bodily off the floor and clasped securely against a broad, masculine chest.

It was not Great-uncle Oswald's chest. It was not the duke's. Prudence hoped very much it was the butler, Bartlett, who was holding her with such apparent effortlessness, but Bartlett had seemed more cushionesque than otherwise. She sniffed surreptitiously. There was no telltale scent of musk. There was—she sniffed again, just to be sure—a faint aroma of spirits and tobacco, a tang of soap and starch from his linen, and, most intriguing of all, the scent of . . . She was hard put to recognize it, but it was most appealing. Could it be, the scent of . . . a rake?

Reluctantly, Prudence allowed her mind to recognize what her body had known instantly. It was Lord Carradice who had snatched her thus. Against whose chest she was nestled. It was a very broad and comforting chest, she had to admit. She felt an overwhelming desire to curl up against it forever, but apart from the fact that she had no business feeling anything so shocking, she knew that within that chest beat a heart that was quite without proper feeling of any kind.

Great-uncle Oswald had called him a famous—nay, an *infamous* rake, a scoundrel, and a reprobate. And he hadn't denied it. He'd even seemed quite proud of having such a dreadful reputation. It seemed quite conclusive.

And Prudence had the evidence of her own eyes that he took nothing seriously. He ought to have been shocked by her wicked forwardness. Instead he had casually entangled them both even further in deception, embroidering on her initial lie with merry abandon, adding layers and layers of further complication, without, apparently, a thought for the consequences.

She did not excuse her own part in creating the lie in the first place, but she at least had been driven by desperation. He seemed to have joined in for . . . for fun! He'd even taken most shocking advantage of her duplicity by using it to steal a kiss. Moreover, a kiss that had not only taken her by surprise, but that had undermined her own sense of lady-like behavior.

She could not quite rid herself of the suspicion that she had pressed herself against him in quite a forward manner. And there was no denying that the experience—though shocking!—had been pleasurable. There had been several instants after he'd stopped kissing her before she'd remembered to push him away.

And those dark, wickedly dancing eyes told her he knew it, every time he looked at her. It was most ungentlemanly of him.

He seemed to have very few notions of gentlemanly behavior. In fact, judging by his demeanor throughout, he seemed to thrive on deception. She supposed rakes must—else how would they be rakes? Ladies, surely, did not wish to be ruined; there would have to be deception or trickery involved. Wouldn't there?

She sighed, feeling the very appealing strength of the arms that held her. It was suddenly much clearer to Prudence how an otherwise virtuous lady might find herself wishing to be ruined.

She waited for him to put her down, knowing that a pony-girl had to be too heavy for any man to carry for more than a few seconds. So she held her breath . . . and waited . . . and waited . . . and he showed no sign of needing to do so. Prudence had never felt so delightfully delicate and feminine in her life. She knew she was not, of course, but the sensation was indescribable.

It was a very good thing that gentlemen in general were not encouraged to carry ladies about, otherwise there would be even more sin in the world than there was already, she decided.

She kept her eyes firmly closed, lying limp against his chest, in absolute certainty of his strength supporting her. If she looked up, she knew she would find herself looking into a pair of dark, laughing eyes. And from this distance, she would find him extremely difficult to resist. And that would be fatal.

She dangled bonelessly in his arms and listened to the flurry of activity around her. Bartlett had apparently produced some feathers and was wishing to burn them under her nose.

Lord Carradice objected to that, saying the smell of burned feathers disgusted him.

Bartlett said that was the point.

Lord Carradice responded that he did not wish to be disgusted at such an ungodly hour, that he had had quite enough to deal with as it was, and that Bartlett would oblige him by putting the feathers away and fetching a glass of water instead.

Bartlett sniffed. The scent of musk receded and Prudence concluded that he had gone to fetch the water.

Uncle Oswald was searching through Prudence's reticule, muttering that women's indispositions were very disconcertin' things for a man to deal with—very disconcertin'! And why the deuce wasn't she carryin' her dratted smellin' salts?

The duke, it appeared, had fetched Prudence's maid and seemed to be expecting Lily to do something, but Lily, overwhelmed by the grand company in which she found herself, said to the duke over and over again, "I dunno to be sure, Your Highness. She ain't never fainted before."

Prudence felt another giggle coming on. She stifled it and abruptly felt herself squeezed in the most alarmingly exciting manner.

"If you dare to laugh now, I shall drop you in the fire along with my tailor's bills," he murmured under his breath, his mouth against her ear. "You have carried the whole thing off beautifully, but if you giggle, you shall ruin everything."

He *knew* she was feigning insensibility. And yet he continued to hold her in this shockingly intimate fashion. Prudence stiffened with indignation. And then the meaning of his words sank in.

His tailor's bills? The love letters he had tried so heartrendingly to rescue from the flames were his tailor's bills? She compressed her quivering lips together, hard. Oh he was a devil, to be sure. She had felt so guilty at burning them. His tailor's bills!

"Put me down at once," she hissed through stiff lips.

He made no move to do so. Instead, he jiggled her in his arms in a most provocative fashion.

"Put her down, at once!" Great-uncle Oswald's voice echoed her words uncannily.

"Oh, there's no danger of me dropping her," said Lord Carradice casually and jiggled her again. "I am merely trying to get more air in her lungs. Oh, well, if you insist, I shall place her here, on the settee."

Prudence felt herself being lowered onto something long and padded. Cleopatra's barge, she thought. As his arms released her she sighed. With relief, she told herself.

"Should we not fetch a carriage and take her home?" said the duke's soft voice.

"Yes, yes—her sisters will know what to do," exclaimed Great-uncle Oswald in obvious relief. He sounded quite flustered. "Ladies' indispositions best left to ladies, after all! You, gel, whatever your name is! See to your mistress while—demmit! I sent the carriage home. Thought I'd be here longer." He turned to the duke. "It will have to be a hackney, if one can be procured. But your man will need to inspect it first. Last time I used a hackney it stank shockin'ly of onions! And check the seats. If m'great-niece is to lie on the seats—oh, hang it. I'll inspect it m'self. I need some fresh air after all this botheration." He turned back to Lily and barked, "Don't leave her side for a moment, gel!"

"Yessir, Sir Oswald." In her mind's eye, Prudence could see Lily bobbing a curtsy. She heard the duke and Great-uncle Oswald leave the room. Silence fell. She was alone, then, with Lord Carradice and Lily.

Prudence lay still, her eyes tightly closed, trying to decide when would be the best time to make her recovery. She had no wish to allow Great-uncle Oswald to have second thoughts about her so-called broken betrothal with the false duke, Lord Carradice. On the other hand, she did not think she could cope with being carried out to the carriage by Lord Carradice. It was too . . . unsettling.

Motionless, eyes closed and breathing gently, Prudence considered her options. Cleopatra's barge was surprisingly comfortable. She was lolling on it, she realized suddenly, and had to suppress a spurt of laughter.

"Lily, is it? I wonder, could I trouble you to you pop out to the kitchen and desire Mrs. Henderson, the housekeeper, to give you a bottle of smelling salts?" said Lord Carradice in a soft, deep voice that was all liquid charm.

"Oh, er, well, sir, it's just—" Lily hesitated.

Lord Carradice chuckled. "You don't think I'm going to do your mistress any harm, do you Lily?" His voice was pure, dark honey.

Prudence stiffened. No woman could resist that voice, let alone a simple country maid like Lily. She decided to give Lily an incentive to stay and moaned a little, as if she were about to come around.

"Look there," said Lord Carradice instantly. "See, she is coming to. Run and fetch those smelling salts instantly, there's a good girl."

"But Sir Oswald said . . . Shouldn't I stay?"

"What if she should fall over again, Lily? You would not

be able to catch her, a frail little creature like yourself. I think I had better stay."

Frail little creature indeed! thought Prudence furiously. Lily was a good fourteen stone at least, and had been known to knock a cheeky footman on his ears with one blow! Oh, he was a rake indeed! Wickedness incarnate. There was not a word of truth in him!

"Yes, o' course, sir," murmured Lily in a dazed, adoring voice. "That would be best. I'll fetch those smelling salts, sir, no trouble at all."

"And perhaps a reviving cordial," suggested Lord Carradice in a solicitous voice. "Mrs. Henderson will know which one."

The room fell silent. Prudence felt a sudden warmth against her leg. He'd had the cheek to seat himself on the settee right beside her. So close beside her, in fact, that she could feel the heat of his body right through her skirts. Cautiously, she opened her eyes and immediately found herself gazing up into the darkest, most alive pair of eyes she had ever beheld in her life. He bent over her, his hands gripping the gilt edging of Cleopatra's barge on either side of her, not actually touching her, but imprisoning her all the same. If she tried to sit up, she would have to push against him and she already knew his strength. She had never in her adult life been carried so effortlessly.

"Feeling better?" He smiled down at her.

There ought to be a law against smiles like that, Prudence thought dazedly. But he had no doubt smiled in just such a caressing way at her impressionable maid. She rallied her defenses. "You know perfectly well that I didn't faint. In fact, you should be grateful to me for it."

"Oh, indeed I am," he said, grinning irrepressibly, and somehow she just knew he was recalling the shocking way he had jiggled her in his arms.

Prudence tried to strain away from him, pressing into the padding on the settee. She felt completely breathless. His eyes smiled knowingly at her, as if he could somehow read her secret thoughts and desires. As if he knew they were at war with her principles. In defense, she dropped her gaze to his mouth. It was a very nice mouth, she thought breathlessly. Finely chiseled and made, it seemed, for laughter. And for kissing. She glanced up at him again and instantly took fright.

"Go away!" She wriggled and thrust her hands against his broad, warm chest. "Let me up!"

"It's no use you looking at me like that," he said softly. "It's far too late to attempt escape." And with that, he lowered his mouth to hers.

Chapter Five

∞

*"O nothing is more alluring
than a levee from a couch in some confusion."*
WILLIAM CONGREVE

IT WAS NOT LIKE THE FIRST KISS HE HAD GIVEN HER—THAT SWIFT, startling stolen kiss that had wiped her mind as blank as a new slate and left her lips tingling many minutes afterward.

This was altogether more . . . more . . .

Just more.

She had been kissed before, yes, but not like this . . . not with the whole mouth. His lips were firm and sure, effortlessly robbing her of her will. Domination by pleasure. His tongue was like warm velvet, stroking, seeking.

She could *taste* him! She tasted the brandy he had drunk a short time before. But beneath that, there was hot, dark, irresistible . . . enticement.

With each stroke, Prudence's resolution dissolved a little more. Without conscious volition, her body arched against him. Her fingers tangled in his hair.

She ought to stop this . . . but whatever it was that he was doing seemed to have robbed her mind of every coherent principle . . . and all resolve. It was magic . . . It was bound to be sinful. It was . . . Prudence could not think. She could only hold onto him, helplessly . . . entranced . . . as sensation swamped her.

His tongue moved in a slow relentless rhythm. A feverish rush of pleasure engulfed her. She'd never felt like this, her mouth and body possessed, fueled by heat and magic.

After a moment Prudence realized he had stopped kissing her. She battled to marshall her wits, but all she could do was blink and stare at his mouth, so close to hers, and wonder at the turmoil it had caused within her . . . was causing still. Who would believe what mere lips could do? And tongue. She flushed again, as a wave of heat passed through her.

She fought for breath, battling to regain her composure, aware of his looming physicality, his gaze hot upon her, still scorching her awareness so that she was unable to look up. Unable to look anywhere, in fact, except at his disheveled cravat. Only she could not help seeing his mouth as well.

She hadn't realized a man's mouth could be so masculine and yet beautiful as well. She thought about the way that mouth had transported her and closed her eyes for a brief moment. The scent of him teased her senses; would she ever be able to forget it after this? A faint odor of brandy and cologne and man and desire.

He'd imprisoned her in a cage made of his body. And hers. Each place their bodies touched burning into her consciousness like a hot iron. His hard right hip pressed against the softness of her thigh. His strong arms were braced on either side of her, one long-fingered hand resting against her shoulder, the other so close beside her left cheek that she could feel its warmth; if she only turned her head a little, her face would be resting on his hand. He bent over her, his chest just inches from hers, and he was breathing heavily, raggedly, as if he had just run a race. And each time he breathed in, his waistcoat just brushed her breasts. Each faint, feather-light sensation sent a quiver right through her body, all the way to her toes.

Prudence held her breath and closed her eyes. She had no desire to escape. She knew she ought to, but she felt so deliciously languid . . . and yet hot, flustered, and tense with expectation at the same time.

She opened her eyes again and forced herself to look at him. She had to see, to know what he was thinking. He was staring down at her, for once no gleam of humor in those dark, dark eyes. He seemed almost . . . shaken. A faint frown creased the space between his brows. His gaze pinned her, intense, slightly puzzled, as if she were some enigma, some mystery.

"Who the devil are you, Miss Prudence Merridew?" he murmured.

Like a bucket of icy water dashed against her overheated skin, his question brought her back to her senses. She focused with all her might. "I'm sorry, Lord Carradice. I didn't mean to cause anyone any trouble," she said in a shaky voice, suddenly perilously near to tears. "I lied to protect my real betrothed. He is a younger son with meager prospects and dependent on my great-uncle's good will."

"That's not what I meant." His voice was deep and vibrated through her body.

She felt suddenly breathless and took an abrupt, shaky breath. Dazed by the turmoil of feelings, she groped for some sort of composure, swallowed, for her mouth was unaccountably dry, and licked her lips. A mistake, she realized instantly, for his gaze heated, and his mocking, beautiful mouth twisted with an unknown emotion, and before she could say a word, she was being kissed once more.

Prudence felt her body rise to meet his, her mouth open to receive the hot, spicy heat of him and as the dark vortex of sensation whirled around her consciousness again, the cool texture of his waistcoat and the cold metal of the buttons bit into the thin fabric covering her breasts. The heat and power of his body radiated through the clothes, and she quivered again, a long shudder of awareness.

Suddenly his hand was on her breast, caressing, teasing, causing the most exquisite sensations to ripple and shudder through her. She trembled and sighed under his hand and he groaned softly.

It was the groan that did it.

It sounded to Prudence's ears like the purr of a self-satisfied cat. An extremely self-satisfied cat. Deep and low, seductive and . . . wicked.

It brought her to a shocked awareness of what she was doing. Here she was, in a strange man's house—a strange duke's house!—lying in an abandoned manner on a decadent Egyptian sofa receiving the most intimate and shocking liberties from a man whom she had only just met. A man, moreover, who was a known rake. A man whom she had seen for herself cared nothing for the usual proprieties or canons of good behavior. And he knew she was betrothed.

Good grief, what had she allowed him to do? She did not even know him, and what she did know should have been enough to make her shun him. He had deceived her, lied about his identity, mocked her great-uncle. He was disheveled, carelessly dressed. His chin was rough with bristles . . .

Prudence tried not to think of how deliciously abrasive those bristles had felt against her skin.

He had been out carousing all night. He drank brandy at breakfast time. The sharp, hot taste of his brandy was now in her own mouth. She felt the blood rise in her cheeks at the thought of it. He was a well-known rake . . . and Prudence Merridew, within minutes of meeting him, had allowed him unimaginable intimacies.

His hand even now stroked her thigh through her thin dress. The other one cupped her breast, his long fingers rubbing, teasing . . . And worst of all—

Worst of all was not that she'd allowed it—it was that she liked it. More than liked it.

Women are nothing but weak, untrustworthy vessels, slaves to their base animal instincts! Grandpapa's voice echoed in her mind. Prudence froze. She had fought against Grandpapa and his horrid strictures all her life. She was no weak vessel, no helpless female. She was a slave to no one and nothing. She'd prided herself on it.

Yet now, look at her! Sprawled helplessly beneath a man who had just taken the most shocking liberties—and she was wishing, most wickedly, for more!

Even though she was betrothed . . . How could a decent, betrothed woman possibly enjoy the illicit advances of a stranger? All her principles and resolve had simply gone up in smoke, vanquished by the casual skill of a rake.

He bent and kissed her again. His tongue lapped at her closed mouth, his teeth nipped gently at her lower lip, demanding entrance. And her body longed to open to him, allow him whatever he wanted.

. . . *slaves to their base animal instincts* . . .

It was not her first experience of her base animal instinct, but Prudence would be no man's slave. She'd been taken unawares, but she was a woman of principle. Or she tried to be. She pushed his face away.

"Unhand me sir," Prudence said crisply. "I wish to get up." Unfortunately, the words came out feebly, almost dreamily, and with a complete lack of conviction. She was mortified to realize her hands still cupped his face. She could not seem to let go.

He took a deep breath, blinked, stared down at her, and the look in his eyes made her gasp. He seemed to shake himself, then his expression changed. It was as if a shutter came over his eyes, that gleam of laughter returned. He sat back a little, took another deep breath and—unforgivably—chuckled. "I doubt if you can stand, yet." There was knowledge and self-satisfied male pride in his eyes, as well as amusement. And a certain careless possessiveness.

He thought her his for the taking.

The realization galvanized her resolve like nothing else could. He might be a rake, but Prudence Merridew was not a loose woman! Even if she had behaved like one for a moment or two. Or three.

Good heavens! At any minute Lily or that odious butler—not to mention Great-uncle Oswald and the duke—could walk into the room and find her carousing with a known rake! She would rather die than allow that to happen.

"I said, unhand me, sir!" This time her voice sounded much more crisp and authoritative, she noted with satisfaction. Even if her body was still feeling deliciously languid and shivery and enjoying the sensation of his arms around her far too much.

He smiled, shook his head provocatively, and tightened his hold. He leaned down, clearly intending to kiss her senseless once more. She could not allow it. Not even one kiss, much as her body might crave it. She simply had to break away from his possession of her. The longer she stayed in such intimate contact with him, the feebler her resolve. And the stronger the desire to feel his mouth on hers again . . .

Prudence panicked. "Let me up! I have had quite enough of your manhandling, sirrah!" Her tone was pure Great-uncle Oswald, she reflected, but it was the best she could do.

His brow quirked. "Manhandling?"

Prudence flushed. "I wish to stand up, sir. I am no longer, er, indisposed." She could not quite meet his eyes.

"But it's been so delightful, er, reviving you like this. Are you sure you are, er, recovered?" he purred provocatively.

That did it. He was playing a rakish game! All of Prudence's resolve rallied. "Set me free, sir!" She raised her hands to push him back. Her reticule, still attached by the strings to her wrist, bumped against her arm.

"No." He grinned. "I think you require a little more, ah, reviving."

"Please let me up!"

He shook his head.

"Then if you will not do the gentlemanly thing—" Prudence said sweetly and hit him over the head with her reticule. It collided against his skull with a most satisfactory clunk. Grace had used very good quality pasteboard and had lacquered over the heathenish Egyptian designs very thoroughly.

"Ow! Blast it, what—"

She tried to push him away, but he kept her imprisoned still. She hit him again.

"Dammit—" He lifted a hand to ward off the reticule, and his grip on her loosened.

Prudence took the opportunity to wriggle out from beneath the cage of his body and slide awkwardly to the floor. She stood up and found her knees a little wobbly, so she retreated behind an ebony inlaid desk and used it to support herself unobtrusively. "How dare you—you—assault me like that!"

"Assault you?" He rubbed his head. "You have the nerve to accuse me of assault after attacking me with that blasted thing? What the devil is it, anyway?"

Prudence ignored him. "I am not for the likes of you, Lord Carradice!"

Lord Carradice stopped rubbing his forehead for a moment. He looked at her with spaniel-dark eyes and said with mock reproach, "Now, Prudence, I thought it was apparent to us both that you *like* the likes of me." And then he grinned in an infuriatingly appealing way.

Prudence ignored the appeal and concentrated on being infuriated. "Well, you are wrong. I most emphatically do not like the likes of you!" she said in what she trusted was a convincing voice.

A devilish look came into his eyes, and he prowled toward her. "I'm certain you are mistaken. I think we should test that theory again."

Oh heavens, he was going to kiss her again! His eyes had that hot look of dark intent she was beginning to recognize. She could not let him touch her. Prudence retreated behind the table. "Stop that at once! I am not for you, Lord Carradice."

He looked crushed, most unconvincingly. "Oh, but after all we have meant to each oth—"

"I *told* you I am betrothed!" Prudence reiterated in desperation.

"Oh yes, so you are. I quite forgot." Lord Carradice grinned, rubbing his head again. "You are engaged to the Duke of Dinstable—or me—or some younger son with no prospects. I forget which."

"You know perfectly well I was never engaged to either you or the duke," Prudence snapped. "As I explained, it was—it was a mistake!"

"Not removing that blasted reticule from your wrist was the mistake," said Lord Carradice in an aggrieved voice. "What the deuce is it made of? Wood?"

"Pasteboard! Though I do not know what concern it is of yours—"

"It's my concern if I get biffed over the head by it. It has a dozen sharp corners and is as heavy as lead! And besides which, it is dam—er, deuced ugly. Why the devil you must carry a thing that weighs a ton and is absolutely hideous to boot, is quite beyond me."

"The reason I carry it should be obvious, even to you," Prudence retorted waspishly. "A girl clearly *needs* a strong reticule in London, does she not? Especially when she comes visiting! Besides, it is not hideous. It was a gift, a labor of love by my little sister and therefore is, to me, *much* more beautiful and valuable than all the hideously expensive furniture in this decadent, horrible room!"

"Oh, I quite agree."

Prudence looked at him through narrowed eyes. She trusted his instant agreement not a whit!

He grinned unrepentantly. "The furniture is horrible. Edward's mother had it all done up like a pharaoh's dinner some seven or eight years ago, in the expectation of him entering London society, but then—for reasons we shall not go into—it all came to naught, and here is this house, filled to the brim with hideous furniture that is now quite out of date! And the worst thing is, Edward has no interest in furniture, so he leaves it like this, to lacerate the sensibilities of people of taste! At least you have an excuse for carrying that frightful reticule, since it was foisted on you by an infant."

"Grace is *not* an infant, and it was *not* foisted on me. Besides, I happen to be very fond—" She stopped herself and took a deep breath, mastering her temper with difficulty. "We will not speak of my reticule," she said with dignity. "My reticule is not the issue here."

"Tell that to these bruises."

She could not prevent herself glancing at his forehead. There were indeed several faint red marks, where a pasteboard corner had dented his skin. Guiltily she met his gaze—only to find laughter spilling from wicked, dark eyes. There was not a trace of a contrition in the wretch.

Prudence opened her mouth to speak. She would wipe that confident smile off his face.

"Ahh, I see you have quite recovered," the duke interrupted from the doorway.

Prudence wondered how long he had been standing there. Something about his expression, a lurking expression of stifled amusement, made her think he might have observed more of her dealings with Lord Carradice than she would wish anyone to witness. She felt an embarrassed flush rise.

"Yes, your color is returning," the duke murmured in a voice of such blandness that it confirmed her suspicions.

"Sir Oswald has finally managed to procure a satisfactory hackney cab, and your maidservant awaits you in the hall with some smelling salts."

"And your betrothed will escort you to the door," Lord Carradice added affably, "*if* you will just inform us which of us he is." He extended his arm to her in a mockery of polite behavior.

The man was impossible. "You know perfectly well I am not betrothed to either of you!" Prudence lifted her chin and prepared to march out the door.

Lord Carradice laid a restraining hand on her arm. "Oh, but if you've been pining for me for the last four and a half years, I really think you deserve a fiancé."

"*Pining?*" Prudence was outraged. "I would *never* indulge in such spineless behavior! And even if I did, I would never pine for *you*, Lord Carradice, as you very well know!"

"Oh, but now you have come to know me so much better . . ." He waggled his eyebrows at her. "You will pine, Prudence, you will."

It was an outrageous thing to say, especially when she could still feel the imprint of his mouth on hers. And the taste of him. Prudence glanced from his dancing eyes to the long strong hand lightly clasping her arm.

He was quite incorrigible.

And impossibly charming. But she would *not* be charmed for the amusement of a lighthearted rake! "Oh, will you release me!" she said crossly.

"No, never, my heart. I never release my betrotheds," he said soulfully.

"Oh stop it! I told you the truth!" she snapped, tugging unsuccessfully at her arm. She turned to the duke and explained hastily, "I am deeply sorry for the imposition, Your Grace. For the last four and a half years I truly *have* been betrothed—to a man called Phillip Otterbury and Lord Carradice knows why I was unable to tell my great-uncle about it!" She tugged again to free her hand from Lord Carradice's grasp. "Now, will you let me go!" And with that, she swung her reticule at his head for the fourth time.

Gideon was better prepared this time. Releasing her arm, he ducked, and the cardboard sarcophagus bounced harm-lessly off his shoulder. He looked up, laughing, to see her storming out of the house with not a backward glance. A moment later he heard the front door slam.

"That," the duke said thoughtfully, "is a most unusual young lady."

Gideon grimaced ruefully. "She is indeed."

"I don't believe I have ever seen a female repulse you so decidedly."

"No." Gideon rubbed his jaw.

"I find it rather refreshing."

"Yes, well, you would. It is that perverse streak in the Penteiths."

The duke smiled absentmindedly. "I collect that despite the farrago of nonsense her elderly relative was spouting, your acquaintance with the girl is of recent duration."

Gideon chuckled and glanced at the clock on the mantel. "Yes, recent is the word. I would say I've known Miss Prudence Merridew for all of about forty minutes."

The duke arched an eyebrow. "She is not one of your . . . er . . ."

Gideon laughed again. "Oh, good Lord, no, she is not one of my *ers*. You should know better than that, Edward. My *ers* may be many and various, but they are never young innocents and without doubt Miss Prudence is a young innocent. Besides, no self-respecting *er* would dream of enacting such a ludicrous scene."

The duke nodded. "Yes, I thought she was not your usual type. Do you . . . ah, have an interest in her yourself, Gideon?"

Gideon looked blank for a moment. He opened his mouth, then closed it. He frowned, thought for a minute, opened his mouth again, then closed it. Then he shrugged carelessly. "You know I have no interest in innocents."

"Are you sure?"

"Yes, of course I'm sure," Gideon snapped, irritated. "Why do you ask?"

"If you have no interest in her, I may decide to pursue my acquaintance with Miss Merridew."

Gideon glanced up sharply. "Good God, why?"

"Have you so soon forgotten the reason for my trip to London?"

Gideon scowled, crossed one long leg over the other, and smoothed the fabric of his buff pantaloons with elaborate care. "Of course not. You have dragged yourself away from your beloved moors and mountains with some ludicrous desire to thrust your head into a matrimonial noose."

Edward smiled gently. "If I choose properly, it will be no noose."

Gideon snorted. "Properly! How can you choose properly? How can anyone—man or woman—choose properly? Do you and I not have the evidence of our own lives that marriage is no safe choice for anyone—man or woman?"

"Yes, but—"

"No one knows what they are getting themselves into when they wed. The mere notion of choice is one of fate's nastier jokes."

"Yes, perhaps, but still it must be done."

Gideon snorted.

"Mine is an ancient name, Cousin. There is that and the dukedom to be considered. My own wishes and fears are unimportant by comparison. I have a duty to marry. So do you, though I know you have set your mind against it."

Gideon snorted again. "Duty!"

The duke continued, "So far as choosing a wife is concerned, I have thought the matter over very carefully, in order that I may minimize the risk. Naturally, I do not want a beautiful bride—we both know why. A plain and convenient bride will suit me, someone I can simply be friends with. If there are no strong emotions on either side, all risks will be minimized. Besides, beautiful women make me nervous."

Gideon frowned. "Yes, I know. So why do you speak of pursuing an acquaintance with Miss Merridew?"

The duke looked at his cousin in surprise. "She is no beauty, at any rate."

Gideon sat up. "What? She's no commonplace society belle, I'll grant you that, but—"

"Indeed, quite the contrary. I find her most comfortably ordinary."

"Ordinary?" Gideon was disgusted. "Good God, man! What the devil's the matter with you? You said yourself she was refreshingly unusual."

"Yes, of course," Edward murmured in a bland voice. "I mean ordinary looking. Almost plain."

"Plain! Is there something wrong with your eyes? She's not the slightest bit plain! Those eyes, that smile, that hair— from top to toe, Prudence Merridew is a rare little gem!"

"A gem, you say?" The duke observed his cousin thoughtfully and smiled. "Quite. I phrased it badly. At any rate, she doesn't make me nervous."

"More fool you, then." Gideon rubbed his head feelingly. "She makes me damned nervous! Never know what the chit is going to do next." He subsided into a chair with a faint, reminiscent grin.

Edward steepled his fingers carefully and said, "She seemed to have an interest in dukes. I see no reason why I should not allow her to pursue it."

Gideon looked narrowly at his cousin. "I wouldn't refine too much upon it, if I were you. I cannot be sure whether she thinks she wishes to marry a duke, or whether she wishes *not* to marry a duke, but whatever it is, you shall put her from your mind forthwith, Edward."

"Oh, but if she is interested in dukes, what a happy coincidence. I am a duke, after all, come to London to further my acquaintance with the female sex. It was your idea, Gideon, if you recall."

"I must have been castaway at the time."

"Miss Merridew is the only female I have met in London so far."

"That shall soon be remedied."

"And since she is refreshingly unlike the females I have met in the past, I think I should call on her and Sir Oswald this afternoon."

"It is a very bad idea," Gideon said firmly.

"Why?"

Gideon groped for an acceptable reason why his very wealthy, very eligible cousin should not make a respectable call on an unmarried lady of the ton in the company of her great-uncle.

"I believe her to be deranged," he said finally.

The duke's mouth twitched, but he responded solemnly, "Ah. You think so?"

Gideon stood up and took several paces around the room. "Well, of course she is! She comes here, uninvited, at the crack of dawn—"

"Half-past nine."

"Exactly! The crack of dawn! Claiming to be betrothed to *you!* Then she mistakes me for you—and then, as soon as her great-uncle arrives, she rails at me for a faithless beast, snatches up my tailor's bills, rips them up in my face, and dashes them into the fire. Finally, not to be outdone, she stages a faint, and when I save her from falling and try to resuscitate her—what does she do? Biffs me over the ear with a hideous miniature Egyptian coffin that weighs a ton, announces she is engaged to some other blasted fellow, and storms out!"

There was a short silence as both men recalled the scene.

"Yes," agreed the duke calmly. "As I said, refreshingly unusual."

The cousins glanced at each other and, as one, collapsed into laughter. After a time, the duke rang for coffee to be brought in.

They drank it in silence, each man pondering the events of the morning. Gideon could not stop thinking about the kisses he had stolen from Miss Prudence Merridew. Or rather, his own reaction to them. For a few seconds, he'd felt like a callow boy, out of his depth, stirred more deeply by a simple kiss from an unknown girl than anything had ever stirred him before.

It drew him like a magnet. It fascinated him. It terrified him.

"Another cup, Gideon?"

With difficulty, Gideon forced himself back into the present. "Not for me, thank you." He yawned. "I'm for my bed. I shall see you this evening. We go to . . . where is it?" He frowned and then pulled a face. "Oh Lord, yes! Almack's."

"No, Almack's is tomorrow night," the Duke reminded him. "I have a little time yet before I must gird my loins, screw my courage to the sticking place, and offer myself up to the matchmaking mamas at Almack's."

"Shakespeare at the crack of dawn!" Gideon shuddered "Vile habit. And if you had any consideration, Cousin mine, you would not mention matchmaking mamas."

"You need not go to Almack's if you don't care for it."

"I don't care for it at all, as you very well know, but we do need to go there. You want to meet eligible young ladies and Almack's is stuffed to the ceiling with them!"

"Indeed, but I don't need you to hold my hand, you know. I am quite capable of braving the terrors of the marriage mart by myself, though it is kind of you to offer. Besides, I may not need to brave Almack's at all. I told you, I have a mind to further my acquaintance with Miss Prudence Merridew," said the duke guilelessly and lifted his coffee cup to his lips.

Gideon frowned. "Miss Prudence Merridew wouldn't suit you at all! You say you want a nice, steady, plain, quiet girl. She's none of those. And she has a frightful temper. You should have seen the way she ripped into me only for offering an aesthetic judgment on that blasted ugly reticule, all because the damned thing was made by her little sister. I mean, if I had a sister who perpetuated such artistic atrocities, I wouldn't go around brandishing them in public, let alone attacking harmless fellows for the crime of being honest."

Edward chuckled.

Gideon shook his head earnestly. "No, no—you may laugh, but Edward, be warned! The girl might have a sweet face and a bucket load of charm, but underneath she's a regular little shrew. Whereas"—he gestured with one hand like a stage magician producing a rabbit from a hat—"there are *dozens* of females at Almack's, most of them nice, steady, quiet girls, some as dull as ditchwater, if that's what you really want. And since you have no desire for a beautiful bride—and I don't at all blame you for that!—I can even introduce you to some positive antidotes, if you want! And almost all of the girls at Almack's will be plainer, richer, and altogether more eligible for your purposes than Miss Prudence Merridew!"

"Oh, I am not such a high stickler." The duke smiled tranquilly. "And I don't care for an antidote for a bride. No, Miss Prudence Merridew is . . . interesting. And you know, I formed the impression that she would like to marry a duke, so if I can avoid hurling myself into the fray of the marriage mart—"

"She has no idea of what she wants!" snapped Gideon. "And neither do you. She is not the woman for you, Edward!"

The duke clapped his hands. "Famous! I never thought to see this moment! And to think I always considered London to be so dull. Oh, Cousin mine, how the mighty are fallen!"

Gideon rolled his eyes. "Pah! You know I am not in the market for a wife. I have no taste for marriage, duty or not. I might, perhaps, indulge myself in a mild flirtation, but that is all. And you know perfectly well I do not make sport of youthful innocents."

His cousin inclined his head. "I do know it, dear boy. That is what makes the whole thing so very interesting."

Gideon scowled, but said nothing. Edward was wrong. Nobody had fallen anywhere. She might have stirred him unexpectedly but he was not going to pursue the matter. He did not need to be stirred. He did not wish to be stirred. He was content with his life as it was. To further his acquaintance with Miss Prudence Merridew would be courting disaster. He was far too sensible to do that.

"And then, of course, there is the Otterbury factor," added the duke.

"You believed her?" Gideon said scornfully. "A moment before, she was claiming to be betrothed to the Duke of Dinstable, and you know how genuine that was! This is just another one of her faradiddles."

The duke shrugged. "Sounded genuine to me. Certain note of conviction in her voice."

"Nonsense! She was just putting me in my place."

"Yes." The duke smiled, adding, "It worked, too, didn't it?"

Gideon shoved his hands in his pockets, crossed his legs at the ankle and glowered at his gleaming Hessian boots. It had worked, dammit. Their little sparring match had stirred his blood. No woman had ever repulsed him so vigorously, particularly after being kissed, and he had to admit he was intrigued. Or he might have been if he wasn't being sensible.

The duke chuckled. "I don't believe she pulled that name out of a hat. One doesn't keep names like Otterbury in hats. Sounded to me like it burst out of her like . . . like some secret she's been keeping for a long time. Perhaps for four long years."

"Four and a half." Gideon scowled and hunched down in his chair. There was substance to what his cousin said. Otterbury. She had tossed the name down like a gauntlet and stormed out. Could she really be betrothed to a man called Otterbury? Not that he was interested, of course. Merely curious, as anyone might be.

Otterbury must be completely ineligible. A cit, perhaps? Someone hopelessly below her in station. Whatever his station, he had to be someone damned special for a woman like Prudence Merridew to wait for him for four and a half years . . .

The duke rose and patted his cousin's cheek provocatively as he passed. "Sweet dreams, dearest Coz."

"Damn your eyes, Edward!" responded Gideon absentmindedly.

The duke left, chuckling softly.

Gideon, lost in thought, stared at his boots.

Chapter Six

"I hope you do not think me prone to an iteration of nuptials."
WILLIAM CONGREVE

THE CARRIAGE ROLLED AWAY FROM THE DUKE'S RESIDENCE.

"Now, missy, I'll want an explanation for this extraordinary——"

Prudence rolled her eyes silently in the direction of Lily, sitting tense and upright on the leather seat beside her, a wooden expression on her face.

But Great-uncle Oswald was made of sterner stuff. To men of his upbringing and generation, servants did not count. "Well?"

"I shall explain all when we get home, dear Great-uncle Oswald," Prudence murmured. "Only I am still feeling a little . . ." Her voice died away, and she lifted the vinaigrette to her nose, a silent reminder of her recent episode of feminine delicacy.

"Hmph!" Great-uncle Oswald subsided.

Prudence closed her eyes, snatching at the brief reprieve. She needed to come up with a way out of this mess, fast. Her small, simple plan had spiraled quite out of control.

Besides, her indisposition was not completely feigned. At the moment she could barely think straight. Her whole body was still trembling. With righteous indignation, she told herself. Of course she was upset. Who wouldn't be, mauled in such a . . . a . . . lascivious manner by a perfect stranger . . . a perfect rake.

Although *perfect* was the wrong word. He was by no means perfect at all!

Her legs were still trembling. And her hands. Even her insides seemed to be quivering.

Not surprising, she told herself firmly. She'd had to use her reticule to defend her honor. Any gently born lady would be unsettled after such an experience.

She didn't feel unsettled. She felt . . . invigorated. Excited. A deliciously sensual shudder passed through her.

Great-uncle Oswald spoke suddenly. "Got the shivers, too, eh? No doubt you are sickening for something—"

Her eyes snapped open, and she felt herself blushing.

"It's not every day a gel gets herself into a mess like this one, missy, so I'm not surprised if you're havin' palpitations." Great-uncle Oswald leaned forward in the carriage and observed her closely. "A slight hectic touch about the cheeks, too, I see. I have no doubt it's all worsened by that dratted ham you will eat at breakfast. Red meat at any time of the day is not good for young gels. Inflames the passions. I expect you need a purge."

Declining to comment, Prudence rested her head on the leather squabs and closed her eyes. It wasn't a slice of ham that had inflamed her passions, it was—

No. She would not think about Lord Carradice. It was her indignation that had become inflamed, not her passions! She would put him very firmly out of her mind. Besides, she had to find a solution to this mess she'd created; her sisters' future depended on it.

But as soon as she closed her eyes, she could think of nothing but the way his eyes had seemed to darken as his mouth came down over hers . . .

On arrival home, Great-uncle Oswald, declaring she looked distinctly feverish, had sent her instantly upstairs to lie down and recover herself. A few minutes later, he brought up a nasty-smelling herbal draft, a purge that he declared infallible, and ordered Prudence to drink every drop. Having no choice, Prudence obediently drained the cup and lay on her bed to ponder her problems.

They whirled around in her brain; she could see no way out. There had to be some way she could support her sisters. She turned the problem over and over in her mind. She could gain employment as a housekeeper, or a governess perhaps . . . but even if she could earn enough, which was doubtful, she would hardly keep a job with four younger sisters in tow.

Try as she might, the unpalatable truth stayed the same: one of her sisters had to marry. Somehow, she *had* to get Great-uncle Oswald to break his decree.

Eventually she did what she had done every time she had failed to come up with an adequate solution; she began another letter to Phillip. His long silence could contain a message. On the other hand it was also true that letters from India had been lost or delayed, some by years. Deliberate silence or accidental delay? She had to know—one way or another—where she stood, and all she could do was write and ask.

She finished her letter just as her maid scratched at the door and peeped in. Seeing Prudence was up and clearly recovered, she bobbed a curtsy and said, "Please, miss, Sir Oswald says if you're recovered, he would be obliged if you was to present yerself in the yellow saloon at four o'clock."

Prudence felt her heart sink. "Thank you, Lily. Please inform Sir Oswald that I shall attend him."

Lily turned to leave, but Prudence stopped her. "Lily, you didn't get into trouble, did you? For accompanying me, I mean? You must tell me if you did, so that I can make amends for it."

"Oh, no, miss. Sir Oswald was a little snappish about it, to be sure, but he knows as how I was only following your orders."

"So you didn't get into trouble?"

"No, miss. Old Niblett gave me a bit of a jaw-me-dead about it, but I don't care for that."

"The butler? Oh, dear. I will speak to him. I am truly sorry to have involved you in my troubles, Lily."

"Oh, no, miss, don't you fret none about old Niblett." Lily grinned and smoothed her apron demurely. "He was just jealous 'cause he's never been inside a real duke's house and I have, coarse and ignorant country hoyden that I am! *And* I spoke to the duke—face-to-face! *And* his handsome cousin the lord called me *a frail little creature*, what's more! So old Niblett is jealous, fit to bust!" She winked at her mistress and bounced out of the room.

At precisely four o'clock Prudence stood outside the yellow saloon, took a deep breath, and knocked on the door.

She hurried into an explanation as soon as she entered. "I am so sorry, Great-uncle Oswald. I hope you're not too upset. It was all my fault, I know. I have been thinking and thinking about how I could have made such a foolish error, and I have come to the unwelcome conclusion that Lord Carradice probably paid me a few graceful compliments, and I must have refined too much upon it—building castles in the air, you know. We girls tend to be very romantical at that age."

Great-uncle Oswald's face softened. "Yes, and I don't doubt that you were unused to receivin' compliments. No wonder the wastrel was able to turn your head so easily."

Swallowing her pride, Prudence nodded. "In any case, I have not seen him for more than four years, so there is no need to worry."

"Are you sure, missy?"

"Oh yes, I promise you. This morning was the first time." That was the truth, at any rate.

"Well, I don't pretend to like it. And I cannot understand why the fellow told you he was the Duke of Dinstab—"

"I think that was my fault too," Prudence jumped in. "It was my initial mistake, and he simply never corrected me."

"But to let you go on addressin' him incorrectly for four and a half years." He shook his head.

Prudence felt herself coloring. The kindness in his tone was harder to bear than any amount of shouting.

"No need to flush up, my dear," said the old man gruffly. "I expect it was all love nonsense and not about names and titles at all. Am I right?"

Bright red, Prudence shrugged.

"Thought so. Dashed loose manners the young reprobate has! Now, before I let it go, I'll ask you once more—it occurs to me you might not have wanted to admit such a thing with your sisters present—did the rascally knave touch you in any improper manner? You know what I mean, missy?"

Missy thought of the way the rascally knave's mouth had almost devoured hers. She thought of a long-fingered hand cupping her breast and stroking it in a way that made a shiver pass straight through her, leaving her toes curling at the mere memory. Yes, she knew all too well what he meant. Prudence, knowing she had turned scarlet, hung her head, and said in a low voice, "No, Great-uncle Oswald, Lord Carradice never touched me in an improper manner."

"Hmph! Didn't suppose so. A rake like Carradice wouldn't waste his time dallyin' with a plain and virtuous gel," Great-uncle Oswald said gloomily. "Pity."

Prudence stared at him in shock. *Pity?*

Great-uncle Oswald saw her look. "Full o' juice, Carradice."

Prudence still didn't understand.

"Not that I approve of such goin's on, for I don't, but all the same, if there had been hanky-panky, it wouldn't have been a bad match for you," Great-uncle Oswald explained. "Settled you right and tight."

"But would Lord Carradice wish to be settled right and tight?" Prudence said with an edge to her voice. "I cannot imagine it—not if he has such a famous reputation as a rake."

"Ah, well, as to that, marriage gives a rake respectability."

Prudence couldn't think how, for it seemed to her that if a man had been trapped into marriage he would have no incentive at all to change his dissolute habits. It seemed likely to her that in such a case a rake would most likely continue in his rakish ways. And she pitied the woman married to that rake, for she would probably be miserable.

Probably.

There might be some compensations, she thought wistfully, recalling the exquisite sensations she had experienced on Cleopatra's barge.

"But since he didn't attempt any hanky-panky, we won't force the rascal's hand."

Prudence sat up. "I would *never* allow anyone to *force* a

man to wed me, hanky-panky or not. The very thought is utterly repugnant. It would be completely humiliating."

"Hmph! You can't call a splendid match like that humiliatin', my gel. Don't matter how it came about, a good match is a good match, and I don't deny Carradice is a better match than even I'd hoped for—for you."

"I think it would be a perfectly frightful thing," Prudence declared hotly. "Married off to a man who cares not a button for you, merely in order to prevent a little scandal!"

"You've led a sheltered life," Great-uncle Oswald said simply. "You don't understand these things." He sighed. "It don't matter, anyway—question is entirely academic, since he never laid a finger on you, nor promised anything in a letter. I suppose we have to be grateful that he didn't come across your lovely sisters in Norfolk." He snorted. "Though I suppose they were mere children at the time. Deuced good thing, too. Couldn't see a blasted libertine holdin' back with one of those little beauties in his arms. Lucky it was you, eh, Prue?"

Prue just looked at him. Not even to get out of this mess would she admit to being grateful for being too plain for even a rake to seduce.

"What am I saying?" Great-uncle Oswald said apologetically. "I don't mean it was lucky at all. He bruised your tender heart, didn't he? Not used to admiration from any man, let alone a London rake. Like putty in his hands, weren't you, poor little lass?" He reached out and patted her knee clumsily. "A few stray compliments and you took him at his worthless word. Turned your little head, didn't he, Prue?"

Prudence gritted her teeth, mortified. The fact that the picture was false didn't make it any better. She might not have had her head turned by Lord Carradice as a girl of sixteen, but this morning, at the advanced age of almost one and twenty, she'd acted no better than her gullible maid, and allowed a libertine to—to take liberties with her person. Worse; she'd flowered under his touch.

It was pathetic when she thought about it.

She *was* unused to compliments from men. Grandpapa was virulently uncomplimentary, and Phillip was the practical sort, not given to flowery speeches. Great-uncle Oswald freely gave her compliments about her noble soul, but since they were interspersed with comments about her plainness, they failed to turn her head.

She probably was susceptible to a cozening rogue. She *had* been putty in his hands, the softest, most pathetically eager putty, right up until the last few moments, she realized bitterly.

At least plain Prudence Merridew had summoned enough self-respect to reject the irresistible Lord Carradice in the end.

Prudence sighed as her customary honesty reasserted itself. It was not self-respect that had made her reject him. It was neither respectability nor virtue. It was simply the fear of discovery that had put a particle of common sense back into her foolish, dazzled brain. Had there been no danger of discovery, she would probably have allowed him anything. And reveled in every minute of it.

. . . slaves to their base animal instincts . . .

It must have been instinct, she told herself, recalling the way her body had molded itself to his without any consciousness on her part. The sensations she had experienced in his arms, delicious as they were, certainly had nothing to do with reason or logic or any of the other principles so important to enlightened humankind.

"Never mind, Prue." Great-uncle Oswald patted her knee again. "We all make fools of ourselves at some time." He peered at her in a gruff, kindly way.

Prudence felt tears pricking behind her eyelids. He looked so much like Grandpapa, but there was no comparison. Beneath the noise and bluster and foppish appearance, Great-uncle Oswald was a dear. She had spent all her life braced against hostility and harshness. She had no defense against kindness.

"The duke seemed a decent-enough fellow, don't you think?" Great-uncle Oswald asked with a touch of anxiety. "I'll have to be polite to him, my dear. I don't mind cuttin' a rake like Carradice if I have to, but I don't think I could cut a duke, Prue."

Prudence nodded vaguely. She had no interest in dukes. She had been momentarily dazzled by a rake with as much morality as a cat and a smile that ought not to be legal. But she knew the dangers now. She felt a sudden twinge in her stomach; Great-uncle Oswald's herbal purge making its presence felt. She grimaced and rose hurriedly, wishing there was an equally effective herbal remedy against rakes. But she had an uneasy suspicion Lord Carradice would not submit to a purge the way her breakfast undoubtedly had.

As she stood, the butler, Niblett, threw open the door. "The Duke of Dinstable," he announced in a sonorous voice.

Prudence glanced at Great-uncle Oswald in horror. Why would the duke come calling so soon? What would he say? Would he demand an explanation? What would she say? And would he be accompanied by his cousin? She held her breath and stared at the door.

The Duke of Dinstable, dressed in neat, buff breeches, gleaming Hessian boots, and a coat of dark blue superfine, quietly entered the room. "How do you do, Sir Oswald, Miss Merridew," he said, bowing politely.

Slightly bemused by the unexpected visit, Great-uncle Oswald invited the duke to be seated. With some reluctance Prudence resumed her seat. One did not rush from the room the instant a duke entered it, and her dilemma was not one she could raise in polite company

"I came to inquire about Miss Merridew's health," said the duke. "Miss Merridew, have you quite recovered from your indisposition?"

Miss Merridew, finding the urge of Great-uncle Oswald's herbal purge most insistent, hastily assured him she was indeed completely recovered.

The duke expressed himself delighted to hear it. He then made a comment about the weather they had been having and asked Prudence's opinion of it.

Prudence responded that it had been quite delightful, such glorious sunshine, such balmy breezes for this time of year, and wondered desperately how soon she could leave the room without causing offense. She would never again swallow one of Great-uncle Oswald's herbal concoctions.

Great-uncle Oswald rang the bell and ordered refreshments. Peppermint tea and plain oat biscuits. The duke blinked but said nothing.

The herbal concoction within asserted itself again and Prudence leaped to her feet abruptly. The two gentlemen instantly leaped to theirs, politely.

She stared at them wildly. "I, er . . . I need to . . ."

Just then the door opened and Charity, the twins, and Grace entered, the latter three talking animatedly between themselves.

"Oh Prudence, dear, there you are," Charity said. "We were planning to walk in the park and were looking for you to see if you cared to come with—oh!" She broke off, staring at the visitor.

The visitor stared back. The other girls stopped their chatter and broke into hasty curtsies.

"Oh dear." Hope rose carefully from her curtsy. "We didn't realize you had company, Great-uncle Oswald."

"Yes, we thought Prudence was alone. We're very sorry for barging in like this," Faith added.

"Quite all right, my dears. Let me introduce you to our distinguished guest, the Duke of Dinstable."

The girls gasped, bobbed another curtsy, and with one accord, turned their horrified faces to Prudence.

Prudence had no interest in their horror; she was entirely occupied with the effects of herbs. "I—I shall see to the refreshments. Pray, excuse me a moment, Great-uncle Oswald, Your Grace." And she rushed from the room.

Great-uncle Oswald frowned. "Don't know what's got into the gel. Butler can bring 'em in perfectly well and what she thinks cooks, maids, and footmen are for, I don't know!" Shaking his head, he continued, "Your Grace, may I present my other great-nieces? This is Miss Charity Merridew, the second oldest."

His face blank of all expression, the duke bowed over Charity's outstretched hand. "M-Miss Charity."

"Then there are the twins, Miss Hope and Miss Faith."

The duke didn't move. He held Charity's hand, staring. Charity, blushing prettily, tugged gently at her hand.

"Miss Hope and Miss Faith." Great-uncle Oswald repeated in a loud voice.

The duke started, glanced at Great-uncle Oswald, dropped

Charity's hand, and swiftly murmured polite greetings to the twins.

"And this is the baby of the family, Miss Grace Merridew."

The duke murmured vaguely, "How do you do, Miss Grace. Er . . . You were planning to walk in the park this afternoon, you said? All of you? Together?" His gaze flickered briefly.

"Yes, Hyde Park. All the fashionable people go there at this time of the day—on the strut, you know," Grace explained artlessly. "It is so interesting to see everyone dressed up in their finest."

"Yes, quite. Er, perhaps we shall meet there, one day," the duke said, looking at no one in particular.

It was midafternoon when Gideon finally gave up all pretense of sleeping. He ought to have slept. He was tired; he'd been up all night playing piquet. And he'd had quite a bit to drink, which usually ensured him a sound sleep. But something—or rather, someone—had prevented him from sleeping.

A small, curvaceous someone with huge gray eyes and curly copper hair whose soft, surprised little mouth had made him forget who he was for several long, unforgettable moments . . .

A small, determined whirlwind, most improbably called Prudence. He smiled to himself and stretched languorously in his big, wide bed. Whoever had named her Prudence was way off the mark. *Imprudence* was more like it. He chuckled again. Miss ImPrudence Merridew. He liked it. What would she have to say to that, the next time he saw her?

He stretched again, enjoying the energy that surged through his body, and thought of the next time he'd see her. Because of course there would be a next time. And soon.

He couldn't get that kiss, those kisses, out of his mind. In those few moments, with Prudence on the couch, he'd lost all sense of himself, or where he was. There was only her . . .

He couldn't recall when that had last happened. He wasn't sure if it had ever happened.

He would see her again. He could remain sensible and indulge his curiosity at the same time. There was no danger. He glanced at the slabs of afternoon sunshine sliding imperceptibly across the floor, snatched his watch from the bedside table, and flicked it open. Nearly four o'clock. Just enough time to pay a call on Miss ImPrudence Merridew and her Great-uncle. Suddenly energized, he bounded out of bed, calling for his valet, and for hot water and his razor to be brought in. And his phaeton to be ordered for half-past four.

Miss Prudence may have made the acquaintance of an unshaven shag bag this morning, but this afternoon she would receive a call from an immaculate Corinthian.

Not that he had any intention of pursuing her; he didn't dally with innocents and marriage was no part of his plans. But . . . he had to find out whether that kiss was a fluke or not, find out whether he would find himself lost in sensation again . . .

Besides, he owed it to Edward to discover what game she was playing.

His first thought on meeting her—his second, actually; his first had been what a sweet face she had—had been that it was some kind of plot to entrap his cousin. He'd expected trouble since that mention of him in the *Morning Post*. A young, wealthy duke, as yet unwed and newly come to town, was a temptation, not simply to matchmaking mamas, or ambitious great-uncles.

But Prudence had repeatedly ended the false betrothal. Even when Gideon's levity had threatened his own head with a matrimonial noose, she'd dragged it back out of danger.

Why had he done that? He pondered the matter deeply and could come up with no satisfactory solution. It must have been the brandy. He could think of no other reason for such a burst of insanity. Brandy had never before incited him to flirt with the possibility of marriage.

Thank the Lord she'd continued to repudiate him.

Although when he'd kissed her, it was a different story . . . Her hesitant, surprised, instinctive response to him was not only intensely arousing, it had somehow struck a chord deep within him.

His reaction had been so primitive it shocked him. She was his. *His!* But he'd never been the possessive type.

How had that happened? How had he allowed it to happen? His brows drew together. He would have to warn Edward about that particular batch of brandy. It obviously had very peculiar effects.

He owed a debt of gratitude to Miss Prudence Merridew.

Gideon could not imagine any other young unmarried woman of his acquaintance passing up the opportunity to snare, if not himself, then the Carradice fortune. In any case, the number of women who'd rejected him in any way was gratifyingly small. Yet Miss Prudence Merridew had most unmistakably rejected him. Several times. Wielding that damned lethal reticule like a little Amazon, to emphasize her point.

Now he came to think of it, that reticule was something of a gauntlet. Carradices never backed down from gauntlets.

Gideon was waiting in the hall for his phaeton to be brought around when the butler coughed discreetly at his elbow. "Excuse me, my lord. A message from the stables: A crack in the wheel of your phaeton has been discovered, and your man has taken it to the wheelwright to be mended."

"Blast!"

At that moment the duke walked in the front door, his expression slightly glazed.

Gideon turned to him. "The most irritating thing, Edward—there's a damned crack in my phaeton wheel, and I was planning to drive out just now. Could I borrow your curricle?"

The duke didn't reply. With a preoccupied air, he allowed Bartlett to remove his driving coat.

"Wake up, Cousin! I asked you a question." Gideon eyed his reflection critically in the hall looking glass and adjusted his hat to a more dashing tilt. "I presume you've finished with your curricle. Can I borrow it this afternoon?"

Edward nodded. "Hmm, yes, of course. But the curricle is being repainted. I'm using my mother's landau. Send a message to Hawkins, Bartlett."

The butler bowed and snapped a finger to a waiting footman, who sped off.

"The landau! That stodgy—but there, I'm being ungrateful. The landau it shall be." Gideon frowned critically at his own reflection. "Everything all right, Edward? You look like a stunned mullet," he said with vague cousinly concern as he adjusted the high-standing points of his collar. "Where did you go?"

"Er, paid a call."

"Did you now?" Gideon said cheerily, making a minor alteration to a fold of his neckcloth. "Brave fellow, I thought you dreaded—" He whirled around and eyed his cousin narrowly. "Who did you call on, Edward?" he said in quite a different tone.

Edward looked a little self-conscious. "I'm in a hurry, Gideon. I am going out again."

"*Who,* Edward?"

But Edward had apparently discovered a piece of fluff on his coat and was engrossed in removing it. When he looked up again, his face was tinged with pink.

Gideon frowned in darkest suspicion. "You called on Miss Prudence Merridew, didn't you?"

Edward raised his brows haughtily. "If a lady becomes indisposed in my house, it is only polite to enquire after her health."

"Don't raise those Penteith brows at me, Edward, I'm immune to 'em. As for her being indisposed, you know perfectly well that faint wasn't genuine. There's no use trying to flummery me—you tried to steal a march on me with Miss Merridew!"

The duke shrugged and said mildly, "Steal a march, dear boy? How very vulgar. We of the house of Penteith never steal anything. We've never needed to. It was the Carradices who distinguished themselves as—what was the euphemism?—border raiders, was it not?"

"Don't change the subject."

The duke smiled. "Dearest Coz, you claimed to have no interest in Miss Merridew, and naturally, as a gentleman I took you at your word. Now, I really must leave."

"But you just got home!" Gideon frowned as his cousin set a curly-brimmed beaver carefully on his neatly pomaded locks. "For a reputed hermit, you've become very sociable all of a sudden. Where are you going now? Do you need the landau to drop you off?"

"No, you take it. I'm going for a walk in Hyde Park."

"A walk! You never walk!" Gideon glanced at the hall clock. "And at this hour Hyde Park will be teeming with humanity—all the ton will be there. You will hate it, Edward."

"Will I?" the duke said blandly. "We shall see."

Gideon shrugged. "Don't say I didn't warn you." To tell the truth, he wasn't much interested in where his cousin was going now; he was much more interested in where he'd been and whom he had talked to. And whether she'd been impressed with his . . . his dukishness, damn him!

He could not forget that it had been a search for a ducal fiancé that had first brought Prudence into his orbit.

Fifteen minutes later, the duke's driver, Hawkins, drove the landau into Providence Court for the second time that afternoon. It halted in front of number 21. Gideon made a quick survey of his person to ensure there was no hint of shag bag, took a deep breath, seized the brass knocker with a bold hand, and rapped smartly.

And waited.

He was absurdly nervous. It was ridiculous for a man of his address and experience to be feeling nervous, Gideon told himself. He had made hundreds of morning calls. Well, dozens at any rate. Rakes did not make morning calls, as a rule. They dropped in on their friends' lodgings, called in at their clubs, visited their mistresses, popped in to Jackson's for a bout or two with the gloves. They left polite little ritualistic morning calls to others. And thought it was ridiculous to call an afternoon visit a morning call.

His neckcloth felt unaccountably tight. Some idiot had starched his shirt points so that they felt like knives, waiting to cut into his chin if he so much as slouched. Not that he was planning to slouch, of course. Gideon resisted the urge to run a finger around his collar.

He was a grown man, for heaven's sake! He could drink tea and nibble cakes with the best of them. They might even serve him a glass of wine.

Great-uncle Oswald abhors the Evils of Liquor!

No. He sighed. *It would be tea.* Or . . . Gideon felt himself blanch. They surely wouldn't expect him to drink ratafia,

would they? He swallowed and felt his shirt points dig warn-
ingly into his jaw.

Why the devil were they taking so long to answer the
blasted door? He reached up to rap the knocker again just as
the door was opened. An ancient butler stood there, eyeing
him expectantly. "Sir?"

His hand hung foolishly in midair for a second, then
Gideon collected himself. "Lord Carradice to see Sir Oswald
Merridew." He presented his card and made to step over the
threshold.

"I shall henquire, my lord," said the ancient retainer in a
sonorous voice and, taking the card, he closed the door in
Gideon's face.

Gideon blinked. He had never in his life had a door shut
in his face. Well, once, by an irate woman, but never by a butler. "Senile old fool," he muttered, and feeling a little foolish
at being kept waiting on the doorstep like a tradesman, he in-
spected his nails, whistling lightly under his breath in a carefree manner.

After what seemed like a very long time, the door opened.
"Sir Oswald is hat 'ome and will see you now in the yellow
saloon."

Gideon followed the butler inside and detained him a moment. "What about the young lady—the young ladies?" he
corrected himself, recalling there were sisters. "Are any of
the Miss Merridews at home?" He smiled at the butler in a
man-to-man fashion.

The butler regarded him balefully.

"Listen here," Gideon began in a confiding tone that had
won over many a butler before. "It's actually Miss Prudence
Merridew I have come to see. Nip upstairs and let her know
I am in with Sir Oswald, would you?" He pressed a folded
banknote into the butler's ready hand.

The butler stared down his nose, quite as if his hand
hadn't pocked the note in a flash, shrugged, then opened the
door to what was obviously the yellow saloon.

Sir Oswald greeted Gideon bluntly. "Have to admit I
never looked to see you come callin'."

Gideon bowed. "How do you do, sir?"

"Eh? Oh, how-de-do, Carradice. Sit down, sit down. I'm

just about to take a cup of healthful tea. Here." He handed Gideon a cup. "Now, I presume you've come to explain that disgraceful scene this mornin . Not to mention your havey cavey dealin's with my great niece."

"Ah, indeed." Gideon sipped the tea, wondering how to answer, then almost choked. What the devil was this filthy-tasting stuff? "Have you had a chance, yet, to talk with Miss Merridew?"

"I have." Sir Oswald frowned, balefully.

"Ah." Gideon swallowed another hideous mouthful, wondering what tale Miss ImPrudence had come up with now and hoping there had been no mention of an Egyptian couch.

"You ought to be ashamed of yourself!"

"Ah, yes. I am, I am," Gideon assured him. From the expression on the old fellow's face, the Egyptian couch had featured after all.

"A man of your experience, flirting with an innocent young gel like little Prudence. You ought to have known a gel like that would misinterpret your intentions."

Ah, that was it. He was accused of flirting. No mention of kisses or couches, Egyptian or otherwise. Suddenly his neck-cloth felt a lot more comfortable. "I know, I know," he said in a rueful, man-of-the-world tone and set his cup down.

Sir Oswald refilled it. "Fellow of your vast experience with women ought to know better than to dally with young gels . . ."

The old chap was off and running in a splendid tirade. Gideon glanced toward the door.

". . . a sheltered young miss doesn't understand . . . rascally rake . . ."

How long did it take that blasted butler to climb the stairs, dammit! Prudence ought to be here any moment.

Sir Oswald glared at him. "A decent man would make amends, do the decent thing, see the girl right."

Gideon was not paying attention. Was that a soft, feminine footstep at the door? He glanced at Sir Oswald's face, realized some response was expected of him and with an effort recalled the last thing the elderly man had said; something about seeing the girl. He nodded in agreement. "Oh yes, sir, I quite agree."

"You do?" Sir Oswald seemed stunned.

Gideon smiled at him winningly. "Indeed I do."

"And that's why you're here now? For Prudence?"

"That's why I'm here now." He smiled again. What did the old fool think—that he'd come to make a morning call on an elderly man? Of course he'd come to see Prudence!

"Well, by jove! that's more like it!" Sir Oswald jumped out of his chair and shook Gideon by the hand. "Well done, Carradice. I knew there was some good in you!"

"Eh?" Feeling as though he'd missed something crucial in the conversation, Gideon allowed his hand to be pumped energetically.

"Wondered if I hadn't been mistaken in you when you arrived here in your courtin' clothes."

"What?" Horrified, Gideon glanced down at his immaculate outfit. *Courting clothes?* He opened his mouth to explain.

Sir Oswald winked at him merrily. "Can't fool an old man, Carradice. When a man changes overnight from shag bag to elegant sprig, there's courtin' in the air. You won't regret it. Damn fine little gel, Prudence. Make you a fine little wife. A very fine little wife indeed!" He rang the bell and called for the celebratory dandelion wine to be brought in.

Gideon said nothing. He felt slightly hollow. Somehow, while making innocuous chit-chat, this dandified old lunatic had gained the impression he wanted to marry Prudence, a girl he had known less than a day. How had that happened? He ran over the conversation in his mind. There were some disconcerting blanks in his memory; the perils of a momentary lapse or two in concentration.

Had he merely been given permission to court Miss Prudence Merridew, or had he unknowingly agreed to something more binding? He had an uneasy suspicion it was the latter. The old chap was making very free with the word *wife*. Gideon repressed a shudder. He ought to stop it right now. Clarify the whole thing. Clear up the misunderstanding.

But for the life of him, Gideon couldn't bring himself to ask what it was they were celebrating, let alone deny it.

He would sort it out later, when the old fellow had recovered from his transports of delight. On second thought, he might not need to—Prudence would deal with the whole thing more effectively, he was sure. She would deny him as she had previously and he would be safe again. What a relief.

It took fifteen interminable minutes and several glasses of the most peculiar tasting wine Gideon had ever swallowed before he could escape Great-uncle Oswald's raptures. The ancient butler escorted him to the front door.

Gideon stepped onto the front step and recalled something. He detained the butler by the sleeve. "Where the devil is Miss Prudence? Didn't you give her my message?"

The butler turned, a faint malicious smile on his face. "She's gone out. Not one of the Misses Merridew is hat 'ome. They left about ten minutes before you harrived." The smile became a smirk as he shut the door in Gideon's face for the second time that day.

"Damn and blast the fellow!" muttered Gideon as he retraced his steps toward the waiting landau. Gone out! Where had she gone in his hour of need? Shopping? The park, perhaps? It was the fashionable hour to be parading, dammit!

The reason for Edward's bizarre desire to take exercise suddenly became crystal clear. Gideon leaped into the landau. "Hyde Park, Hawkins. And spring 'em!"

Hawkins, knowing the respect due to a vehicle bearing a ducal crest and having placed both the duke and Lord Carradice on their first fat ponies twenty-odd years before, declined to spring anything but condescended to urge his beauties in the direction of Hyde Park at a decorous trot. Behind him his passenger chafed and cursed the muleheadedness of old retainers and the deviousness of dukes!

Chapter Seven

∽

*"Think of what it will mean
For your good name and mine, if you do this."*
SOPHOCLES

THE LANDAU PASSED THROUGH THE WROUGHT-IRON GATES OF HYDE Park and entered a throng of people and carriages almost as bad as the traffic on the streets they had just left. Gideon sat bolt upright, cursing the low sprung vehicle; if he'd had his high-perch phaeton, he could have seen over the heads of this lot and spotted the perfidious Edward in a trice.

"There he is, blast him! Lurking among that gaggle of yellow-haired chits there. Pull over, Hawkins!"

Hawkins negotiated a halt beside the crowded path, and Gideon jumped down and thrust his way through the crowd to where Edward stood in the midst of a group of ethereally fair young ladies. Loitering suspiciously around the group were a dozen or so young bloods, several of whom Gideon knew very well to be rakes of the highest order. He knew well their quarry, for hidden right in the midst of all of them, where his cousin clearly imagined he could conceal her, was one small, delightful lady dressed in a silver gray pelisse with dark green trim.

As he had suspected, his conniving cousin had made an assignation behind his back with Miss Prudence Merridew! The gray pelisse was an exact match for her glorious eyes;

the green the perfect foil for her magnificent hair, all but a few curls of which was currently hidden by an elegant bonnet with a dark green feather.

Furiously, Gideon shouldered his way through the pack of rakes, edged past the gaggle of fair young things, plastered a surprised expression on his face, and made the guilty pair an elegant, sarcastic bow.

"Edward, Miss Merridew, what a charming and unexpected surprise. Miss Merridew, permit me to tell you how very charming you look." He bared his teeth at her in an attempt to smile. The wolf catching Red Riding Hood in a flirtation with a beagle.

"How do you do, Lord Carradice. Thank you," Prudence responded with composure. "Permit me to tell you in return, sir, that you look rather different from our last meeting also. More . . ." She paused, as if searching for a word.

Elegant, supplied Gideon silently. *Dashing. Stylish.*

"Tidy," said Miss Merridew.

Tidy! Gideon concealed his chagrin behind another bow of elegance and grace. Blast it, did the girl not know how long he had taken to tie his neckcloth? Could she not see the cursed thing was a miracle of precision and style? Was it not apparent to her that his coat was so much the crack he was barely able to breathe and that his collar points were so highly starched they practically decapitated him? And all she could say was that he looked *tidy!*

Edward spoke. "Cousin, I believe you have not yet met Miss Merridew's sisters."

"Sisters?" Gideon looked around vaguely and realized that their conversation was being observed with great interest by several young ladies; two in pink, one in blue, and the other in white, all with yellow hair, though one had more red than yellow.

"Permit me to introduce them," continued Edward. He gestured to the one in blue. "This is Miss Charity Merridew."

Gideon bowed over the blue girl's hand, aware that Prudence had a faint, worried frown on her brow. Hah! Feeling guilty, was she? So she should! If she was such a pattern card of virtue, she shouldn't be meeting Edward in secret.

The duke indicated the two in pink. "Allow me to present Miss Faith and Miss Hope Merridew, who you will perceive are twins, and this is Miss Grace Merridew, the youngest of the family."

Gideon bowed perfunctorily over the hand of each girl, fully aware of his cousin's game. If Edward thought that tossing a bunch of yellow-haired chits at him would distract Gideon away from Prudence, he could think again. And if strategy was the name of the game, Edward had met his master.

Gideon smiled down at the cluster of blonde young things. "You have all come to London recently, I think."

There was a soft chorus of feminine agreement.

Gideon smiled again, feeling quite avuncular. "London is made the fairer by your presence." He shot a look at Prudence to see how she was reacting. She was glaring at him like a cross little hawk. Hah! Sauce for the gander, Miss Im-Prudence! His smile encompassed all the young ladies. "Are you enjoying your stay, ladies?"

One of the pink ones gave him to understand that they were, but said they had hoped to mix a little more in society than they had hitherto been allowed.

Gideon recalled Prudence telling him her sisters wanted to get married. He had no objection; the sooner she was free of the worry of them, the better. Right now, the girls were very much in the way. "Ah indeed, indeed," he said. "I don't suppose any of you young ladies would care to take a turn around the park in a landau, would you? Only, mine—well, actually it is my cousin's—is sitting over there, blocking traffic, and Hawkins, the driver, is looking daggers at me, wishing to be on the move again. Would any of you care to be taken up for a circuit or two?" He smiled encouragingly.

Prudence's faint frown turned into a glare. "No tha—"

"Oh yes, please," chorused the pair in pink.

"It would be of all things, delightful," said the one in blue, whose name Gideon had forgotten. He was much more fascinated by the way the sun gleamed on the stray curls of Prudence's hair, revealing a hundred different colors in the silky tresses. "Delightful," he murmured, and then recalled himself as Prudence swept militantly toward the vehicle, ushering her sisters before her like a small, furious whirl-wind. He strolled after her, enjoying the way her deliciously rounded hips swayed in her hurry.

Like a busy little governess, she supervised her sisters as they climbed into the landau, darting him swift glances of reproof if he so much as offered to assist them. Gideon tried hard to repress a grin. She knew what he was up to, of course; knew he was trying to get rid of the girls so he could be alone with her, and so she'd gathered them around her in a protective flock, hoping to escape his attentions. Her defensive strategy would prove futile. Even Prudence could not get more than four into a landau, five, with the little one in white. The two pink ones had almost bounded into the low-slung vehicle, and the blue one climbed gracefully in after them, followed closely, almost hastily, by the duke.

Gideon beamed as his cousin seated himself in the landau beside the blue one. Good old Edward, family loyalty coming to the fore at last! Sacrificing himself to a drive with a bunch of chattering girls so his cousin could further his acquaintance with Miss Prudence. If a plain and dull wife were what Edward wanted, then Gideon resolved to find him the nicest plain, dull girl the ton could produce! He winked at his cousin. Edward did not appear to notice. He looked a little glazed about the eyes. Poor fellow, he was unused to female company.

There was barely room even for the littlest one. Gideon waited for Prudence to realize it. There would be no space in the landau for Prudence at all—not unless she forced them to squash together in a horribly undignified manner. Her sisters were eager for the promised treat. She could not order them from the carriage at this stage.

Instead of hiding among her sisters as she'd no doubt planned, she would be separated from them. Apart from the milling crowds of fashionable promenaders, her only other acquaintance was her footman standing stolidly, observing events a few yards away. She was caught effectively alone in the park with him. There was not the slightest whiff of impropriety—but she was trapped, nevertheless. Common politeness would force her to stroll with Gideon, to accept his proffered arm, to participate in low and intimate conversation, all the while respectably under the eye of the ton, and with her footman at hand.

Prudence, her hand on Grace's shoulder, watched as the twins carefully tucked in their skirts to make room for their little sister. She'd seen for herself the impact her beautiful sisters had made on Lord Carradice. He'd barely looked at them—a move that had instantly raised her suspicions. *Everyone* stared at her sisters. They were so beautiful that people could not help it. Then he'd instantly tried to tempt them away from her protection by offering them a ride in his elegant landau.

She would scotch his rakish game! She had no intention of letting him take her sisters for a ride. She had evidence enough from that . . . that *incident* on Cleopatra's barge that his reputation as a rake was well deserved; she would protect her innocent and lovely sisters from his advances if it was the last thing she did!

"Come along, Grace dear," she said. Once Grace was seated, there would be no room for anyone else. Prudence shot Lord Carradice a look of pure triumph . . . and was shocked to receive a blazingly triumphant smile in return.

What on earth could he be so pleased about? He must see by now that there was no room for him in the landau. She had rescued her beautiful sisters, had cleverly bundled them out of his way, with the assistance of his quiet, eminently respectable cousin the duke . . . and left herself alone with a rake with only a footman's protection, she realized suddenly. Surely *she* could not be his prey?

But there was a distinctly wolfish gleam in his smile as he helped Grace up the steps, a gleam that started a thrumming in Prudence's blood. She remembered Cleopatra's barge, and swallowed.

She could *not* be alone with him.

She was not alone, she told herself firmly; there were hundreds of people in the park; respectable people, people who would ensure nothing could happen to her. And she had a big burly footman at her command. James would protect her from any untoward advances Lord Carradice might make toward her.

The trouble was, Lord Carradice didn't need to make any

advances. He set her heart a fluttering with just a look, a glance. And his lazy, wicked, crooked smile. Dear Lord, what that smile did to her insides . . .

She must not be alone with Lord Carradice, not even in a crowd of hundreds in the middle of Hyde Park with James the footman at her elbow. It was not safe. She snatched Grace back to the ground, almost tumbling her out of the carriage in her anxiety.

"There is not enough room in the landau, Grace, dear," she said firmly. "If you try to squash into it you will crush your sisters' gowns. Stay and walk with me, my love."

Grace's mouth opened to protest but Prudence hurriedly nipped her arm and her little sister subsided. She glanced from Lord Carradice back to Prudence and frowned. Prudence avoided the question in her gaze. Grace might be young and innocent, but she was not at all stupid.

The landau moved off, the sisters gaily waving, the duke looking stunned to be seated among such a gathering of femininity. Prudence watched them go, then in a determined fashion, linked arms with Grace.

"Oh, no, that is not at all the fashionable mode of promenading," Lord Carradice said, and in an instant he had inserted himself casually between the sisters, taking one on each arm. He smiled down at Prudence, and his arm tightened, pressing hers to his big, warm side. "This is how it's done, Miss Merridew. Is it not much better?"

Prudence shivered. No, it wasn't better at all. She could feel his strength, his warmth, could smell the faint smell of clean linen and freshly shaven man. It was much worse.

"You know I am betrothed," she reminded him in an elaborately casual tone.

He chuckled, deep, low, and lazy. Prudence felt it vibrate clear though to her bones.

On the other side of him, Grace gasped. "Prue! I thought that was supposed to be a deadly dark secret!"

Hastily Prudence changed the subject. "Lord Carradice was most interested in the Egyptian reticule you made for me, Grace. He thought it very unusual."

Gideon glanced down at the young girl on his arm. "Aha! So you are the perpetrator of that—"

Prudence gripped his arm hard. "Yes, indeed, Grace. Lord Carradice admired the workmanship immensely." She sent him a severe look and added, "Didn't you sir?"

"Er, yes, quite," Lord Carradice responded. "Tremendously solid, er, workmanship, Miss Grace. I was much struck by it." He paused then added, "Very much struck."

Prudence spluttered a little at his effrontery.

He sent her a mischievous look and added in a thoughtful tone. "In fact, I do not recall when I was so much struck by something as—solidly artistic." He removed his arm briefly from Grace's and rubbed his head meditatively. "Your workmanship made a powerful impact on me, I must say. Quite . . . stunning!" He sighed, and linked arms with Grace again. "I don't suppose you'd think of making another one for your sister, only in netting. Extremely fashionable at the moment, netting reticules."

Prudence tried very hard to remain serious. It was a severe struggle. They walked on in silence for a few moments, bowing here and there at passing acquaintances. Finally Prudence mastered herself enough to continue the conversation. "My sister is fascinated by ancient Egypt, my lord. As are we all." Perhaps if he thought them a family of bluestockings, he would lose interest. Gentlemen disliked studious women; she knew that from Phillip.

"Did you truly admire my reticule, sir?" Grace squinted suspiciously up at the tall elegant man.

Gideon glanced down at the creator of the instrument of his downfall and softened. The child looked a lot like Prudence when she frowned. "Yes, Miss Grace, there was much fascination with things Egyptian, after Napoleon invaded that land, though as a fashionable topic, it is quite passé now."

The little girl's face fell and, aware of Prudence's hand tightening on his arm, Gideon hastened to repair the damage. "Of course, the frivolous world of fashion cannot keep anything in its silly head for long. People of sense will wish to study the world of the ancients for many years to come."

The look of warm approval Prudence bestowed upon him almost took his breath away. It was followed almost as swiftly by a frown as he bent to draw Miss Grace out about her interest.

A mercurial little creature, Miss ImPrudence. More and more she fascinated him.

Just then Prudence was hailed by a pair of ladies in a carriage: Lady Jersey and another lady Gideon didn't know. Gideon bowed in the ladies' direction but remained where he was. He was in no way inclined to be questioned by one of the most garrulous leaders of the ton. Bad enough she'd seen in him the park walking with Miss Merridew and her sister.

However, Prudence, being newly come to London and still dependent on Lady Jersey's approval, had no option but to go over. She gestured to Grace to come with her, but Gideon kept Grace's arm linked in his, and said, "No, no. You go ahead and chat to the ladies, Miss Merridew. Miss Grace will not mind staying behind to entertain me, will you Miss Grace?"

Miss Grace agreed placidly enough. Miss Prudence, on the other hand, gave him a searing, mistrustful glare as she stepped forward to greet Lady Jersey and her friend.

Gideon grinned. He would now find out the truth about Miss ImPrudence's so-called betrothal. He looked thoughtfully at Prudence's little sister. She stared back at him with open candor, a small, solemn angel with strawberry blonde curls and celestial blue eyes. He'd never had much to do with young girls, having no sisters or female cousins, but he flattered himself he could handle females of all ages.

"Er, do you have a doll, Miss Grace?"

"I used to have a doll, but Grandpapa burned her."

"Ah," Gideon did not know how to reply to that. It occurred to him there might be an opening there for bribery. "Would you like to have a new d—"

"My sister was worried about being alone with you. She made me come with her instead of going for a drive."

Gideon was nonplussed by such plain speaking. "Oh well—"

"You're the man who pretended to Prudence that you were really a duke, aren't you?" The angelic blue eyes were fixed on his face.

Gideon made a careless gesture. "A small misunderstanding—"

"But you did, didn't you? You pretended to be the Duke of Dinstable." The small angel smiled up at him seraphically.

"Well, yes, I did," admitted Gideon, "but it was a mere— Ouch! What the devil!" He bent down, rubbing his shin, and stared at the angel in shock. "What the dev—er, deuce did you do that for? It hurt!"

"Good," said the angel. "I was afraid these new shoes would not be sturdy enough."

"Good?" Gideon repeated indignantly. "Look here, I don't know what you did in the country, but in London you can't go around kicking people on—"

"Why not?" demanded the angel, a pugnacious tilt to her chin.

"Well, er, it's just not done!"

"But if people deserve kicking, what else can I do?"

Gideon rubbed his bruised shin and considered this fraught path. "In what way did I deserve kicking?"

"You played a horrid trick on my sister Prue. And—"

"Your sister is chock-full of tricks herself—Ow! Will you stop that!" He rubbed the other shin.

"My sister Prudence is *not* full of nasty tricks! She looks after us all and protects us from Gr—people. And she is good and kind and always tries to help everyone, and nobody ever helps her. She risked everything to get us to London and had a perfectly splendid plan to save us and then Great-uncle Oswald ruined everything, and poor Prue blames herself, but she cannot help being plain and—"

"Plain? Why the devil does everyone keep saying she is plain?" declared Gideon in exasperation. "Do you all need spectacles?"

Grace's diatribe stopped. She stared at him as if considering something. Gideon edged back, mistrusting the look in her eyes.

"You don't think Prudence is plain?" she repeated.

"Of course I don't! Rash, yes. Mercurial, certainly, but plain?" He snorted.

Grace frowned. "But you've seen her with the others, haven't you?"

"What others?"

"My sisters," She gestured in the direction of the long-departed landau.

"Oh, those yellow-haired chits? Yes, I saw them. What about it?"

Grace tilted her head and eyed him with solemn consideration. "So, you think Prudence is pretty . . . "

Gideon gave her a severe look. "You'll not distract me so easily, miss. When I have something to say I'll say it to your sister, not to some brat who goes around kicking people."

She seemed to find this a satisfactory answer. "Grandpapa used to call me a limb of Satan," she confided.

He eyed the offending foot pointedly. "Perfectly understandable. And that would be the limb he meant, I'm sure."

"I never kicked him. I wish I had, though," she said darkly. "And I will if I see him again."

Gideon rolled his eyes. "If you go around kicking people, you'll never take in society and it will embarrass your sisters sorely, I assure you."

She grinned. "I won't kick you anymore—as long as you don't hurt or upset Prudence. I don't like it when people are horrid to Prudence."

Gideon couldn't help warming to the sprite, in spite of his aching shins. He wouldn't like it if anyone hurt Prudence either, and if they tried he would do a damned sight more than give them a kick! He held out his arm to her. "I assure you, Mistress Limb, I have no intention of harming your sister in any way. Quite the contrary, in fact. And if I did, I should deserve far more than a kicking. Now, shall we stroll on a little?"

She took his arm happily.

"Do you enjoy observing ducks, perchance?" he inquired politely. "There is a duck pond over there."

"No."

"In that case we shall not visit them. Let us await your sister on this bench, instead." They sat down and observed the comings and goings of the fashionable for a time. He glanced across to where Prudence was chatting to the ladies.

She was watching him. Gideon felt warmed by her attention. He smiled at Prudence and patted Grace's hand where it rested on his arm, silent reassurance that he would take good care of her little sister.

Prudence glared back at him horribly. Gideon wondered what unkind things the ladies were saying about him. Gossip was a shocking thing!

He wondered how he could broach the matter of Prudence's betrothal with The Limb. He didn't want her to become suspicious again. Neither did his shins.

"Lord Carradice," The Limb interrupted his musings abruptly. "If you were madly in love with someone, would you become engaged to them and then go off to another country? And expect them to wait for years and years and not even write them very interesting letters?"

He turned to look at her. This was the opening he had hoped for. "Have you been reading your sister's letters?"

She flushed. "Only a few. And only because I'm worried. But—would you leave someone if you were madly in love?"

He shrugged. "Couldn't say. Never been madly in love."

She frowned at him. "But if you were engaged, would you leave the lady behind you for more than four and a half years?"

He shrugged again. "Depends on the lady. If I didn't want to marry her, I might."

"What if she were Prudence?"

Gideon scuffed a pattern in the raked path with his foot. It would be most discreet to say nothing. Instead, he heard himself saying, "Any man who leaves a girl like your sister for four and a half years is a thrice-blasted fool . . . You never know what she might do—waltz off and snag the nearest duke!"

Grace poked his side crossly. "Oh pooh! That was for us, not her, silly!"

Gideon couldn't see how a false betrothal to his cousin would benefit anyone. He considered it a moment and then, recalling the small angel's penchant for physical violence, asked diffidently, "I don't suppose you'd care to explain it all to me."

She frowned. "I don't think I should. It is a secret, you know. A deadly dark one."

"Yes, I *do* know," Gideon reminded her. "If you recall, your sister mentioned it just a moment ago in front of me. I'm simply curious as to how my cousin the duke was brought into it." He smiled down at the young girl, so endearingly like her sister, and added, "Come now, Miss Limb, you may trust me. My shins are at your mercy."

Grace hesitated a moment, then capitulated. "The thing is, Great-uncle Oswald will only bring my other sisters out after Prudence is safely betrothed. And of course, she cannot tell him about being betrothed already, because she promised Phillip she wouldn't, and Prue never breaks a promise, you know."

Gideon silently filed that interesting little fact away in his mind.

Grace continued, "When Prue turns one and twenty—that's next month—we can live with her, but unless one of us marries by then, we shall have no money to live on. And if Grandpapa finds us he will take us back and we shall never get away again. Grandpapa is a very terrible person, you see. We have run away from him."

Gideon did not really see; it was a garbled tale at best, but he persisted. "Why does your uncle insist Prudence must be the one to be betrothed first? If he's trying to fire them all off, why not bring them all out together?"

"Great-uncle Oswald says my sisters would ruin Prue's chances of marriage. He is excessively fond of Prue, you know. But he says no man would want to marry Prudence once he'd seen my sisters. And it isn't fair, because Prudence is the dearest, kindest, nicest, bravest person in the world!"

Dear little soul. Gideon patted her hand again. There must be something wrong with the other sisters, something peculiar that would put off Prudence's suitors from wishing to marry her. No doubt that was the reason she'd rushed them into his landau, so he wouldn't notice.

"So . . . Prudence needs a *fiancé* in order that her sisters may find husbands," he said slowly. "Because if one of you doesn't marry within the month, you will all be taken away by Grandpapa."

"Yes." Grace shivered and snuggled a little closer to him. "But Prue will fix things. She always does."

Gideon was disturbed. The child was a little Viking. What would put that look on her face? He put a comforting arm around her. "It's all right, I'll—" He broke off in sudden shock. He'd been about to assure her he would look after them. What had got into him lately? "You have no parents?"

"No. They died when I was a baby," Grace explained. "Grandpapa brought us all back from Italy after they died . . . But Prue takes care of us. She always promised us that when Phillip came back from India, she would take us all away from Grandpapa, only . . ."

There was that look again. Gideon was beginning to have serious misgivings about Grandpapa. "Only Phillip hasn't come back," prompted Gideon.

"I think he must be dead," Grace confided. "India is very dangerous, you know. There are all sorts of things that can kill you. He could have been stung by a scorpion, or bitten by a cobra—that's a snake. They keep cobras in baskets in India—they're frightfully poisonous—and play music to them. Or he could have caught one of those terrible tropical diseases, where your nose falls off—or is that something else? But I think he has been eaten by a tiger or trampled by an elephant," she ended with apparent relish. "There are hundreds, even thousands of tigers and elephants in India, and I think it very likely Phillip has perished at their—you can't say hands, can you? What would you say—tusks? Fangs?"

Gideon was not prepared to speculate. He cut to the heart of her artless speech. "Why do you think he is dead?"

"Because he has not written to Prue for months and months. And though Prue says the mail from India is very unreliable, what with storms and ships sinking all the time and people drowning—"

He cut off her ghoulish recitation. "It is very unreliable."

"Yes, and Prue says to break off a betrothal to someone working in such terrible conditions as Phillip is in India is as bad as breaking your promise to a soldier who is away at war. And I perfectly understand that. It is a matter of honor, isn't it?"

Gideon nodded thoughtfully. So Miss Prudence had considered the possibility of severing her betrothal, had she?

"But he has never taken so long to respond to her letters before, and you would think he would, wouldn't you? Particularly when our need is so great."

"Hmmm." Gideon's mind was spinning. "Yes, I can see your need is indeed great . . ."

Prudence smiled and nodded, responding automatically as her acquaintances quizzed her gently about being seen walking in the park with a famous rake. She bore the polite chit-chat as best she could, watching her sister and Lord Carradice from the corner of her eye. She was itching to get back there. Grace would be blabbing all sorts of things. That man could charm information out of a post and Grace was no post! Her little sister was laughing and chatting away merrily, while Lord Carradice gave her his full attention. What was she telling him?

Prudence's feelings were so mixed. On the one hand it was wonderful to see Grace looking so happy. She had become so quiet and almost morbid during the last year or so at Dereham Court, but a few moments in Lord Carradice's company, and she was smiling and chattering like any other ten-year-old girl. She'd even heard her giggle once. Prudence hadn't realized how long it had been since she'd heard Grace giggle. For that alone, she owed Lord Carradice her gratitude.

It wasn't simply careless charm, either. He had been kind to Grace, sensitive to her fascination with ancient Egypt. Many fashionable types would have scoffed at her interest in a fad no longer current, but he'd reassured Grace and made her feel important. And now he looked as though he was listening to her with every appearance of interest. Not many sophisticated men of fashion would bother drawing out a child. It would be more common for their eyes to roam the park, seeking more interesting diversions, but as far as she could see, Lord Carradice's eyes had only strayed from

Grace to Prudence. Again, it ought to have earned her gratitude, for Grace needed to experience masculine kindness, to
know that all men were not like Grandpapa . . .

All of these were excellent reasons why Prudence should
feel warm toward Lord Carradice. Instead they made her
more determined than ever to avoid him. She didn't need
Lady Jersey's warnings that he was a fatally charming rattle-
snake and she could place no dependence on his constancy.

She knew about his fatal charm. He effortlessly drew her
to him—the rake in him seemed to call to some dreadful female weakness in her. The animal instincts Grandpapa had
spoken of so often and that she'd never believed in—until
Lord Carradice.

To be in the grip of such instincts should be alarming,
and indeed, when she was in a calm and rational state and
out of reach of his rakish wiles, she was alarmed. But when
she was with Lord Carradice . . . her deplorable animal instincts seemed to just take over.

But that was only part of his danger. Prudence's short
time in London had taught her that growing up as she had in
an atmosphere of cruel harshness, she had few defenses
against kindness. Lord Carradice's careless kindness to her
little sister was devastating. It threatened to undermine all
her resolve.

It was the most dangerous wile of all. All the more dangerous because she suspected it wasn't a wile at all.

She watched him charming her little sister with kindness
and tried to harden her resolve. Kindness wasn't everything.
He was perfectly capable of taking advantage of whatever it
was that Grace had confided, only to tease Prudence. And
the trouble was that even while she *knew* he was only teasing, she . . . she felt things. Things a betrothed woman had
no right feeling for another man.

He was not the slightest bit serious about her. How could
he be? He was a gazetted rake and she was no beauty to en-
tice him into fidelity. He had no respect for the concept; he
knew she'd been engaged to Phillip for years. He should
have realized her mind was firm and resolute and not to be
swayed by a rake's easy charm, but did he care?

She thought of Cleopatra's barge: Her mind might be resolute, but her body was only too easily swayed. And it could not be!

As Lady Jersey had told her, he was simply bored, like the rest of London society, and thought he would entertain himself with her for the season. But like him or not, Prudence would be no rake's idle entertainment. For her own peace of mind and self-respect, she would have as little to do with him as possible.

She broke away from the two ladies as soon as politeness allowed, ready to send Lord Carradice on his way. But as she walked toward them, her decision faltered. Her little sister sat happily arm in arm with Lord Carradice, her eyes fairly blazing with excitement. Prudence blinked. Surely any man who could make Grace look so happy could not be all bad.

His eyes, too, gleamed with laughter and anticipation. That look ought to warn her, she reminded herself. Just so had he looked before he had first kissed her. His eyes had glinted that way as he pressed her back on a certain Egyptian sofa.

She couldn't trust him an inch.

"Thank you for keeping Grace company," she said brightly and seized Grace's hand. "However it is late, and we must find our sisters and get home. Good-bye, Lord Carradice."

She began to march toward the exit, but Grace dragged at her arm, saying, "Prudence, Lord Carradice and I have come up with the most brilliant solution to our problems!"

"It is so kind of Lord Carradice to be concerned," she said sweetly, flinging a look over Grace's head that told Lord Carradice that she wished him to take himself off. "However, I don't wish to trouble him with our private family affairs. I'm sure he has much more important matters to take care of." She hurried on.

"Not at all." He ambled along beside her and quite casually added, "Grace and I have decided that the best thing is for you and I to become betrothed—purely for your sisters' sake, of course. Nothing binding."

She stumbled a moment in shock. "You must be mad, Lord Carradice! I couldn't possibly agree to anything so absurd!"

She tried to lengthen her pace, as if to escape his outrageous suggestion. Beside her, Lord Carradice strolled along, his long legs easily outpacing hers with no apparent effort.

"Why not?" he asked in a reasonable tone.

"Yes, Prue, why not? I think it is a splendid plan," said Grace enthusiastically, skipping along beside them.

Prudence darted her a quelling glance. It was not a splendid plan, it was impossible! Quite ridiculous! She hurried on through the park, peering around in an effort to see that landau with her sisters in it. Unfortunately, there were so many other people, she could not see over them. "I'm a little worried that your coachman may have become lost with my sisters."

"Hawkins is never lost, and besides, my cousin is with them. Now don't change the subject. We were discussing our betrothal, " said Lord Carradice calmly.

Prudence came to an abrupt halt. "Hush!" She glanced around. "People might hear you and not know you are funning, and then we should really be in the suds!"

He shrugged. "I don't care if they hear—"

"Well, I do!"

He took her hands and smiled down into her eyes, a sort of lazy, knowing smile that weakened her resistance quite disgracefully. She snatched her hands away.

He lowered his voice slightly. "Grace and I are agreed. Your sisters must have their coming-out before Grandpapa's ankle is healed, and since Great-uncle Oswald is so pigheaded about firing you off first, and since Otterbottom is in India, giving some poor tiger indigestion—"

"Mr. Otter*bury* is not!" Prudence glared at Grace. "Did you have to blurt out everythi—"

"Or oozing up between the toes of some miserable elephant," Lord Carradice continued imperturbably, "you have need of a *fiancé faux* to foil Great-uncle Oswald's foolish dictum concerning your sisters' coming-out, and thus I humbly offer my services."

"Humbly!" She snorted. "It's impossible!"

"Why is it impossible? I'm frequently humble. I do humility extremely well. Ask anyone! I was voted the most humb—"

She interrupted his nonsense. "I meant, your offer is impossible. I wouldn't do at all."

"Why not? Grace likes me, you like me, Great-uncle Oswald —"

"Grace is an impressionable child, easily deceived!" Prudence ignored an indignant gasp from her sister and continued in a heated tone. "And you cannot possibly claim that Great-uncle Oswald likes you. He despises you. He called you a smoky knave and an unshaven lout!"

He passed his hand across his chin. "You will perceive I possess a razor."

"He also called you a vile deceiver, a cowardly impostor, and a shocking humbug!"

"Pah! Sticks and stones!" Lord Carradice dismissed Great-uncle Oswald's strictures airily. "And it was *shockin' humbug*, not *shocking*. In any case, men of his age are not at their best at such an ungodly hour of the the morning. I think you will find he is singing rather a different tune now."

"Pooh!" snapped Prudence inelegantly. "Why would he have changed his tune so suddenly?"

Lord Carradice managed to look wicked, smug, and saintly, all at the same time.

"In any case," Prudence added belatedly, "*I* don't like you!"

He shook his head at her, a deep smile lurking in his dark eyes. "Oh, Prudence, here I thought you were a truthful girl! Relatively speaking. All dukes aside."

Prudence found herself reddening under his suddenly intent and knowing gaze. She turned away, suddenly flustered. She did *not* like him! Not one little bit! She couldn't possibly like such a frivolous person! She refused to!

He added in a purr, "I'm sure you do like me. I'm very likeable, once you get to know me. Grace liked me after only a few minutes, didn't you, Miss Limb?"

Her traitorous little sister nodded enthusiastically.

"See! Even Great-uncle Oswald came to like me once he knew me better. I grow on people, you see—"

"So do warts!" she snapped. "And I never gave you leave to call me Prudence. I am Miss Merridew to you, sir! And I will *not* enter into a false engagement—or any other sort—

with you! Come, Grace! Come, James!" And gesturing to
the waiting footman, she marched imperiously off, dragging
Grace by the hand.

He strolled along beside her, seeming to take one step to
her three. "It is most unfashionable to scurry through the
park, you know."

"I am not scurrying!" Prudence moderated her pace in as
dignified a manner as she could.

"No?" he said as if it were the most ordinary of conversations. "Would you say scuttling was more accurate? I
wouldn't have thought so, but—"

"I will not bandy words with you," Prudence said frostily, tugging her giggling sister along.

"No? What will you bandy with me, then? I'll bandy
whatever you like, I don't mind." His voice lowered sugges-
tively, bringing an irresistible image to Prudence's mind of
those stolen wicked moments when he had driven every
proper thought from her head and swamped her body with
wondrous sensations . . . And her mind, ever since, with impossible dreams . . .

Prudence could not bring herself to answer him. It was a
ridiculous situation, she thought crossly. Like fleeing from a
tiger, only the tiger persisted in loping along beside her,
making conversational banter and looking at her in a way
that made her hot and flustered. With fury, of course. She
strode on toward the exit nearest to Great-uncle Oswald's
house, Grace skipping along on one side of her, Lord Carradice strolling on the other, and James, the footman, stolidly bringing up in the rear.

She suddenly remembered something and confronted
him with it. "Why do you think Great-uncle Oswald's dictum is foolish?" she asked, and then cursed herself for her
own foolishness.

He gave her a direct look. "Your sisters' entry into society could make no difference to your own likelihood of finding a husband. A beauty need not worry about attracting
suitors. Sir Oswald is a man of enterprise. If there is a fly in
the ointment, he will no doubt find a dowry large enough to
sweeten the pot."

It was as if he'd slapped her. It was not as if she didn't

know she was plain and undesirable; she had known it all her life. Still, the careless words, so casually uttered had . . . hurt. Deeply.

It was a warning that she would be very foolish not to heed, Prudence told herself. This man had the power to slip past her barriers. They were barely acquainted and yet he had already hurt her unbelievably, simply by uttering words—words she *knew* to be true.

It wasn't only her fashionable Great-uncle and London's leading mantua maker who thought her too plain to be desired in marriage; this was from a rake—a man who really would know. A man who had been teasing her from who-knew-what motives. Teasing. Flirting. Putting foolish, impossible dreams in her head. Making her feel attractive, desirable, almost pretty.

And then telling her she was a fly in the ointment.

How could she have thought he was kind?

She didn't want his double-edged admiration. She didn't need his false, foolish dreams or his false betrothal. She had a betrothed; Phillip. Phillip, who did not care that she was plain and had given her a ring to prove it. Four and a half years ago.

She strode blindly on, blinking fiercely to prevent the sudden uprush of scalding, *stupid* tears she could feel prickling behind her eyes and in her throat, just waiting to spring forth in front of . . . in front of everyone and humiliate her.

She stumbled over a cobblestone and his hand was there to support and steady her. "What is wrong?" he said, in a low, concerned voice. "What have I—"

She shook off his hand fiercely. "I have the headache. Just leave me alone," she snapped. "Just go away!" She heard her voice crack. "Stay away from me, in future, Lord Carradice! And stay away from my sisters, too!" And snatching her sister's hand, Prudence hurried away.

Gideon stared after her. "What the—" He glanced at her footman and received such a look of contempt that he was stunned. "What did I say?" he demanded.

But the footman merely shook his head and marched off after the two girls.

Chapter Eight

∞

"There is nothing more unbecoming in a man of quality than to laugh;
'tis such a vulgar expression of the passion."
WILLIAM CONGREVE

"ALL I DID WAS OFFER TO ACT AS HER BETROTHED, SO THAT HER wretched sisters could make their coming-out." Gideon had arrived in the dining room that evening to find his cousin already seated at the table, gazing abstractedly at a silver bowl of fruit set in its center. "And she sent me packing and stormed off in a huff!" It was more than a huff. What the devil had he said that upset her so?

"Very unsettling," responded Edward. "Shall I ring for the first course?"

Gideon frowned. Edward seemed a little preoccupied. Perhaps he was finding the whirl of London society a little overwhelming. But he had no time to worry about his cousin. His last words had upset Prudence, and he could not for the life of him imagine why. He'd gone over their conversation a dozen times in his head already, and still he was none the wiser.

He ought to have put it out of his mind. It was what he usually did. Women were odd creatures and often did get upset by the strangest things. But for some reason he couldn't put it out of his mind. He decided to consult his cousin.

"I thought it was what she wanted, but she behaved for all the world as if I'd mortally insulted her." He shook out his napkin and cast a worried look at the duke. "Even her footman gave me the blackest look. Am I so notorious?"

Edward shook his head. "I wouldn't call you notorious. A terrible flirt, perhaps; a little too free with other men's wives on several occasions—though it has to be admitted that the wives do seek you out—but notorious, no. What exactly did you say to her?"

Gideon made a frustrated gesture. "I simply assured her that her sisters could not make the slightest difference to her own marriageability, that beauty would always find suitors. And that if there was a fly, or flies, in the ointment, Sir Oswald would sweeten the pot with a fat dowry. And she behaved as if I'd insulted *her!*" He shook his head and helped himself to the nearest dish. "I'm sorry about foisting them on you this afternoon, by the way, but I wanted to get Prudence alone."

The duke looked up and smiled, a smile of peculiar sweetness. "Oh yes. I didn't mind. Not at all." He sighed and helped himself to a dish of buttered crab with smelts.

Gideon, frowning, spooned something onto his plate. "So tell me, Coz, what's wrong with them?"

The duke frowned. "Wrong? The crabs are excellent."

"Not the crabs, the sisters. The flies in the ointment," Gideon said impatiently. "What's wrong with them?"

Edward blinked. "There's nothing wrong with them, Gideon."

"Not cross-eyed, or simple, or obviously deranged?"

Edward stared. "No, they're quite, quite perfect."

Gideon shrugged. "They must take fits, then."

"Why in heaven's name would you think so?"

"Apparently Sir Oswald is adamant that the other sisters would ruin Prudence's chances—he doesn't know about Otterbury, by the way—so he's insisting that Prudence be fired off first. And underneath the bluster, he's pretty shrewd, so there must be something to it. If he says the sisters could ruin her chances, there must be something very wrong with 'em."

"No, it will be their looks that have him worried."

Gideon raised his brows. "Ah, a trifle on the gargoyle side, are they?"

"On the gargoyle—" Edward paused, the fork halfway to his mouth. "Do you mean to say you didn't notice?"

"Notice what?"

Edward shook his head in disbelief. "Far from being gargoyles, Prudence's sisters are all quite extraordinarily beautiful."

Gideon frowned. "Beautiful? Are they? Are you sure?" He lifted his fork and paused. He glowered down at his plate. He had unaccountably filled it with stewed cucumbers. He detested stewed cucumbers.

"They quite dazzle the eyes," confirmed his cousin.

"As lovely as Prudence?"

The duke's jaw dropped. After a moment he recovered himself and said, "Much lovelier than Prudence. That, I surmise, is the problem. Each one of her sisters, even little Grace, would outshine Prudence in every respect."

Gideon stared at him in a moment's disbelief. "I might not have taken much notice of the other sisters, but I did spend upwards of half an hour with young Grace, and though she's a nice little thing and quite pretty, she's not a patch on Prudence."

Edward observed him solemnly for a moment and then gave a large, satisfied sigh. "This," he said, "promises to be vastly entertaining."

"What does?" Gideon asked, unaccountably annoyed by the smug expression on his cousin's face.

But the duke would not explain.

"I don't understand what you are hinting at, but you are wrong. I have no interest in Miss Merriweather. You know how I feel about marriage. And this is not about marriage, anyway. It's merely a ruse to enable her sisters to find husbands." Gideon speared a veal olive viciously. "I don't pretend to understand why the whole thing must be shrouded in such mystery and subterfuge, but if a stand-in *fiancé* is what she needs, I'll do it. I don't mind helping her out—as long as it's not the real thing, of course."

"Very selfless of you, cousin."

"You may scoff, but I think it is quite altruistic of me,"

Gideon said. "There's not many men who will risk parson's mousetrap out of sheer disinterested helpfulness—"

"Extremely sheer," the duke murmured.

"—to a female who is, after all, very little more than a stranger. But she is an orphan, you see, and—"

The duke was overcome by a sudden choking fit.

Gideon waited until he had subsided and added in an austere tone, "If she needs a false betrothed so badly that she must come calling on *you* to get one, there's no reason why she cannot accept *my* assistance."

"None at all, dear boy. Call on her great-uncle, by all means."

"Well, as a matter-of-fact, I did earlier this afternoon, and he assumed I was there to ask for her hand. Silly fellow."

"So what did you tell him?"

"Oh, well, it was complicated," Gideon said in an off-hand manner. "He was practically frolicking with delight, and I could not get a word in to disabuse him of the notion. But now, since the damage is done, Miss Prudence may take advantage of the misunderstanding. I don't mind, if it will help her sisters out."

"They being orphans, too," the duke agreed in a choked voice.

"I don't see what there is to amuse you so, Edward," Gideon said crossly.

"Nothing. Nothing at all, to be sure," the duke murmured solemnly. His lips twitched. "I don't suppose Sir Oswald gets his brandy from the same supplier, does he? He might have received a bad batch, too."

"He doesn't drink brandy," Gideon said, "but he did serve the filthiest-tasting wine."

Prudence was cross. More than cross, she was furious. The moment she had arrived home from the park, Great-uncle Oswald had called them all into the front parlor and congratulated Prudence on her great good fortune. Lord Carradice, it seemed, had done the decent thing and had agreed to a betrothal with Prudence. And since they were all so keen on it, Charity could now begin her coming-out, starting tonight, in fact, by accompanying him and Prudence to Lady

Ostwither's private musical soiree. He had already sent Lady Ostwither a note.

"There must be some mistake," Prudence had said, amid the general excitement caused by this announcement. "Lord Carradice has no interest in me." Lord Carradice, in fact, had just told her she was more or less unmarriageable. So what was his game?

"On the contrary, my dear, the fellow is not such a scapegrace as I thought him. He must have a conscience, after all, for he was here, in this very room, dressed to the nines in his courtin' clothes and announcin' that he fully intended to do the decent thing by you, Prudence, my dear, dear girl. And of course, I gave my permission. Twenty thousand a year!" Visibly moved, Great-uncle Oswald embraced her.

With Great-uncle Oswald wreathed in delighted grins, blinking back tears and speaking ecstatically of the Carradice fortune, Charity fretting in instant pleasure-panic about whatever would she wear to Lady Ostwither's, and the twins skipping in delight around the room predicting their own imminent coming-out and twittering on about how handsome Lord Carradice was, there was not much Prudence could do except grit her teeth and smile.

The wretch!

He was making mock of her, that was clear. One moment he was wheedling secrets out of her ten year-old sister, the next he was suggesting a false betrothal to Prudence—and in the next breath had told her she was plain and unmarriageable! And now— No, hold. Prudence frowned on a sudden thought. He must have spoken to Great-uncle Oswald *before* he met up with them in the park. It must be some devious ploy of his. But to what purpose?

She was brooding about the sequence of events when her great-uncle made an announcement that shocked her out of her reverie.

"I shall send a notice to the *Morning Post* immediately!"

"No!" exclaimed Prudence, horrified. "You must not!" Grandpapa would see it.

"Why on earth not, m'dear? You've made a conquest of a fellow the tabbies have been stalkin' for years! Why not puff it off to the world? Nothin' to hide, have we?"

"No, no, of course not. It is just that . . . er," Prudence snatched an excuse from the air. "Lord Carradice is in mourning."

Great-uncle Oswald looked surprised. "I'm sorry to hear that. I hadn't heard. Who was it who died, m'dear? And if he is in mourning, come to think of it, why does his raiment not proclaim the fact? He was wearing a blue coat—dash it all—*blue!* 'Pon my soul, the fellow is a careless dresser!"

Prudence thought frantically. "Ahh, his great-aunt died. But . . . she had a horror of black so she requested that her family continue to wear colors for her."

Great-uncle Oswald pulled a face. "Dashed peculiar, these modern notions. Colors for mourning. Pshaw! Which great-aunt was it? Not Estelle, was it? Or Gussie? I hope it wasn't Gussie—although come to think of it, Gussie is Carradice's aunt, not a great-aunt at all. Well, that's a relief! Always been fond of Gussie."

Belatedly, Prudence realized Great-uncle Oswald was likely to be acquainted with all of Lord Carradice's more elderly relatives.

"Ah, no, I don't think it was Estelle or Gussie. I, er, I think this great-aunt lived a very retired life . . . in Wales."

"Oh, Wales, that explains it," said Great-uncle Oswald, quite as if Wales were Outer Mongolia. "And you didn't catch the name, eh? No mourning! Dashed odd business all around. Still, if he wants a quiet betrothal, I'll not oppose it. Twenty thousand pounds a year! I think that calls for a toast."

"Lord Carradice must have meant what he said in the park, Prue," whispered Grace while Great-uncle Oswald poured them each a celebratory half glass of dandelion wine. "About wanting to be your *fiancé faux.*"

Prudence nodded slowly. "Yes, but why? That's the question, Grace, my love. Why would Lord Carradice want to enter into a false betrothal with me? I trust him not at all."

Grace looked solemn. "I don't think he wants a false betrothal, Prue. I think he really likes you."

Prudence sniffed. "Nonsense! What he likes is playing games! He's just teasing me, dearest. The man is frivolous to his bones! He knows I am promised to Phillip."

Hope had come up behind them and overheard Grace's words. "Of course he likes you, Prue! Why, in the park, he could barely take his eyes off you!"

"He didn't even look at Charity," added Faith. "Or any of us, except you."

Prudence raised an eyebrow at Charity for confirmation of this incredible tale.

Charity shook her head. "I'm sorry, Prue, I didn't notice. I was a little distracted by the other sights in the park."

Hope and Faith burst into giggles and went into a huddle of whispers. Charity turned a little pink.

"Charity also has an admirer!" exclaimed Hope slyly.

"Oh, don't be silly, Hope," said Charity, but she looked a little self-conscious.

"Eh? What's that? Young Charity made a conquest already, has she?" exclaimed Great-uncle Oswald in great good humor. "Don't surprise me at all, such a dazzling creature you are, m'dear. I'm sure we'll have 'em comin' around in droves, soon enough! Now that we've got Prudence and young Carradice sorted out!" Beaming, he raised his glass of dandelion wine. "To the happy couple!"

Prudence set down her glass. She could not drink, not even to a false betrothal, and to a man who had clearly done it all just to tease her. She felt wretchedly guilty about Great-uncle Oswald's delight in her marrying into a title and a fortune. He would be horrified to learn she would actually marry a penniless younger son of undistinguished family.

"Come on, Prudence m'dear, drink up. Do you a power of good, dandelion wine. Strengthens the blood, you know." Great-uncle Oswald lifted his glass. "To the future Lady Carradice!"

That was a toast Prudence could drink to. She could drink with a clear conscience to his unfortunate future wife. She heartily pitied the poor woman, whoever she would be.

She sipped obediently, then returned to the subject of Charity's mystery beau. "Now, Charity, tell us about this admirer." She did not know what devious game Lord Carradice was playing, but if it meant that Charity had the chance to be safely settled, she would do her best to turn it to her advantage.

"Never fret, Prudence my dear," exclaimed Great-uncle Oswald. "We'll fire young Charity off with no trouble at all—no trouble at all. Ravishin' creature, she is! It was you I was worried about, but you've done us all proud, m'dear—twenty thousand a year! I couldn't be more delighted, 'pon my word, I couldn't. Our little Prudence, settled at last. Drink up, gels, drink up!"

He raised his glass and drained it of every last drop of dandelion wine. "I'll speak to Carradice and work out when we can have the betrothal celebration. If he's gaddin' about the town in colors, I can't imagine his Welsh great-aunt would object to a small, tasteful party."

Prudence drank mechanically. As long as it remained a family secret, there should be no difficulty. She was confident she could carry off a false betrothal. She was almost confident she could manage Lord Carradice. Forewarned was forearmed, after all. All she had to do was keep Great-uncle Oswald happy and ensure Charity made a good marriage to a kind and loving man.

In the meantime, she needed to know more about this mysterious admirer in the park. Charity had a streak of self-lessness in her that could be fatal. Prudence didn't want her lovely, gentle sister to be dazzled into marriage, nor to sacrifice her own happiness in order to make her sisters safe.

Marriage was supposed to be joyful. Prudence had learned that by observing her loving parents; her younger sisters remembered only the harshness of Grandpapa and duty. Charity desperately needed to be loved. All her sisters did, to make up for the terrible childhood they'd had. Prudence had promised them the sunshine and laughter and love and happiness her parents had had, and she was determined that if Charity married, it would be for love—nothing else would do. If necessary, Prudence would find another way to save them all from Grandpapa.

She turned back to her sister. "Charity dearest, pray don't be shy. Tell us about this admiring gentleman."

Charity blushed. "Oh, Hope exaggerates. There wasn't anyone in particular," she said. "Several gentlemen asked to be introduced in fact."

"No one in particular! What a bouncer!" interrupted

Hope. "Why, a certain gentleman could not take his eyes off you, Charity, and you were looking right back—"

Charity, cheeks rosy, shook her head vigorously. "Hush! it's nothing, just . . . nothing. You must not refine upon it. He—they were just being polite, that's all."

"Who couldn't take his eyes off Charity?" asked Prudence.

Hope opened her mouth, but Charity shot her a look that silenced her. "Nobody! The twins are talking nonsense." She looked daggers at her giggling twin sisters. "You are such children!"

But Prudence didn't believe her denials. "Hope, who you are talking about!"

Hope waved her hand airily. "That pudgy little duke, of course. Lord Carradice's cousin. Hermit Ned. The Duke of Dinstable. He couldn't take his eyes off Charity, from the moment they were introduced. And she was all cow's eyes in return."

"He is *not* pudgy!" Charity pounced on her sister with fury. "He's not the *slightest* bit pudgy! He's solid! And strong! And he's handsome. And kind. And intelligent. And—"

"And worth thirty thousand a year, b'gad!" exclaimed Great-uncle Oswald.

Prudence stared at her sister in amazement. She'd never seen Charity so vehement. So protective. So passionate.

"The Duke of Dinstable?" she said. "But how . . . when—?" She broke off. It must have happened when he took the girls for the ride in the landau.

"The Duke of Dinstable! I think that calls for a little more dandelion—no! Hang it! If we're celebrating a duke, it had better be the very best stuff!" Great-uncle Oswald gleefully yanked on the bell cord. "A bottle of our finest cowslip, Niblett. We are celebrating! What a day! What a day! A baron already hooked, and now the nibble of a duke on our line! Romance is in the air, girls! To the tune of fifty thousand a year! Bless my soul! I haven't had so much excitement in years!"

·   ·   ·

Lady Ostwither's soiree was just what Prudence would have wanted for Charity's first appearance in society. The gathering was small—only about fifty or so people—but very select. And since Lady Ostwither's own daughter was making her coming-out this season, Lady Ostwither had made certain many of the guests were wealthy and eligible young gentlemen.

Having met Prudence, Lady Ostwither was rather disconcerted when Sir Oswald Merridew's second orphaned niece turned out to be a Diamond of the First Water. She collected her face with commendable dignity and said in a voice that grated only a little, "You might have warned me, Sir Oswald!"

However, being a kindly lady she made both girls welcome. And if it galled her to see so many of the young men she'd earmarked for her daughter now vying to find Charity the best seat, the most refreshing lemonade, and anything else that should take her fancy, she didn't allow it to show for more than a moment or two.

Prudence watched the buzz around her sister with satisfaction. There would be plenty of young men for Charity to choose from. If Hope and Faith were wrong about the Duke of Dinstable, there were other fish in Charity's sea.

And though her sister was surely the most beautiful and sweet-natured girl, Prudence could not really see her becoming a duchess. A duke would expect to marry within his own rank, surely. Charity was only the granddaughter of an obscure and unfashionable baron, a girl, moreover, whose father had made a *mésalliance* with the daughter of a tradesman; Grandpapa had drummed that flaw into them time and time again. Would inferior breeding matter to a duke?

What nonsense, she told herself. There was no reason to fret at this point. She had no real cause to think the duke was interested in Charity—only the mischievous reports of a pair of silly young girls. And Charity's blushes and vehement defense of him. If there was truth in the report, Prudence would do what she could to promote the match, but in the meantime, it was important that Charity meet a variety of eligible gentlemen.

And then there would be the twins to be settled. As for herself . . . She would look after Grace.

She wondered whether a letter had arrived from India. She'd left money with the scullery maid, to give to her brother in the village, and had written out Great-uncle Oswald's address for him, but she was not sure how well the lad could read and write, and if he copied the address wrongly, well . . .

How frail a thing was a letter, to carry such weighty responsibilities. And with so many possibilities for something to go wrong . . .

All the more reason for trust and faith to remain strong, Prudence reminded herself firmly.

"That particular shade of sage is exquisite on you, my Prudence," a dark velvet voice murmured in her ear.

She whirled. "L-Lord Carradice." He was staring at her in a way that made her feel hot all over, even though her gown was rather thin and she had been feeling a little chilly. She tugged her shawl around her.

He did not move, but it was as if his eyes caressed her all over.

Prudence felt the heat spread.

"I asked you to stay away from me."

He simply smiled, and Prudence could see why so many women had made fools of themselves over him. Well, she would not be one of them!

"I would appreciate it if you would stop . . . stop . . . *ogling* me like that," she hissed, tugging her very modest neckline higher. "It is very embarrassing." She folded her arms across her breasts defensively.

He tried to look contrite. "It wasn't me," he confessed. "It was my eyes. They are bold and easily led and have no sense of propriety." His eyes wandered back to where her arms were folded, and he added softly, "Besides, you are so lovely. My poor eyes cannot resist the temptation you give them."

Prudence went breathless with pleasure at the unexpected compliment. *You are so lovely.* She tried to squash the small surge of delight. It was utter foolishness to believe a word he said, of course. Such empty flattery no doubt came to his lips as easily as breathing. In the park earlier he'd implied she was too plain to attract a husband. A fly in the ointment. He was flirting, and only naive country nobodies would fall for it. She pursed her mouth in what she hoped was a governessy fashion. "You are talking nonsense. A short time ago you said I was a fly in the ointment of my sisters' marriages and that—"

"I said nothing of the sort!" he interrupted indignantly. "Why would I say anything so patently ridiculous?"

"You did, too. In the park."

"I did not! In fact I distinctly recall telling you that you would have no trouble finding a husband—beauties like you invariably attract suitors in droves—and that whatever is wrong with your sisters, it wouldn't lessen your own chances."

She stared at him suspiciously. Beauties like her. He couldn't possibly mean it. Was he just trying to make up for lost ground. "What do you mean whatever is wrong with my sisters? There is nothing wrong with my sisters!"

"No, that's what Edward says, too. So you've no need to worry." He heaved a satisfied sigh. "So that's why you were cross with me! Because I insulted your sisters. I wondered about it all evening. I'm sorry. I'm sure they're very nice girls and you'll manage to find someone for them eventually."

Prudence couldn't think of a thing to say. He'd thought her beautiful sisters were the fly in the ointment? He called Prudence a beauty. He couldn't possibly be sincere. But he sounded sincere. Was his eyesight defective? She peered into his eyes, wondering.

Instantly they got that dark, sleepy-intent look in them, the look she knew meant she needed to be wary. They ran over her in a caressing manner that made her shiver, and not from cold.

His voice deepened. "Have I told you how lovely you look tonight in that sage gown? It brings out the glorious color of your hair and makes me imagine that I could drown in the crystal depths of your eyes, quite happily."

"Yes. But I think you talk a lot of nonsense. And I asked you to stay away from me. And will you please stop ogling me!" She tried to sound severe, but oh, how his compliments went to her head.

He instantly looked crushed, but as she had seen him produce the exact same expression for Great-uncle Oswald, his cousin, and a butler, she was in no way fooled by his apologetic mien. His eyes gleamed with laughter. The man had not a contrite bone in his body.

"I would if I could. But it's my eyes. They cannot resist you, but see, I will beat them for their forwardness." He batted his lashes rapidly, then gave her a sleepy, wicked look, purely sinful.

Prudence found her own lips twitching with amusement. She fought to keep a straight face. He was an incorrigible rogue. She should not encourage him.

But oh, Lord, how was she ever to resist him? Her upbringing had armed her against brutality, scorn, and harshness; she had no defense against the pleasures of compliments and warmth and laughter. And being told she looked lovely.

"I will have you know I was raised according to rules of the *strictest* propriety," she told him severely.

"No? Were you?" he said sympathetically. "Never mind, that's the nice thing about growing older. One can escape the results of one's upbringing."

Escape our upbringing. His words jolted her. Suddenly all her problems rolled back into place. She ought not be standing here flirting—yes, that's what she'd been doing, flirting with Lord Carradice.

He added lightly, "Things change. People change—some of them, most delightfully." His eyes ran over her appreciatively.

Feeling a wave of warmth as a direct result of his look, Prudence released her breath slowly. And some things didn't change unless you made them happen. She had to make Lord Carradice go away. She couldn't think straight while he was near.

She moved to the room where people were gathering for the musical recital. Lord Carradice followed. Twice now she'd asked him to stay away from her! And did he take the slightest bit of notice? She recalled her other grievance.

"I have another bone to pick with you."

"Oh we can do better than bones, surely." He prowled forward.

She backed away, giving him her frostiest, most repellent look.

His eyes narrowed in amusement. "My word, what a peculiar expression. Eaten something that disagrees with you, my dear?" he said in a solicitous voice. "Not surprising, that frightful weedy tea stuff your great-uncle serves."

Remembering the purge, Prudence flushed, then recollected that Lord Carradice had not witnessed that little debacle. "I wish he had served you something much worse than his tea!" she declared callously. "Something poisonous."

"He did. Some atrocious dandelion wine. Ghastly."

"How dare you sneak off behind my back and arrange to get yourself falsely betrothed to me."

"Did *I* do that? How very shocking of me!" Lord Carradice purred. "And all the time I thought that was *you*, arriving at my cousin's house, all of a twitter because you'd claimed to be betrothed . . ."

"Oh." Mortified, Prudence felt her face heat even more. "That."

"Yes, that." His eyes quizzed her so shamelessly that Prudence felt quite irritable.

"It was very bad of me, I know. However I have already apologized several times for it, and since you are so uncivil as to continue reminding me of the fact, I shall repeat myself: I am very sorry for embroiling you in my problems."

"Oh but Prudence." His voice was like warm, rich chocolate. "I'm happy to be embroiled in anything of your—"

"I did not give you leave to use my first name, sir," Prudence cut him off primly, certain by the look in his eyes that he was going to say something vastly improper.

He led her to a small group of chairs. "No, you didn't, and you are quite right to point it out to me," he said, pulling a chair forward for her. "A singularly inappropriate name it is, too. I shall not use it in future."

It was one thing to dislike your own name and quite another for him to cast aspersions on it, but Prudence decided not to take issue. She had other fish to fry. She allowed herself to be seated, then said, "Now, about your visit to my great-uncle this afternoon—"

"Did it upset him?" He sat down beside her.

"Well, no."

"He wasn't distressed, concerned, offended, or enraged?"

Prudence gritted her teeth. "No, of course not, but—"

"He was, in fact, quite pleased?"

Prudence refused to answer. It was difficult enough to deliver a reprimand without having to admit that his visit had made her elderly relative perfectly, quite vulgarly ecstatic.

"Whatever my great-uncle may have thought, you had no right to suggest that I have agreed to a betrothal," she said severely.

"I didn't."

"It was bad enough—" She broke off. "What did you say?"

"I didn't."

"Didn't what?"

"Suggest that you had agreed to a betrothal," he said. "In fact I don't recall saying anything of the sort. It never even crossed my mind."

Prudence scanned his face intently, unsure of whether he was teasing her or telling the truth. He was a very difficult man to read. He seemed to find everything amusing.

"The whole thing was Sir Oswald's idea." He shrugged and stretched out his long legs in front of him. "He simply decided I was wearing 'courtin' clothes' and given our previous four-year history, leaped to the conclusion I had finally come to ask permission to wed you. I didn't ask, but he gave it anyway and seems to think it a done deal." His eyebrows rose in polite enquiry. "Tell me, does he always make such ludicrous leaps in logic?"

"Oh." Prudence didn't know where to look. It sounded very plausible . . . She could easily imagine Great-uncle Oswald jumping to false conclusions. And if the misunderstanding was anyone's fault, it was hers, for precipitating the whole ridiculous mess with her lies.

She glanced across at Charity, surrounded by beaux. Prudence might regret the lies, but she could not regret the results. Even if too close an acquaintance with Lord Carradice was one of them. She felt a wave of warmth pass across her skin.

She turned back to him. "I owe you an apology. Again."

He waved his hand airily. "Not at all. In any case, since Grace so kindly explained everything to me in the park, I have decided to remain betrothed to you, so you need not fret your mercurial elderly relative any more."

Distracted as she was by the interplay between Charity and her companions, it took a moment or two for his words to sink in. She swung around. "You've decided *what?*"

He smiled slowly, a smile that made her breathless, even as she wanted to strangle him. "Yes, I've decided to overlook your cavalier treatment of my love letters and forgive you, and so we remain betrothed. Great-uncle Oswald and I are in perfect accord, for a change."

"They weren't love letters. They were tailor's bills. And we are *not* betrothed!"

"Ah, but the old gentleman thought the burning of the letters most affectingly romantic—so did I, for that matter. That tailor grossly overcharges. And besides, you know you need me, Imp."

"I don't need you. And—what did you just call me?"

"Imp. It's short for ImPrudence—much more appropriate. Whoever named you Prudence was ill-advised. There is not a shred of prudence or caution in you!" He observed her indignant reaction with patent approval, then commented affably, "You know, huffing and puffing like that shows off your bosom very prettily."

Prudence instantly stopped breathing. He smiled, a slow, devilish invitation to wickedness. "It's a very nice bosom. You should show it off."

"I was not show—"

"There's no point arguing—you know you need me, Prudence."

"I know no such thing!" she hissed. "Now hush, Miss Ostwither is about to perform on the violin."

He laid his hand on her arm soothingly, and murmured, "You don't need to admit it here and now; you can wait until we are alone." His thumb stroked her skin, sending warm shivers down her spine.

She shook his hand off furiously. "I shall take care never to be alone with you again, Lord Carradice," she whispered frostily.

He leaned forward and murmured, "Is that a challenge? I love a challenge. So, how will you admit your need of me?" His warm breath heated her skin. He was far too close.

She edged away. "I will never admit any such thing!"

He gave her a heated look from beneath his dark lashes. "It will be our little secret, then," he purred. "I love secrets."

"Oh hush!"

Chapter Nine

∞

"Eternity was in our lips and eyes
Bliss in our brows."
WILLIAM SHAKESPEARE

HE SAT BACK AS THE PERFORMANCE COMMENCED, ONE LONG LEG crossed over the other, his arm resting casually along the back of her chair. His hand dangled an inch or so from her bare skin. Did he know she could barely think, let alone speak, for awareness of the proximity of his fingers?

Of course he knew. He was a rake. This is what he did; flustered virtuous ladies merely by his proximity. And shameless conversation. Prudence refused to be flustered. She concentrated on the concert and utterly ignored the way his fingers occasionally brushed her skin. If she shivered occasionally, it was caused by a draft!

After some moments, he leaned forward and whispered in her ear, his breath warm against her skin. "If we were not betrothed, your sister would not now be sitting with my cousin, drinking Lady Ostwither's vile ratafia and listening to that girl inflict on us that excruciating noise she alleges is something Mozart created."

"Hush! She is our hostess's daughter."

"Yes, but from the sounds emanating from her, she must be standing on a cat, and I don't approve of cruelty to animals—or ears! But you digress," he reprimanded her. "We were discussing the necessity for our betrothal to stand."

"*I* digress!" Prudence whispered indignantly, then bit her tongue. She would not take his bait. It was both impolite to her hostess and unwise, tactically. His words were true; if Great-uncle Oswald realized Prudence and Lord Carradice were not betrothed and never had been, Charity wouldn't be here, attended by several very eligible gentlemen. She glanced across at her sister. It was time to change the topic.

"Tell me," she whispered, "who is the gentleman standing near my sister just now?"

Lord Carradice glanced over. "Which one? There's a crowd of 'em. Carver is the tall yellow-haired fellow standing behind her, the soppy-looking thin one in the atrocious yellow velvet coat is young Hopeton, and as for the medium-sized duke on her left, weren't you betrothed to him at one point?"

"Thank you," she whispered frostily.

Miss Ostwither finished her piece and was politely applauded. She lifted her violin again and Lord Carradice groaned. As Miss Ostwither murdered Mozart once more, he leaned across, his mouth so close to Prudence's ear she could feel his heat, and whispered, "Whoever that girl's music master is, he should be hanged, drawn, and quartered—preferably while she plays him a dirge on that thing."

Unsuccessfully, she smothered a giggle.

"Pray, do not be so frivolous as to giggle at a serious musical event," he murmured austerely. "Innocent cats gave their lives for this." She giggled again, and several people shushed them.

The hand that had been resting so perilously close to her bare skin moved and she felt the light touch of one fingertip. Her body burned with awareness of it. She tried to shrug it off. It hovered, then returned, stroking her skin in tiny, thistledown circles. The sensation was deliciously unsettling. Prudence shivered. How could a shoulder be so sensitive? She moved in her seat. The fingertip caress followed. She tried to wriggle away from it.

"You'll fall off that seat if you move much farther," he whispered.

Prudence sat very straight on her seat for the remainder of the recital, clutching her reticule on her lap. She would have liked very much to biff him with it, but the circumstances made it impossible. There was nothing she could do. The man was incorrigible. He had no conscience at all. She tried to focus her attention on Miss Ostwither. It was not possible. Tiny sensations of pleasure rippled through her, spreading from that one tiny point to the rest of her body. Prudence fought them.

A second finger joined the first.

She sat up in rigid indignation, a silent message of virtue outraged. Unfortunately it brought the rest of his fingers in contact with her skin. Now four long, strong fingers and a thumb sent tiny, hot ripples of sensation through her. Prudence immediately slumped in her seat to sever the connection. Some things were more important than elegance.

He shifted casually and the long, wicked fingers once again trailed featherlight twirls across her skin. Prudence sat hunched in her chair, fighting each insidious shiver of pleasure his touch created. She became hotter and hotter and crosser and crosser.

Finally Miss Ostwither's recital came to a screeching climax and an interval was declared. Prudence almost leaped from her seat and hurried away from Lord Carradice as fast as she could. He strolled after her and with no ceremony, tucked her hand in his arm and resumed the conversation. "Are you still sniffy with me over the resumption of our betrothal?"

"I am not sniffy. And I don't wish to discuss it. Or anything else with you. I have had quite enough of your company, thank you!" She tried to tug her hand out from his.

He ignored her. "Now, Miss Imp, you must be betrothed to somebody; after all, you can't wait around forever for a fellow who goes off and gets himself squashed by elephants. Very careless sort of fellow, this Otterclogs—won't do for you at all. You need somebody reliable. On hand. Like me."

"Reliable? You?" Prudence made a rude sound under her breath and bowed politely to a passing acquaintance. "And his name is Otter*bury*."

He gestured to his long, elegant form. "At least I have the decency to remain unsquashed by elephants."

"I doubt even an elephant *could* squash you!" she snapped, goaded. "Besides, Phillip has *not* been squashed by an elephant!"

"How do you know?" He moved forward, towing her inexorably with him.

"I would have heard from his mother. She was our neighbor in Norfolk, you know."

"Ah, then it must have been the tiger that got him."

"It was not a tig—! This is a ridiculous conversation."

"It is indeed, but you're the one who brought Otterbottom up in the first place. I have no idea why we're wasting time discussing some stupid fellow who went off to live with elephants—he must be addled in the brain. If you were mine, I'd never leave you, Prudence. I couldn't."

For a moment, Prudence couldn't breathe. His words were so enticing, his voice so deep and dark and sounding so very sincere . . . His arm felt strong and warm and hard under her gloved hand, and the faint scent of his cologne teased her senses. She tried to tell herself it was the aftermath of those wicked caresses.

How could such a light touch have such a pervasive effect on her entire body?

She glanced around. Somehow as they'd strolled, he'd maneuvered them toward a secluded alcove without her realizing. Dark red-velvet curtains draped across it. She backed against them, instinctively needing the support of the wall or window the curtains covered, but found herself floundering in red-velvet folds instead. He reached across her shoulder and brushed one of the curtains aside.

She glanced around. No wall or window, the curtains concealed a door. He prowled toward her, so close she could feel his breath on her skin. She found herself backing away, into the room behind. It was a small room, dim and private. The red velvet folds fell back into place; he closed the door behind him and she heard a key click. The sounds of the ball receded. All Prudence could hear was the sound of her own heart thudding.

Mere minutes after she'd sworn it would never happen again, she was alone with Lord Carradice.

Breathless, flustered, and suddenly unsure of herself, she glanced up at his face. His eyes were warm and unfathomable and seemed to wrap her in their velvety depths. No laughing devils in them now, to warn her away. He bent, and suddenly Prudence knew he was going to kiss her.

She held up her hands to ward him off and somehow, they simply came to rest against his chest. His hands caught her around the waist and drew her to him until they were hip to hip, chest to chest, and almost mouth to mouth.

Oh, where was the pasteboard reticule when she needed it? Why had she brought the silk one?

"Lord Carradice," she began.

"Gideon," he corrected, and captured her mouth before she could utter another word. The tip of his tongue traced her lips, teasing, exploring, probing. Soft and tender at first, he grew more demanding.

She felt herself softening, melting under the sweet onslaught of his mouth. She'd always understood kissing was a simple matter of lips meeting . . . and yet there was nothing simple at all about these kisses.

She'd thought she knew what it was like to be kissed by him. She was wrong.

A long, delicious shudder passed through her body. She gasped and he possessed her mouth fully, lavishing himself on her, in her, ravishing her senses with delight. Prudence grew dizzy with pleasure.

She could taste him inside her, the unique, intoxicating flavor of Gideon. And desire. She could taste it in the growing urgency of his kisses, in the fevered need of his embrace, in the searching, caressing mouth. A hunger deep within him. For her. For Prudence Merridew.

Deep, lavish hunger.

His need consumed her. It called to something deep within her and the last shreds of her resistance melted. She clung to his shoulders and kissed him back. He was addictive.

Her hands slid over his clothing, warmed by the rock-solid muscles of his chest. His heart pounded under her fingers. Her knees weakened and she leaned into him for support. His stomach was tight and hard, his long, hard thighs cradled her softness.

She slid her hands up his body and wound them around his neck. Her fingers slipped into his hair.

His hand slipped into her bodice.

She froze. And remembered who she was. And what she owed.

"No," she whispered.

He drew back slightly and seemed to read something in her face, because his mouth twisted, ruefully. His breath came in ragged gasps. His eyes burned, dark embers of heat. His desire was as powerful and potent as ever.

He laid the back of his fingers against her cheek, and slowly, slowly trailed them down to her jawline. It was the lightest of sensations, the most exquisite of caresses.

Prudence tried very hard not to melt at the simple tenderness of the gesture. She did her best not to drown in the heat of his eyes, so dark and intense and full of need. She told herself she should be warned by the small, possessive smile that played about his lips as he watched her shiver under his hand.

But she couldn't make herself move away.

His touch engendered feelings in her; unnameable, yearning feelings. Feelings she shouldn't, mustn't, didn't want to have.

Not for him.

She licked her lips and tried to muster her resolve. It was pitifully small. But her conscience burned. She stepped around him and made herself walk to the door on legs that still trembled. As she turned the key in the lock, she recalled how he'd said he loved a challenge.

"It's not fair," she whispered.

"What's not fair?" His voice was soft.

"Tempting me like this. Toying with me, with my feelings."

He opened his mouth to respond—some flippant, rakish comment, she was sure, and she couldn't bear it if he did, she was so swamped with emotion herself. So she cut him off and said in a rush, "I've told you and told you I'm not free, and you take no notice of me. I know you think I'm a liar and—"

"I don't! You have no idea what I think—but I'll tell you this, Miss Imp, I don't think of you as a liar!"

She gaped. How could he not, after all the lies she had told?

He flicked her chin lightly, and her mouth closed. "I don't count that nonsense you told your uncle. You had good reason, I gather. But you're a rarity in the London ton, an honest woman. I shan't forget that morning in the duke's house, when your uncle came in. You could have snagged me, claimed I'd compromised you, and though I'm no bargain, you could nevertheless have gained a fortune and a title." He smiled a little raggedly. His chest was still heaving. She tried not to watch.

"You promised me it wasn't a trap and you kept your word. I couldn't name another woman who would do that, Miss Imp, couldn't name another woman whose promise I would trust."

She heaved a great sigh; frustration mixed with relief. "Then *please* do not play these seductive games with me. I know it's just a bad habit you've got into, but truly, I cannot bear it! I am not of your world. I don't know how to play such games, and I don't know how to—" She broke off abruptly. She'd been about to admit she didn't know how to resist him. That would be fatal.

He paused a moment, then said, "What makes you think it is a game?"

"It can be nothing else," she said simply. "You say you believe in my promises. And I am promised to Phillip Otterbury." She looked at him, expecting he would acknowledge her words.

He said nothing. A slight frown knotted his brows.

She drew out the thin gold chain she always wore. On it was strung a golden ring of outmoded design, a large red stone glittering at its center. "Phillip's great-grandmother's betrothal ring. It is given to the first bride of the family each generation. It represents the sacred promise I made him, a promise I will not break, no matter how you may fluster me with your seductive wiles and caressing ways." She flushed and added, "I am bound to Phillip in other, more private ways, but this is the visible symbol. I have worn it for four and a half years. I have *never* taken it off. Can you understand that, Lord Carradice?" She gazed up at him, earnestly. "Can you respect it?"

"I can but try," he said slowly. He gave her a crooked smile in which regret was mixed with wry self-knowledge. "Though I confess, my bad habits may get the better of me."

Prudence sighed, tremulously. He couldn't help himself. Even the man's apologies were seductive. She clutched Phillip's ring like a talisman.

"Friends, then?" she said with valiant resolve.

He heaved a gloomy sigh. "Very well, friends it shall be, though it will ruin my reputation if it gets out."

She smiled shakily at him and he slipped her arm through his.

"Our betrothal *faux* still stands, of course," he added, "though outside the family, it shall be as secret as the grave." He drew her through the red velvet curtains, out into the alcove.

The grave. His words jolted Prudence's memory. She opened her mouth to inform him of her latest folly—his imaginary mourning—but was interrupted.

"Lord Carradice, you wicked, wicked man—I thought I recognized those divine shoulders—where have you been hiding?" A light, brittle laugh and a knowing look accompanied the words. A dark-haired lady with a bodice half the size of Prudence's laid a hand on Lord Carradice's other arm.

He bowed instantly, all light-hearted charm again. "Mrs. Crowther, you look very dashing tonight. Red is certainly your color."

So much for his compliments, Prudence thought, feeling cross that they'd been interrupted. Sage was her color, red this Mrs. Crowther's. Too practiced by half.

Lord Carradice introduced Prudence and though she was polite enough, Mrs. Crowther obviously thought her of little account. Soon they were surrounded by Mrs. Crowther's friends. Lord Carradice's friends, too, it appeared.

All the women were beautiful, or if not precisely beautiful, extremely attractive. And sophisticated. And the men looked Prudence over with bored, speculative eyes, glancing from her to Lord Carradice and back. Their suave, knowing looks made her palm itch to slap them.

"Now, my dear Carradice," exclaimed Mrs. Crowther, "you must come and settle a question my friends and I have been debating!"

"Oh yes, do," gushed a lady whose name Prudence couldn't recall. "You are such an exquisite judge of what suits a lady best."

Prudence tried not to pull a face.

"You must decide which is more frightful: Lady Bentick's ridiculous turban with so many plumes she looks like a funeral hearse—"

"—or the dowager duchess's *cornette* with the green velvet peaks, frothing with lace and sprouting daisies at the top, for all the world like a lace-encrusted mountaintop!"

"We have wagered on it, you see."

"Yes, please do go, Lord Carradice," Prudence said immediately. "I see my sister signaling me. I must go to her." It was almost true. Besides, she needed to meet the other gentlemen who were dancing attendance on Charity.

She stood on the edge of Charity's circle and watched Lord Carradice and Mrs. Crowther from across the room. There was much laughter and drinking, and to her intense annoyance, a lot of touching of Lord Carradice's arms and hands by the ladies. And once, by Mrs. Crowther, a most familiar pat on his jaw! It was apparent to her that Lord Carradice and several of these ladies had been—were still?—on extremely familiar terms.

Prudence didn't like Mrs. Crowther or her friends, she decided, but she was grateful to her for reminding her of a truth she'd been in danger of forgetting: Lord Carradice was a practiced charmer, a frivolous tease. Women flocked to his side, touched him in a familiar manner, laughed with him intimately, flirted with him.

And he flirted back. Because that's what he was, she told herself sternly. She wasn't condemning him for it, it was simply the way he was. He was a rake. And as such, not to be taken seriously.

And never to be trusted.

Gideon watched Prudence tend to her sister, smiling to himself at her little mother-hen stance. He'd released her half reluctantly. He didn't want her to leave, but he also didn't quite like Prudence talking to Mrs. Crowther and her flighty friends.

Theresa Crowther had a nasty tongue on her and an eye for gossip and her friends were loose and silly. He didn't feel comfortable seeing them and Prudence together. He allowed himself to be led across the room and smiled absently through the remainder of the conversation, wondering what he'd ever seen in Theresa Crowther, and whether he'd ever really enjoyed this shallow, vapid company.

"My sincere condolences, Carradice," a voice behind him said.

Gideon turned, startled. "Condolences? For what?"

A pained look crossed Sir Oswald's face. "For *whom,* I think you meant, Carradice. It's perfectly shockin' the way you younger fellers mangle the language." He eyed Gideon's severe evening dress with approbation, "At least you've had the decency not to wear colors tonight, though I am a believer in respecting the wishes of the dead."

Gideon stared at him blankly. The wishes of the dead? What dead? Could the old chap be talking about Brummell, who'd introduced the fashion of black evening clothes, and who'd recently disappeared from society? "As a matter of fact, I never wear colors in the evening," he said. "But he isn't dead, Sir Oswald. He's living on the Continent somewhere, fleeing debts."

Sir Oswald frowned. "Fleein' debts? There's no reason to go into mournin' for people fleein' debts, Carradice. Or is that what they do in Wales? Dashed peculiar!"

All at sea, Gideon decided to ignore the bizarre Welsh references. "I'm talking about Beau Brummell," he said.

"Brummell? What's he got to do with it? Why the devil are we talkin' about Brummell?"

"Didn't you say he was dead?"

"No! Is he? Can't say I'm surprised. Living among for-eigners is a risky business, I know; did it myself for years. Well, well, old Brummell, eh? What took him off? The drink, I'll be bound." Sir Oswald pursed his lips disapprovingly at the glass of champagne Gideon held in his hand.

Gideon, feeling as if he was having a conversation in Bedlam, said carefully, "I didn't say he was dead. As far as I know, he is still alive and living on the Continent."

Sir Oswald's bushy white brows bristled with indignation. "Well, dash it all, man, I *knew* that! The whole of the ton knows it. Known it for ages! What the devil are you regaling me with news so old it has mold on it, eh?"

Gideon drained his glass and looked around for a servant. He needed something a little stronger than champagne to cope with this conversation. But not brandy. "My apologies, Sir Oswald. Shall we start again? Who is dead?"

"Your great-aunt, of course!"

"My great-aunt?"

"Yes, sorry to hear about it. My condolences, Carradice. I didn't know her myself, but I'm sure it's a great loss. When was the funeral?"

Gideon opened his mouth to explain that as far as he knew Great-aunt Estelle was currently abroad, scandalizing most of her relatives by traveling unchaperoned with an Italian count.

A small, breathless female squeezed suddenly in between Gideon and Great-uncle Oswald: Miss Prudence Merridew, looking flushed and beautiful and conspicuously guilty. Of course. The moment conversations made no sense, Miss Im-Prudence would be at the bottom of it. He should be used to it by now.

He smiled down at her, tucked her hand under his arm, and signaled a passing waiter to bring her a drink.

Sir Oswald beamed benevolently at the gesture. "Ah, Prudence, m'dear, I'm just askin' Carradice here about the funeral. In Wales, I suppose it was, Carradice? Never been to a Welsh funeral."

Prudence said hurriedly, "It was a very small, private affair, I believe, was it not, Lord Carradice?" She sent him an urgent look.

Gideon nodded. "Oh yes, Sir Oswald. It was very small—so tiny in fact that it almost didn't exist." A small hand squeezed his arm, not with affection, so he added, "And completely private. Wales, you know."

Great-uncle Oswald nodded understandingly. The hand relaxed.

"And which great-aunt was it? For a moment I thought it might be Estelle. Gave me a nasty turn. But Prudence said no. I didn't know you had any relatives in Wales."

"She lived a very retired life, I believe," Prudence said.

"Oh *very* retired," Gideon agreed. "The family hardly knew she was there at all."

The waiter arrived with the drink Gideon had requested. Across Prudence's head, Sir Oswald waggled his eyebrows at Gideon in a man-to-man fashion. Gideon, not knowing what else to do, waggled his back.

Sir Oswald stared, his bushy brows beetled slowly upward. "Oh, like that, was it? Packed off to Wales, was she? I see now why the whole thing was kept so dashed quiet. Take your point, Carradice. I'll say no more about it, then. Ladies present and all that. Now, Prudence m'dear, you surely aren't goin' to maudle your insides with that shockin' stuff, are you? I thought you was gettin' her lemonade, Carradice!" He glared at the champagne Lord Carradice had ordered and removed the glass from Prudence's hand. "I sent some of my special rhubarb tonic to Lady Ostwither—I'll go and roust up one of those fellows to fetch some for you now. Tonic for the blood, you know, rhubarb." He hurried off.

Prudence turned to Gideon, her brow furrowed and her mouth pursed in the most delightful way. Gideon longed to kiss her. He cast a quick, furtive glance around the room.

"What is it?" Prudence said anxiously.

"Just checking to see if anyone would notice if I kissed you now."

She took a step backward. "Don't you dare do such a thing! You said you'd stop teasing me! We agreed to be friends!"

He gave her an injured look. "I was thinking of a very *friendly* kiss."

"You know what I mean." She made a praiseworthy, if unsuccessful attempt to keep her mouth in a severe line.

Gideon shrugged and tried to look guilty. "Habits aren't so easy to change, Miss Imp."

He studied her, a smile playing round his lips. She was three parts fierce, one part adorably flustered, and the whole of her completely irresistible. And that dimple, peeping out just when she was trying to look most straitlaced and puritanical. He took a small step forward, closing the gap between them. She held her ground and lifted her reticule, not high, nothing to draw any vulgar attention to them—just a small reminder to him of what she would do if necessary. Little Miss Imp, ready to do battle with the big, bad rake.

He sighed, mournfully. "You have no sense of adventure, do you, Miss Imp?"

"Don't call me that! And don't you dare do anything improper. Now, what did Great-uncle Oswald mean about your great-aunt being packed off to Wales?"

Gideon shrugged. "I have no idea. I've never packed a great-aunt off anywhere, and if I tried, I'd come a cropper. A lady of backbone and fortitude, my Great-aunt Estelle. Terrifying female. Nobody could pack her off anywhere. Someone tried once, I believe . . . poor fellow was never heard of again."

"But Great-uncle Oswald said—"

"Excellent things, eyebrows. One waggles them in a mysterious fashion and people jump to all sorts of conclusions. I've no idea what your esteemed relative thinks about my imaginary aunt, and care even less. The point is, he dropped the subject."

"Yes, thank goodness. Do you think ladies' eyebrows can communicate as well?" she asked.

"No, they don't have sufficient thicketry," he said with authority.

"Thicketry?"

"Yes, that is the official term. Now, while dear Sir Oswald is fetching you some disgus—er, delightful tonic, I don't suppose you'd care to enlighten me as to why I needed a recently expired Welsh relative in the first place. Not that I'm not ungrateful, you understand. A thoughtful, if unusual gift. Nor do I wish to exhibit vulgar curiosity, but if I'm to be acquiring dead relatives at the drop of a hat—"

"Oh, pray, stop! There is no need to rub it in, I know it was wrong of me, and I meant to tell you earlier, but was distracted."

"Distracted, eh?" His smile was rather smug, she considered.

"By your friend in the inadequate scarlet dress," she corrected him. "The thing is, Great-uncle Oswald was going to put a notice of our betrothal in the *Morning Post*. Your being in mourning was all I could think of at the time to prevent him. I'm sorry. "

Gideon looked at her in admiration. "No, you did very right. So I'm in mourning, eh?"

"Yes, but you don't have to go into black, because I said your great-aunt had an aversion to black and the trappings of mourning, so her will instructed everyone to wear colors. And to go to dances and so on."

"I'm particularly relieved about the 'so on,'" Gideon assured her. "What a wonderfully resourceful girl you are!"

Prudence blushed. "I suppose you think I'm a dreadful liar, but—"

"Not at all," exclaimed Gideon, "I thought I recently reassured you on that point. Resourcefulness is to be admired."

Prudence bit her lip.

"But you have grossly compromised my character, Miss ImPrudence, and now you'll have to make it up to me."

"Make it up to you? In what way, pray?" Prudence asked, darkly suspicious of his sudden injured-saint expression. "Compromised your character? I didn't think such a thing would be possible."

Gideon took her hand in his. "Not possible to compromise my character!" he exclaimed, deeply shocked. "How can you ask such a thing? First you paint me as a pudding-hearted suitor with a sad want of dash—which is appalling, for I am particularly known for my aversion to pudding and my eloquence in dash! Next you break my tailor's heart by consigning his *billets-doux* to the fire and then you kill off my relatives willy-nilly and refuse to allow me to go into mourning—"

"They were bills, not *billets-doux!*" Prudence objected.

"To a tailor," declared Gideon in an austere manner, "it is the same thing! Now, allow me to escort you in to supper, and over crab patties, partridge poults, and lemon tartlets, I shall give due consideration to the matter of compensation owed for the blackening of my good name."

Prudence looked mulish.

"I thought you said we were to be friends," he reminded her.

"Yes, but your view of how friends behave and mine seem to be chalk and cheese."

"Then you must educate me on the matter, immediately, before I disgrace myself by lapsing into bad habits again. And while you offer me knowledge on the etiquette of friendship, I shall offer you crab patties, which are food for angels. Not cheese. Plebeian stuff, cheese. Quite unworthy of you." He tucked her hand back into the crook of his arm and proceeded to steer her gently but firmly toward the supper room, explaining, "You shall nourish my mind while I feed your body."

How did he *do* that? Prudence wondered as he swept her in to supper. He'd not only overcome her scruples about going in to supper with him, he'd made her laugh. And he'd also managed to make the innocent consumption of crab patties sound like some sort of seductive rite, and she had no doubt he could make it so!

She resolved to stick to bread and butter. And perhaps just one lemon tartlet.

Chapter Ten

∽

*"Thus I am not able to exist either with you or without you;
and I seem not to know my own wishes."*

OVID

IT WAS BARELY A WEEK SINCE CHARITY HAD ATTENDED HER FIRST society function, and already she was a success, thought Prudence proudly. Now, attending her first ball, her sister was a picture of grace and beauty, seeming to float effortlessly through the complicated figures of the dance. Only Prudence knew the significance of the faint frown marring the marble smoothness of Charity's brow. At least the tip of her sister's tongue wasn't visible, as it was wont to be when Charity was concentrating hardest.

For the days leading up to the ball, all five sisters had run the dancing master ragged, practicing and practicing until they knew all the steps by heart. It would be mortally embarrassing if Charity or Prue made a misstep or forgot the movements of the dance. They were determined not to look like the ignorant country misses they were. They had even practiced the wicked waltz, though neither of them expected to perform it yet.

The dancing master might well have saved his shoe leather, thought Prudence with a wry smile. The Merridew girls might have performed their part in the dances with sufficient grace and skill to pass muster, but Prudence had danced several dances with veritable clodhoppers and now the flounce on her new ball dress was torn so badly that she needed to pin it up.

Charity seemed to gain confidence with every step. Prudence smiled, watching. Who would have thought that after spending a childhood where to dance or sing was to court a whipping from Grandpapa, her sister would prove to have so much natural grace? She appeared perfectly at home in a ballroom, as if, like the other girls here, she'd been preparing for it all her life. The dance drew to an end, and Charity's partner led her from the floor. Several gentlemen came forward offering her sister refreshments. Charity seemed unfazed by the attention.

Observing her sister shyly responding to masculine gallantry, Prudence felt as though she would burst with pride. Her younger sister was a picture of beauty, confidence, and grace. It was a personal triumph over Grandpapa and all his meanness. Her sister was like a rose, who, having spent most of her life in a harsh and bitter environment, emerged into sunlight unfurling her delicate petals, untainted by the vicissitudes of the past. Prudence prayed that all her sisters would be as unscathed.

She was watching Charity so closely, she knew to the minute when the Duke of Dinstable walked into the room. Their eyes must have met, for in an instant, her sister changed from a shy young girl at her first-ever ball to a glowing creature who seemed lit from within.

Prudence blinked. She had never seen her sister thus. Charity was radiant.

She glanced from Charity to the duke and back again. It was amazing. Hope was right, after all. The duke gazed at Charity in much the same way as she was looking at him—as if entranced. There might well have been nobody else in the room, for all the two of them noticed.

Was that how it was, love at first sight? It had been that way with her mother and father. One look and he'd known, Papa used to say. Mama would laugh and say it took at her least three good, hard looks at Papa before she'd decided he was the one. And Papa would laugh and kiss Mama and call her his beautiful slow top. Slow top indeed, Mama would retort in playful indignation—she was simply being discerning! And she would give him a look, and Papa would look back and after a moment they would laugh and kiss again.

Prudence sighed. Even though she'd been a child, she had never forgotten those intense, magical looks. The look of two people in love.

Now her beautiful younger sister and a shy, neat duke were exchanging just such searing, magical looks. A lump formed in Prudence's throat. It was exactly what she had dreamed of for her sisters: the love that Mama and Papa had known, the love that only Prudence could remember. The love that Prudence had once dreamed of for herself.

She watched the duke bow over her sister's hand and the breathtaking smile her sister gave him and prayed that their magic, at least, was real. And enduring.

Prudence took a long swallow of ratafia. She'd feared so much that her anxiety to see them safe might influence Charity into agreeing to the first possible man who offered for her. But if appearances were to be believed, and the duke did offer for her, there would be no sacrifice.

The duke seemed a very decent man—what little she knew of him. Quiet, a little shy, yet with unmistakable dignity and the assurance of rank, he was looking at her gentle sister with the kind of tenderness that made Prudence feel like weeping. And her sister was looking right back at him.

For that look in her sister's eyes, Prudence would tell a hundred more lies.

The duke was surely not a rake like his cousin; in fact, that newspaper report about him she'd read had suggested he'd come to London in search of a wife. Prudence closed her eyes and said a little prayer. When she opened them, he was leading Charity toward the terrace, escorting her as if she were some sort of fragile bloom in need of care and protection.

No, the duke was not a rake like his cousin, Lord Carradice, thank goodness. He was totally sincere.

So why did she feel so suddenly . . . bereft?

Recalling the torn flounce, Prudence made for the ladies' withdrawing room. She drew a packet of pins from the new netting reticule that Grace had made her and began to repair the damage.

"Torn your flounce, Miss Merridew? Do you want me to pin it for you?" It was Mrs. Crowther, the woman she had met at the Ostwither soiree. Without waiting for Prudence to respond, Mrs. Crowther bent down and took the pins from Prudence's hand. She was wearing red again tonight, a brilliant, low-cut silk gown that pooled around her as she knelt.

Prudence had little choice. She thanked Mrs. Crowther and stood quietly while the older woman pinned the flounce with quick, efficient movements.

"That should hold it," Mrs. Crowther rose from the pool of crimson silk. Her dress molded around her sinuous figure like a flame.

Prudence, in her gown of creamy satin with dainty green and white snowdrops embroidered around the hem, felt like a gawky schoolgirl by contrast.

"Thank you." She put on her evening gloves again and made to leave.

"Not so fast, my innocent." Mrs. Crowther placed a long-fingered hand on Prudence's arm.

"I beg your pardon?" Prudence raised an eyebrow, hoping she looked haughty. She did not like Mrs. Crowther or her tone. She tried to move but found Mrs. Crowther was holding her fast. They were not alone in the room and Prudence did not want to make a scene.

"A quiet word of warning, from one woman to another."

Not knowing quite what to say, Prudence merely arched her eyebrows again.

"I think the situation calls for a little more privacy." Mrs. Crowther led Prudence into the adjoining sitting room, currently empty.

"What situation?" asked Prudence, feeling annoyed with herself for allowing this woman to waylay her. But in truth she did not know how to avoid it without being impolite.

"The situation with Lord Carradice. You have been seen with him on several occasions."

"I do not see that it is any business—"

"Lord Carradice and I are friends. Intimate friends, you

might say," Mrs. Crowther purred, sliding her hands voluptuously over the silken folds of her gown.

Prudence stiffened. If she'd had the courage to make a small scene in the withdrawing room earlier, she would not be having to deal with this distasteful conversation.

"So I thought it only fair to warn you, my dear young lady: Men are such careless beasts. Of course he is only amusing himself with you but—"

"How do you know he is only amusing himself? He may not be," interrupted Prudence, suddenly furious. She knew Lord Carradice was only amusing himself, but she was not going to allow this flame-wrapped harpy to say so. "Or if so, it may not be *me* who is his little amusement." She allowed that to sink in and then added pointedly, "You are married, are you not?"

Mrs. Crowther laughed, a brittle yap of scorn. "Don't tell me you think he is serious in his attentions to you! He couldn't possibly be, my dear!"

Her tone was woman-of-the-world to simple schoolgirl and while Prudence privately agreed with the sentiments, Mrs. Crowther's sophisticated dismissal flicked Prudence on the raw. She raised her eyebrows and said in a calm, interested voice, "Why not?"

Mrs. Crowther smiled and preened herself. "If you had *any* knowledge of dearest Gideon at all, my dear child, any truly *intimate* knowledge of his history, you wouldn't have to ask that."

The woman oozed smugness. Prudence couldn't bear it. She said in her silkiest tone, "Perhaps you have misread the situation, Mrs. Crowther." As if bored by the conversation, Prudence frowned critically at her gloves, held them out, and smoothed them back to her elbows.

Mrs. Crowther watched with narrowed eyes. Prudence fussed with her gloves until she thought the other woman would burst with impatience and then added, "Are you sure these gloves are not crooked? There is something in their fit I don't quite—"

"The gloves are irrelevant!" snapped Mrs. Crowther.

Prudence gave her a thoughtful look, then shook her head. "Oh, I don't agree. An elegant pair of gloves quite sets off a ball gown . . . or ruins the effect. Now, what were we discussing? Oh yes. Have you considered that *dearest Gideon*, as you call him, could be an old family friend?"

She adjusted the gloves again and added casually, "I don't suppose it occurred to you that our mothers might have been bosom friends as girls . . . And if that were the case, would there be any surprise in him keeping a friendly eye on my sisters and me for their sake?" It was not precisely a lie, Prudence told herself. More a statement of possibilities.

It wiped the smile off Mrs. Crowther's face. "You knew his mother? So you must know about what happened. The old scandal."

Prudence had no idea what the woman was referring to but decided not to compound her deception any further. She raised a disdainful eyebrow. Even without masculine thicketry, eyebrows were useful things, she decided; people read so much into them.

Mrs. Crowther frowned and said half to herself, "It would explain why Dinstable is squiring your sisters around, too, for if your mother had known Lady Carradice she would have known the duchess also. So you must know about that business . . ." She straightened and added briskly, "In which case, you must also know that Gideon will never marry, and why. And since he has never shown any interest in"—she glanced at Prudence disparagingly—"debutantes, you would be foolish indeed to nourish any expectations."

"Expectations? Of Lord Carradice?" Prudence laughed incredulously as she opened the door. "Good heavens! What an odd notion! Set your mind at rest, Mrs. Crowther, I have no expectations concerning Lord Carradice at all!" It was the truth, after all. She sailed from the room.

"Miss Merridew!" Lord Carradice stood in the hallway.

She wondered how much he had overheard.

"Sir Oswald and your sister have been wondering where you were," he said stiffly. "You must be more careful of the company you keep at such affairs, Miss Merridew. Mrs. Crowther, you will excuse us?" He bowed.

Mrs. Crowther let out a peal of laughter. "Oh, it is too, too amusing: Rake Carradice, playing the role of duenna. I vow, nobody would believe me if I told them! I see you spoke the truth, Miss Merridew—your mothers would be proud!" To Prudence's intense irritation, she trailed long, white fingers familiarly along Lord Carradice's arm as she passed him. And he did nothing to prevent her!

"What the devil was that all about? Why are you talking to that woman?" Lord Carradice took her arm as if he owned it and drew her farther along the hall and into a small, private room. He shut the door firmly behind them.

Prudence glared at him. He seemed to know where every small, private room in the building was. He was such a rake! And yet he had the audacity to criticize her behavior!

Holding his gaze in a silent challenge, she began to strip off her long white satin gloves. Let him reprimand her! If he dared. She loosened the tip of each finger with a small, angry tug, one by one. His eyes were fixed on hers, but she could tell by the slight flaring of his nostrils that he was aware of each movement, disapproving, no doubt. The combination of his intent observation and his silence inflamed her temper further.

She drew each long, elegant glove down her arm, baring the skin in a long, slow sweep, then tucked the gloves through a loop in her reticule. She was ready to do battle.

"What business of yours is it who I decide to talk to? You are not, despite what Mrs. Crowther said, my duenna!"

Gideon felt his temper flare. He'd been unaccountably worried about Prudence's absence, fretting lest one of the rakes who'd attended the ball had lured her aside and was taking advantage of her. He'd gone in search of her, on the terrace, in the garden, and through numerous small rooms and hidden alcoves, his anxiety mounting all the time.

And then he'd found her with Therese Crowther, and the sight of his former mistress in conversation with Prudence had caused a reaction in him he didn't quite care to examine. And it was not helped by the damned seductive way she'd removed her gloves. He felt defensive yet aroused. It was not a felicitous combination.

The duenna taunt had cut; still, he found himself saying, "She is not fit company for you!" He sounded ridiculously prissy. His frustration increased a notch.

"Not fit company? Then why did you introduce us the other night?"

He had no answer to that. "It was an error of judgment."

"I thought she was a friend of yours. An *intimate* friend," she said.

Gideon gritted his teeth. "Yes . . . no . . . not anymore. Hang it all, Prudence, I didn't come here to argue with you! You are an innocent. Just take it from me that Mrs. Crowther and her like are not fit companions for—Where are you going?"

Eyes snapping with temper, Prudence tried to storm past him. He blocked her exit with his body.

She pushed at his chest crossly. "I'm leaving. Since Mrs. Crowther and her friends are not suitable company for me, what does that make you, Lord Carradice? As her *intimate* friend! Even less suitable! And so—" She shoved at him with small, determined fists. "I'm leaving. Or trying to!"

Gideon stared down at her, taken aback by her words. She was right. He'd known instant discomfort the other night when she'd met, even briefly, with the set of people he called his friends. Only they weren't really friends at all, merely companions in boredom. And vice.

She railed at him, "I don't need protecting. I'm not at all the innocent you imagine me. And you have no right to decide who I may or may not talk to."

Gideon rolled his eyes. "Compared with that crowd, any decent woman is an innocent."

His words inflamed Prudence's ire. How dare he compare her with his glamorous mistress and then call Prudence a *decent woman!* He might as well call her dull and drab! In her girlish gown with the demure snowdrops!

She wished she had a scarlet silk gown. Then she would show him!

On second thought, she didn't; scarlet would clash horribly with her hair. And no doubt on her, that tissue-thin silk would cling in all the wrong places. Life was so unfair!

But she would show him anyway! Without hesitation she reached up, pulled his head down to her level, and kissed him soundly on the mouth. It was a clumsy kiss and in her haste she'd landed a little off center, so she did it again, remembering how he had kissed her the last time. This time she found her target, dead on.

She kissed him openmouthed and felt the familiar, delicious shivers pass through her as he responded. She thought of scarlet dresses and kissed him in the most wanton way she could imagine.

Remembering what he had done with his tongue, she reached inside his mouth and stroked deeply and rhythmically. He tasted of wine and heat and Gideon. Their tongues tangled. He moaned deep in his throat and tried to take control of the kiss, but she wouldn't let him.

She held his head in her hands and kissed him again as if her life depended on it. His arms lifted, dropped, and then wrapped around her, drawing her body up against his long, lean strength. One of his hands stroked up and down the line of her spine and came to rest on the curve of her bottom. He pressed her to him and she felt his hard, aroused body straining against her.

Her palms framed his jaw. She pushed herself tight against him, loving the friction of his hardness against her softness, kissing him with everything she had in her.

When her knees started to wobble beneath her, she realized that she was about to reach the point of no return. She hung on to her self-possession with all the resolution at her command, broke the kiss, and pushed herself out of his embrace.

They stood facing each other, breathing fast as if they'd been in a race. The laughing devils had gone from his eyes, and he stared at her in a stunned fashion that Prudence found deeply satisfying. She'd expected to be shaken by the kiss; she always was after kissing Lord Carradice. But this time, she was not the only shaken one. He looked positively stupefied.

She felt a spurt of deeply feminine triumph. Ha! Perhaps she was not so dull and dreary, after all!

He reached for her and she stepped back, smoothing her dress with hands that were not quite steady. "No. No more. It was simply meant to demonstrate that I am not the innocent you seem to think me."

The dazed look disappeared and a narrow look took its

place as Lord Carradice retorted, "If you think that so-called demonstration convinced me that you are in any way fit to be part of Theresa Crowther's circle, you are mistaken. Those kisses proved nothing—nothing except your innocence."

"Oh, you are impossible!" She stamped her foot in frustration. She knew she'd botched the first kiss, but the second and third ones had nearly knocked her on end! She'd put everything she knew into them. And he still thought her a know-nothing miss in need of protection!

He smiled wolfishly, seeming to read her thoughts, and prowled closer. "There is no need to look chagrined. I found your kisses more than delightful. But if you truly wish to increase your experience, you are very welcome to practice on me. We are betrothed, after all."

She skipped out of his way, and once there were a few feet of space between them, faced him with hands on hips. "It is a sham betrothal, if you recall. And an excellent thing, too, for a blind beggar could see we two should not suit, the way we quarrel."

The smile lines deepened, and he took a few steps toward her. "I would not necessarily call it quarreling. And even if you do, quarreling is not necessarily a sign of incompatibility. It can be a sign of . . . passion."

Prudence sniffed and moved even farther away. "My parents never exchanged a cross word. And neither do Phillip and I."

He raised a sardonic brow. "From what I can gather, you don't exchange words with Otterboots at all. Must be terribly dull for you. But then he seems like a dull sort of fellow—and you say he can't even muster a decent quarrel?"

He was right, Prudence realized suddenly. She could not even imagine having such an exhilarating exchange of temper with Phillip. And her argument with Lord Carradice did feel very . . . passionate. And as for that kiss she'd initiated . . . Her confidence drained. She would *never* have jumped on Phillip like that! Whatever had made her behave in such a manner? Her wretched temper! How could she let him provoke her so easily?

He had this way of getting under her skin. He didn't even

try to breach her defenses; he simply slipped under them and turned them to his own advantage. It was . . . it was unacceptable. She would never have allowed it with any other man. The only time Phillip had breached her defenses, he'd used his masculine strength. Lord Carradice never used physical force. It was something more insidious. Inciting her animal instincts . . .

She was having doubts, thought Gideon, watching her intently. About Otterbury, he hoped, rather than about himself. But if they were about himself, there was only one way of dissolving them that he could think of. Kiss 'em away. He moved subtly closer, and before she had time to avoid him, he had her in his arms again and kissed her thoroughly.

She gave one indignant squeak. He could feel her trying not to soften against him. She was losing the battle. He kissed her just long enough for her to realize it.

"See," he said softly as he released her. "If this is a quarrel, you have to admit it's a lot of fun."

"I will admit nothing of the sort," she said loftily, trying not to let him see how rattled she was. "Nor will I discuss Phillip with you. And as you so kindly pointed out, I shall, in future, be more careful of the company I keep." She gave him a waspish little smile; she was not referring to Mrs. Crowther and her ilk. She pulled on her gloves like gauntlets. "Now, I must return to my sister." And before he could react, she sailed out of the room like a cross little hawk. With adorably ruffled feathers.

Gideon did not rejoin the party for some time. He sat down and considered what had just happened. In one sense it was a scenario he was more than familiar with; a few stolen kisses, a few illicit caresses in a secluded room during a party or ball. On the other hand . . .

Lord! Who could believe that a man of his experience could be knocked all on end by a couple of clumsy, heartfelt kisses, delivered in anger—or so she claimed. One had even almost missed his mouth.

But he had been utterly bowled over by them. Because those sweet, clumsy kisses had brought with them a revelation that had shocked him to his back teeth.

He didn't want it to be a false betrothal. He really wanted

Prudence. As his lover. But not as his mistress. There was only one solution he could see to that conundrum.

After some time he stood and left the room. He wandered through the crowded ballroom like a man in a daze. He was reeling. His whole life plan had been turned upside down.

He left the ball and walked out into the dark streets. Eventually he found himself staring at the knocker on his cousin's door and realized he had no memory of walking home. He would have been easy meat for Mohocks and footpads.

What did that matter when the fundamental premise of his whole life had been suddenly overturned?

He broached the matter in oblique fashion to his cousin the next evening. "Found any likely prospects yet, Edward?"

The duke started. He'd been in a brown study, staring off into middle distance. "Likely prospects?"

Gideon looked at his cousin. "In your search for a suitable bride." He frowned. "*Suitable* being the operative word. It must be damned difficult. I mean, our parents charted their courses to marriage in all innocence, and look now that ended up!"

Edward smiled ruefully. "I know. But now I've decided we have no choice except to do what they did: marry and take a chance."

Gideon sat up. "What? You don't mean . . . ?"

"Yes, Gideon, I've found my suitable bride." Edward looked a little sheepish.

"Excellent!" He topped up his cousin's glass. "Who's the girl? Anyone I know?"

Edward hesitated. "If you don't mind, I won't mention her name until I've addressed the question to her and received an answer."

Gideon frowned. "You needn't fear I'll blab it about own. Dammit, Coz, you know me better than that."

"Oh, of course. You know I'd trust you with my life. It's not that, it's just . . . tempting fate, I suppose you'd call it."

"Oh, well, if you're steeped in superstition, Edward, that's your affair. It's not as if you're likely to be turned down. But tell me, do I know her?"

His cousin considered the question. "Yes, you've met her several times."

"And she's everything you said you wanted? Plain, quiet, dull—er, docile? Not the sort to stir up unpleasant emotions?"

"That's not exactly how I'd describe her. But she is the bride for me."

"Excellent. So she's nice and plain?"

Edward's mouth quirked. "You were not struck by her beauty, at any rate."

Definitely plain, Gideon decided, for he was quite a connoisseur of feminine beauty. It was natural that Edward would not wish to dwell on the girl's lack of looks. He was going to marry her, after all. Gideon swirled the port in his glass, eyeing the candle flame through the ruby liquid, and cast his mind over the many plain girls he recalled from this year's crop of debutantes. There were too many to recall any particular plain Jane who'd been singled out by his quiet cousin. In fact, it was an especially dull batch, he decided; there was only one beauty who sprang to mind, Miss Prudence Merridew, and Edward had not paid her any particular attention, he was sure.

"What are your plans for the morrow, Edward? Going to speak to the girl's father?

"No. I have an engagement to escort the Misses Merridew to Astley's Amphitheater in the afternoon and am promised to Featherstonehaugh for dinner—"

Gideon looked up. "Astley's Amphitheater? Whatever are you going there for?"

The duke shrugged. "It came up in conversation last week, and the young ladies expressed great interest in it. They haven't seen many of the city's delights as yet, and Miss Faith and Miss Hope in particular were very eager to observe the lady equestriennes. So I offered to escort them."

"Is, er, Miss Prudence to be one of the party?" Gideon said in a casual tone.

"I think so. Certainly she seemed as eager as her sisters when informed of the prospect by Miss Charity."

Gideon picked up an ornament and toyed with it. "Sounds like rather a lot for you to handle, Edward. One

lone gentleman escorting so many young and excitable females. Would you like a hand with them, by any chance?"

His cousin smiled. "Why Gideon, how very kind of you
to offer. But there's no need to worry about me. I can manage. They're not all that excitable, you know. No, no, dear
boy—you stick to your own plans."

"Oh, there's nothing that cannot be put off," Gideon said
decisively. "I wouldn't dream of leaving you to cope with a
gaggle of young girls all alone. I'll come."

The duke observed him in silence a moment and then
said in a voice that had the tiniest quaver in it, "I'm touched
by your thoughtfulness, Cousin. Such noble self-sacrifice."

Gideon's eyes dropped ruefully before the gentle irony in
his cousin's. He set down his glass and dragged his hands
through his hair in exasperation. "Hang it all, Edward, I
haven't the faintest notion of what to do. I'm in desperate
straits, here. You've no idea!"

"Oh, I think I do understand," said the duke gently.
"You're not alone in those straits, you know."

Gideon looked up, startled. "You mean your plain and
sensible choice—"

"Is not the slightest bit plain! In fact she's a diamond of
the first water. Probably the most beautiful girl in the ton,"
Edward told him glumly. "And the worst thing is, I'm head
over heels in love with her. It is exactly what I feared would
happen and there's absolutely nothing I can do about it."

"Good God!" Gideon reached for the decanter and refilled both their glasses.

"I know. And we both swore never to let it happen. How
did it happen, Gideon? How, after all these years and all this
careful avoidance, did it happen? Because one minute I was
sailing along perfectly happily, my nice, safe course char-
tered and the next minute I was knocked all a'beam and in
well over my head."

Gideon shook his head, gloomily. "Yes, that's it exactly.
Drowning in her eyes—and happy to do so."

"After one look, one glance! And despite all my plans."

Gideon sighed. "That's all it took with me, too. One look.
Oh, I fought it for a time, but now . . . besotted!"

Edward sighed. "I shall seek an appointment with her great-uncle the day after tomorrow."

Gideon sat for a moment, pondering their confessions, and slowly his cousin's words filtered through to his brain. A beauty with a great-uncle! He exploded suddenly from his chair. "Speak to her great-uncle, you said! Dammit, Edward, you can't be in love with Prudence, too, blast you! Because if you are—"

Edward waved his anxieties aside. "No, no, calm yourself, cousin, it's not Prudence. It's almost worse than that. It's Charity."

Gideon sank back in his chair. The relief was overwhelming. It was a few moments before the appalling significance of Edward's words struck him. "Charity? You cannot mean it. Not . . . her *sister?*"

Edward nodded. "Yes—the gossips will have a field day. History repeating itself all over again. We shan't have a moment's peace, once word gets out." He heaved a gloomy sigh. "You know how I hate a fuss!"

Chapter Eleven

⌒

"Let us not love in words or speech but in deed and in truth."

JOHN 3:18

"THAT," HOPE ANNOUNCED AS THE CARRIAGE PULLED UP IN FRONT of Great-uncle Oswald's house, "was the the most exciting thing I have ever seen! The music, the spectacle, the lady riders—and the way that man rode on the horse's back standing upright. How I would like to try that."

"And he wasn't even holding on to the reins!" her twin agreed. "He was quite handsome, too, in a barbaric sort of way, didn't you think?"

The carriage door opened. Gideon stepped out and proceeded to hand down the ladies. The twins alighted first, followed immediately by Prudence. She accepted his hand but refused to meet his eyes. Gideon suspected she couldn't. He had an idea that his little hawk was flustered beyond anything by her forwardness in kissing him at the ball. If he was any judge of feminine behavior, she was mortified as much by her obvious response to him as with her out-of-character actions. And so she was pretending it hadn't happened. Ever since the kiss, she had treated him with reserve and a great deal of formality. She was, in fact, thought Gideon with an inner chuckle, doing her very best to pretend that they'd never even met.

But if she thought severe formality would force him to

keep his distance, she was in for a disappointment. She was adorable as a formidable little dowager. If she treated him with much more of her disdain, he'd have to kiss her again.

Gideon held her hand a moment or two longer than strictly necessary, and she stood there waiting for him to release her, refusing to look at him. Finally she lifted her gaze and glared up at him, tugging her hand in vain. He lifted her gloved hand to his lips, turned it over, peeled back her glove and kissed the naked flesh revealed, all the while quizzing her wickedly with his eyes.

A fiery blush lit her cheeks, and she snatched her hand back and stepped briskly away from him. A moment later a maidservant darted up the side steps onto the wet pavement and thrust a piece of paper into her hand.

Gideon turned to help the next girl down, but his cousin was there before him.

"Miss Charity," Edward murmured reverently.

Charity laid a gloved hand in Edward's and stepped down.

"Did you enjoy the show?" the duke inquired gravely, still holding on to her hand, even though she had alighted safely. Gideon smiled to himself. The flags of the pavement were slightly uneven, after all.

Charity's face glowed with pleasure. "I thought the horses were the cleverest, knowing exactly what to do without anyone telling them. If anyone had told me that horses could perform a dance with perfect timing and execution— well, I wouldn't have believed them! To think I have seen an equestrian ballet! Thank you, Your Grace, for taking us. It has been a truly wonderful experience." She smiled, and suddenly Gideon could see her resemblance to Prudence. It was obvious to him now why his cousin thought Charity a diamond of the first water. Her smile was the same as Prudence's.

"The pleasure was all mine," the duke declared, flushing. Gideon observed his cousin compassionately, seeing the glazed look, the distinctly codlike helplessness and devotion. Yes, they were both well and truly hooked.

Gideon turned to assist Grace, but she had scrambled down unaided. She hooked her arm through his in a friendly manner. "I liked the battle scenes best—all that smoke and the cannons and the soldiers so brave and smart in their uniforms," she declared.

But Gideon's attention was suddenly caught as he realized Prudence had frozen, stock-still. She was as pale as the crumpled piece of paper clutched in her hand. As he watched, she swayed slightly, as if suddenly faint.

Gideon sprang forward and wrapped his arm around her waist. "What is it, Prue? Bad news? Are you ill?"

It spoke volumes for Prudence's state of mind that she did not seem to notice his intimate hold, let alone his use of her name. She held up the paper and in a sombre voice said to her sisters, "It's from Mrs. Burton."

It was as if a small flock of happy chicks had suddenly spotted a snake above them, he thought. The carefree excitement of a moment before was extinguished by a sudden tense silence.

The twins moved closer, their hands linked in unconscious solidarity, their eyes fixed on Prudence. Grace turned as white as her sister. Prudence stepped away from Gideon and gathered the little girl to her protectively. Charity stood biting her lip, then quietly stepped away from the duke and went to stand on the other side of Grace, so that Prudence and the child were enclosed.

Gideon exchanged glances with Edward and with one accord, they stepped closer to the huddle of girls, in time to hear Prudence explaining, "Mrs. Burton doesn't know how he found out. She thinks the new boot boy let something slip, but when she wrote this"—she checked the letter again—"the day before yesterday, he'd ordered the coach to be made ready for a long trip. He's coming to London to look for us. She sent this note with one of the stableboys, who rode on the mail. He cannot be far behind."

The girls looked wildly around as if he—whoever "he" was—might be anywhere. Prudence swallowed and continued in a calm voice. "It is all right. We shall be safe, I promise you."

"We will have to flee, won't we Prue?" Charity said quietly.

Prudence hesitated, then nodded. "I can see no other alternative."

"Won't Great-uncle Oswald help us?" Grace asked.

Prudence looked troubled. "He would try, I'm sure, darling. But he is entirely dependent on Grandpapa financially and he has been so kind to us, I don't think we should ask him to risk his very livelihood."

"And he is not so strong or as vicious as Grandpapa," Hope stated bluntly. "Grandpapa would just knock him down and start on us."

"He might not even believe us," added Faith. "Nobody ever did before. Not until Dr. Gibson saw Grace with his own eyes."

"Besides," Charity added practically, "Great-uncle Oswald is away for the day and Grandpapa could arrive at any minute."

"What's going on, Prudence?" Gideon scanned her face worriedly. She looked so frightened, dammit! They all did. He wanted to snatch her back in his embrace but she was surrounded by sisters. He clenched his fists. What the devil was happening and why did they seem to think that flight was their only alternative? He glanced at Edward, who returned his look with a worried shrug.

"We have to leave—now," Prudence said in a flat voice. "Thanks to Mrs. Burton we are forewarned, and by the time Grandpapa comes we shall be gone."

"What do you mean?" Gideon tried to catch Prudence's eye but her eyes were only for her sisters. Like a little mother hen she swept them all up the front steps into the entry hall.

"Quick girls, upstairs and pack a portmanteau, as fast as you can. Pack for me, too, if you can. Hope, will you fetch down my special box, please? I will make the other arrangements. And I'll leave a note for Great-uncle Oswald, explaining everything. Now hurry, hurry! If he catches us, all will be lost!"

Before Gideon or the duke could say a word, Charity, Hope, and Faith raced up the stairs and disappeared.

"Grace, my love, all will be well if you just hurry," Prudence urged.

Grace's arms folded defensively, hunched into herself. "Oh Prue, what if—" The little girl looked, to Gideon's eyes, suddenly a great deal smaller and younger. Pale and pinched and defenseless. He found his fists clenching harder.

Prudence gathered the child into her arms and hugged her tightly. "He shan't find us, Graciela, I promise you. I will . . . I will kill him myself before I let him take us back. I will soon be one and twenty, and he cannot touch us then. Now run along and pack. We will leave as soon as I can find a carriage to take us out of London." She gave her little sister a gentle push toward the stairs, and Grace hurried off.

Gideon grabbed Prudence and swung her around to face him. "What the devil is the matter? I gather your grandfather is coming to town but why do you fear him so?"

Prudence shrugged him off. "I'm sorry, I don't have time to explain. We must get away from here. I have to get some money. And find a carriage. And write a letter."

"But I want to know why—"

She flung off his hand, clearly distracted. "We have to get away! Please, just leave. I thank you for your concern, Lord Carradice, and your kindness, too, Your Grace, but we must—"

"Hang my concern, I'm not going anywhere!" snapped Gideon. "Do you imagine for one minute that I could leave you in such obvious distress? Whatever it is, I'm at your service. Now, what do you need me to do?"

Prudence could hardly believe her ears. She stared up at Lord Carradice a long painful moment. "Do . . . do you mean it?" she stammered. "Y-you will help us?

His face softened and he gently smoothed back a lock of hair from her face. "Foolish Imp. You don't imagine I could see you so obviously facing trouble and just stroll out of here, do you?"

Prudence shrugged. Not since she was eleven had anyone seemed to care about her distress, and certainly nobody had simply offered to help. She bit her lip and stared at him dumbly, her eyelids prickling.

"Come, my love, don't cry now. Plenty of time for that later, if you want. I'm with you all the way in whatever you want." His smile was a touch rueful. "Will I help you? Try to stop me!"

"I, too, wish to offer my assistance," added the duke.

Prudence's face crumpled, but she managed to master herself. She fiercely blinked back tears, forcing herself to become businesslike. "Thank you. I would be extremely grateful if you could find us a carriage. We need to get away from here on the instant and Great-uncle Oswald has taken his to visit friends in Richmond."

"What sort of carriage?" asked Gideon.

Prudence looked at him blankly.

"Where are you planning to go?"

She shook her head. "I don't know. I hadn't thought that far ahead. Out of London. It depends . . ." It depended on how much money she had. She'd meant to sell some of her mother's jewelery before this, but she'd put the moment off, hoping it would not be necessary, after all. And now, see where her procrastination had got her!

Gideon glanced at the duke. "What about your mother's old traveling carriage? It's a bit antiquated, but it's solid enough and should fit five young ladies and their possessions. And if you order my phaeton, that should cover all eventualities."

"An excellent notion," agreed the duke. "I shall nip home immediately and see to it."

"Oh, and Edward, tell your man and mine to throw a few things in a valise for us. And a roll or two of soft. Doesn't hurt to be prepared."

"Good idea." The duke hurried out the door.

Gideon turned back to Prudence, explaining, "You see, Edward customarily drives a curricle, and the landau is too—" He broke off. She looked quite distracted, frowning with fierce concentration, completely unaware of his presence. Her hair had fallen out of its customary knot and loose tendrils were spiraling outward. The half-dozen freckles across the bridge of her nose stood out against her pallor like bread crumbs scattered over snow.

She looked small and worried and bedraggled and beautiful, and the forlorn expression in her eyes squeezed his heart in his chest.

"It's all right. Tell me what needs to be done," he said in a bracing tone. "I am yours to command."

"We need to be gone from this place as soon as possible. While the girls pack and your cousin finds us a carriage, I'll write the letter for Great-uncle Oswald, and you can . . ." She frowned. "Actually, there's nothing you can do at the moment—unless you want to help with the packing?"

He sighed. "I'm not much use at packing feminine apparel, unless you don't mind it all crushed, but I will fetch and carry bags." He added with a glimmer of wry humor, "I was hoping for a little more scope for my chivalrous instincts. Porter was not exactly the role I had in mind. Are you sure you don't need any dragons slain?"

He said it as a joke, but her face dimmed, as if a shadow had passed across her eyes. He couldn't bear it. In two quick paces he had her wrapped in his arms. She clung to him briefly with ragged vehemence, then stepped back, as if to isolate herself from him.

Gideon stroked her cheek lightly with the back of one finger. "Tell me about the dragon, Prue," he said softly. "Your grandfather. Why has he got you all in a pother? I didn't think you were afraid of anything."

She shook her head, not meeting his eyes, saying nothing.

"Grace seems terrified," he said. "I always thought her a little Viking, afraid of nothing."

She didn't want to tell him, he could see. She was determined to deal with it on her own. Gideon was just as determined to find out what caused a happy flock of garrulous girls to become pinched and fearful and silent.

"What makes a child like Grace so frightened?" he persisted softly. "What would make my courageous little Miss ImPrudence flee in such anxiety?" The backs of his fingers caressed her skin with tender insistence.

Prudence shivered. She closed her eyes, a brief, almost defeated look. Then she swallowed and said simply, "Grandpapa is very harsh."

"He beats us all," Hope said from the doorway. "Violently, often, and for no good reason. He beats Faith just for singing and me if I use my left hand. But he *thrashes* Prudence. And lately he has started on Grace in the same way. I *hate* him! Prue, here's the box. And Faith wants to know if we can take our new Kashmir shawls."

There was a moment of silence in the room. The very matter-of-fact way in which Hope had referred to the beatings chilled Gideon's blood. *He thrashes Prudence?* For a moment he could not think.

Prudence stirred, pulled away from Gideon's touch, became almost brisk again as she took a battered wooden box from Hope. "Thank you. Yes, take the shawls if you want. They are warm as well as fine, and you might need them in the carriage. But take only what you can fit in one portmanteau. We cannot carry any more. Now hurry!" Hope ran off.

Prudence sat down at the writing desk, picked up the pen, and began to write. She didn't look at Lord Carradice, but she could see him from the corner of her eye.

He was very still. Hope's words had shocked him, she could tell.

But she didn't have time to reassure him. And besides, there was nothing to say. What's done is done and no use repining. It was now that counted, not the unhappy past. And right now, she had to get this letter written to Great-uncle Oswald.

Poor Great-uncle Oswald. This morning he'd left a house full of girlish laughter; he would return to find it empty. He would read the tale of their lies and deception. And then he would have to face an enraged elder brother.

It was poor thanks for the kindness and generosity he had shown them. Prudence vowed to make it up to him one day.

She continued to write. Behind her and slightly to her left, Lord Carradice stood as if frozen. He remained still and silent for several long moments. Then she felt him moving toward her, felt his hands enclose her shoulders and gently turn her to face him.

"He thrashes you?" His voice was deep and soft, but it contained a note she had never heard in him before. She'd thought him only capable of pleasant nonsense and laughter.

She was wrong.

"Why does he thrash you?" he asked again, in that soft implacable voice. "And why has nobody stopped him?"

His anger was a little frightening, to tell the truth. Frightening, and yet comforting at the same time. Because although she didn't understand such silent, cold rage, and had never experienced such a thing, she knew it was entirely on her behalf. She'd never experienced that, either. A rage that protected instead of attacked.

She had no idea how to deal with the feelings his response had engendered, had no idea how to respond. She could not look him in the eyes. She shrugged awkwardly, and tried to bend over her letter. "It is nothing, just some stupid prejudice he has about my hair," she mumbled.

"What about it?"

"He thinks the color is a sign of the Devil in me. A sign that I am wanton and wicked . . . and evil." She stared blindly at the letter she was writing. There was some truth in Grandpapa's accusations. He had cause for his condemnation of her—oh, not about her hair, but about . . . other things.

She heard the quick, shocked intake of his breath and felt his palm curl around her nape, tenderly, possessively, comfortingly. His long, strong fingers slipped through her tumbled curls, loosening the final remnants of the knot, stroking and caressing as he murmured, "Your hair is beautiful, Prudence. It's glorious. Like a sunset over an autumn forest. Like tendrils of molten copper, fresh from the forge. I've never seen more beautiful hair in my life "

The writing in front of Prudence shimmered and blurred. Of course, he was only saying it to comfort her, but still . . . he must admire it a little at least, else how would he think of such beautiful things to say . . . *Tendrils of molten copper, fresh from the forge . . . A sunset over an autumn forest.*

She treasured up his words in a small, secret corner of her heart.

He pressed a warm kiss on the nape of her neck, and she shivered with fleeting pleasure, awash with weakness in the wake of his tenderness. Oh, where was the flippant rake when you needed him? She could resist him . . . just.

But this Lord Carradice, with poetry and tenderness on his lips . . . and protective rage in his heart.

She still couldn't bring herself to look at him. She didn't

know why she felt so ashamed that he knew part of her shabby little secret, but that was how she felt. She'd wanted nobody to know how viciously her grandfather beat her.

She felt . . . besmirched. She knew she should not, that Grandpapa had no moral right to continue beating her.

And yet . . . And yet . . .

She was not an innocent. Not like Grace and her sisters.

Four and a half years before, Prudence had, by her own actions, broken rules she knew Grandpapa had held sacred. Her actions had pushed him over the edge from habitual harshness to extreme and deliberate cruelty. Her physical punishment was, in some peculiar way, an expiation.

That was what made her most ashamed of all. As if there was some sort of vile complicity between them . . .

But then he'd started on Grace . . . and *that* she could not bear. That was when she'd started to fight back.

Lord Carradice moved around to stand beside her and waited for her to look up at him. Prudence bent over the letter, trying to disguise the fact that her eyes were full of unshed tears.

"Prudence, my Prudence," he said softly.

She closed her eyes a moment, forcing the tears back. He lowered himself, slowly, with fluid deliberation, until he was kneeling before her. He took her hands in both of his, warm, strong, filling her with his strength. His face was on a level with hers; she could tell by the faint stirring of his breath against her skin.

She took a deep, shaky breath and opened her eyes.

And found herself drowning in his dark, fathomless gaze. There was no lurking twinkle, no glimmer of mockery.

"No one shall ever again harm so much as a hair on your head, my Prudence, nor that of your sisters, not while there is breath in my body to prevent it."

It was a vow. Prudence felt like a medieval queen, with the knight of her heart declaring himself her vassal. She stared into the liquid heat of his gaze and saw there a refuge, and a haven, and love.

And the tears finally spilled from her eyes, for she was not entitled to his refuge or his love. She belonged to Phillip, was bound to him by the promise she had made in the churchyard, and by a later promise, even more sacred. His ring rested hard and heavy against her breast, reminding her of the weight of her oaths, even now.

"Oh dear, look what you've made me do," she wailed, searching in vain for a handkerchief and dashing tears from her cheeks with embarrassment. "I almost never cry, and have no time to do so now, in any case. I need to be strong, for my sisters' sake, as well as my own."

He pulled out a pristine white handkerchief and gently mopped up her tears, while she tried to scrub them away with her hands.

"I know," he said quietly. "And you are strong. But I don't care who you think you are betrothed to. At this moment, you are mine to protect—and for the rest of my life, if you wish it."

She shook her head distressfully and he tipped up her chin and smiled ruefully. "Don't fret, love. I haven't forgotten Ottershanks. I don't mean to press you at this inopportune time. Just know that you are no longer alone in this, or any other difficulty." And he lifted her hand and kissed it with the same formality—almost with reverence. Renewing and reaffirming his vow.

Prudence snuffled into his handkerchief, unbearably moved.

"Now . . ." He stood up and said in a very different voice, "You mustn't disdain the protection of a frippery shag bag and a medium-sized duke with a tendency to stoutness. We can be formidable fellows when we try, you know." He rubbed her back lightly and added in a soft voice, "Dry your eyes, Miss ImPrudence. We have letters to finish, bags to pack, dragons to rout!"

Prudence gave him a tremulous smile. Having a friend who was young and strong and independent of Grandpapa's influence *and* willing to stand up for her was a new experience.

"I gather Sir Oswald does not know the situation."

Prudence shook her head and explained, a little shamefacedly, "No. We deceived him when we came here. I . . . I forged a letter in Grandpapa's hand. Great-uncle Oswald welcomed us with open arms and showed us more kindness

than my sisters have ever seen in their lives—since Mama
and Papa died, that is." She stopped a moment, unable to
speak for the lump in her throat. "Grandpapa is our legal
guardian, at least until I come of age—which is the week
after next. Once I turn one and twenty, by my father's will,
I am entitled to become my sisters' guardian." She did not
mention the need to support them as well.

"Then why not ask for Sir Oswald's support until then?"

"I could not ask it of him. My sisters are right. Grandpapa
would not hesitate to lay violent hands on Great-uncle Oswald—he nearly killed a groom once, for some mistake
with a horse."

"But—"

"And though Grandpapa is the elder brother, he is
stronger and fitter, for he hunts regularly. Great-uncle Oswald lives a sedentary existence."

"I would not allow him to harm your uncle."

She smiled mistily and shook her head. "Thank you, but
that is not all. As a younger son, Great-uncle Oswald is entirely dependent on Grandpapa's good will for his income,
you see. I could not bear it if he were thrust into poverty as
a result of trying to help us."

Lord Carradice did not look convinced, so she continued,
"Great-uncle Oswald probably would defy Grandpapa, but
with no income of his own, he could not support us, and
though I shall have money from the sale of some jewels, I
couldn't possibly support Great-uncle Oswald in the style he
currently enjoys. He is rather extravagant, you know." She
shook her head decisively. "No, far better that we simply
take ourselves out of Grandpapa's reach until I turn one and
twenty. And if Charity and—" She broke off. Edward had
not yet asked Charity to wed him. It could still come to
naught. "Your cousin said he would help us. A duke is quite
powerful in some ways, is he not?"

"Yes," said Lord Carradice. "And so are the cousins of
dukes."

That brought a glimmer of a smile to her lips. Gideon
continued, "So, we are to embark on a journey. And what is
our destination to be?"

"I hadn't though that far ahead," she admitted. "I just

want to get away before he gets here—oh, and I will need to sell some jewelry. I will not have sufficient—"

"You need not sell your trinkets," he began. "I shall advance a sum—"

"I'm sorry, but I could not possibly accept money from you," Prudence interrupted him firmly. She added in a softer voice, "Your help is most welcome, Lord Carradice, and I will gladly borrow your cousin's carriage, but you know it would be most unseemly for me to borrow money from you."

"Bah! Propriety be hanged—"

"I have jewelry set aside for just this purpose," Prudence insisted. "And I would appreciate it if you would assist me in the selling of it, for I must confess I do not know where to start." She looked at him, her eyes troubled. "It's not that I don't appreciate—"

Gideon scowled, then sighed and smiled at her ruefully. "I know, and you are quite right. I'm sorry, I should not pinch at you for your scruples. I shall help you sell your baubles, though it goes against the grain. Finish your letter, my dear, and don't give it another thought. I think I can hear my cousin's voice in the hall, which will mean your carriage awaits you."

He left the room to check arrangements with his cousin.

It didn't take long for Prudence to finish the letter to Great-uncle Oswald. She left it propped up on the mantel in the drawing room, sealed with wax, his name on the front. She hurried upstairs to see to the packing of her things, but there was nothing left for her to do. Her maidservant, Lily, had done it all for her; the bedchamber had been swept clean of her possessions, the portmanteaus were packed and strapped onto the Duke of Dunstable's somewhat antiquated but undeniably large traveling carriage. Also in the street, being walked up and down by Lord Carradice's groom, was a dashing phaeton drawn by two magnificent grays.

"Miss Merridew and I have a small commission to perform in the city," announced Lord Carradice. "We shall travel in the phaeton and catch up with the rest of you."

"I hope there's room for me, Miss Prue," declared a loud voice behind them. Lily stood in the hallway, clutching a bundle to her chest. "I'd rather be skinned alive with a blunt knife and me innards eaten by rats than left behind to face old Lord Dereham!"

"It's all right, we wouldn't do that to you," Prudence assured her. "Of course you shall come with us."

Lily glanced from the carriage with the crest on the panel to the dashing phaeton and hesitated. "Which carriage are you ridin' in, miss?"

Lord Carradice said softly, "Lily, it would be best if you traveled in the main coach with the duke. Miss Prudence and I are using the phaeton."

Prudence opened her mouth to suggest that she needed Lily as chaperone but he caught her attention, and gave her a significant look that encompassed the battered old box. She subsided. He was right. She didn't want a witness to the shame of having to sell her mother's jewelry. It was bad enough he knew what straits she was reduced to, but Lily, good soul that she was, would gossip. And besides, she told herself, it would be an hour or so in an open carriage with a groom in attendance. No chaperone was necessary.

Lily's face fell. "But don't you and Miss Prudence need me here, me lord?"

"We do, of course, but I think my cousin the duke would be sincerely grateful for your assistance. One mere man with so many young ladies . . . He's relying on you, Lily." He smiled winningly.

"Ah, well, if the duke needs me," said Lily with the air of one accustomed to the helplessness of dukes. She handed her bundle to a groom and took her place in the carriage, swelling visibly with pride as the duke helped her to mount the steps.

James, their loyal footman, stood in the evening shadows, watching the whole proceedings, doing his best to look nonchalant. Prudence saw the longing in his eyes and realized he was too proud to ask to come with them. "James, we wouldn't dream of leaving you behind," she said softly. "Please come with us—if you want to, that is."

"Oh, thank you, miss. O' course I want to!" James bowed with alacrity and raced up the servants stairs to fetch his belongings.

"Is there a chimney sweep you'd like to invite, too?" Lord Carradice murmured, and Prudence turned defensively.

But his gaze upon her was warm and lit with approval and understanding, so she explained, "James has been one of our only friends . . ." She looked up at him. "Until now."

There was a lump in her throat, making it difficult to speak. Back in Norfolk, many people knew of their situation but had turned a blind eye, leaving five young girls at the mercy of a harsh and twisted man. She cleared her throat and continued, "James risked his position many times in order to protect us—Grace, in particular. We could not possibly leave him behind to face Grandpapa's wrath."

"No, of course not," he said softly. "Loyalty is your middle name, is it not, Miss Imp?"

James came clattering down the stairs with a bundle under his arm. He tossed it up to the roof and climbed up beside the coach driver. Good, thought Prudence. The duke was a welcome escort, but he was not very athletic looking, and Charity was his priority. If James was with them, there would be a strong, masculine arm for Grace and the twins as well.

Her sisters peered out of the coach, looking a great deal less anxious now that the excitement of travel was upon them.

The butler watched the whole thing with a dour expression. He tweaked Lord Carradice's sleeve and muttered something under his breath. Prudence raised her brows in enquiry.

Lord Carradice explained, "Niblett here is concerned that my cousin and I are kidnapping you and your sisters, not to mention half the staff. I hope you will reassure him."

"Of course nobody is being kidnapped, Niblett," Prudence assured him. "We've been called away on an urgent family matter. I've left a letter for my great-uncle in the drawing room. Please make certain he gets it on his return. I shall write again when we arrive at our destination."

"And where would that destination be, miss?" inquired Niblett.

"Oh, it's all in the letter," she said vaguely. Even had she decided on a destination, she wouldn't tell Niblett. He was the sort of butler who loved gossip and who would tell her grandfather everything at the drop of a guinea, or perhaps five.

"Oh, you can tell Niblett, my dear."

Prudence tried frantically to catch his eye, but Lord Carradice seemed oblivious.

"My cousin and I have planned the journey in detail. We are going initially to my lodgings, for there is something I must drop off. Then we're off to my house." He added helpfully, "To my house, in Derbyshire. And thence, north, to my cousin Dinstable's seat, in the far reaches of Scotland."

Prudence groaned.

"Oh, Niblett won't betray us, my dear girl," Lord Carradice assured her. "Will you, Niblett?" He slipped a folded banknote in the butler's direction.

Niblett bowed in majestic, creaky assent and pocketed the banknote without a flicker of awareness.

Prudence was aghast. "I wish you had not done that," she said as he assisted her into the phaeton. "Niblett is not to be trusted with any secret. The moment anyone offers him even the paltriest sum of money, he will tell all."

"I'm sure we can rely on Niblett to do exactly what we wish." Gideon took Prudence's hand in a firm, soothing grip. "Trust me, Miss ImPrudence, I am an excellent judge of character."

Prudence looked unconvinced.

Lord Carradice put on his driving gloves and picked up the ribbons of the phaeton. He nodded at his cousin, who signaled back, and the large coach rumbled away over the cobblestones, everybody waving madly. Lord Carradice signaled his groom, who released the horses' heads and leaped up behind as the phaeton moved off down Providence Court.

Behind them, Niblett smirked as he closed the front door.

Chapter Twelve

"The very instant I saw you, did
My heart fly to your service."
WILLIAM SHAKESPEARE

As the carriage wheels rattled over the cobbles, Prudence's hand stole to her breast where Phillip's betrothal ring hung hard and heavy against her heart.

It ought to be Phillip who was helping her now, not Lord Carradice.

And it ought to be Phillip who dominated her dreams at night and her thoughts by day . . . not Lord Carradice.

Gaslights illuminated his profile in momentary flashes as the phaeton twisted and turned through the maze of streets. She held herself rigid and apart from him but could not prevent herself from bumping lightly against his shoulder and thigh each time the high-slung carriage swayed and rocked. She tried to ignore the unsettling sensations each moment of contact caused her, tried to keep her back ramrod straight, but it was difficult. What she really wanted was to cling to his arm and feel his strength supporting her.

Once off the main thoroughfares, the streets were eerily quiet. Though they were by no means the only ones abroad at this hour, they were the only open carriage. She shivered, though the night was not at all chilly.

She leaned back a little to get a clearer view of Lord Carradice's profile and observed him obliquely, disturbed by the tenor of her thoughts. Over the past few weeks she'd done her level best to dismiss him from her mind and heart, telling herself sternly that he was frivolous and unreliable and that she was foolish and faithless and wanton at heart, as Grandpapa said.

She'd been warned by Lady Jersey and others that Lord Carradice had merely been entertaining himself with her until something better came up. Bored persons of the ton did that, they'd explained: Take up a person for a time and make much of them, then drop them for no reason, cutting them dead the next time they met. It was the way of the the sophisticated world.

And yet tonight, she'd entrusted herself and her sisters' safety to them without a moment's hesitation. A notorious rake and his supposedly misanthropic cousin. And now she was alone in the darkness with the rake and far from fearing for her reputation, she took great comfort from his presence and his words of reassurance.

Who could have known the frivolous rake would turn out to be such a source of strength and comfort? It had been hard enough to withstand his blandishments before . . . Now it was going to be even harder.

"Is it far?" she asked.

He glanced at her sideways. "The jewel broker, you mean? No, not far, in fact, just around the corner." His grays slowed and turned into a narrow street, where the buildings were crowded together. It was the sort of neighborhood where no gaslights burned. Were it not for Lord Carradice's carriage lights, the darkness would have been total, for none of the houses showed even a single light burning.

Prudence clutched the battered box tight against her. "I never imagined it would be possible to sell jewelry at this hour of the evening. Are you sure it can be done?"

He smiled and eased his horses to a walk in front of a tall, narrow building. "I'm sure. I have done business with this fellow many a time. He will not mind being disturbed."

Prudence nodded. The sharp edges of the box bit into her chest. It was foolish, she told herself firmly; she'd known for weeks, months, that she would need to sell her mother's jewelry, and yet now that the moment had arrived, she wanted to cling to it, to the last physical mementos of Mama and Papa.

Lord Carradice jumped nimbly down, secured his horses, and held up a hand to Prudence. She took a deep breath and laid hers in his outstretched hand, but to her surprise, he shook his head, kissed her hand lightly, and returned it to her lap.

"T'will be better if I see Sitch alone," he said. "Just hand me the box and I'll see to it."

"You need not spare me —" she began.

"No, it isn't that. Sitch is a canny devil. If he sees there is a lady involved at this hour of the evening, he will surmise that the situation is urgent and use the knowledge to drive the price down. However, if I stroll in, apparently on my way to a gaming hell and needing to convert a few assets into cash, well, he is used to such scenarios from clients." Lord Carradice held out his hand for the box.

Prudence bit her lip. She opened the lid for the last time, took out the pile of handkerchiefs and fiddled with a hidden catch. "There is a false base," she explained.

Despite the dark, she could almost see Lord Carradice's brows rise.

"It was necessary," she said defensively. "Grandpapa searched our belongings. He took Mama's diamonds when I was eleven, said Mama was wicked and evil and her baubles an abomination of Jezebel." She glanced at him briefly, fiddling in the dark with a hidden catch. "Only she wasn't! She was good and kind and beautiful, and he was the evil one!"

She took a deep breath and continued. "I made a stocking purse and hid it under my skirts, with the rest of Mama's precious things in it. They belong to my sisters and me, not him! But it was too difficult to carry them all the time—they are quite heavy, you know—so I got the stableboy to make a false bottom for this shabby old box."

She darted him a faintly mischievous look. "I kept it open, in full sight on my dressing table, holding handkerchiefs, and Grandpapa never suspected a thing, though he was certain there must be more jewels hidden away—

Mama's papa was wealthy, though not well born. And Mama took her jewels when she and Papa ran away."

"Aha, a runaway match."

"A *love* match," she corrected him. "A very great love match. Mama's papa didn't want her marrying into the dissolute aristocracy, and Grandpapa didn't want his son to marry a cit. So they ran away to Italy."

The catch finally shifted, and Prudence removed the false base of the box. She dipped her fingers into the small trove of family treasure. She knew each piece by heart. Here was the sapphire necklace and earrings . . . such an intense, vivid blue—the exact color of Mama's and Charity's eyes. She'd always imagined Charity wearing them for her wedding, as Mama had at hers . . .

And here was the heavy, smooth coolness of the pearl choker that Mama loved so much. She closed her eyes a moment and remembered Papa fastening it around Mama's long and elegant neck, for the clasp was always stiff and difficult. It was always an event of laughter and teasing, but each time, Papa would kiss Mama on the nape after he had fastened it . . . a slow and lingering caress . . . and the laughter would fade, and an odd, exciting tension would fill the room.

Prudence had not understood it as a child, but now suddenly, years later, sitting in a phaeton in a dark London street, she realized what the tension was that had hummed so tangibly between her parents . . .

Desire.

She glanced at Lord Carradice standing silently watching her and as their eyes caught, a sudden silence hummed between them.

The moment stretched. His hand reached toward her and she wanted more than anything to take it. Even as her hand lifted to reach out to him, one of the grays snorted and stamped restively and the carriage jerked. Prudence grabbed the side to steady herself, and Lord Carradice went to the horse's head to assist his groom.

"It were a rat, me lord, a big 'un," she heard Boyle say. "Ran right under 'is hooves, it did."

Prudence shivered. She watched Lord Carradice murmuring soothing sounds to his horse, calming it with his hands while his groom calmed the other one.

The moment was gone. Prudence knew she needed to ensure it never returned. She took one last, long look at the contents of the box, blinking away the tears that stung her eyelids. Prudence and her sisters were her mother's true legacy. What were cold jewels and metal compared with the happiness of Mama's daughters? And memories—her memories were in her head, not this dear, shabby old box . . .

"There is nothing you want to keep?"

Her fingers lingered on the locket. It was broken, though the catch could be mended, no doubt. It was quite large and made of gold, so it would fetch a neat sum, but to her, the most precious part of it was inside. She opened it. One last look at the faces painted inside, a silent renewal of her promise to Mama as she died, that she would take care of her sisters.

"No, there is nothing," she tried to say, but the words choked in her throat. She shook her head and, with shaking fingers, closed the locket and made to replace it in the box. They were not good likenesses anyway, she told herself.

His hand stopped her, closed around her fingers, enclosing the locket. "Keep it." His voice was oddly harsh. "If you need to sell it later, you can, but for now, keep it."

Her fingers tightened thankfully about the old gold trinket. She shut the lid of the box carefully and handed it to him. "Make sure you get a good price," she whispered.

Be damned to a good price, Gideon thought. Did she think he was the sort of man who would haggle over the price of a woman's bits and pieces? He almost snatched the box from her, so uncertain was his temper. It was unbearable to see her so vulnerable yet so determined not to accept his help.

He yanked on the doorbell, sending it jangling noisily in the nether reaches of the house. After a few moments, an upstairs window opened. Old Sitch peered out, a nightcap on his head.

"Who is it?" he quavered.

"Carradice," Gideon barked.

Grumbling under his breath, the old man disappeared and a few minutes later he unbolted the door. "'Tis an unusual hour for you to come calling on me, me lord! No trouble, I hope."

Gideon thrust the box into the man's hand. "Have these cleaned, reset, and restrung—whatever is needed to bring them up to scratch again."

"Cleaned and reset?" Old Sitch stared at the collection of jewels, then scratched his head, bemused. "You came at this hour to ask me to clean some jewels."

"And reset any that need it, yes," Gideon said brusquely. "I am leaving town this night, immediately, and need the job done by the time I return."

"You're never fleeing the country, me lord?"

"Fleeing the country? Good God, no!" Gideon stared, then realized he needed some sort of rational explanation. "I—er, was called away urgently, but recalled I'd promised to get these fixed. No time to delay, you know. They'll be needed pretty urgently when I return."

"Very good, me lord. I'll have them sparkling and perfect again for the little lady." Sitch shuffled to the door and opened it.

"There is no little lady!" Gideon said meaningfully.

Sitch peered out into the street. Prudence sat bolt upright in the phaeton, looking anxious, fretful, and to Gideon's eye, wholly adorable.

"Quite right, me lord. Trick of the light. I never saw no little lady."

"Good man." Gideon took his leave. Prudence looked so relieved to see him, it took all his self-restraint not to snatch her into his arms and kiss the jitters out of her. Instead, he climbed aboard the phaeton, concentrating on sang froid.

"Here you are," he said in a terse voice. "I hope it is sufficient for your needs." He pulled a thick roll of notes from the pocket of his greatcoat and handed it to her.

The thickness of the roll made Prudence's eyes widen. "London prices must be much higher than elsewhere. You've done better than I expected. Thank you."

He shrugged, a trifle embarrassed by her misplaced gratitude. "Sitch has done business with me for years. I knew he would not let us down. Now, we'd best make speed to catch up with Edward and your sisters." He lifted the reins. "Are you going to hold that money in your hand all the way, or do you have somewhere to put it?"

She started. "Oh, yes. Of course." She carefully peeled off half a dozen notes and placed them in the Egyptian reticule. Gideon waited with interest to see what she would do with the rest. "Turn your back, please," she said briskly, looking a little self-conscious.

Gideon quizzed her with a look, then shrugged. "Boyle, turn your back," he called to his groom, then he also turned his back, or as much of it as the seat of the phaeton would allow. There was not a lot of room for maneuvering. A shame he was bred a gentleman; he was dying to know where she planned to hide the rest of the money. He felt her wriggling beside him. A sharp little elbow nudged him high on the shoulder. "Sorry," she gasped. "Stay where you are. I'm not finished yet."

From the angle of that elbow, her bodice was the fuller by several hundred pounds, he surmised. He chuckled to himself. He couldn't imagine how she thought her bosom would hide that much money; her curves might be delightful but they were not so full as to be able to disguise a thick wad of banknotes.

"Not yet!" she hissed.

He heard the slither of fabric and a surge of velvet cloak and muslin gown frothed across his lap. Gideon grinned. Unless he missed his guess, Miss ImPrudence Merridew had just exposed her legs to a London street—a silent and empty street, to be sure, but a public thoroughfare just the same. He grinned.

"Cooling your limbs, Miss Imp?" he murmured.

A gasp and a flurry of fabric being hastily tugged down was his reward. "I asked you not to look! If you were a gentleman—"

"Rest easy, Miss Imp. I didn't cheat."

"Then how did—"

"I turned my back as you asked, but I'm not deaf, and when this falls across my knees—" He gestured to the folds of her dress and cloak. "I put two and two together."

"Oh," she said. "Well, it is true, I did pull my skirt up a

little. But there is nobody here to see, and I keep my stocking purse under my petticoat, for safety."

"Very sensible. Now, may I turn around so we can resume our journey?"

She made a small sound, which he took for assent, so he turned back to face the front again. He whistled to his groom, and as the horses moved on, Gideon glanced at her and smiled. "So, how much is your bodice worth? I'm guessing"—he glanced again—"fifty pounds."

Prudence blinked, then clapped her hand to her bodice with a small shriek. "You *did* watch, you . . . you rogue!" She thumped him on the shoulder furiously, and he laughed, denying it.

"Not at all! You must acquit me of everything except excellence in surmise. You bumped me with your elbow, and it was in such a position that I worked out the rest."

She narrowed her eyes at him. "Perhaps, but how could you possibly know there was fifty pounds in my bodice?"

He gave her a slow, knowing look, as if to say, *Work it out, my dear.*

She blinked. He must have . . . to have noticed a change in the size of her bodice, he must have *looked* at her! *Intimately!* Prudence blushed. He was indeed no gentleman!

"Exactly." He seemed to have read her thoughts. "Any change in your bodice, and I would notice."

"That—that's . . . You are quite outrageous!"

"I know." His tone was apologetic, but Prudence wasn't fooled for a minute. "I've told you before of the trouble I have with my eyes," he continued. "The poor things are anxious, you see—too anxious for their own good."

She was silent for a minute, frowning while she debated whether to maintain an aloof dignity or satisfy her curiosity. It was fully three blocks at a smart pace before curiosity won.

"What do you mean, anxious? Your eyes don't look anxious to me at all! As far as I can see, they are bold and perfectly wicked!"

He edged the grays to a walk while they negotiated a jumble of handcarts and barrows, nearing a market. "Ah, but that is their tragedy. All that bold wickedness is just a brave front, you see. Underneath, they are sadly anxious. Particularly about your bodice," He paused a moment, then added, "I mean, what if something should fall out? It's very worrying, I can tell you!"

She gasped. Casting him a darkling look, she drew her cloak together and beneath its shelter, folded her arms across her bosom. "You are quite incorrigible!"

But Gideon could see the dimple lurking in the corner of her mouth, even as she glared down her masterful little nose at him.

"I should turn it off without a character, if I were you," he said in a conversational tone. "It betrays you every time."

There was a long pause as she turned the comment over in her mind. "Turn what off without a character? What are you talking about? I don't think I could ever turn anyone off without a character reference."

"You really should, you know; it betrays you time and time again."

She turned to him, puzzled and not a little suspicious. "What does?"

"That dimple."

She flounced her shoulder away from him and observed the road in silence for the next moment or two.

"See, there it goes again," he said softly. "Every time you try to be cross and schoolmistressy and put me in my place, out it pops, betraying you!"

The dimple disappeared for a moment, then returned as she struggled for propriety.

"I find it adorable," he murmured and put an arm around her to steady her as they turned a corner at a smart trot. Muffled in the voluminous folds of her cloak, she was unable to fend him off as he could see she would prefer to do.

"I would hate you to fall off," he murmured and tightened his hold. "So undignified, not to mention dangerous."

She made a halfhearted effort to wriggle away from him, then sighed and allowed herself to be held firmly against his side. A stern look gave him to understand she would tolerate no further encroachment, but after a few moments of stiff resistance, the warm curves of her body relaxed into him, swaying with the movement of the carriage in perfect synchronization with his.

Gideon smiled to himself. It was the closest he'd got to her in ages.

They turned onto the turnpike road, and Gideon set the grays to at a steady clip, driving one-handed, unable to bring himself to release her. She would be cross with him again when she discovered he hadn't sold a thing. But he was damned if he'd let her sell her precious bits and pieces only for some nonsensical notion of propriety.

He'd had every intention of selling them for her, hadn't thought twice about it initially. What were jewels, after all, but hard pieces of metal and glittering stone; a decorative form of business transaction. Men and women traded jewels all the time in his experience; a diamond necklace for favors granted, sapphire ear bobs for an apology, an emerald bracelet as a silent farewell. Oh, women had always spouted stuff about symbols of love, but he'd always thought it a lot of nonsense, a polite lie to disguise basic avarice.

Until now.

He recalled the soft look in her eyes as she'd gazed into the box, the tender wistfulness with which she'd handled each piece, as if saying a silent farewell to it. The women he knew would have been most reluctant to give up the diamond and sapphire sets—they were clearly the most decorative and valuable pieces. Yet the piece Prudence had handed over with most reluctance had been a scratched and worn old locket with two amateurish portraits inside.

There had been tears in her eyes as she'd handed them over, he was sure of it, even in the dark. Something about the husky tone of her voice and the way she wouldn't look at him directly.

Tears. Over a scratched old locket with two bad portraits.

He hadn't been able to get a clear look at both pictures, but one of them was of a man's face. Her parents? Or was the man in the locket Otterbury? If she hadn't been battling to hide her tears he might have asked her about it. But now was not the moment.

•   •   •

The lights of London soon dropped away behind them. They passed through several sleepy villages at a fast clip, the only light that of the moon and the carriage lanterns. The sound of the horses' hooves rang in the night, disturbing a few dogs here and there, leaving them barking in the distance. To Prudence, it felt like they were the only people awake in the world.

She had done little traveling as an adult and found the pace of his lordship's phaeton a little alarming, to tell the truth, particularly on the turnpike road. It was very disconcerting to be driving pell-mell into the night, not knowing quite where they were headed, so she was very grateful for the occasional light of the moon when it came out from behind the clouds.

The moon! Recently risen, the heavy, creamy globe shone from behind directly along the road they were traveling.

"Lord Carradice, we are driving away from the moon!" Prudence exclaimed.

"So we are."

She tugged at his sleeve. "But the moon rises in the *east!*"

"So it does, and very romantic it is, too, don't you think?"

"But Derbyshire is to the *north*."

"Correct again, Miss Merridew," Lord Carradice congratulated her. "I can see you're a whiz at geography. Shall we play at geographical question-and-answer to while away the miles, then? I do so enjoy discussing geography, don't you?" He tucked her hand into the crook of his arm and continued in a chatty tone, "Did you know that there is a place called Goatfell in Scotland, for instance? One can only surmise that a noble goat gave its life for—"

Prudence snatched her hand back and said in exasperation, "But you told Niblett we were going to your seat in Derbyshire. So why are we traveling west instead of north?"

"Because if we want any supper, we must hurry along. Are you hungry? I must say I am—"

"Oh, for heaven's sake! What are you talking about?"

"You mean you're not hungry?"

"Yes, of course I am, but—"

"Well then, we'd better make haste. It doesn't do to keep a lady hungry."

He urged the horses to even greater speed, and Prudence was forced to grip his sleeve again, this time for security. It really was a frightful pace, but she managed to say in a firm enough voice, "Lord Carradice, I insist you explain why we are traveling west!"

He turned his head, and his smile glinted wickedly in the moonlight. "My cousin has sent a man ahead to bespeak rooms and a late supper for us all at The Blue Pelican in Maidenhead. Granted, it is not very far out of London, but you cannot wish to travel through the night like the mail does."

Prudence relaxed a little, relieved to hear that her sisters and the duke were also apparently heading for Maidenhead, though the choice of destination seemed a bizarre one. "Whether or not we travel through the night is immaterial to me, as long as my sisters are safe, but that is not the point! Why Maidenhead? It is nowhere near Derbyshire."

"Neither it is," agreed Lord Carradice, apparently much struck by the notion.

"But you told Niblett we were going to Derbyshire! And you paid him handsomely not to tell!"

"I did say you could trust my judgment of his character, but, no! You wouldn't heed me." He attempted to look downcast by her lack of faith in him, but a tiny curl of his lips gave him away.

Prudence's jaw dropped. "You mean you bribed Niblett not to tell . . . but told him a lie, knowing he could not be trusted, anyway?"

Lord Carradice looked affronted. "Of course I trusted him—trusted him to pass on the information instantly."

"How did you know he would not honor the bribe?"

Lord Carradice tapped the side of his nose and looked wise. Prudence wasn't fooled. "You have tried to bribe him before!"

"You have a very suspicious mind, Miss Imp." Lord Carradice looked as if butter wouldn't melt in his mouth.

Prudence nodded, satisfied. "I thought so. It is very wrong to bribe servants, you know, but in this case you did the right thing. Let us hope Niblett will not suddenly turn over a new leaf. It would be most unfortunate if he decided not to tell."

"No chance of that," murmured Lord Carradice, adjusting the reins in his grip. "I only gave him five guineas."

"Five guineas?" Prudence exclaimed in horror. "But that is far too much!" She knew exactly how much five guineas would buy, and it seemed foolishly improvident to squander it on bribing a devious and untrustworthy butler.

"Nonsense. It is sufficient to make him realize the information was worth something, but believe me Miss Imp, Niblett holds himself a great deal more expensive than five guineas. He will be insulted by the paltry nature of the sum and will hasten to inform your grandfather of our supposed destination. And thus, if your grandfather pursues us, he will head directly for my seat in Derbyshire, and my people there will have received the message to send him on to Scotland. Alternatively, he may decide it is too far and give up."

Prudence shivered. "He will pursue us," she said in a low voice. "There is no doubt of that."

Lord Carradice frowned at her sober certainty and laid one hand over hers. "He may pursue you," he assured her firmly, "but he shall not find you."

She gave him a look of the bleakest misgiving. "In my experience, Grandpapa does not give up easily. And he is very good at intimidating others. Your people might be too in awe of him to deceive him."

"I doubt that," he began, and then, seeing she could not be convinced of that, added, "and if by some mischance he does find you, he shall not lay so much as a finger on you, that I promise you. You are safe with me, my Imp, and so are your sisters."

His voice was deep and sure and steady, and Prudence was comforted, despite herself. She ought to have removed her hands from his grasp, but she could not bring herself to do so; it seemed as if strength and calmness flowed into her from him. She had an overwhelming impulse to lay her cheek against his shoulder, as if she could, just for a while, lay all her burdens on that broad, strong resting place.

But she couldn't. It was just a momentary weakness on

her part. He thought his assistance, his gallantry, and his wonderful generosity in helping her would make a difference—and it did, but only to her feelings. He thought it was only a matter of time before she broke her vow to Phillip. But then, Lord Carradice was used to ladies who thought nothing of breaking vows, even marriage vows.

To Prudence, such vows were sacred.

And even if her feelings had changed, even if what she once felt for Phillip was a pale shadow of what she feared she now felt for Lord Carradice, she could not betray Phillip's years of loyalty. She and Phillip were joined, even if not in the eyes of society and the law; a ring had been given and accepted, and promises made in the churchyard, under the eyes of God.

And the bond had been sealed by blood.

If she was ever to come to Lord Carradice—and deep in her heart she acknowledged that she wanted to—she would come to him free and clear and wholeheartedly, not as an oath-breaker. Love was too precious to be tainted.

She buried her hands in the folds of her cloak. She had managed on her own before; she would manage again. Even if Grandpapa did find them, and used the law to get Prudence and her sisters once more under his control, she was determined to defy him. She would turn one and twenty soon.

And if Charity and the duke wed—as she hoped they would—perhaps the duke would help her to force Grandpapa to sign over the money. Lord Carradice might try, but a duke, especially if he were a relation by law, would have more power. *If* the duke and Charity married.

In the meantime, Prudence could protect her sisters, surely.

Assuming Grandpapa was not so enraged he beat her insensible again . . .

She swallowed. She must not dwell on her fears. Fears sapped your strength. If she stayed strong, Grandpapa could not get the better of her. That other time, she had been ill, feeling lost and abandoned, and he'd caught her at her most vulnerable. She would not allow that again.

Chapter Thirteen

⧣

"The curfew tolls the knell of parting day . . .
And leaves the world to darkness and to me."

THOMAS GRAY

THEY CHANGED HORSES AT BRENTFORD AND THE PACE WAS NOT quite so fast or so smooth, the horses being not so well matched nor as smooth-gaited as Lord Carradice's. A few miles farther on, the land opened up before them, an endless, bleak expanse of silver and shadows lying silent and cool under the moon.

"Hounslow Heath," said Lord Carradice, apparently responding to the tightening of her hand on his arm. She had found it easier to ride thus, holding on to his arm—purely for security, of course. The light carriage was very well sprung, but it did tend to bounce around a little on uneven patches of the road.

"It has an infamous reputation, has it not?" she asked.

"Yes, for highway robbery, but you need not be anxious, Miss Imp. It has more or less ceased to be a problem these days. Since Bow Street formed their Horse Patrol a great many offenders have been caught or driven to make a living in some other way. The rule of the gentlemen of the high toby is a thing of the past. Besides, dusk is the most dangerous time, and we are well past that."

"I am not unused to banditry," she said. "In Italy when I

was a child, we encountered them many times. In some parts of the country, where poverty has been a fact of life for generations, banditry is a way of life for whole families, indeed whole villages."

"Indeed?" He sounded surprised by her matter-of-fact tone. "It sounds fascinating, if a trifle disconcerting. Did you like living in Italy—bandits aside, of course?"

"Oh, yes. It was wonderful. We were all so very happy there." She sighed. "Each place we lived in seemed always to be full of sunshine and flowers and laughter and singing. People sang all the time. Well, I don't suppose they did, but they *seemed* to. The servants, the workers in the fields often sang as they worked. And Mama and Papa loved music and we children used to put on concerts for them every Wednesday night. In English and Italian—we learned lots of folk songs—and Mama used to sing the babies to sleep every night." She smiled, reminiscing.

"Do you remember so much about it, then? You were only a child when you lived there, were you not?"

"Oh yes, but we left when I was eleven, and I can remember so much. And of course, I've told my younger sisters all about it, over and over, so that they can remember, too." She added, "It's very important to remember happy times; it makes you stronger inside when things are . . . less happy. Of course, as children, we probably had the best of it; Italians are extremely indulgent toward children, you know. I expect we were terribly spoiled."

He chuckled. "I see no evidence of that. And I imagine you and your sisters made a charming little choir. Do you play, as well as sing?"

She paused a moment, watching the faint shadow of the clouds scudding over the moonlit heathland, then said lightly, "No. We are all woefully ignorant in that area. Grandpapa does not approve of music, you see. He considers it sinful, except in church, and even then . . ." She shrugged. "The way we lived in Italy was very, very different to life in England."

She shivered, remembering what it had been like to come from the warmth of Tuscany to cold and desolate Norfolk.

Five bewildered little girls, newly orphaned and left to the mercies of a bitter, hate-filled old man . . .

"Cold, Miss Imp?" Without waiting for her response, he put an arm around her and drew the fur traveling rug more securely around her.

"No, I'm not cold," she said, but she allowed his arm to remain around her and even leaned a little against him. She knew she oughtn't, but there was something about the moor and the moonlight and the memories of her lost childhood that was making her melancholy. The warmth and strength of his arm and the feeling of his solid body against hers was very comforting.

Besides, she was tired. She glanced at his moon-silvered profile. He didn't seem the slightest bit sleepy. He was probably accustomed to staying up late. She recalled the first time she'd met him; he'd been coming home at half-past nine in the morning, and regarding it as the end of the evening.

There was something about traveling in the night, with shadows and moonlight and the rhythmic clip-clop of the horses' hooves, which was very conducive to the exchange of intimacies.

"Tell me about your childhood," she said. "What were your parents like?"

He stiffened immediately, so that the horses checked their pace. He flicked them back to their normal pace and glanced at her, a wry expression on his face.

"My early years were happy enough," he said after a moment. "The usual sort of childhood, I imagine; nurses and nanny and tutors and the like. Learning to read and write and ride and shoot. And then when I turned eight, I was sent off to school."

Prudence frowned. Servants and tutors, things to be learned and then sent to school at eight! It was not her idea of a happy childhood. "Were you happy at school?"

He shrugged. "Is anyone happy at school? It wasn't bad. Edward was there, too—my cousin, you know. We are much the same age."

"That must have been nice for you both—a little less lonely," she said. "And what about your mother and father?"

His profile seemed to harden. "Not happy," he said after a while. "They married the wrong people."

"Oh." She wanted to ask more, but there was such a forbidding expression on his face, she didn't like to.

He glanced down at her, and his arm tightened around her. "You could say they worked it out in the end."

There was a long pause. Prudence could feel the tension in him. She said nothing. "I suppose you might as well hear the whole blasted story," he said at last. "With your sister and Edward tying the knot and—" he broke off. "The old gossip will no doubt be dredged up again, and someone is bound to fill your ears. You may as well hear the truth." He took a deep breath and said in a light tone, quite as if it didn't matter to him, "My mother eloped with Edward's father when we were fourteen."

She must have made some small, shocked sound, because he looked down at her. "Yes, it was pretty frightful. Caused a huge scandal. They were sisters, you see, Edward's mother and mine, which made it worse somehow."

"Yes," whispered Prudence. "A double betrayal—of sister and husband."

"Exactly." The horses' hooves thudded rhythmically on. A light breeze had sprung up, not cold, but very fresh, chasing the clouds across the night sky.

"It must have been dreadful for you and Edward."

He shrugged carelessly but did not respond. Prudence was not deceived by his careless manner. He cared too much to speak of it seriously. "How did your father cope?" she ventured after a while.

He flicked the reins and said in an offhand manner, "He pursued them at first, but lost them on the Continent. He was very fond of my mother, you see. You might say he loved her to distraction." His voice, under the light, conversational tone, held a note of bitter savagery. They drove on for several miles. Prudence could feel the tension vibrating in his body. He had not finished his story. She laid her hand on his knee and leaned into his body, offering silent comfort.

The cool breeze picked up. The hooves rang out on the roadway.

Finally Gideon spoke, "He returned home a broken man, became a recluse . . ."

Prudence bit her lip and gripped his knee harder.

Gideon glanced down at her. "He shot himself in the end." The reins were wrapped so tightly around his hands, they must be biting into his flesh, yet he did not pull on the horses at all. Control.

There were no words for such a story; she could only offer him the comfort of human warmth. She slipped her arms around him and hugged him and he stiffened and then slowly relaxed.

After a moment he said in a choked voice, "He simply couldn't bear the loss . . . He loved her, you see. Truly loved her . . . And the loss of her drove him to the point of madness. Killed him."

They drove on for several more miles, Prudence tucked against his chest, her arms around him in silent comfort, his arm holding her tightly against him. The heath stretched before them, a bleak prospect of wild and uncultivated land dotted here and there with dense thickets of brush and stunted trees.

"It must have been terrible for you and your cousin, too. And your aunt."

"Yes, well, she went into a decline for a while, then when she heard they'd both been killed on the continent, she—"

"They were both killed, your mother and the duke's father?"

"Mmm, yes." He nodded. "Drowned in a boating accident on Lake Geneva about six months after they ran off. That was when my father shot himself, actually—when he realized there was no hope of ever getting my mother back." He added, as if to himself, "I'd always believed my father to be a strong man, but . . ."

"I'm sure he was a strong man," Prudence assured him warmly. "But he needed your mother." She stared up at his unmoving profile a little anxiously. "We all need love, you know. It isn't a weakness—it's the most wonderful source of strength. And if people fall apart for a little while when it is taken from them, well, that is understandable."

"You did not fall apart when your parents died."

"No, because I was just a child and I did not perfectly understand how much my life would change. And besides, I had my little sisters to look after. Grace was still a baby, so I had no time to brood—" She broke off as it occurred to her that Lord Carradice's father had had a son to look after, a son who would have been just as devastated as his father, a son who needed support and love.

Prudence's sisters had needed support and love. And by loving them, she had been healed of her grief.

His son's needs hadn't stopped Gideon's father from brooding, it seemed. Where had Gideon been when his father shot himself?

He seemed to know what she was wondering about because he said, "He was alone in the house when he did it. A quick, clean shot, I'm told."

After a moment, Lord Carradice continued, "I was at school when they ran off and Father went after them. I never saw him . . . never said good-bye. Nobody told us anything until they received word of the drowning accident."

"But that's terrible!"

"I suppose they chose not to distress us with what, after all, was mostly rumor at that point. It was a wasted effort, however."

She felt the tension rising in his body again and laid her cheek against his shoulder. He glanced down at her, and an indescribable expression passed over his face.

"The ton will always gossip, you see. It feeds on such stuff. And it trickles down to the children of the ton."

Prudence bit her lip and watched his face. It seemed to harden as he said, "Edward and I were treated to any number of lurid tales about our parents' elopement from the other boys—not to mention all sorts of other scandalous doings."

He gave a bitter, self-mocking laugh. "Of course, we didn't believe a word of it. We were convinced both our parents were devoted couples. Edward believed his father the soul of honor and my mother—well, both our mothers were above rubies—you know what boys are." He shrugged ruefully. "We had a great many fights, defending my mother's honor until Edward's house master told us it was true— Mama had indeed run off with Uncle Frederick."

Prudence was appalled. Poor little boys, to be left to tend for themselves in ignorance. And to be told such dreadful news in such a horrid fashion. "And then I suppose you went home to your respective parents."

He gave her an ironic look. "No, for why would anyone want two unhappy boys underfoot at such a time? We stayed at school until Christmas. "

Prudence hugged him tighter. At such times you needed family around you—but she knew all too well that family could not always be relied upon. It was easy in the drama of the hour for the needs of children to be overlooked . . .

"It must have been terrible for you both."

"More so for Edward than me. He loathed the notoriety, of course. The gossip and teasing absolutely flayed him— boys at that age can be very cruel, you know, and he is a great deal more sensitive than I am."

Prudence doubted that. Some people showed sensitivity; others put up a defensive shell and pretended not to care.

"He was a fool. He showed them how much their taunts upset him, you see—lost his temper every time. You wouldn't know it to look at him, but quiet, gentle Edward can be a tiger when roused. Or he was in those days. He fought every blasted one of them! Fatal, of course! And naturally I fought alongside him, even though I knew there was not a particle of use in it."

He shook his head. "I told him and told him he should ignore them, try to laugh it off. . . . Show a bunch of boys you care about something, and it is an open invitation to a kicking. Edward suffered. He really suffered. . . . It got so that he wouldn't speak to anyone except me for months. Not that we ever discussed it. One doesn't, you see . . . And finally . . . finally, Christmas came . . ."

"And you went home—"

He interrupted. "Papa shot himself two days before I came home."

Prudence made a small sound in the back of her throat. Two days before he came home. Two days before Christmas. He must have known his son was coming. Poor, poor little boy to come home to that. "What did you do then? Did the duke's mother—?"

He shook his head. "No. She went into a decline and didn't leave her bed for nearly a year."

There was a long silence, broken only by the sound of the horses' hooves and the creaking of the phaeton as it bowled along the road. He shook his head and said in a light, shaking voice, "When I left for school, Papa was away for the day; my mother and the servants saw me off. The next time I went home, Mama, Papa, and Uncle Frederick were all . . . were all dead, and the servants called me master . . ."

He shrugged and added in a bracing tone, "There was a great deal to be seen to, for the estate had been neglected while Papa had been chasing after Mama."

His words touched her deeply. She could picture it so clearly. The young Gideon, fourteen years old, arriving home, confused, devastated, both his parents having been snatched from him under circumstances of which a young boy could have little understanding. His closest relative, his aunt, prostrate with helpless grief, his cousin withdrawn into a protective shell. And their world prattled of their tragedy as if it were the most delicious of gossip.

The phaeton swayed around a corner. Clouds scudded across the moon.

The servants had called a grieving young boy master and looked to him for orders. No one had comforted him, no one had put their arms around him, or let him weep or rage like a grieving young boy should.

So a shattered, sensitive boy had become a careless, flippant, laughing man, determined to show the world he cared for nothing and therefore could not be hurt. Prudence understood now. She hugged him in silence, her face wet with tears.

"I didn't see Edward for months after the funeral. He never went back to school, never went to Oxford, had himself educated privately, away from the malicious tongues and quiet whisperings. He more or less buried himself on his most remote estate, in the wilds of Scotland; in fact, for a while he became the hermit you accused me of being that first day." His voice lightened deliberately as he said, "How long ago that day seems . . . Ah, look—see that milestone? We are but a mile from Cranford Bridge and thus have come safely across the heath. It is a mere ten miles more to Maidenhead—but of course, you would know that, with your talent in geography. "

He was trying to turn the subject, but she wanted to know more. "Is the duke's mother still alive?"

"Oh, yes, she survived. She even tried once to get Edward to come to London for the season, but it all came to naught—well, not quite." He laughed, a short, dry laugh. "While she was in London, turning the house into a fashionable Egyptian nightmare, she met a fellow, an American, rich as Croesus, and he married her and took her back home to Boston. Delighted to marry a duchess, you see, and she was delighted to leave the old scandal behind her and start afresh in a new country."

"So you and your cousin both ended up alone," Prudence said softly.

They passed through the sleeping village of Longford, woke an ostler at Colnbrook, and paid him well for his pains as they changed horses. The night continued fair and cool and though she was very tired from the long journey and late hour, Prudence's mind was spinning. In this short time she had gained such insight into him . . . and it had thrown her heart into turmoil.

"Salt Hill ahead," Gideon said softly. "On the other side of it lies Maidenhead." They had fallen silent for the last few miles. Miss Prudence was tucked into his shoulder like a drowsy little owl. Unless he missed his guess, she was almost asleep. It had been a long and exhausting day for her, and she would be tired out from her anxieties as well. It would be a long, slow haul up the hill, even for the light phaeton, but in less than an hour they would be at The Blue Pelican and the chambers and light refreshments Edward had bespoken.

She straightened, yawned sleepily, and moved a little away from him. "Have we passed Windsor Castle yet? I believe it is visible from the road."

"No, not yet. It's a little farther on."

"The poor king, I wonder how he is—"

From out of the darkness came the sudden thunder of hooves.

"What the—?"

Two horsemen burst out upon the road ahead of them and bore down on their vehicle as if it wasn't there. At the very last minute, one of the horsemen swerved and passed on a short distance, but the other seemed as if he wished to impale his horse on the shafts of the phaeton. He wrenched to a halt mere inches away.

With the angle of the hill and his horses plunging in fright, it was all Gideon could do to keep them under control. "Blast it, man, what do you think you're—"

"Stand and deliver!" The voice rang out with startling clarity. There was a moment's confusion as the horses continued to plunge and rear. The man in front of them wore a dark muffler wrapped around the lower part of his face. Moonlight glinted on the long barrel of a pistol, aimed straight and steady at the passenger.

At Miss Prudence Merridew.

Gideon's heart froze. Cursing under his breath, he fought to calm the horses. Behind him he sensed his groom moving furtively. "Easy, Boyle," he snapped. "I can handle the nags. No need to get down."

"Right you are, sir," Boyle growled. "Easy and waitin'."

Gideon nodded. Boyle had got the message. Gideon was not talking about the horses. There were two guns under the seat at the back, kept for just such emergencies. And from Boyle's response, he had them in hand and was alert for the first opportunity to use them.

In other circumstances, Gideon might relish the prospect of a fight, but the presence of Miss Prudence sitting silent and still and no doubt terrified on the seat beside him gave him a frantic new sense of caution. There were two highwaymen, spaced well apart; one sat his horse right beside the phaeton; the other lurked several yards behind it, farther back off the road. With the robbers dispersed like that, his groom could probably account only for the one behind them.

Gideon could jump the first man and risk it, of course, but with Prudence sitting motionless and silent, looking down the barrel of the long-nosed pistol, Gideon was not prepared to attempt anything that might endanger her. Silently he cursed himself for not carrying his own pistols. He usually did when traveling. Miss Prudence's anxious need to flee had driven more rational thoughts from his mind, and he'd forgotten them, dammit! Unforgivable carelessness!

Gideon—brainless, besotted Gideon!—had come unarmed, and by doing so had endangered his love!

"What the devil do you think you're about?" he growled at the highwayman. "There's a village just ahead. If you shoot, you'll be heard."

"Aye, mebbe," agreed the robber. "But they be nicely tucked up in bed, and I have a good fast 'orse, so if you'll be so good as to hand over your val'ables, we'll be on our way." The pistol jerked toward Gideon suddenly. "Nice an' easy, me fine gent—no sudden movements. You 'aven't forgotten me partner, 'ave you? 'E's watchin', nice and quiet-like. Nervous, 'e is. Finger very light on the trigger, if you get my drift."

Gideon put his hands where the highwayman could see them, one hand wrapped around the reins, the other resting protectively on Prudence's knee. The robber was no fool, damn the fellow's eyes! He'd made sure Prudence was between himself and Gideon. If Gideon tried anything, Prudence would be caught in the cross fire. Gideon was nicely hamstrung.

"Come on, missy, hand over the pretties, now."

She didn't make a sound. Gideon watched her out of the corner of his eye. She was sitting bolt upright, one hand clutching her reticule tightly to her, the other hidden in the folds of her cloak. He glanced at her face. She looked extremely pale, but that could be the moonlight. As he took in the expression on her face, Gideon's heart sank. She was going to refuse to hand over her money; he could see it in her eyes and the stubborn, angry set of her jaw.

"Don't argue with the fellow, Imp," he said quietly. "Your safety is not worth the paltry sum you carry in your reticule." He spoke loud enough for the robber to hear.

She glanced at him mutinously. Oh, Lord, he thought in

frustration. Why risk herself for such a small sum when the majority of her money was in the stocking purse concealed beneath her skirts? He was going to have to somehow push her out of the way before he could tackle the robber. Perhaps if they appeared to wrangle over the reticule, it might distract the robber. He hoped Boyle would be able to deal with the one to the rear of them.

"Look, Sis, I know it's your pin money and all you have left for the quarter," he said, affecting a peevish tone, "but really, it isn't worth it. Now give it over, do."

He heard a cross little snort beside him. He turned to the robber and smiled ingratiatingly. "My sister is a little frightened." He squeezed Prudence's knee meaningfully.

"Runs in the family then, don't it, sir," the robber said mockingly. "Now hand it over. I'm out o' patience."

Gideon drew his purse from his pocket and tossed it to the robber. It contained a few guineas only; the majority of his money was in a secret pocket in his greatcoat.

"And I'll take that little box thing on yer lap, miss."

Prudence glared at the robber but handed over the Egyptian reticule without fuss. Gideon felt his breath release. Thank God. She was going to be sensible, after all.

"Right. And now I'll 'ave that gold chain round yer pretty neck."

Gideon felt Prudence stiffen. Her betrothal ring was on the end of that chain, he suddenly recalled. Oh, Lord, she was going to be difficult. If only the damned robber was on his side of the phaeton.

"'Urry up!" the man behind growled.

The man closest to her said, "See, my friend's getting impatient, and when he's impatient, missy, his finger gets tighter on the trigger. A hair trigger it is, too, and liable to go off at the slightest touch. Now hand over that gold chain!"

"I won't. It is my chain, and you shan't have it"

Gideon groaned inwardly. She was going to get herself killed for the sake of blasted Otterbury's blasted ring. He loosened his hold on the reins, looping them inconspicuously around the brake handle on his right.

The robber gaped. "What did you say? Can't you see

there's a pistol pointin' straight at your heart, girl? Now hand it over!"

She lifted her chin. "No. It's not very valuable, and you wouldn't get much money for it, but it is personally very precious to me, so I shan't give it to you." She placed her hand protectively across her chest.

The robber blinked and swore under his breath. "Stubborn little piece, ain't you? Well, in that case, I'll just 'ave to help meself." He urged his mount closer to the carriage and reached across to grab her.

It was Gideon's chance. With one hand, he shoved Prudence backward and scrambled across her to take a flying leap at the robber.

Something slammed into his shoulder and he missed the robber and plummeted into the road. Something banged against his skull. A flurry of shots rang out. People were shouting. The horses reared and stamped, and the carriage moved jerkily back and forth in response. Gideon, confused and for some reason unable to stand, managed to roll aside to escape the wheels, but it was as if he'd rolled into white-hot coals of fire, the pain in his shoulder was so sudden and intense. There was a lot of cursing, then a thunder of hooves followed by relative silence.

"Steady those horses," he heard Prudence call. "Now, or else your master will be crushed under the wheels."

He heard Boyle respond, though the words were indistinguishable. There was a swish of fabric, and suddenly he was surrounded by softness, the acrid tang of gunpowder, and the smell of gardenias. Prudence gardenias. And a Prudence angel gazing down at him, all blurry and golden and beautiful, with a halo of gold. He gazed, momentarily entranced.

"Put the lantern in front so I can see his wound," snapped the angel. The halo abruptly shifted, and Gideon was forced to squint against the sudden glare as a lantern was placed beside his head.

"He is alive," she called, then murmured softly, "I'm sorry, oh, I am so very sorry . . . I did not mean . . ." She fumbled with the buttons of his waistcoat and then ripped open his shirt. "Oh, good God, the blood."

Blood? He opened his eyes a crack and gazed up into her

lovely face. She was frowning blackly. It was hard to tell if she was blazingly angry or frantically anxious. He tried to smile and pat her hand in reassurance.

She said, "Do not move, I beseech you! Any movement will make it worse!"

He could not argue with that. Whatever it was, it hurt like the very devil. There was a series of ripping sounds, and then she pressed down on his shoulder, hard.

It felt like someone had plunged a red-hot poker into his shoulder.

"Oh, sorry! I know it hurts, but truly I must do this to stop the bleeding."

He had no idea what she was doing, but if she wanted to plunge a red-hot poker into him, he supposed he deserved it for forgetting his pistols. He concentrated on not making a sound. After what seemed like an eternity, the pressure eased slightly, though the poker was burning hotter than ever. She lifted a blood-soaked pad and peered at his shoulder. The face of his groom intruded into his view as well.

Gideon tried to say something, but for some reason his tongue wasn't working.

"Looks like a flesh wound," Boyle said.

"Oh, that's good, isn't it? I mean not good—for, of course, any wound is frightful, but it means no bone has been damaged."

"Aye. Bones is one thing," said Boyle, "but he could bleed to death yet from that little hole."

There was a small, feminine gasp, and Gideon felt the grip on him tighten convulsively. His senses ebbed and flowed. Vaguely he heard Boyle say, "Sorry, miss, didn't mean to alarm you, but I was a soldier, see. We'll have to get him up in the phaeton, get him to a surgeon fast as possible. But first, we'll see what we can do to stop that bleeding. Now if we can just bind that pad back in place . . ."

Gideon felt a sharp wave of pain. As if from a distance he heard, "That's it, miss, good and tight so as it'll stanch the bleeding . . ." Above him, Prudence's face wavered for a moment as the flaming poker was plunged in his shoulder anew.

When he opened his eyes again, he heard Boyle say,

"I've secured the horses so they can't move, so if you'll move, miss, I'll see if I can pick him up."

Pick him up? As if he was a helpless child? Gideon tried to instruct Boyle to do no such thing, and to announce that he would mount the carriage himself, thank you very much! But even as his thick and muzzy tongue tried unsuccessfully to form the words, he felt Boyle's arms slide under him, there was a jolt, and everything went black.

Prudence peered worriedly at Lord Carradice. He was still extremely pale, though not as pale as when Boyle and several sleepy ostlers had carried him into The Blue Pelican at Maidenhead the previous night and had laid him out on the settle in the parlor. He'd been as pale as death then.

She would never forget that dreadful drive—the groom whipping the weary horses over Salt Hill and stopping to waken the inhabitants of the first house they came to and asking for the direction of the nearest surgeon, only to be told the closest one was at Maidenhead, another five miles farther on. So on they'd journeyed, at as fast a pace as the poor horses could manage; Boyle swearing, the whip cracking, the carriage swaying and bounding, and Lord Carradice lying warm and heavy in Prudence's arms, bleeding to death, for all she knew, with darkness all around.

Prudence had clutched his prone body to her, hugging him tightly against her heart. He lay sprawled across her body, insensible, his head cradled in the hollow between her chin and her breast. With one arm she'd held his body securely against her; with her other hand she pressed as firmly and steadily as she could on the pad that covered his wound, the wound that welled warm sticky blood over her fingers the whole time.

She felt so miserable, so frightened, so guilty. If he died . . .

But he had not died.

Now he lay in bed, his eyelashes dark crescents against the pallor of his skin. He lay propped up against his pillows, a bandage around his head and shoulder, and a loose brocade dressing gown draped around him for warmth. Apart from the dressing gown, he was naked from the waist up. The surgeon had advised against trying to clothe him until his gunshot wound was a little better. It was a flesh wound, which was a blessing, she'd been told. But even with the smallest of wounds, there was always a danger of infection and fever, said the surgeon. They were to watch for fever, especially. The head injury was another matter; until he awoke, no further diagnosis could be made.

Prudence lightly touched the skin of his chest. It felt warm, not hot, dry, not clammy. That was good, was it not? She pressed her whole palm to his skin. It felt good.

Too good. She had never touched a man's naked chest, never even seen one. Not Phillip's, even with the intimacy they'd shared, and not any other man's. At Dereham, even the farm laborers worked fully clothed at all times, no matter how hot the weather.

Her fingers stroked through the hair that was sprinkled lightly across his chest. Starting in a wedge, the darkness seemed to arrow down, down below the sheet tucked so firmly around his midriff. It was fascinating to be so close to him. She ought not to be so fascinated; she was supposed to be checking for fever only. But she couldn't seem to help herself.

His eyes opened.

Prudence leaned forward and laid a hand on his arm. "Oh, Gid—Lord Carradice, thank heavens! I've been so worried. How are you feeling?"

Lord Carradice smiled faintly. She'd almost called him Gideon. "All the better for seeing you, my Prudence."

She frowned anxiously. "Yes, but how do you feel? You look frightfully pale."

Gideon reached out and patted her hand. "I feel perfectly well, my dear," he lied. Her fingers clutched his convulsively, and he felt a great deal better.

She gazed at him, her expressive little countenance reflecting a series of emotions: relief, distress, guilt, anxiety. That worried pucker was back between her brows, blast it, deeper than ever. Damn that robber! "I'm sor—" he began.

"I'm so very sorry about what happened," she blurted

distressfully. "I truly never meant you to be injured like that."

He squeezed her hand, wishing he had more strength to gather her against him and smooth out her worries with his other hand. "Do not wrinkle your lovely brow over my injuries, my Prudence. I'm as right as rain. I'm impervious to highwaymen; it's only beauteous redheads I have a weakness for."

She seemed to flinch at that, and avoided his gaze. Gideon frowned, but before he could ask her what troubled her, she said, "I know, oh, I know. I am so very sorry. Indeed, I could not regret it more deeply, I assure you! I would give *anything* for it not to have happened."

Gideon smiled at her passionate tone. The extreme degree of guilt she was exhibiting, the very heartfelt nature of her distress—it could signify only one thing. His gallant defense of her had broken though the barrier of her propriety. His act had forced Miss Prudence to acknowledge there was more between them than simple dalliance, and now she felt guilty for so misjudging him. If that was the case, it was worth getting shot for. He caressed her fingers gently. "So you finally admit it, do you?" he said softly. "About time, Miss Imp."

She snatched her hand back. "Of course I admit it. I have confessed freely to the fault. But you cannot deny you are at least a tiny bit responsible for what happened. Why did you have to jump across me like that at that moment?"

Jump across her? He frowned until he realized she was back to talking about the highwayman. He gave her a very masculine look and explained, "You were in between that blackguard and me. I had to get across you to get to him. It's not your fault."

"No, but if you had warned me at least, signaled your intention in some subtle fashion, it would never have—"

The role of protector suited him, Gideon decided. He rather enjoyed her feminine flutterings after the event, her concern for his well-being. "My dear girl, how would warning you have changed the situation?" His tone was pure indulgence.

"If I had known you were going to leap across me like

that," she said with a thread of acid, "I would no doubt have taken more care not to shoot you."

It took a moment for her words to sink in. *"Taken more care not to shoot me?"* His brows snapped together. "What the devil do you mean? That blasted robber shot me! You had nothing to do with it!"

She shook her head. "No. I shot you. I was aiming at the highw—"

"You shot me?" Lord Carradice's face was a study of bemusement and disbelief. *"You shot me?"*

Prudence bit her lip. "Yes, my lord."

"With what? If that scoundrel Boyle passed you a pistol—"

"No, I used my mother's pistol."

"Your mother's p—"

"Yes, it was hidden under my cloak. It's quite small and handy, see?" She bent down and took a small silver pistol from a basket beside the bed and showed it to him. His hand reached for it, then hesitated.

"It's all right," she assured him, "it's not loaded anymore. And I've cleaned it."

He looked at her from under his brows. "Thank you, I have handled a pistol before." He picked up the pistol, examining it carefully.

"Mama and Papa always carried pistols when we traveled in Italy—even for quite short trips. I told you we'd encountered *banditti* in Italy several times when I was a child. Don't you remember?"

He waved a vague hand, signifying something.

"So naturally, I packed it."

"Oh, naturally. Your mama's pistol . . ." He put the pistol down, leaned back against the pillows, and covered his face with his hands. "Go on." His voice was muffled.

Prudence looked at him doubtfully. He seemed suddenly weaker, and his chest was heaving in quick bursts. "Yes, I had it in my reticule of course, but—"

A muffled sound came from Lord Carradice.

"Are you feeling unwell again, sir?" Prudence bent forward.

He shook his head and mumbled from behind his hands, "No, no. Continue, if you please."

She frowned, but sat back and folded her hands. "Very well. I took the pistol out of my reticule when the robber first rode up and had it hidden under my cloak. I am extremely sorry. I did not mean to shoot you, of cour—"

"Oh, well as long as you did not *mean* to . . ." His shoulders heaved.

"You're laughing!" Prudence accused.

He moved his arm to reveal a face that was indeed alive with laughter. "Who, me? How could I possibly laugh at such a situation? Shot by the woman I was trying to defend, by gad! And I imagined myself such a gallant devil, wounded while protecting one of the weaker sex!" His dark eyes danced with mischief. "And all the time the weaker sex had winged me!"

She frowned at him and he instantly added in a pathetic voice, "I am a wounded man. You've mistaken laughter for pain—extreme pain. I need someone to soothe me. My pulse is tumultuous with pain—see? Lay your head here, Miss Prudence, and you will hear how my heart is pounding." With one hand he patted his chest, while the other feebly beckoned her closer.

She looked at him mistrustfully, guilt warring with annoyance and anxiety. He was funning . . . but he *was* wounded. She had never seen anyone bleed so much. For all his nonsense he might be in more pain than she believed . . . He was the kind of man who joked to hide his deeper feelings, after all. Should she check his pulse?

When she didn't move, he sighed deeply. "I see, you don't care if I expire. You did mean to shoot me, after all."

"Of course I did not mean to," she assured him indignantly. "I was aiming at the highwayman, meaning to wound him in his shooting arm, only for most of the time his horse's head was in the way so I could not get a clear shot at him. That's why I got him to come closer—"

"Got him to come—" He sank back against the pillows and stared at her in silence for a moment. "You mean that little piece of insanity was a *deliberate ploy to get an armed highwayman to come closer to you?*"

Prudence avoided his accusing stare. "Well, not exactly a deliberate ploy. I did have no intention of giving him what was on my chain."

"That blasted ring!"

She flushed. "No, not the ring. But I do admit it was convenient for him to move."

"Convenient!"

"Yes! And it would have worked, except you leaped in front of me, banging my arm just as I was shooting, and so . . . so the wrong man got shot!"

"The wrong man . . ." Gideon sank into the pillows and put a feeble hand to his forehead. "What a relief. And here I was wondering if you had come to my bedchamber to finish me off."

She gave him a schoolmistressy look. "I may very well change my mind and do just that!"

He looked at her soulfully. "You're a hard woman, Miss Prudence. So, are you responsible for the lump on my head, as well?"

Since he clearly didn't recall the whole of what had occurred, Prudence's conscience forced herself to finish telling him the tale, no matter how mortifying it was. "No, of course not. When I . . . er—"

"Shot me," he prompted helpfully.

She gave him a look of reproof, threaded with guilt. "I know. There is no need to keep repeating yourself!" She smoothed a wrinkle in the bedcovers and continued, not meeting his eye, "Well, after that, you plummeted off the carriage, startling the highwayman's horse—"

"Remiss of me."

She gave him a single, piercing look and he sat back, satisfied. "It reared in fright, and we are not sure whether that is how you hit your head or whether one of your own horses kicked you a few moments later, for—"

"Oh, undoubtedly my own nags. Everyone joining in the fun, it seems."

"Nonsense! We were all very upset—"

"Even the horses?"

"Particularly the horses. It must be excessively upsetting

to have somebody rolling around beneath your hooves while guns are being fired."

The amusement dropped from his face. His hand shot out and grabbed her by the wrist, "Guns, you say? More than one? Did that blasted swine shoot back at you?"

His gaze ran over her intently, anxiously, and Prudence felt herself flushing at his warm concern. She was unused to protectiveness in a man and found it unutterably appealing. She shook her head. "No, I am perfectly well. The shots were from your man, Boyle, who, in the confusion, managed to fire at the highwayman and his partner. They took fright and galloped away. In fact, our robber," she added confidingly, "got such a fright when I fired that he dropped my reticule and Boyle retrieved it for me. So that was lucky, wasn't it?"

He gave her a look and said in a dry voice, "Oh, extremely lucky," and closed his eyes.

There was a short silence, and she wondered what he was thinking.

He opened his eyes and fixed her with a suddenly intent look. "What did you mean, *'not the ring'*?"

Prudence pretended not to understand. She gave him a blank look and smoothed his sheet busily. "Are you thirsty? Do you need anything?"

"Stop avoiding the question. I thought you'd chosen to risk your life rather than hand over Ottershank's blasted betrothal ring. But when I said so just now, you said, *'No, not the ring.'*"

Prudence shrugged in embarrassment. "I'd already given the robber the ring. I'd taken it off earlier. It was in my reticule."

He gaped at her, and she added defensively, "I couldn't risk everyone's lives for a ring, even if it is valuable and an Otter*bury* family heirloom. So I handed it over. Phillip would understand."

Lord Carradice sat up, but before he could ask the question that sprang to his lips, she added accusingly, "And as for risking your life, well, I didn't think you'd be in any danger, because I was between you and the man's pistol—except that you took it into your head to jump in front of me, that is! And if anyone is to be castigated for taking insane risks—"

"Well dash it all, Imp, it's my job to protect you! Of course I jumped the blasted villain! As soon as he mentioned that blasted ring, I knew you'd—"

"Chain," she corrected him. "He only mentioned the chain. And I don't expect you to protect me. I can protect myself, thank you. I have been doing it for years."

Gideon flung her an exasperated look. What the devil was he to do with such a woman? Protect herself, indeed! It galled him unbearably to reflect that she had remembered to provide herself with the means of protection when he had neglected to do so. He attempted to harness his temper and said in a clear, reasoned tone, "At the time I believed the chain was attached to the blasted ring, and I knew—at least I imagined—you wouldn't hand that over!"

A thought occurred to him. "And while we're explaining things, would you mind telling me why you would happily hand over a ring you told me you made a sacred promise on? You told me you hadn't taken it off for four years, so I would have thought that of all things—"

"Yes, I know," she jumped in hastily. "And I wasn't *happy* about it, not at all. But, after all, it is the *promise* that is sacred, not the ring. The ring is a token and a symbol, but it represents something that cannot be stolen—my promise to marry Phillip."

"That doesn't explain why you took it off." There was some significance in it, he was sure. There had to be.

To his fascination, she blushed and began to busy herself smoothing his bedclothes, fussing around him like a small, anxious hen, but hovering at the end of his bed, well out of his reach. "I took the ring off the chain when we were back in London, when you were inside that house."

And she'd given the highwayman Otterbury's ring.

"So you risked your life for a simple gold chain?"

He watched as she tucked the sheet tight around his feet, as if her life depended on it, head down to hide her blush. "In truth, I hadn't intended using the pistol, unless it looked like he was going to shoot one or all of us. But when he noticed the chain and demanded I hand it over—"

"Can you adjust these covers? They feel dashed tangled."

Absentmindedly she moved to the head of the bed and started straightening his bedclothes as she explained, "I simply couldn't hand it over, just as I knew I couldn't sell it. I mean, it's not as if he would value it, because it isn't very valuable to anyone except me—and my sisters of course. To us it is priceless."

"Ahh, that's better," murmured Gideon. "Oh, and there's a devilishly uncomfortable wrinkle under here that's most . . ."

She bent to tug at the undersheet. "And so I did risk it, and while I did not intend it, you were hurt, and for that I most sincerely apologize."

"Oh that's all right, Miss Imp. I survived. Maybe if I move like this and you bend down you could get it . . ."

She bent over him obediently, striving to remove the nonexistent wrinkle. Her hands brushed underneath his legs. He could smell the scent of her hair, the faint gardenia fragrance of her soap.

"Show me what is on the chain," he murmured in her ear.

She hesitated, then reached inside her bodice and drew out an old-fashioned locket attached to the gold chain.

Gideon nodded and wrapped his arm around her waist, drawing her closer as he peered at the locket. Of course, the locket. He'd seen her face when she'd placed it with the other jewels for sale, remembered the loving way she'd cupped it in her hands, her yearning reluctance to lose it. It had cut at him, even though he knew she would lose nothing.

Prudence moved to pull the chain over her head, but he stopped her with his hands. "No, don't take it off. I can see it well enough from here." He pulled her closer against him, so she was half sitting, half lying on the bed beside him. His arm around her, he fumbled awkwardly with the locket.

"The catch is faulty," she said. "I've been meaning to have it mended." Her fingers brushed against his as she opened it for him.

There was a short silence as they both gazed into the locket. Gideon could feel the softness of her body relaxed against him. Her scent was intoxicating. He could feel her warm breath on his skin; his own breathing was becoming increasingly ragged. He forced himself to focus on the two slightly lopsided images in the locket. They meant so much to her. A man and a woman with old-fashioned hairstyles. The painting was clumsy. He wondered who they were. He wondered whether she'd painted the miniatures herself. He wondered whether he'd ever be able to let go of her . . .

"It is Mama and Papa. The only pictures of them we have." Her thumb ran caressingly around the gold rim of the locket. "The likenesses are not perfect—they were painted by a young Italian boy who lived in the village and hoped to become a painter. Papa was to be his patron . . ." Her voice caught and wavered on a sob.

Gideon could not bear it.

She bit her lip and said, "I know I should not have taken such a foolish risk, but the thought of never—"

"Hush," Gideon said gently as he tipped her face up to receive his kiss.

Chapter Fourteen

∞

"A woman would run through fire and water for such a kind heart."
WILLIAM SHAKESPEARE

SHE DID NOT PULL AWAY.

He gave her no time to think, but covered her mouth with his, gently, possessively, tenderly, so as not to startle her into flight. She hesitated a moment, then he felt her body relax against him, and she leaned into his embrace. A sharp pain shot through his shoulder, but he ignored it, and his arms tightened around her. He felt her lips soften under his as she began to return his kiss softly, uncertainly, surprise blossoming into desire.

She kissed him gently, carefully, as if he was on his deathbed, not simply suffering a minor flesh wound. He would suffer a dozen such wounds for another of these tender, heartfelt kisses. She tasted of warmth . . . and tears . . . and just a faint hint of tooth powder. Lord, but she was sweet. He could not get enough of her.

Slowly he took the kiss deeper and deeper, the warmth and generosity of her shy response overwhelming him. He had been anticipating this moment since the last time he'd kissed her, but still, it took him unawares. The heady rush, the surge of . . . of *feeling*. Hauntingly familiar and yet piercingly, achingly new.

How many women had he kissed? He did not know. He did not care. None of them had been Prudence.

She put her hands up to hold his face as she kissed him back and at the feeling of those two small, cool hands cupping his cheeks so earnestly as she pressed warm, damp kisses against his mouth, he felt something inside him dissolve. He wanted to shout from the rooftops, he wanted to hoard her like a secret. Had any woman ever left him feeling so . . . so simultaneously powerful . . . and yet so . . . so helpless? He did not know, could not think. All he could do was to kiss her, to hold her . . . and fight the need to possess her, for though they were alone and on a bed, this was not the moment. He knew it.

His much-vaunted seduction techniques—where were they? He could not think straight enough to recall a single move. This was pure instinct, pure aching emotion . . .

Her fingers tangled in his hair, and he felt a fresh surge of tenderness as he coaxed her lips apart and deepened the kiss. Part of him felt like a boy, trembling on the brink of life, and yet another part of him looked on, immensely old. When had he ever been content to merely hold and kiss? When had a kiss not been the first step in a well-rehearsed dance of seduction and pleasure? His body knew the moves, craved them, even if his mind was as scrambled as his morning eggs.

So where had these scruples come from? He could seduce her in an instant, he could feel it. And he needed, more than anything in his life, to possess her, to make her his, flesh of one flesh. And yet . . . and yet . . .

Each careful, moist kiss was precious to him. Each touch of her hand, along his jaw, in his hair, around his neck. The soft, eager press of her body against his, innocent, ignorant of the effect on him. And therein lay the problem. He would rather have a dozen heartfelt, hesitant kisses from her than one night of passion and a morning—possibly a lifetime—of regret. Miss Prudence must come to him with a whole heart and in her own time. There could be no regrets afterward.

That was the difference, he suddenly realized. He was going to spend a lifetime with this woman, and he wasn't going to rush his fences and jeopardize a moment of it. He would harness his urges and savor every instant, every small caress, each loving, untutored kiss.

And so he allowed the embrace to end. He watched her slowly come to her senses, watched the dazed, wide gray eyes focus and awareness slowly flood her. "Oh!" she exclaimed. "Oh, dear!" She pulled herself suddenly out of his arms, jumped up, and began straightening the bedclothes, darting swift, embarrassed glances at him and looking away. Finally she stopped, took a deep breath, and looked him in the eye.

"We . . . I shouldn't have done that," she said at last.

"Should we not?" Gideon could not help but smile at her flustered expression. "Why not?

She sighed. "You know why not. I am not free."

Gideon shrugged. "A few kisses. You make too much of them," he said lightly. "You were sad. I merely comforted you."

She thought about it for a moment, and her brow crinkled uncertainly. "Was that truly the reason?"

"What else?" The casual tone of his words were belied by the look in his eyes. Or was that just her own confusion? Prudence wondered. Her own wishful thinking. She was still trembling deep inside from those few moments of what he called comfort. If that was comfort, then . . . she understood nothing . . .

"Although you might want to check again—I'm certain I must be feverish." He took her hand and laid it to his forehead. A tender smile belied the dark promise in his eyes. He turned her palm inward and pressed it gently to his face. The hollow of her palm cupped his cheekbone, her fingers brushed his smooth brow. It was perfectly cool and not the slightest bit clammy or feverish. Prudence didn't move. Her chest felt suddenly tight. The tips of her fingers just touched the thick, dark, springy hair. She itched to run her fingers through it again, but she couldn't bring herself to move.

His hand lay over hers, warm, strong, and possessive. Slowly, he brushed her hand down over his cheekbones into the hollow of his cheek, warm, male, and unshaven.

Prudence wondered vaguely how a failure to shave could be so wonderfully exciting, but it was, making him seem darker, more dangerous, and excitingly masculine. She shivered as he caressed her hand slowly and sensuously with his face, rubbing against her like a big, lazy cat, his eyes never leaving hers, mesmerizing, enchanting, as skin to skin, the embrace moved along the strong line of his jaw until it reached his lips.

He paused, for what felt like an aeon, and she waited, as if on a precipice, feeling his firm, warm mouth beneath her trembling fingers. Then, slowly, he turned her hand until her palm cupped his mouth. He pressed one kiss into the hollow of her hand, and it was as if her insides turned to melted butter. He pressed another, and her knees began to buckle.

That was what saved her. As her legs trembled and threatened to give way beneath her, she snatched her hand away for balance, for security, for safety. At least that was what she told herself afterward.

She sagged against the end of the bed, clutching at the rails at its foot, and fought for composure.

She tried to make herself angry, but she couldn't.

She tried to convince herself he had taken unfair advantage of her, but she didn't believe it. The truth was, she wanted to fling herself back into his arms and have him kiss her on the mouth again, instead of the hand. And later, maybe she could kiss him on the palm and see if he felt it clear through to the tips of his toes, the way she had.

But she couldn't.

She might wish to be free to to love Lord Carradice, but she wasn't. She'd given Phillip a sacred promise. They'd exchanged rings and . . .

And they'd plighted their troth.

Promises were not to be given lightly. She gave few promises, and when she did, she honored them. She'd been able to control few things in her life; she had no choice in where she lived, with whom, what she wore, who she saw, what she ate, or how she and her sisters were treated. The only thing she truly owned or controlled was her honor.

In any case, her sacred vow did not only involve herself and Phillip. Old and bitter grief began to well inside her. With shaking hands, she fussily began to straighten the items on his bedside table. Some things were too painful to dwell upon.

"What is it?" Lord Carradice frowned as he watched her sudden nervous activity.

Aware of his eyes steadfastly observing her, she snatched a pillow from under his head and plumped it violently, the pillow hiding her face from him.

"Ouch! Take care. That's the head the horse kicked, remember? Now tell me, what has disturbed you?"

"Nothing," she muttered and briskly plumped the next pillow. Activity was better than emotion. When you were busy, you had no time to think.

"Doesn't look like nothing to me," he persisted. "Your eyes are like smoky pools of crystal; every feeling and emotion is reflected in them."

Prudence stopped in mid-pillow-fluff. *Smoky pools of crystal* . . . Nobody had ever said anything half so beautiful to her before. She'd always considered her gray eyes dull and colorless, but *smoky pools of crystal* . . . She averted her gaze abruptly, recalling that they also apparently reflected her thoughts. And if they revealed thoughts, they might also reveal secrets . . .

He reached out and possessed her hand. "Tell me."

It occurred to Prudence for a fleeting moment that she ought to tell him. Though she did not know if she could bear the way he would look at her afterward, she might as well tell him and get it over with, because she didn't think she could withstand his tender assault on her virtue much longer. But as she gazed into his dark, concerned eyes, the coward in her put the moment off a little longer.

"It's not fair of you to undermine my principles, to disregard what I have told you about my betrothal."

"Haven't you heard, Imp, all's fair in love—"

She cut him off. "But you have all the advantage here!"

He touched his bandage and regarded her soulfully. "I do?"

"Yes! And stop looking at me like that. You know perfectly well what I mean. Phillip can't compete with you. He is far away across the sea, and you are here." He did not conceal his satisfaction at that, so she added crushingly, "Always underfoot! He was little more than a boy when I saw him last, whereas you are a man of practiced charm. Very practiced!"

He grimaced.

"You need not pull that face. You know it's true, whether you like the fact or not. And pretty compliments drip easily from your tongue—"

He ostentatiously wiped his mouth.

"—while poor Phillip writes staid and matter-of-fact letters. But not all men can be poets and it would be shallow of me indeed if I abandoned him because he does not make my head whirl with pretty compliments and you—" She broke off, seeing by the look in his eyes that she'd said too much. "Whatever, it does not matter. I am not so shallow nor so dishonorable as to jilt Phillip in his absence, so we shall drop the subject henceforth, if you please."

Apparently he didn't please. "If he doesn't make your head whirl—and I'm not referring to compliments—he's not the man for you, Imp. Duty and honor is a dashed dry foundation for a marriage. Oh, I know many make it, but you deserve more, my Prudence. You need—and deserve—to be most thoroughly and completely loved. And by a man who makes your head whirl."

His words and the look in his eyes as he said them robbed her momentarily of breath. Prudence avoided his gaze. She felt shaky. Blast the man—just as she had bolstered her resolution to resist him, he must go and say something else that made her yearn for her life to be different. To have been different.

"I have to go," she said. "I shall order a nuncheon to be brought to you."

A slight frown wrinkled his brow. "Something else is disturbing you, and I intend to discover what it is. I don't like to see those shadows in your lovely eyes, my Prudence."

"I am *not* your Prudence," she retorted, taking refuge in propriety.

He did not argue, just smiled at her in a deeply masculine way that annoyed her, even as her insides melted.

"I'm not!" she argued, flustered.

He arched an eyebrow at her.

"I don't understand why you persist with this nonsense! I thought we'd agreed to drop the subject!"

He sent her a sizzling look. "You agreed. I didn't."

"It is not for discussion. I can do nothing until I see or hear from Phillip. I'm sorry, but that's how it is. Besides, there are things between him and me that..." She broke off. "Well, never mind that."

"I shan't mind if you don't," he agreed. "But I'll not let you go, Prudence. I'll not pester you, but know this: I will wait until you choose to listen to your heart."

"Pshaw." It was a feeble effort. She took a deep breath and tried again. "Humbug! How can you presume to know my heart?"

He smiled a slow, devastating smile. "You *are* my heart." He lifted her hand and kissed it. "And our hearts beat in tune. I know it—I, who used not to believe in such things. And you know it."

She shook her head but was too shaken by his words to say anything. *Our hearts beat in tune. I know it—I, who used not to believe in such things.* Did that mean what she thought it meant? That he, a notorious rake, now believed in love . . . even after what he'd told her of his parents? Because of her?

Oh, dear Lord, what a mess she was in. Promised to one man and bound by honor and duty to keep that promise. And yet . . . and yet . . . Oh, unruly heart!

Even if he wasn't being rakish, even if he meant what he said, that he could perhaps have feelings for her, he didn't know her whole situation. He would think differently about her if he did. She tried to comfort herself with the reflection. Cold comfort . . .

She had learned enough about the world that in some matters, at least, Grandpapa and society were as one.

"Don't fret yourself, my dear," he said. "I know you hold your promise to Otterbottom sacred and I cherish you the more for it. Kept promises have not figured largely in my life till now, so I value one when I see it. But I *shall* wait for you."

Prudence just looked at him. *I cherish you the more for it.* Oh, why must he use such words? He would not cherish her if he knew . . .

She would have to tell him. It was the only way. Only then would he stop this relentless, tender wooing that was tearing her apart. She swallowed and took a deep breath, then closed her eyes.

No, she could not do it, not now. Not yet. She could not

bear to tend him in his sickbed while he stared at her in disappointment. Or condemnation. Or worse.

She would not even think the words her grandfather used so freely on her.

But it would flay her alive to have Gideon say them—or even think them. She would have only a little time more with him. It was cowardly of her, she knew, but she would not tell him the truth until he was well again, and she could flee his condemnation in good conscience. She gave his bedclothes one last vague, distracted swipe and turned to leave.

His hand shot out and caught her wrist. "Trust me, Imp." His voice was deep and dark and soft with sincerity.

Her heart seemed to seize in her chest like a hard, cold ball. She froze, closing her eyes. He was right. It was time. She could put the moment off no longer. And if he . . . after he knew the story, if he . . . well, her sisters could tend him. They'd be glad to, she knew.

"Very well, since you insist, the whole story." She fetched a hard, wooden chair from the corner of the room and sat a few feet from the edge of his bed. She didn't think she could do it if he was too close and able to reach out and touch her.

Folding her hands in her lap, she looked at him for one last moment, drinking in the last moments of his warm, unshadowed gaze. After this there would be a different kind of knowledge in his eyes, and she didn't think she would care to look into his dark, dark eyes again and see it there. Not with the memory of tenderness and laughter. She took another deep breath, then with trembling lips, began to burn her bridges.

"I never thought any of us would marry. Grandpapa said our blood was inferior and we should not spread the mongrel taint."

Gideon stiffened, but before he could say anything, she held up her hand and continued, "It's all right. We know we are not mongrels. He hated our mother, you see, and considers her blood tainted, but there was *nothing* at all wrong with her," she added in an impassioned voice. "She was beautiful and loving and—" She broke off and took a deep breath. "Mama's family was not gently born. Her grandfather began as a butcher and his son, our grandfather, was also in the butchery trade, so they were what Grandpapa calls cits, though immensely rich ones. We do not care, of course, but because of his prejudices, Grandpapa would not allow us to go about or to attend any of the local functions—except for church, and even then we had services in our private chapel when possible. But the point of all this is that we girls grew up not knowing many people.

"Phillip's parents owned the property next to Grandpapa's. We did not know him, for he and his older brother were away at school, but we did know Mrs. Otterbury from church, so we knew of him. Anyway, one day while we were out walking, we met him. His horse had gone lame and Phillip was leading it home, taking a shortcut through the Court—that's Dereham Court, where we lived—to spare the horse, so of course, we started talking and, oh! You have no idea how wonderful it was to talk to someone other than my sisters, someone of my own age!" Her eyes shone with a soft, reminiscent glow. "That day I walked with him to the edge of the property and we just talked and talked—about everything and nothing."

"How old were you?" Gideon interjected, feeling ridiculously envious of that glow.

"Oh, about fifteen, I think," she said. "And from then on, we met often, in secret, of course. His mother used to visit occasionally, which was unexceptional, since she did not bring Phillip. And though Grandpapa did not like her coming and was shockingly uncivil to her, there was no actual reason for him to forbid her visits." She smiled reminiscently. "She is very kind, Mrs. Otterbury, and put up with all sorts of rudeness in order to visit us."

It occurred to Gideon that Mrs. Otterbury recognized an opportunity for her younger son when she saw it. Each of the Merridew girls were reputed to be handsomely dowered; an ambitious mother would certainly brave more than incivility to secure a fortune for a son otherwise unprovided for. His Prudence was too unworldly to see a more mercenary motive in her neighbor's sudden friendliness.

Prudence continued, unaware of his cynical thoughts, "The little ones, particularly, loved her visits, as they have few memories of Mama, and Mrs. Otterbury was so warm and kind and . . . and *motherly*. You know, she even cuddled them sometimes, and it was so wonderful—little girls need to be cuddled frequently, you know."

"So do big ones," he said softly and held out his hand to her.

She shook her head, but her color heightened. "You think there are only a few shared childhood memories binding me to Phillip, don't you, apart from the promise and the ring? There is more. I did not plan to tell you . . . but perhaps if I do, you will understand and cease this . . . this . . ."

"Courtship," prompted Gideon.

She gave him a look he couldn't interpret. "Just let me explain."

"Very well." Gideon leaned back and folded his arms and prepared to listen.

"Phillip's departure for India was very sudden. I had no idea he was going anywhere until just a day or two beforehand."

Young men just didn't up and leave on the spur of the moment to take up a position in India, thought Gideon. It wasn't like taking the stagecoach to London; the trip to India took months. There were all sorts of arrangements to be made: passages to book, clothes to be fitted, special supplies to be purchased, such as remedies against tropical diseases; the list was long. He'd wager Phillip had been busy preparing for his journey for some time; he simply hadn't chosen to inform Prudence.

"It was very distressing," Prudence said. "I didn't know if I would ever see him again—it's terribly dangerous in India."

"So Miss Grace informs me," Gideon murmured.

"Yes. Phillip wanted me to marry him and go, too, but of course I was too young to be able to wed without permission, and in any case, Grandpapa was growing more . . ." She hesitated. "I suppose you would call it . . . harsh. So I couldn't leave the children with him, and Phillip said India was too dangerous for the younger girls."

"Not too dangerous for a sixteen-year-old?"

"Oh no, for I am not at all frail or helpless. Besides, Phillip said he could protect me from danger."

Gideon managed not to snort. He was hardly in a position to criticize, after all.

"But it was not practical for all five of us to go, even with the assistance of my dowry—Papa's will leaves us money even if we marry without permission, you see—for that is what he and Mama did."

Gideon nodded. He did indeed see. Otterbury tried to persuade a lonely sixteen-year-old to wed him on the sly, knowing she came with a handsome dowry.

"Phillip proposed to me at The Cairn —that's what we call Mama and Papa's grave—and don't look like that, it isn't really their grave, but we girls made a pile of stones in a corner of the Merridew family burial yard. It is next to the Dereham private chapel, so nobody goes there except family and the gardener who keeps it tidy. We planted flowers around The Cairn and when we were lonely or unhappy, we used to go and talk to Mama or Papa. It was a comfort, you see. We'd tell them things, just small items only of importance to family—like girlish secrets and Grace's teeth."

Gideon frowned. "Her teeth?"

Prudence smiled, "Every one of her baby teeth was added to The Cairn with great ceremony. Teeth falling out are exciting for a child, and no one else at Dereham was interested, but Mama and Papa were always listening. That's what we thought, anyway." She smiled to herself, a little misty-eyed.

"So that's where Otterclogs proposed?" Gideon said. *Cunning bastard,* he thought.

"Yes, he asked their permission first and then—" She broke off at the sound of a soft knock on the door.

"How is our wounded hero?" a low, feminine voice called. Gideon swore under his breath.

"It is Charity!" she explained, clearly flustered by the interruption. "I—er, I didn't tell them it was I who shot you! They think it was the robber!"

Gideon nodded. "Your bloodthirsty tendencies are safe with me, Miss Imp." Dammit, she'd been about to explain the hold that blasted Otterbury had on her. He was in no mood to entertain visitors, but he could see she'd snatched at the interruption like a drowning man snatches at a straw.

She jumped up and opened the door. Charity entered on tiptoe, carrying a covered tray. "Is he awake?" she whispered.

"I'm awake, Miss Charity," Gideon responded.

"He's awake!" A cluster of golden heads peered around the door and in seconds his bed was surrounded by sisters and his cousin.

Prudence, suddenly recalling his chest was naked but for the bandage, quickly whisked the sheet up around his chin and tucked it in firmly, watched by four pairs of curious female eyes.

"How do you feel, Coz?" asked Edward. Gideon winked, and Edward relaxed.

"Oh, you poor, brave man, thank heavens you're recovering. I've brought you some nice, hot gruel." Charity set the tray on a nearby chest and lifted the cloth to reveal a spouted invalid bowl, containing an ominously gray liquid.

Gideon pulled a face. He had no intention of drinking gruel.

"Oh look, he's in pain," exclaimed Faith. "You're very brave, sir."

"Is it very painful?" asked Hope.

"Of course it is," said Grace scornfully. "He bled everywhere, all over the landlady's best sofa. It's absolutely ruined!" she pronounced with relish. "Did you kill any of the villains, Lord Carradice? Prudence wouldn't discuss it."

"That's quite enough, Grace, dear," interrupted Prudence hastily. "We don't want to exhaust Lord Carradice, do we?"

"Oh, Lord Carradice wouldn't mind," the invalid murmured. "A little exhaustion, in a good cause . . ."

Prudence blushed and seized the invalid bowl. "This gruel will help you get your strength back, sir."

"No, I thank you, some beef and burgun—"

The spout was deftly inserted between his teeth. Gideon spluttered and tried to object, but the vile stuff was poured gently but ruthlessly down his throat.

His visitors stayed and chatted for some few minutes, and pleasant though it was, Gideon soon found that he was indeed exhausted.

Prudence picked up on it instantly. "I think our invalid needs to sleep now," she declared. When the visitors had left the room, she came back to his bedside, gently smoothed his pillows, and tucked him in. Like a babe, he thought in disgust.

"Sleep now," she whispered, passing a hand across his brow.

He caught it and held her hand against his cheek. "I still don't know what your terrible secret is, my dear, but there is nothing you could tell me that would make a difference. You have led a sheltered life—" He held up a weary hand. "No, don't argue with me. I have no doubt that what you think scandalous and unforgivable would not be so very dreadful to a man such as myself. I shall wait. It will make no difference to me."

He subsided, and Prudence turned to leave. His words stopped her in her tracks. "I shall wait for you until I am old and gray if I must. But I'll have you in the end, my Prudence. And you'll come to me with a whole heart, you'll see."

Prudence was stunned. He would wait for her until he was old and gray? The look in his eyes caused her heart to pound. She put out a shaking hand as if to hold him off, though he wasn't touching her, and hadn't made a move toward her. "But you are a rake," she whispered.

He gazed into her eyes for a long, long moment. "Yes. And when a rake finally falls, he falls forever." He let her digest that for a moment and then added solemnly, "Besides, you should not scorn my rakishness. Having a rake about the place will come in extremely useful."

She frowned in puzzlement. "Useful?" It was an odd word to use. "What do you mean? What possible use would I have for a rake?"

"I could tidy up all your fallen leaves each autumn."

It took her a moment to perceive the jest. Laughter and tears trembled on her lips at the same time. Oh, what to do with him? How could anyone love such a wicked, funny, foolish man?

How could they not?

Prudence left the room.

Chapter Fifteen

∞

"But having done whate'er she could devise
And emptied all her Magazine of lies
The time approached . . ."
JOHN DRYDEN

THE CITY OF BATH ROSE FROM A GREEN AND VERDANT VALLEY, THE afternoon sun seeming to gild the rows and rows of terraced houses rising in serried ranks like the steps of an amphitheater.

"I had no notion Bath was so beautiful, so very splendid!" exclaimed Prudence.

Hope and Faith peered out from the coach windows on one side, while Prudence and Grace peered from those on the other. Lord Carradice observed the young ladies indulgently, pointing out various sights along the way, lounging on his seat, his coat slung around his shoulder in a careless style that disguised the bandaging.

"No, indeed!" agreed Grace. "I was quite misled by the name. Bath!" she pronounced in mild disgust. "Who would expect such a dull name to be given to such an interesting looking place."

"Ah, but the name has a romance of its own, Miss Grace," explained Lord Carradice. "You see, since ancient times people have traveled for miles to drink from and bathe in the mineral springs here. Even the ancient Romans valued it and built a fine city here. Can you imagine brave Roman centurions bathing here, Miss Grace, after a battle with the wild barbarians of the north?"

"Oh, yes. Washing away the blood of battle!" Grace nodded, shivering deliciously.

Lord Carradice chuckled. "Bloodthirsty little wench! I suspect they washed that off long before they got to Bath!"

"It is almost as if the Romans are still here, so grand and beautiful some of the buildings are," said Faith. And indeed, there was so much classically inspired architecture in evidence, the town did boast a decided Roman character.

Once Lord Carradice was well enough to travel, they'd completed the journey in easy stages, stopping a night in Hungerford before continuing on to Bath in the morning. Prudence and Lord Carradice rode in the duke's carriage with the girls, while the Duke drove Lord Carradice's phaeton, Charity seated beside him. Lily and James sat atop the carriage, enjoying the sights in the mild weather.

It had been an unexpectedly merry journey—more like a picnic excursion than an illicit flight from their legal guardian. There had been no further accidents, and no highwaymen or injuries. Lord Carradice, who seemed unfazed by his wound, had proved to be a most entertaining companion, telling ridiculous tales, which had Prudence and her sisters in fits of laughter, teaching the younger girls to make up scurrilous rhymes about the various acquaintances they'd made along the way—the waiter who sneezed on the tureen of broth and then wondered why it came back untouched, forsooth! Lord Carradice had argued strenuously on behalf of that *forsoth* rhyme, claiming that when he was a boy, everyone pronounced it so!

Howled down, he then demanded the girls soothe his bruised pride with music, and then when he discovered how few songs they actually knew, he set himself to teaching them. So they'd arrived in Bath a happy, laughing, singing throng.

Prudence could have hugged him. Not since their parents had died had her sisters laughed and sung and giggled with such riotous glee. More than anything, it quelled her anxiety about whether she was doing the right thing. Even if it all ended in disaster, at least they'd had this.

The carriage wended its slow way through the steep streets of Bath. The girls stared, entranced at the sights to be seen at this still-fashionable watering place. Charity and the duke were ahead of them by some hours, having left earlier in the faster, lighter phaeton.

They were hanging out of the windows, exclaiming over the sights, when suddenly Hope exclaimed, "Good gracious! It can't be! No, it is, I'm sure of it. Prudence look! It's Phillip!"

"Phillip?"

"Phillip Otterbury, you goose! What other Phillips do we know?"

"It can't be. He's in India."

"Well, obviously he's returned," retorted Hope impatiently. "He's there, in the street—walking away from us now, do you see? In the brown coat and a curly-brimmed hat!"

Prudence peered out of the coach, as did all her sisters. "I can't see anyone in a brown coat."

"There's a young man in a bottle-green coat who looks a bit like Phillip, only much shorter," offered Faith.

"Not the one in bottle-green, hen-wit! The brown coat—oh, he's turned the corner and gone now. Didn't *any* of you see him?" Hope demanded in exasperation. But none of the others had seen anyone who even slightly resembled Phillip Otterbury.

"You must have made a mistake, Hope." Prudence sat back on her seat and smoothed her skirt. She was feeling quite shaky.

"I didn't. It was Phillip, I'm sure of it!" insisted Hope.

"How would you know after all this time?" asked Faith. "It is so long since we saw him, I certainly don't have any clear recollection of how he looked."

"Don't you?" Hope frowned. "I'm sure I remember him. He was very good-looking—surely you remember that?"

Lord Carradice frowned.

Hope continued, "And this man looked just like him . . .

extremely handsome, only a little bit older. And thinner. And browner," she added with clearly diminishing confidence.

"Hope, dearest, even I have trouble recalling exactly how Phillip looks," Prudence said gently.

"Indeed?" Lord Carradice murmured. "How very interesting."

Prudence ignored him. "I'm sure this man in the brown coat did look a little like Phillip, but you know, we have only been gone from the Court six weeks and if Phillip had been expected home, Mrs. Otterbury would have informed the world as soon as she'd heard. You know what she's like. The whole district would have known of his planned return within hours of her receiving the letter. Even if a letter came the day we left, Phillip would still be weeks or more behind it, I'm sure, and we would have heard."

Hope sighed. "That's true. I suppose it wasn't him, after all. For what would he be doing in Bath, anyway?"

Faith put an arm around her sister. "No doubt Phillip being so much in our minds of late, you wanted him to be here and were caught by a passing resemblance."

Hope nodded. "If Phillip were here, he'd be able to save us."

"Well, Lord Carradice is saving us instead!" declared Grace fiercely. "And I'd much rather be saved by him than Phillip, any day!"

"Thank you, Miss Grace. One does hope one's poor efforts are appreciated," murmured Lord Carradice. He sighed lugubriously, and somehow everyone's eyes were drawn to the injury he had received while saving them. Only he and Prudence knew who had actually shot him.

Hope exclaimed, "Oh, sir, I hope you did not think me ungrateful!"

"No, no, Miss Hope, not at all." Lord Carradice waved her apologies away. "Now, up there on our left is Milson Street, where all the fashionable shops are to be found." The girls peered out in the direction he'd pointed, while he lounged back against the seats and gave Prudence a quizzing look.

Prudence found herself blushing. Grace had uncannily given voice to Prudence's own thoughts. She would indeed

much rather be rescued by Lord Carradice than by her betrothed! She stared out the window and tried to put the
thought from her mind.

"Here we are," said Lord Carradice. The carriage drew up in
front of a long row of terraced mansions, built of creamy
gold stone and laid in a magnificent arc around a circular
park enclosed with iron rails.

"Which house is it, sir?" asked Grace eagerly.

Which *house?* Prudence felt a sudden twinge of anxiety.
She had been utterly remiss in agreeing to this! They could
not stay in a house owned by Lord Carradice or the duke.
Not under the same roof as an unmarried man. An unmarried
man who was in no way related to them. An unmarried man
who had a reputation as a rake! Not even with four sisters to
play chaperone. It simply could not be done.

Traveling with Lord Carradice and the Duke of Dinstable
had been almost unexceptional—even the highest sticklers
would not have had much to cavil at five unmarried girls
traveling with their maid and footman and escorted by two
unmarried gentlemen, even if the gentlemen were unrelated
to them. She squashed the thought about traveling in the
phaeton at night with an unmarried man and his groom—
after all, it *was* an open carriage. And there was no room for
anyone else. And it had been an emergency. And besides,
nobody knew . . .

But to reside, even for a short time, under the same roof
as those gentlemen, no! It could not be done. Even if Charity were to marry the duke, Prudence would not wish it
whispered about that the duke had been forced to do so, having compromised the lady.

They would have to stay at a hotel. Or take rooms with a
respectable landlady.

"I don't think we—" Prudence began.

"The three houses with the yellow doors are ours," interrupted Lord Carradice, in answer to Grace's question. "The
one on the left is mine, the one on the right is my cousin's,
and the one in the middle is where our Aunt Augusta lives.
She's expecting us—I sent a message ahead when I was laid
up on my sickbed. You'll love Aunt Gussie, I know. She's

the very best of our mothers' family." He glanced at Prudence and added wryly, "Had Aunt Gussie not been living in Argentina at the time, I doubt our parents would have made such a mull of it all. But she's only recently arrived in Bath and is finding it dull after being abroad for so many years. She is, no doubt, in transports of delight at the prospect of guests."

"You mean we are to stay with your aunt?" gasped Prudence in relief. "And not with you and the duke?"

He gave her a reproachful look but said nothing as the twins began to alight. Then, as Grace stepped down the carriage steps, he shook his head and added in a voice of injured innocence, "Stay with me and the duke? I am shocked at the suggestion, Miss Imp, shocked! I may be a rake, but I do have a passing acquaintance with the rudiments of propriety, you know. And you would not wish to stay in Edward's house, for his mother's decorating genius reached here also, and the inside is distressingly Egyptian. Roman outside, Egyptian within." He shuddered. "I fear any resident other than Edward would be obliged to resort, like Cleopatra, to an asp! He, of course, is inured to it."

He leaped lightly from the carriage and held out an imperious hand to assist her to alight. As she stepped down he bent low toward her and murmured in her ear, "In fact, I did plan for you to stay at my house—purely for protection, you understand—but Edward would not have it, you see. The stuffy fellow is such a stickler for the proprieties! Can't imagine how we can be related." He stepped back, winked, and offered her his uninjured arm.

Prudence didn't respond. She couldn't. A lump in her throat prevented her. He'd planned for them to stay with his aunt all along. She was beginning to perceive the pattern of it; whenever she was worried or fretting about something, he produced some piece of nonsensical impropriety to shock her and thus tease her anxieties away . . . kindness and thoughtfulness buried beneath a disguise of bold and flippant rakishness.

She mounted the steps in silence.

The middle yellow door was flung open, and a short, immensely round lady dressed in purple and gold silk bustled down the steps.

"Ladies, I would like to present my aunt, Lady Augusta Montigua del Fuego. Aunt Gussie, may I present the Misses Merridew. This is Miss —" began Gideon, but the lady cut across him.

"Not now dear, it's far too chilly to be standing about doing the pretty. My dears, come in, come in—you must be starving!" She gathered the girls together like a small, friendly whirlwind and whisked them inside, talking nineteen to the dozen.

"In here, my dears. My how lovely you all are . . . Yes, yes, give Shoebridge your pelisses and hats—and tea and cakes at once, Shoebridge. Gideon, what on earth have you done to your arm? In the back parlor, Shoebridge—so much more cozy, my dears. And Shoebridge, I am not at home to anyone . . . Does anyone wish to visit the necessary? No? Oh, the joy of young bladders!"

She took a deep breath and before anyone could respond, continued without a pause, "Now, my dears, which of you is Prudence—oh, you must be she, of course—such beautiful eyes. Gideon, dear boy, you are a rascal, and I'm utterly delighted!" She gathered the astonished Prudence in a soft, perfumed embrace, adding, "And I am still waiting for you to explain to me this sinister-looking bandage!"

Prudence gave a guilty start. Did this amazing little woman know Prudence was responsible for his injury? She opened her mouth to admit all, but the lady was still speaking.

"And why am I also still waiting for a kiss from the wickedest of my neph—! Oof! Put me down, you wretched boy! You cannot possib—!"

Gideon swept his aunt up into an exuberant one-armed hug, lifting her completely off her feet and swinging around in a circle.

"Aunt Gussie, Aunt Gussie, you are an eternal delight to me! Never, never change!" he said, planting a hearty kiss on each delicately rouged plump cheek.

"Put me down, you dreadful creature!" Dainty slippered feet kicked fruitlessly, six inches above the floor.

All four Merridew sisters stared, openmouthed. Grace giggled first; then the twins joined in. Prudence was too befuddled to do anything except stare. She could see Lord Carradice twirling a short, plump lady, laughing with her and holding her in strong, protective arms, but in her mind's eye, in her heart's secret chamber, the lady Prudence saw Lord Carradice twirling was not his aunt . . .

"Never fear, Aunt Gussie." Gideon whirled her around again. "You're as light as a feather. My injury is not so bad that I can't embrace my favorite aunt in all the world!"

"Pah!" snorted Aunt Gussie, as she emerged from his embrace, looking like a ruffled, thoroughly delighted hen. She added with an assumption of severity, "It's not your arm I was worried about, it was my dignity!"

Gideon let out a shout of laughter and hugged her again.

"Dreadful boy—he never did have any manners, you know," she confided to Prudence as she slapped her nephew away. "Oh stop it, Gideon, do! Make yourself useful and find your young lady a seat! Over there." She indicated a crimson velvet sofa.

Gideon bowed and escorted Prudence across the room with exaggerated solicitude.

Prudence, feeling slightly dazed by the whirlwind of words, not to mention her rogue vision, allowed herself to be led.

Your young lady. She felt like an impostor. She sat down on the sofa. Lord Carradice sat close beside her. Very close. She could feel the warmth of his limbs burning right through her dress. She shifted away.

"I see," he murmured softly. "It is only on carriages you are prepared to snuggle up to me."

Prudence gave him a look of reproof. She said nothing, but his words had conjured up—as he no doubt knew they would—those long hours of extreme intimacy on their journey. He was quite unprincipled in some matters. His leg shifted, and she felt its warmth again. She moved and placed her reticule between them. He sighed ostentatiously.

Aunt Gussie wrapped a plump arm around Grace's waist, beaming. "And you must be little Grace, the baby of the family—oh my, my, what a heartbreaker you're going to be in a few years! And so like your sister, Charity, except for the coloring. She and Edward arrived some hours ago, by the way, and have gone into town on some errand or other. Gideon, you didn't tell me the sisters were beautiful, too! No wonder you and Edward stood no chance. Sisters! Oh, how the ton will talk! But we shall not regard—"

Prudence stared at her, puzzled. Gideon leaned forward and frowned, and his aunt caught herself up hastily, saying, "No, no—I am saying nothing. Grace, child, take this charming little chair here—it's quite my favorite, don't you agree?" Grace nodded, smiled, and impulsively, tentatively gave the little lady's arm a small squeeze. "Oh, you dear, sweet child." Lady Augusta enveloped Grace in a soft hug. "I am so very pleased you've come to stay with me. My scapegrace nephews have done something right, for a change. Several things right, in fact. We are going to have such a delightful time!" She patted Grace's cheek and smoothed a fiery curl back in a motherly gesture. "Such beautiful, beautiful hair you and your sister have. I always wanted Titian hair, you know."

Four pairs of eyes were drawn inexorably to the cluster of brilliant Titian curls perched atop Lady Augusta's head.

Unperturbed, she laughed, patting her own hair. "Oh my dears, this isn't natural! But I always say, if nature won't oblige, a good coiffeur will. My own color is the dreariest mouse-brown, so naturally I couldn't put up with that, for a mousy person I am not nor ever was."

Suddenly Lady Augusta's words echoed in Prudence's mind. *You didn't tell me the sisters were beautiful, too!*

Too? Prudence turned the words over in her mind, carefully. No matter how she looked at it, the words seemed to indicate that Lord Carradice had told Lady Augusta . . . things . . . about Prudence. What had he told her? And more to the point, why?

Notorious rakes surely wouldn't discuss a little flirting and teasing with their aunts . . . would they? And what had she meant when she'd said, *No wonder you and Edward stood no chance. Sisters! Oh, how the ton will talk!* She could only think of one thing: it was a reference to his and Edward's fathers marrying sisters.

Lady Augusta gathered a twin with each arm and marched them across the room. "As for you two pretty peas in a pod—which one is which? No, let me guess—you must be Faith, for you haven't taken your eyes off my piano since you walked in. Your sister told me you loved music and of course you must play it as often as you wish, my dear." She turned to Hope. "And so you must be Hope! The chaise longue is for you two so I may study you at leisure and learn to tell you apart—what a dazzling double debut you will make!" The twins, bemused and vastly entertained, allowed themselves to be seated by the imperious little lady.

With everyone finally seated, the Lady Augusta plunked herself breathlessly down on the nearest chair and beamed around the room. "Edward has already told me the barest modicum of your story—I shall speak to you gels later and receive the whole of it, but Gideon!" She stamped a slippered foot. "How many times must I ask you! How did you hurt your arm?"

Gideon chuckled. "If you had once stopped to draw breath, O Aunt, I might have found an opportunity!" He held up a hand to stop her retort and hastily said, "I was shot in an encounter with highwaymen, a mere flesh wound. Don't look so horrified, Aunt Gussie, there was no real damage done, and nothing was lost!"

Lady Augusta rolled her eyes. "Men! No idea how to tell a tale properly! Miss Merridew, I rely on you to fill me in with all the details later. I understand you were there when the villains accosted you."

"Oh, she was, indeed," said Lord Carradice. "In fact, it wouldn't have been nearly such an exciting adventure without her."

Lady Augusta sat forward excitedly. "Oh, do tell."

Prudence narrowed her eyes at Lord Carradice in a silent message. They had agreed that it would be better for everyone that the truth would remain their little secret. If anyone discovered it was she who had shot Lord Carradice and not the robber, she would become the object of gossip and notoriety. And though Prudence did not give a fig for what people might say of her, she did not wish to draw undue attention to herself and her sisters. They were in hiding, after all.

Lord Carradice responded to her quelling look with one of limpid innocence. "Oh, a gentleman never tells tales, Aunt Gussie."

"Nonsense, Gideon! We are family!" snapped his aunt. "Besides, explaining to your aunt how you were injured is not telling tales. It is your duty as a nephew!"

She was a very forceful little lady, Prudence decided. She glanced again at Lord Carradice, willing him to silence, not trusting him an inch. That mischievous look was back in his eyes.

He opened his mouth, glanced at Prudence in a show of uncertainty, leaned forward, and explained, "No, I am sorry, dear Aunt, but indeed, it would not be gentlemanly." He glanced at Prudence again and added, "Besides, it is not even interesting. Screaming and fainting never is."

Prudence gasped. The wretch! Painting her as a foolish, fainting female was as bad as telling the truth! Worse! She glared at him.

Lord Carradice continued hastily, "However, afterward she gallantly sacrificed her petticoat for the stanching of blood, for which I will evermore be grateful."

Lady Augusta sniffed, unimpressed, and said to Prudence, "Well, I daresay highwaymen can be alarming, but I was never the least bit in favor of fainting as a tactic unless it is to avoid awkward questions—then it is very useful. But I have had many an encounter with ruffians and *bandidos* myself in Argentina, and I am of the firm belief that a cool head and a show of strength is what is needed in an emergency of that sort. "

"Yes, ma'am," murmured Prudence, vowing silently to strangle Lord Carradice the moment she could discreetly do so.

Lady Augusta's voice softened. "Don't look so chagrined, child. You cannot be blamed—in this country, well-bred females are only ever taught to be feeble and decorative—such nonsense! I myself always carry a gun when traveling. You would do well to consider it!"

"Yes, Lady Augusta, I shall in future," Prudence said

with a darkling look at Lord Carradice. He smiled benignly on her in the manner of an elderly uncle.

Lady Augusta beamed. "Good girl! That's the spirit. I shall even instruct you in the use of a firearm, if you wish. I have a small yet deadly pistol, especially made for me."

"Thank you, Lady Augusta," Prudence said politely. "I would appreciate that very much. I can think of a use for a small but deadly pistol. Right now, in fact."

Lord Carradice made a smothered sound, which he tried to turn into a cough.

His aunt's eyes narrowed. She glanced shrewdly from her nephew to the stiffly polite young lady seated beside him. "Oho! So that's it, is it? Gideon, you are as wicked a young rascal now as ever you were. Never mind, my dear. I perceive that this rapscallion has slandered you shockingly— no, there is no point denying it, Gideon. I can tell from the mischief in those wicked black eyes of yours. You never could lie to me!" She turned back to Prudence. "I collect that the edifying story he, er, *didn't* tell us was a complete farrago of nonsense."

Gideon slapped a hand over his heart. "Aunt, you wound me to the quick."

Lady Augusta sniffed. "That confirms it. Miss Merridew, we shall speak later, and you shall tell me the whole—yes? I gather it is not for general consumption, but I assure you, I am the soul of discretion." There was another muffled sound from her nephew. "When it comes to family, I mean!" she added with dignity.

Family? Prudence's head came up at that. She glanced wildly from Lady Augusta to Lord Carradice. What had he told her? Had he told his aunt they were betrothed? Was that why Lady Augusta was willing to have five unknown young ladies foisted on her with no notice?

"Family?" she queried. She had to clarify the matter instantly. She could not accept this lady's generosity on false pretenses. She could not pretend she was betrothed to Lord Carradice—not to this aunt who clearly adored him. Heat rose in her cheeks. "Lady Augusta, I think you should know—"

"Aunt Gussie is referring, of course, to Edward's as yet

unofficial betrothal to your sister," Lord Carradice interrupted in a bland voice.

Prudence blinked.

"Aunt Gussie is Edward's aunt as well as mine. She was our mothers' sister."

"Oh." Prudence nodded. "Of course." She wanted to sink through the floor. Luckily at that moment the door opened, and in came the butler, Shoebridge, and several footmen carrying an immense tea tray and another tray piled high with cakes and other delicacies. The scent of fresh-baked scones filled the room, providing an instant distraction. Lady Augusta poured tea and served scones and jam, adding dollops of clotted cream with a lavish hand.

Prudence ate and drank in silence. Of course, there would be no need to pretend to his aunt that there was an understanding between them. There was no longer any need for that fiction. It had been for Great-uncle Oswald and now its purpose was fulfilled. Charity had made her coming-out and had found herself a husband. Once she was safely married, she could keep the younger ones safe until Prudence came into her own inheritance.

She bit into a scone slowly. Lord Carradice was now free to do as he wished. He'd already done more than anyone could expect, escorting them to safety. He could bow out gracefully if he wanted to, leaving them in the competent hands of his cousin and aunt, and return to the carefree pleasures of his previous reprehensible way of life.

That would be a relief.

He wouldn't bother her anymore. She would no longer have to put up with his nonsense. No more wicked teasing. No more shocking impropriety. No more illicit kissing and fondling to set her pulse leaping and her body tingling. Life would return to its usual serious purpose.

It would be a relief. It would, she was sure.

Once she got used to the idea.

That was the trouble with his sort of frivolity and fun. It was addictive. Her life had been so grim, so serious, so without joy . . . until Lord Carradice came into it. And viewed his way, problems seemed to shrink. Gazing into those dark, laughing eyes, she could believe that nothing and nobody could hurt her again. The trouble was, gazing into those eyes of his, she could believe almost anything—even that she was beautiful. Her looking glass was more honest, however, and her common sense more truthful.

The trouble was she'd needed him more than he needed her. And now he was free to leave.

She was worrying again, Gideon saw. She had that little anxious crease between her brows. He didn't like it, didn't like to see her fretting about anything. His fingers itched to reach out and smooth it away. He could dedicate his life to that crease, to making sure it never appeared.

If she'd only let him, blast it!

Talk about hoist with his own petard. Having spent most of his life making everyone believe him a frivolous fellow who took nothing seriously, the one time he wanted someone to see through the pose for the sham it was, she couldn't. She didn't believe a thing he said, was determined to keep him at arm's length. Even now, he could feel her leaning away from him on the sofa, as if she could be compromised if they so much as touched.

He almost wished she could be so easily compromised. Dammit, he would take her any way he could—well, no, he wouldn't. She had to come to him of her own free will, without pressure, without fear, without hesitation. That was the trouble.

Because of her own free will she had promised herself to Otterbury. Not Gideon. Gideon was only the substitute, the passing stranger, the next best. Dammit!

Just then the door opened, and Charity and the duke came in. "Excellent!" exclaimed Lady Augusta. "You're back just in time for tea. Another two cups, Shoebridge."

Gideon eyed his cousin. Edward looked different: excited, more assured somehow.

"What have you two been up to?" he asked casually.

They jumped and glanced at each other like guilty schoolchildren. The duke looked a silent question at Charity. She nodded, biting her lip in excitement and trepidation.

"We just spoke to the bishop," announced Edward.

"Of Bath and Wells? Whatever for?" exclaimed Aunt Gussie.

"A bishop!" Hope said in disgust. "I'm sure there are much more exciting sights to see in Bath than a bishop's palace."

"Actually, the bishop's palace is in Wells, not Bath," said Aunt Gussie. "Don't tell me you drove all the way to—"

But Gideon understood at once. "And did you get it?"

Edward nodded and patted his pocket.

"Get what? I wish you boys would explain, instead of talking in this odiously cryptic manner," Aunt Gussie said crossly. "Charity, my dear, what are they talking about?"

Charity blushed, glanced at Prudence apologetically, and said softly, "Edward was showing me the sights, when we heard that the bishop was visiting Bath. He thought we should take advantage of the opportunity to apply for a license. Without having to drive all the way to Wells."

There was a sudden silence, broken only by Grace's question, "A license? What for?"

"A license to get married without having to wait to call the banns," Prudence said shakily. "Oh, Charity—you're going to be married!"

Pandemonium broke out. Five females—Lady Augusta included—leaped to their feet and embraced Charity, pelting her with questions and exclaiming in amazement. Tea and scones grew cold, forgotten.

Gideon strolled over to his cousin, who had been pushed to the edge of the excited group of females. "Congratulations, Coz. She'll make you very happy, I think."

Edward, beaming, nodded. "I never believed I could be so happy about tying the knot, Gid, when you think of how we both swore to avoid it. But with Charity, it's different. I cannot imagine life without her. She . . . she's perfect, isn't she?"

"For you, she obviously is," Gideon said. "You're looking extraordinarily happy, I must say." He eyed his cousin thoughtfully and added, "I don't suppose you've done the deed already, have you?"

Prudence heard the soft question. "What? What did you say? *Done the deed already?*" She stared at Edward a moment and turned back to Charity. "Don't tell me you're already married! Charity—you haven't, have you?"

Edward reached out and gathered Charity to his side. "No, we haven't, but it wasn't for want of trying."

Prudence stared at him. "What?"

Edward shrugged. "I could have talked the old boy into doing it then and there, I'm sure—there are advantages to being a duke, after all." He smiled at Charity, who nestled happily into the curve of his arm. "But my bride wanted to wait."

"Of course she did, you silly boy!" exclaimed Aunt Gussie. "She doesn't want a hasty hole-in-the-corner wedding! She'll want to purchase bride clothes and send out invitations and order a special dress and then there's the wedding breakfast—"

"Oh no," interrupted Charity gently. "I don't care about any of that. I would have been very happy to be married immediately. A small and private ceremony is exactly what Edward and I want. And I have plenty of lovely new clothes, thanks to Great-uncle Oswald's wonderful generosity."

"Then what delayed you, child?"

Charity said simply, "When I marry, I want my sisters with me. We've all anticipated this day so much . . ." She flushed and added in a low voice, "Only I never expected it to be such a happy occasion."

Gideon watched as Prudence's lovely eyes grew bright with tears. "You are happy, aren't you, Char?" she whispered.

Charity's eyes flooded. "Oh yes, Prue, I am. Very happy." She wiped her eyes and added, "I never dreamed I could feel like this." She leaned closer into the duke's embrace. "Just like you promised."

Prudence's face crumpled. "Oh, Charity . . ."

Gideon handed her a handkerchief. She clutched at it blindly. He took it back and proceeded to dry her eyes, ignoring her halfhearted efforts to repel him. "Don't fuss, Imp," he said softly. "All eyes are on the bride. Nobody is looking at you."

"You are," she said in a watery voice.

"Yes, but I can't help myself. You couldn't stop me looking at you if you wanted to. And you're beautiful when you're damp."

For some reason, this brought on a fresh flood of tears, and Gideon busied himself with drying them, too.

Aunt Gussie frowned and turned to the younger girls. "We'll get no sense out of this lot for a while, so come and sit over here near the fire and while the gentleman dry your sisters' eyes, we shall plan our wardrobes. Don't worry about the tears, Grace, child—everyone cries at weddings! It's a tradition." She smiled at them all. "I am very glad you gels have come to stay with me. I was bored to death, you know. Bath used to be extremely fashionable before I left this country, but these days the town is crowded with people I've never heard of—dowdies, fossils, and mushrooms and—d'you know the worst thing about it?"

The girls shook their heads.

"Nothing *ever* happens!" Lady Augusta sat back and regarded them with satisfaction. "At least it didn't until the Merridew gels arrived." She raised her voice and said, "Edward, when is this wedding to be?"

"We've booked the church for next Wednesday," he responded vaguely, still preoccupied with his bride.

"Wednesday! That is a bare week from now!" Lady Augusta surged to her feet. "Come, gels, there is much to arrange. A private ceremony is one thing, but it need not be a shabby affair. Your sister may think she has enough pretty dresses, but she's about to become a duchess. And you shall be the sisters-in-law of a duke, and if that is not the best excuse for shopping, I don't know what is!" She sailed from the room, sweeping the twins and Grace in front of her.

Gideon glanced at his cousin and Charity. "I think we should give them a little privacy, don't you?" he murmured.

Prudence, still feeling a little emotionally unsettled, nodded and allowed him to escort her from the room. He led her through a passage and into a small, pretty room furnished in blue and gold. Before she knew it, she was seated on a sofa wrapped in a firm, immensely appealing masculine embrace.

"Oh, no, I shouldn't," she muttered feebly.

"Hush!" He tucked her securely against his chest. "Just

let me hold you for a moment. Just for comfort. There's nobody to see, and I promise you I shall be the soul of propriety."

Prudence gave a watery chuckle. "I don't think the high sticklers would think much of your notion of propriety." Even being alone with him was indiscreet, let alone the way he was holding her. But she didn't care. It was lovely being held like this, even for a short time. Just for comfort, she told herself. For friendship.

"Tell me about this promise Charity mentioned."

"Oh, it was just something I used to tell them when things were at their darkest."

His right hand stroked the soft inner skin of her arm, sending warm ripples through her. "Tell me," he insisted softly.

"Mama and Papa were very happy, very much in love," she began. "And we lived in Italy. I think because theirs was a runaway marriage, and they—and we—were wonderfully happy . . . until they died . . ."

"How did they die?"

She drew in a deep, shaky breath. "It was a fever. They caught it in the city where they'd gone for a party, staying a week or more. Papa died in the city, very quickly. And when Mama returned with the terrible news, it was clear she was ill, from the moment she arrived." She shivered, remembering. "The servants recognized the illness at once and fled. I found Concetta, our nursemaid, sneaking out the back. She told me why everyone else had gone."

He put his arm around her, and she allowed herself to lean against him, just for comfort. She said, "I convinced Concetta to take the baby and the children with her, to safety."

"And you, a child yourself, stayed behind to look after your mother."

She nodded. Her face crumpled as she whispered, "But she died, anyway . . ."

He hugged her tight then, as she wept a few more tears.

"Tell me about the promise," he prompted after a long interval.

"When she was dying, Mama made me promise to look

after the little ones. She promised that no matter what happened in our lives, we would each find great love and happiness . . ." She scrubbed at her eyes, embarrassed at the outburst. "But then we were sent to live with Grandpapa, where there was no sunshine and no love and certainly no laughter, though we managed to have a few moments of happiness. So when life was bleakest, I used to promise my sisters that no matter how bad it seemed, one day we would all live like we did in Italy. With sunshine and laughter and love and happiness."

"I see."

"Yes." She sighed. "And now Charity is the first of them to find love and happiness."

"Is she, indeed?" he murmured, tucking a stray curl behind her ear. "Why do you say 'them' like that? As if you don't believe in that promise for yourself."

Prudence hesitated. "I do not think I was born lucky."

"Why not?" he asked softly.

"Well—I thought I'd found—" She broke off.

"You thought you'd found love when you were sixteen," he said in a deep voice.

She nodded.

"And then you found you'd made a mistake, that Ottershanks had feet of clay and a brain to match."

"Y—No! I don't want to talk about this anymore," she said, suddenly struggling to sit up.

He allowed her to sit up but caught her by her shoulders, facing him. A twinge of protest came from his injury, but he ignored it. Gazing intently into her eyes, he said deliberately, "He left you, Imp. Abandoned you to fate and the mercy of your grandfather who, according to your sisters, thrashes you. Did Otterclogs know about the thrashings?"

Her gaze dropped.

"So he did know and he left you to—!"

"No." She cut him off. "They were never as bad until . . . until after Phillip left."

Gideon's eyes bored into her. "What happened after Phillip left, Imp?" he asked softly. "What happened to make your grandfather treat you so badly?"

"I was . . ." Her face twisted with grief, and she tried to pull away. "No, no, I can't!"

"You can tell me anything, love," he said gently. "What happened after Phillip left?"

"There was . . . I found I w—" She closed her eyes for a moment, swallowed convulsively, took a deep breath, and said, "I discovered I was with child. That is what binds me to Phillip, not simply the promise."

In fact, she hadn't even realized it herself. It was Grandpapa who'd noticed she couldn't keep her breakfast down five days in a row, Grandpapa who'd recognized symptoms of which she was ignorant, Grandpapa who informed her that, like the harlot he'd always known she was, she was breeding a bastard.

It was the worst day of her life. Until now, she'd told no one, no one except Philip. Not even her sisters knew.

Now she'd told Gideon. Without waiting to see his reaction, she fled the room.

Chapter Sixteen

∞

"Love is the whole history of a woman's life,
It is an episode in a man's."
MADAME DE STAËL

PRUDENCE FLEW UP THE STAIRS, HER HEART IN TURMOIL. SHE
hadn't been able to look him in the eye—she wasn't sure
why.

Her grandfather's words came back to her as she sought
the sanctuary of her room. *No man will want another man's*
leavings . . .

Was that how Lord Carradice would see her now? As *an-*
other man's leavings? She shuddered. No! It was an ugly
image, planted in her mind by a twisted old man. She ought
to know better than to think of it. She wasn't anyone's *leav-*
ings. She was herself, Prudence Merridew, no particular bargain, perhaps, but still . . .

She shuddered again. It was a disgusting expression. She
would banish it from her mind this instant.

She opened doors, searching for the bedchamber allotted
her, but her mind worried at the question like a tongue at a
sore tooth. Would this change Lord Carradice's opinion of
her? And if so, how?

Would he still want her now he knew the dreadful truth?
She would find out soon enough. Had he ever truly wanted
her in the first place? She'd been warned repeatedly that he

was a 'here and therian.' That the chase was what he liked. And she had led him a chase.

Dull doubt crowded in on her. Other people's warnings echoed in her mind. Just because he sounded sincere did not mean he was. And just because she wanted to believe him, it did not mean he could be believed. Girls were ruined every day because they believed what men told them. A girl would have to be foolish to take a well-known rake at his very appealing word . . . wouldn't she? No doubt the more appeal, the more danger . . .

No doubt of it at all.

The only use any man would have for the likes of you is as a whore!

Stop it! Stop thinking such vile thoughts! She clapped her hands over her ears, as if the thoughts could be blocked out like that.

Lord Carradice would never think of her in that way, she told herself firmly. He wasn't a bitter and twisted old man. He was more compassionate, more understanding. He wouldn't try to take advantage of her secret. Prudence was certain of it.

She discovered her portmanteau sitting at the foot of a bed in the room in front of her. Her hat was on the bed. She entered the bedchamber, closing the door quietly behind her.

Prudence sat down on the bed, her knees suddenly weak. Lord Carradice had said once that Prudence was too innocent for the company of women like Theresa Crowther. Yet Mrs. Crowther had once been his own mistress. He hadn't spoken of her with respect.

She thought of how hard it already was for him to behave with even a semblance of propriety toward her. Now that he knew she was no virtuous maiden . . . would he still think she didn't belong with Mrs. Crowther and her ilk?

Of course he would, she decided. He was kind. He was not a hypocrite, like many in society. It was good that he knew her secret, knew the final guilty tie that had bound her to Phillip.

She removed her short spencer jacket and hung it in the closet. Grandpapa had painted a terrifying picture of what fallen women suffered.

Had she not lost the babe, she would have learned those consequences firsthand. Grandpapa would have cast her out, never mind the slur on the family name. He'd called the death of her baby a judgment on her.

Prudence's eyes filled with slow, bitter tears. She'd been forced to grieve in silence and in secret. Had she disobeyed, her sisters would have suffered even more for her sin. She was bidden to silence and so had told no one of the child—only Phillip, in two letters that he must not have received, for he'd never responded. She'd spent many an hour at Mama and Papa's cairn, however, weeping alone until her eyes were swollen and dry. She'd added many a small pebble to Mama's cairn, for the baby . . .

Pouring some water out of the ewer on the dresser, she wondered whether, if Grandpapa had cast her out, and if she had by some stroke of chance met Lord Carradice . . . no, the idea was ridiculous! She would have died in a gutter of starvation, no doubt. Or perhaps she would have gone to Mrs. Otterbury, and then Phillip would have sent for her.

Only Phillip *hadn't* sent for her. She splashed cold water on her face. *Why not?* she wondered for the hundredth time.

Mama said you had to seize your chance at happiness. Prudence had been given her chance. She'd refused to run away with Phillip; she hadn't been able to leave her sisters behind. She'd made her choice.

And because of it, her baby had died.

Prudence had to live with that.

A child! Gideon was stunned. It was a bigger barrier than he'd realized to win her. He'd felt quite confident of his ability to win her from Otterbury, but a child! He couldn't compete with a child. She clearly felt the child bound her to Otterbury.

He felt a surge of rage. Dammit, what sort of a loose screw was Otterbury to get a young, gently bred girl with child and then abandon her to seek his fortune!

He wondered about the child. Was it alive still? Many babes did not see their first birthday. He tried to think back to how she had put things. *That is what binds me to Phillip, not simply the promise. That* being the child. *Binds*, she had said, not *bound*. So the child was still alive.

Was it a girl or a boy? And where was it? Not in Norfolk—she wouldn't leave a child with her grandfather and flee herself. So, had the babe been wrested from its mother and hidden away from sight, farmed out to strangers for a few guineas? It was the usual thing in such cases.

Only Prudence was a rare, loyal creature. She couldn't even give up on a man who'd left her alone to face the consequences of his lust, left her for four long years. If she couldn't forget a creature like that, could she forget her own child? Never. Not a woman like his Prudence.

Did she ever see the child? Would she be allowed? Did she even know where he or she was? Was it a boy or a girl? He pictured a tiny girl with Prudence's eyes. He hoped it wasn't a girl. He couldn't bear a little girl with Prudence's face growing up alone and unloved. And if it were a boy . . . He imagined a small boy with curly red hair, a look of dogged determination on his little face, a stubborn little chin, just like Miss Imp's firm little chin.

Oh, God, the whole idea was unbearable. He had to speak to her at once.

"Dammit, Aunt Gussie, she won't speak to me. It's been days now and I haven't been able to get her alone, not even for a moment."

"Well, what do you expect, you foolish boy? She's busy. And so am I. Has it escaped your notice that her sister and my nephew are getting married the day after tomorrow?"

"But this is important."

Aunt Gussie waved a dismissive hand. "Pooh! You can talk to her anytime—a wedding is but once in a lifetime—and don't look like that at me, young man, it is *not* my fault that both my husbands died! Women have more stamina than men, that is all. And stop distracting me! There are a thousand things to be done. Even the smallest, most private ceremony takes a great deal of organization, you know!"

Gideon gave her a blank look. "I don't see how that follows. All you need is a bride, a groom, a parson, and a couple of witnesses, and that's it. So there should be plenty of time for Prudence to—"

His aunt rolled her eyes. "That is exactly what Edward said to me. You men have no idea, do you?" she said. "It is still a very important day in a young woman's life, no matter how small and private it may be. Whether there are to be five hundred guests or five, it must be a day young Charity can look back on without regrets. She is being rushed into this as it is—she has barely had a coming-out, poor child, and if she had, she would have had all London at her feet." She shook her head. "Such an exquisite creature should have been able to spread her wings a little, experience the power of her beauty before tying the knot and being dragged off to the wilderness, as I'm sure Edward will do, the wretched boy!"

Gideon shrugged. "I don't know what plans they have, but Charity seems very happy to me, and Edward is floating on air. But *I* need to speak to Prudence, and she's avoiding me!"

His aunt threw up her hands. "You are all too besotted to understand a thing! So it is left to me to ensure that the arrangements are perfect—there are flowers and food and champagne and all sorts of things to arrange, Edward's house to be set in order, not to mention the matter of bride clothes."

"She said she had plenty of clothes."

His aunt gave him a scornful look. "You cannot possibly imagine that I would allow that beautiful child to be married in a gown she has worn before, do you, Gideon? Have you forgotten to whom you're speaking?" She shook her head in disgust. "I have a reputation to maintain, and it shall not be said that I had the most beautiful creature in England under my care and I allowed her to be married in her old gown."

"Prudence is more beautiful, and anyway, Charity's dress can hardly be old, she said—"

"Pah! Out of my way, you foolish boy, I cannot waste time bandying words with a man who has only one thing on his mind." She swatted him aside like a fly and bustled past.

"Aunt Gussie!" Gideon was shocked.

His aunt turned, her black-button eyes sparkling with

mischief. "Well, you do, don't you, Rake Carradice?" She tilted her head and gave him a very knowing look. "Or are you going to suggest the idea of bedding Miss Prudence hasn't crossed your mind, hmm?"

To his chagrin, Gideon felt his face reddening. "Well, dammit, of course it has crossed my mind—but only in the most honorable way," he retorted.

"Said the man who swore he'd never, ever marry." She peered up at him and laughed. "And you're blushing! The hardened rake is actually blushing!"

"If I'm blushing, it's for your atrocious manners, Aunt Gussie." Gideon scrabbled for a shred of dignity. "It is hardly proper behavior for an aunt to quiz a man on his love life! Your time in the Argentine has—"

Aunt Gussie laughed delightedly. "The libertine lecturing on propriety—oh, I *am* enjoying this. When a rake falls, he falls *so* hard." She reached up and patted his cheek. "There's not a particle of use telling me of your intentions, honorable or not, dear boy—I'm only your aunt. Speak to Miss Prudence about it, and don't waste any more of my time! I have a wedding to organize!"

"Yes, but that's the problem," retorted Gideon, exasperated. "She won't even see me!"

But his aunt was off, sailing from the room like a small battleship in a high wind.

"Well, what about this ribbon? Do you think it matches your new dress or not? Or is it not quite the right shade of blue?" The Merridew sisters frowned over the ribbon.

"Perhaps a shade too much lavender in the tone. What about this one, Charity?" Faith suggested. Charity chewed her lip, undecided.

"Take them all to the window, and we shall compare them to your satin in the daylight," Prudence decided.

They trooped to the window and scrutinized various ribbons carefully against a small piece of celestial blue satin from Charity's new wedding dress. "I think the darker blue will look the best against—" Charity began.

"Look! It's Phillip! It is! It is!" shrieked Hope suddenly.

"Outside, Prudence! In the street there! See! I *wasn't* mistaken the other day."

Prudence looked to where her sister was pointing and froze. Phillip? She stared through the window. It *was* Phillip. Here. Strolling down a street in Bath. Vaguely, she felt ribbons slithering from her slackened hold. Some part of her heard her sisters exclaiming and chattering as her mind tried to grasp it. Phillip wasn't in India. He was here in Bath. Bath. But how? When had he come home? Her mind tried to make sense of it, but it kept slipping out of her grasp.

"Go on, Prue. Don't just stand there. Run out and catch him," Hope urged her.

Prudence turned and blinked. She felt almost dizzy. Hollow. Even a little bit sick.

Her sisters beamed at her. "Isn't it wonderful, Prue?" exclaimed Charity. "Phillip will have no idea you are here. What a marvelous surprise for you both. He'll be thrilled."

"Yes," Prudence said dazedly. She tried to gather her senses. "I wonder what . . . I mean, why . . ." She glanced back out of the window and it was true. Phillip Otterbury was strolling along the opposite pavement, as large as life, jauntily swinging a cane as he perused the contents of various shop windows through a quizzing glass.

"Hurry!" Charity urged, taking the last of the ribbons from Prudence's limp fingers. "Before he disappears again!"

"Yes, yes, I must." Prudence hurried out into the street, then stopped abruptly. What would she say to him after all this time? She took another few steps toward him, and stopped again, suddenly uncertain as questions crowded in again. Why was he in Bath and not in Norfolk? Why hadn't he written to let her know he was returning? How long had he been back in England? Was that why he hadn't he responded to her letters these last few months—because he was in England and her letters had gone to India?

"Go *on!*" Hope gave her a push from behind. "He's right there, Prue! What's the matter with you? Hey, Phillip! Phillip Otterbury!" she called, and waved, oblivious of the curious looks they were receiving.

Phillip turned, a slight smile on his face as his gaze swept the street. His jaw and his quizzing glass dropped as he spotted them. He glanced quickly around him, as if to check whether he was observed, and then simply stood and stared at Prudence.

She stared back. He wasn't moving. Why not? Her gaze swept over him. He looked different, as Hope had said— thinner and browner and not as tall as she had remembered—but he was unmistakably Phillip. He was still handsome—more handsome than she remembered, though not as tall. His golden hair was burnished, brushed into careful curls and looking even fairer against the darkened color of his skin. Phillip was back in England.

"He looks very fine and elegant, does he not?" she heard Faith murmur behind her. And indeed, he was very fashionably dressed in breeches of the palest primrose, high, white-topped boots, and a coat of bottle-green, padded extravagantly at the shoulders, nipped in tight at the waist, and embellished with large, silver buttons. His shirt collar was high and stiffly starched, supporting a starched necktie of complicated design. He wore a very high-crowned hat and carried a black lacquered cane. She didn't remember Phillip as being interested in fashion, but it seemed he now was. It was, after all, more than four years . . .

"Go *on*, Prue! What's wrong with you?" Hope pushed her again. Prudence's other sisters crowded in behind her, murmuring encouragement.

As if in a trance, Prudence slowly closed the gap between herself and Phillip. Why didn't he move? What did that look on his face mean?

And then suddenly they were face-to-face.

"Phillip," she said, then not knowing what to do, held out her hand.

He quickly glanced around him, then took it, frowning. "Prudence, my dear girl, it *is* you! I thought I must have been mistaken. What on earth are you doing in Bath?"

Prudence blinked. Over the years she had imagined this moment hundreds of times. She'd imagined all sorts of places and had enacted many different scenes in her head. Not one of them bore the faintest relation to this mundane meeting in a public street. "My sisters and I are visiting friends here. I could ask you the same question, Phillip."

He cast another glance back up the street and said hurriedly, "Oh, me, too, me, too. Visiting friends—that is to say, colonial acquaintances. Mere acquaintances. Nobody you need worry about." He peered past her. "Good grief. Your little sisters have grown up a great deal, have they not?"

"It has been more than four years."

He laughed heartily, as if at some witticism. "Four years! Yes, indeed, how time does fly." He pumped her hand energetically. "I am delighted to see you, delighted, my dear. Though I might wish our meeting was not in so public a place. I cannot believe you here are in Bath." He gestured, taking in the whole street. "Amazing coincidence."

He seemed very nervous, thought Prudence. Ill at ease. She supposed it wasn't surprising. She felt quite peculiar herself. She couldn't believe that this was Phillip, that he was here in Bath, and not thousands of miles away. "How is your mother, Phillip? Is she here, too?"

"No, she is at home, with my father. Who are you visiting? Anyone we know?"

"Well . . ." Feeling a little awkward about explaining how she and her sisters were fleeing her grandfather, Prudence tried to think of some innocuous way to explain her presence in Bath. "Charity is to be married tomorrow."

"How nice! To whom?" he said, looking back the way he'd come.

"She is to be married to the Duke of Dinstable."

He started. "Good heavens! A duke! How very splendid. I must congratulate her." He waved at the girls, who had been hanging back. At his signal, they hurried forward excitedly, only Grace hanging back. As they drew nearer, he lifted his quizzing glass to observe them and exclaimed, "Well, you never told me Charity had grown into a beauty! She's a regular little diamond! No wonder she snagged a duke, even without the disadvantage of your mother's connections. In fact, all your sisters are dashed pretty, Prudence, if I might say so."

"What do you mean, the disadvantage of our mother's connections—" began Prudence indignantly, but before she could finish, her sisters arrived, and the conversation was swamped as her sisters pelted him with questions, the questions Prudence had been too stunned to ask.

He'd returned to England a couple of months ago. Yes, his mother was well. Yes, he had been home to Norfolk and indeed, he had been extremely surprised to hear they were not at home. And of course, terribly disappointed to miss seeing them, especially since even the younger ones had grown into such beauties! Ha-ha.

No, he hadn't actually heard anything about scarlet fever—although now that he came to think of it, his mother might have mentioned something of the sort. Of course, he hadn't called at Dereham Court, not formally—well, no point in that, after all, with their grandfather being the dashed inhospitable fellow he was. And besides which, since they were not at home, there was little p— How did he know they were not at home? Oh, one of the servants must have told him, he couldn't remember who. Someone had mentioned it, at any rate. Scarlet fever? Well, possibly, that was it. But nobody had suggested they had come to Bath—he would most certainly have remembered that! So had Lord Dereham brought them to Bath to take the waters, after their illness? Oh, they hadn't had scarlet fever? But didn't someone just say—? And he'd heard some talk of the old man having broken his—They'd *what!*

Run away from Lord Dereham?

He turned to Prudence. "Are you *mad*, Prudence? To run away from your legal guardian? Five unmarried girls? I've never heard of anything so ill-judged in my life!"

He held up his hand at the chorus of explanations and justifications that began and said, "Who, may I ask, assisted you in this extraordinary piece of folly? Do you not understand what it will do to your reputations?"

Prudence, casting a minatory glance at her sisters to hush them, said calmly, "The girls exaggerate. It is not the dramatic event you seem to think it, Phillip. Until recently we have been staying with our great-uncle, Sir Oswald Merridew, in London, and were escorted here to Bath by Charity's affianced husband, the Duke of Dinstable. We are staying in the home of Lady Augusta Montigua del Fuego, so you see, there is nothing to cause the least risk to our reputations."

"That's right," Grace butted in, her hands braced belligerently on her hips. "It's not fair of you to speak to Prudence like that when you have no idea what's been happening! She wouldn't have had to rescue us if you'd been there in the first place! But Prudence always looks after us, and she wouldn't let anything bad happen, not even to our reputations, would you, Prue?" She added, "And besides, Lord Carradice escorted us to Bath, too, *and* he saved Prudence from a highwayman, *and* he likes Prudence, *and* he's really nice!"

"Carradice? Never heard of him!" Phillip glared down at her. "Grace, isn't it? Well, why don't you go away and look in the shop windows or something, while your sister and I discuss adult matters?"

Charity glanced from Phillip to Prudence and said hastily, "Yes, let's, girls. Phillip and Prue need to talk privately. Prue can catch up with us in a few moments."

Grace and Hope looked unimpressed by this suggestion, but Charity was firm in her resolve and coaxed them away.

Phillip turned back to Prudence. "The whole thing sounds extremely havey-cavey to me, Prudence. Scarlet fever and highwaymen! Running away—and I don't begin to understand why anyone would imagine you needed rescuing! And as for you staying with these so-called friends—I've never heard of this Carradice fellow, and I can't say I like the sound of him escorting you thither and yon. Where is your great-uncle? And as for Lady whoever Montigua del Whatzit! What sort of a name is that, I ask you?"

"It's an Argentinian name."

Phillip sniffed. "I knew she couldn't be English."

"Lady Augusta Montigua del Fuego is the extremely English aunt of the Duke of Dinstable," Prudence explained in a tight voice. "Her second marriage was to an Argentinian gentleman but, having been widowed, she has now returned to live in England."

"Oh. Well, if she is a duke's aunt, I expect it is all right."

"It is. She has been wonderfully kind to us, Phillip, and I will not have her disparaged in any way," Prudence said in a voice that made Phillip blink at her in surprise.

"Well, I wasn't meaning to—" he began.

"No, I'm sure you weren't," she said briskly. "But the street is no place to discuss of this or any other personal matter. You may call on me at Lady Augusta's house this afternoon."

"Er, yes, very well." He bowed stiffly.

"Here is Lady Augusta's direction." She scribbled on a small piece of paper and pressed it into his hand. "I shall expect you this afternoon. What time would suit you?"

"Er . . ." He glanced around the street again, as if for inspiration. "Two?"

"Two will do very nicely. I will see you then, Phillip. We have much to discuss," Prudence said crisply and hurried off down the street, gathering her sisters as she went, leaving Phillip staring after her.

Her legs were shaking by the time they reached Lady Augusta's, even though it was but a few minutes' walk. Her sisters discussed the extraordinary coincidence of running into Phillip all the way home, speculating on what had brought him to Bath, how he had changed, how fashionably he was dressed, and above all, what his return would mean to Prudence and themselves. They seemed to think all their problems were solved.

Prudence herself said not a word. If asked, she would have had to say she was delighted to see him. But actually, she'd been severely jolted by the encounter. She felt almost . . . betrayed by his return to England, unannounced. How long had he been in England?

She walked slowly up the stairs to her bedchamber. Not even the most optimistic of people could think that little scene in the street was the reunion of long-parted lovers, said the small voice within. But she still wore his ring on the chain around her neck. And he still clearly felt he had the right to reprimand her about her behavior, as an affianced husband might.

After so many years apart, each of them was bound to have changed, grown in different directions. He had become more assertive. As had she. It was only natural.

But what did Phillip expect of her? Had he told his parents of their betrothal? Was she still, for him, *"the sole dream that keeps me going in this hellhole on earth,"* as he had once written? It didn't appear so, but appearances could deceive. He did not seem overwhelmed with emotion, but one could not embrace in the street, after all. It was not surprising if a certain amount of self-conscious awkwardness attended their initial meeting. And if he did still want her, how was she going to deal with that?

Her stomach fluttered with nerves.

At two o'clock they would meet again in private and it would all be sorted out, she told herself. She stared into the looking glass, tidying her hair absentmindedly.

When she thought of the nattily dressed stranger she'd met in the street, she didn't feel anything. She didn't feel betrothed to him. She didn't feel connected to him in any way. And yet they'd made a child together.

Gideon had spent the past hour pacing back and forth, peering out of the upstairs window on the lookout for the return of Miss Prudence and her sisters. Having forced himself to wait until it was a decent hour to call on Miss Prudence again, he'd been frustrated to discover that all the young ladies had gone shopping. Again. He'd returned to his own house and proceeded to wait. As patiently as he could. Which was not very.

He'd made his decision and could not wait to speak to her about it. He would marry Miss Prudence forthwith and fetch her child to her at once. The child would live with them and be adopted as his son or daughter. It would cause a deal of talk, of course, but he had thought it all through; if any scandalmongering did arise, he would simply have it whispered abroad that the child was his, and thus there would be no slur on Prudence. The ton might even honor her charitable nature for taking in his base-born child with so little fuss.

Not that he gave the snap of his fingers what the world thought, as long as that dreadful, blind grief was banished forever from her eyes.

At last he saw the Merridew girls walking down the street, a small knot of bustling femininity engaged in animated conversation. Not Prudence, he saw. She wasn't talking at all. It was a little difficult to see under the bonnet she was wearing, but he thought she looked a little pale, a little solemn and anxious. He'd soon put the roses back in her cheeks.

Gideon ran down the stairs, hurried next door, and sent up a message asking to speak to Miss Prudence. He paced the floor of the front drawing room and awaited her arrival.

Prudence hesitated, her hand on the door handle. She felt drained. First the encounter with Phillip in the street, and now this. She'd managed to avoid him for several days, but now events were crowding in on her. She had to deal with Lord Carradice before Phillip arrived.

His note said *in private*. What did that signify? Something he would not wish to speak of in public, or with a chaperone present? She hoped he wouldn't bring up the child. A true gentleman would simply never refer to it again. He wasn't like Grandpapa, he wasn't. He might not approve of her immorality, but he was kind; he wouldn't condemn her.

She felt sick. He must realize she had to speak to Phillip first, clear things with him before she could think about anything else. Once that was over . . .

The clock in the hall chimed. Half-past one. Phillip would be here in half an hour. She would have to get the interview with Lord Carradice over quickly. She didn't think she could bear it if he was still here when Phillip arrived.

She tidied her hair and straightened her clothes. There was a hollow ache inside her. Nerves, she told herself. She took a deep breath and quietly entered the room.

Lord Carradice strode right up to her, much too close for comfort. "You *are* pale!" he exclaimed. "There is no color in your cheeks at all!"

"I cannot help that," she responded stiffly and took a pace backward. If he so much as touched her she would cave in completely. She had to keep her strength.

He followed her, looming so close she could even smell his cologne water. His face was creased with concern. "No, I know. It is my fault. Oh, Prudence, I am sorry for pressing you to speak about your past—sorry for causing you distress, I mean. I cannot regret learning your story, but—"

"I am glad you found it edifying," she said distantly and stepped backward again.

"Edifying?" He frowned. "A strange word. But never mind that—"

"I won't."

He gave her an odd look, then closed the gap between them again. "Prudence, it doesn't matter—"

She sidestepped him. "I think it does!"

He followed and took her shoulders in a firm, possessive grip. "Yes, of course it matters, but I meant it doesn't make any difference to me. I want you! Let *me* take care of you. Let *me* protect you. I—"

This was what she'd so wanted. One part of her was bursting with joy for him to say such things. For this man to want her . . .

But she was still betrothed. She was promised to Phillip. How could she speak of love with this man before she'd broken off her engagement. If, indeed, she *could* break off her engagement . . .

She must.

"While I am still betrothed I can have no answer for you!" She thrust him away and retreated, panting slightly.

"You don't care about Otterbottom! You don't love him! You can't possibly love a fellow who left you in such a case and stayed away for four long years, leaving you to the mercy of—"

"Phillip is back."

His jaw dropped. "Back?" Black brows snapped together. "Where is he, then? When did he arrive in England?"

That was the number-one question, she thought. She said only, "He is here, in Bath. He will be here"—she glanced at the clock on the mantel—"in twenty minutes."

"Here in Bath!" He looked shocked, but recovered and said in an urgent voice, "You can't possibly just pick up where you left off, Prudence. You haven't seen him since you were sixteen. If you ever did love him, it was a young girl's infatuation, that's all, and even so, if you'd been allowed any normal society, I doubt whether you would have given him the time of day! From what you and your sisters have said, your grandfather kept you all more or less as prisoners, and I've heard prisoners even befriend rats and mice, they are so lonely. Otterboots was your rat, that's all, but you are out of your prison now and—"

"Otterb—Phillip is *not* my rat! He—"

"Only a rat would desert you when you found yourself with child, Imp," he continued ruthlessly.

There was a short silence. She could not think of what to say.

She had to speak to Phillip. To break her promise to Phillip now, without speaking to him first . . .

No. She'd given him her promise. She owed him an interview at least before she fell into another man's arms.

As desirable . . . as irresistible as those arms were . . .

So somehow she managed to shrug, and said only, "Well, he's back now." And she had no idea what to do.

"No excuse," he said. "I would have come back—no, I wouldn't—I'd never have left you behind in the first place."

His persistence was irritating, even as it warmed her heart. She wished he would just go away and let her deal with Phillip and then she would know in what case she stood. Instead he was pushing her toward a declaration she was not ready to make. And she didn't like to be pushed, not even by Gideon! "Hah!" she managed. "You are a notorious rake. You must have left dozens of women behind— hundreds, even!" Her voice grew a little added uncertain and she stepped behind a small footstool. She needed to put some distance between them.

A gleam of laughter crept into his eyes. "Oh, by all means, hundreds, to be sure. My stamina is legendary." He prowled toward her.

"Well, I don't know how many—" She broke off, perceiving that the conversation was in danger of descending into farce. "The point is, Phillip could not help leaving me. The circumstances—"

"He could, Imp." He stepped over the footstool and caught her hands in his good one. She tried to tug them away, but his grip, though gentle, was firm. He looked down at her, and the mischief died away as his eyes caressed her. "These mythical hordes of women aside, I've never seduced an innocent, nor taken up with any woman who wanted more from me than a little lighthearted dalliance."

Prudence just looked at him, trying to work out what he was telling her. Her head ached. Her mind was spinning. Phillip would be here any minute; Gideon was rambling on about rats and seduction. Maybe she'd misunderstood his declaration. Was he trying to tell her *she* was only a little lighthearted dalliance, too?

He continued, "It's not to my credit, I admit, but I've never left a woman worse off for knowing me. And I've *never* left any woman carrying my child."

His words froze her spinning mind. Why was he telling her this? Why did he have to talk about the child again? She could not deal with this anymore. She held up her hand as if to ward him off.

She had to put some distance between them.

"Please, I beg of you, say no more on this subject. I am waiting for Phillip. Until then, I can think of nothing else."

"You don't mean that."

"I do. I really, truly do."

Gideon felt more worried by the minute. She was withdrawing from him, he could tell it by the look in her eyes, the stiffness of her body. What more could he say to convince her? She simply had to agree. He could not bear it if finally, after all these years, he had found his true love and she rejected him because she thought she owed a duty to Otterbury. But she was definitely pulling back. All his skills with women seemed to have deserted him. That was the trouble; she was not "women," she was Prudence. Gloriously, uniquely Prudence. His beloved.

He could not simply walk out now and let Otterbury keep her. For he would, Gideon knew. Seeing Prudence after all these years, Otterbury would fall in love with her all over again.

He had to win her now. Get in before Otterbury renewed his suit. Otterbury had all the winning cards; the ring, a promise kept for more than four years, and a child.

All Gideon had to offer was the heart of a rake. A heart that, by his own admission, had never before been constant or tested in any way.

His mind searched in vain for words to win her over, but he had no words he had not already said. And they had proven useless.

The Bard? Poetry—yes. That was the language of love. But he could think of no Shakespeare except for *Now is the winter of our discontent.* He squeezed her hands again. "Forget Otterboots. Come to me." It was hardly poetic.

Lines from Marlowe came to him, blessedly, and he quoted, *"Come live with me and be my love, and we will all the pleasures prove."*

She stared at him as if confused and as she started to shake her head he hastened to reassure her. "Your babe can live with us and —"

That blank look came to her eyes, one he was beginning to recognize. Gideon felt suddenly frantic. "What is it, Imp? Oh, God, I'm making such a mull of this. What have I said now?"

She shook her head and turned away.

He followed her. "Prue, speak to me. What is the matter?"

She put up a shaking hand as if to keep him at bay. "You misunderstood. There is no child, not living. Grandp— I . . . I became ill and my—" She swallowed. "My baby was born dead before its time."

She added, "I can bear no more of this. Please leave. Phillip will be here any minute." She moved toward the door.

He said in a ragged voice, "I've never felt like this about any woman. I need you with me, Imp. More than I've ever needed anyone or anything in my life." He reached for her again, but she backed away, shaking her head in frantic denial.

It was too much. There was too much filling her mind; filling her heart. She felt torn. She needed some time alone, time in which to think.

"I'm sorry, but I cannot!" She fled from the room.

Gideon walked out of his aunt's house like a sleepwalker. He was shattered. And more deeply in love than ever. A year ago he would not have believed that a woman like Prudence could exist.

It was simply not in her to betray a vow. It didn't matter that she'd made the promise to a man who abandoned her, nor that the witnesses to her vow were dead.

He thought of all the women he'd known who'd broken vows. He thought of his own mother who made and broke promises so lightly, who cared not a snap of her fingers for the vows she had made to her husband, or the duty she owed to her son, never mind that the man she eloped with was her own sister's husband.

How could the son of a woman like that understand a woman like Prudence?

He might not understand her, but oh, how he wanted her.

He was a fribble, a rake, a man who had neither given nor kept a promise to a woman his entire adult life. He was shallow, selfish, and possibly even a little vain. He did not understand her. He did not deserve her.

But he would not give her up! Not to a creature like Otterbury. Otterbury had been given his chance to make her happy and instead, he'd left her in the most dire situation a woman could face—and in the hands of a vicious bully. Otterbury deserved no consideration. Gideon could give her up to a more worthy man, perhaps.

Or perhaps not, he thought darkly. Definitely not! He wasn't giving her up to anyone!

Prudence needed to be made happy. And Gideon needed to be the one who made her happy. He was the right man for the job. He was the only man for the job.

And there and then, Gideon made his own vow, the first of his new adult life. It was private, without witnesses and not even voiced aloud. But he meant it with every fiber of his being: He would marry Prudence Merridew and spend his life trying to give her the promise she had made her sisters—sunshine and laughter and love and happiness.

Chapter Seventeen

∽

"Love never dies of starvation, but often of indigestion."
FRENCH PROVERB

THE CLOCK IN THE HALL TICKED WITH AGONIZING SLOWNESS, THE hand inching toward the hour. Prudence paced back and forth on the landing above. Her head rang with echoes of the conversation with Lord Carradice. She had thought of almost nothing else since he left. Had he truly meant what she thought he had? *"Come live with me and be my love."*

It was a clear declaration. He did want her. Possibly even as much as she wanted him.

Two o'clock chimed. She glanced at her reflection in the looking glass and smoothed back an unruly curl. She'd made herself as neat and tidy as she could, cultivating a serene exterior. She smoothed the fabric of her dress with damp hands. She could do this.

As the last golden chime died away the doorbell jangled in the hall below her. Even as a boy, Phillip had valued punctuality. It was one of his virtues.

The butler, Shoebridge, glided languidly toward the entrance, stopped to adjust a floral arrangement with maddening deliberation, then, as the bell jangled again, opened the door with a dignified sweep. Prudence peered over the rails; the entrance was out of her sight, but she could hear the low murmur of masculine voices, then footsteps on the polished parquet floor, and finally Phillip came into sight.

He'd changed his clothes, she noticed, as Shoebridge took his high-crowned beaver hat, black-and-silver trimmed walking cane, and overcoat before conducting him to the front drawing room. His hair was elaborately curled and pomaded into the latest style. His boots were glossy, and small tassels swung from their sides. His coat fitted tightly, the shoulders wadded broad and the waist nipped in tight. Phillip had become a pink of the ton.

She swallowed. The finale to a four-and-a-half-year prelude. She took a deep breath and slowly descended the stairs. She had been caught unawares in the street. She would do better this time.

For years she had imagined Phillip's return. Now, all she could think of was Gideon and the words that made her heart—belatedly—sing. Ironic that when Gideon was uttering those very words, all she could think about was the imminent interview with Phillip.

She recalled his face when she had asked him to leave. Her anxiety had made her clumsy; still he could have, should have waited until she was free to come to him. Free to say yes to him. She would make it up to him.

She hugged the gloriously romantic words to her heart.

> Come live with me and be my love,
> And we shall all the pleasures prove.

She had no doubt that if anyone could prove all the pleasures, it would be Gideon. She shivered as she thought of it. Further lines echoed in her head as she descended the stairs.

> And I will make thee beds of roses,
> And a thousand fragrant posies;

Beds of roses. There would be an occasional thorn, no doubt, but with Gideon, who would notice? Or care?

> Fair-linèd slippers for the cold,
> With buckles of the purest gold.

She had no need of gold buckles on her slippers. A ridiculous extravagance. Not to mention out of date! Besides, once she was free, she would go to him barefoot!

She reached the drawing room. It was time to put aside the dream of a love without cost or judgment, of proving pleasures and lying in beds of roses with a dark-eyed laughing man. First she had to face what she had done with her life. Only then could she move on.

"Phillip," she greeted him as she entered the drawing room.

"My dear Prue!" Phillip strode across the room, placed his hands on her shoulders and kissed her carefully on each cheek.

It was as if she were standing outside her body, observing the whole with dispassion. He smelled of . . . some exotic scent—patchouli and musk, perhaps? It was oddly redolent of the Duke of Dinstable's butler. How bizarre. Here she was, being embraced by her long-lost fiancé, and his scent reminded her of someone's butler.

At last he released her. "Ah, Prudence, Prudence," he exclaimed. "How you have grown up!" He stared at her for a moment, then placed a kiss on her lips.

Prudence, feeling guilty, endured it stiffly. It was not how he'd kissed her in the past. His lips were seeking, demanding. She kept her own lips firmly closed.

His ardour was very disconcerting. She hadn't expected it. She should have. As far as Phillip was concerned, they were still betrothed.

He loosened his grip and Prudence stepped quickly backward.

"Still a shy little mouse, I see."

She tried to smile, to mitigate her rejection of him. "It's been such a long time, Phillip. I . . . I am sorry."

"I must say, I expected a warmer welcome from you, little Prudish," he said. "We did a sight more than that when you were a girl, if you recall."

"Only once. And I didn't want it then, either," she retorted. "And there were such consequences of that act—" She bit off the words. It was not fair to greet him with complaints and recriminations. Not after all this time. Water under the bridge. She was finished with this man.

She softened her tone. "I am sorry, Phillip. We are not the people we once were. We need to acquaint ourselves with the people we have become. Much has happened since that day we became betrothed."

He frowned.

She drew the ring from the neck of her gown. "I have kept your family ring safe all these years."

He looked a bit nonplussed. "Ah, yes. Good."

This was the moment she had been waiting for. She slipped the ring off the chain and said, "Phillip. I'm sorry, but I cannot keep your ring any longer. I cannot marry you."

There was a short silence in the room. He placed his hands on her shoulders and turned her to face him.

"*You* are breaking the betrothal?" His voice was incredulous. "After four and a half years of wearing my ring?"

She swallowed and nodded. The first promise she had ever broken.

"Why?"

She said nothing. She held the ring out to him. He took it and examined it carefully, hefting it in his hand as if gauging its weight. "Solid."

"Well, it would have to be to have been handed down by all those female ancestors, wouldn't it?"

"Female ancest—? Oh yes, indeed, yes. The ancestors."

He fiddled with it, as if unsure what to do. "Does Lord Dereham know about this?"

"If you mean the ring, no. I kept it hidden, as you instructed. If you mean does he know of the betrothal, no again. In any case, Grandpapa is no longer the issue—we've left his house, never to return."

"Yes, your sisters said this morning that you'd run away. A most foolhardy thing to do, Prudence. He is your legal guardian!"

"In a short time, he will be my guardian no longer. Once I turn one and twenty, I shall take possession of my inheritance, and we shall all be free of Grandpapa forever."

"But why go to these hysterical extremes and risk his displeasure? What if he should disinherit you? It is most unwise, Prudence, most unwise!"

Prudence stared at him in disbelief. She had told him in her letters how harshly Grandpapa treated them. She'd even told him the worst thing, the thing she had told no one else. "You *know* how unbearable it was living with him," she said slowly. "I wrote to you often about it. You can't possibly have forgotten."

Phillip waved a dismissive hand. "I am wise enough in the ways of the world to recognize excessive female sensibility when I see it."

Prudence blinked. *Excessive female sensibility?*

Phillip, oblivious, continued, "It could not have been easy for the old man, having five young females on his hands. If he was a little old-fashioned, well, that is understandable. And a little discipline never hurt anyone. Besides, he must be very old by now. He can't live for much longer, and then it will all be worth it. He's full of juice, you know."

Prudence said slowly, "So that is why you never responded . . ."

"Now, Prue, be fair. I probably didn't get the letters you're talking about. You know how unreliable the posts are to India." Phillip did not meet her eyes. "In any case, if I'd done as you begged me—come home to take you all away—by the time I returned home you would have forgotten whatever little problem it was you'd written about in the first place. A pretty fool I would have looked then!"

He didn't seem to realize he'd contradicted himself. He *had* received that all-important letter.

"So you simply ignored what I said."

"Now, now, Prue, don't be difficult. I was a world away. You have no idea of the hardships I was facing in India."

"But when I told you . . . the baby . . ." She could not speak.

He flushed. "Hush. There is no need to talk of such indelicate matters. How it happened was unfortunate, but it was no doubt for the best."

Indelicate matters. She walked over to the window and stared out of it blindly. She had wanted so badly to share her grief about the baby with him, the father, and now it seemed he felt none.

She turned back suddenly. "So, you think we should have stayed with Grandpapa—for the money? And simply overlooked his cruelty toward us?" She searched his face. "And it *was* cruelty, Phillip, not 'a little discipline,' as you call it."

He shuffled his feet uncomfortably. "Females are apt to exaggerate such matters. If you only knew the hardship, the privations I suffered in India trying to make my fortune—"

Prudence narrowed her eyes. "It's all money with you, isn't it? You think we should have stayed for the money. You did not send for me when I needed you, because you were too busy making your fortune. Were you always like this? Was I simply blind?"

Phillip shrugged and said indulgently, "Now, would I bother you with weighty financial matters when we were courting? Females are well known to be impractical and unworldly—"

Prudence snorted, and misinterpreting, Phillip hastened to reassure her. "We men do find it charming, I assure you. I admit, even last year I might have sung a different tune, for it looked like your grandfather had lost his whole fortune. The company nearly went bankrupt, you know, and we all had an anxious time of it. But then four or five months ago it took a sudden turn for the better and now it is flourishing like you wouldn't believe! He is still worth buttering up, believe you me."

Prudence felt queasy. How could she have ever thought this pompous, mercenary creature was the love of her life? He must have had this mercenary streak in him all along. How could she not have seen it? He did not even care about their child! He'd received the letter and simply hadn't bothered to respond. Her baby was *an indelicate matter*. Its death was *for the best*.

She could barely look at him, let alone be polite to him. Rage and bitter betrayal filled her throat, threatening to boil up out of her and scald them both. She wanted to punch him, to scream at him like a virago. She was unable to speak.

She had wasted years of her life—and worse—on an idol with feet of clay, a vain and shallow man to whom money was more important than Prudence or their child. How could she have been so blind, so stupid? Gideon was right. Phillip had been her rat.

He sat down, smoothing his elegant inexpressibles, seemingly oblivious of her emotional state, and glanced critically around the room. "If you won't stay at Dereham Court, I still don't understand why you are not with another relative, your great-uncle, for instance. These people you are staying with, have they cozened you into this bold and unbecoming independence? Because I'll have you know I made investigations and I cannot like your being here, not one bit! Staying with some woman you don't even know. The relict of some fellow in the Argentine! Good grief, Prudence, don't you know any better?"

Prudence put a firm hold on her temper. "Lady Augusta—"

"According to my . . . my hosts, who are very respectable people, this Lady Augusta del Foreigner simply appeared in Bath one day. None of them had heard of her at all before that. She is not listed in Debretts! She is an adventuress, mark my words!"

"Nonsense—" Prudence began, but Phillip swept on.

"I have had her pointed out to me in the street. She has a head of hair that would shame an opera dancer." He glanced at her own red hair as he spoke. "And she paints her face. Lady, my foot!" He sniffed. "They make up titles over there, you know."

"Fustian! She is—"

He waved her assurances aside with a lofty hand. "Be guided by one who has experienced a great deal more of the world than you have, Prudence. My hosts do not know her, and my own common sense has filled in the rest of the picture."

Prudence folded her arms militantly. Her hands itched to box his pompous ears. Had she been totally blind at sixteen? It was a frightening thought, to realize one could delude oneself so completely.

"In addition, there are serious doubts about this duke your sister is supposed to be betrothed to," Phillip declared. "One of my hosts is second cousin to the aunt of a duke, and is in a position to know such things. They are acquainted with all the most important members of London society and they know that while a Duke of Dinstable is listed in Debretts, he actually lives in the far north of Scotland and never sees a soul. I think that shows you." He sat back and regarded her smugly, but when she didn't respond, he added, "Your so-called duke must be a fraud."

"No, he was a hermi—"

"You have led Charity into a pretty pickle. I'll lay odds her betrothed is a nameless adventurer after your sister's inheritance."

"Poppycock!" snapped Prudence. "Your hosts are mistaken."

"They are extremely respectable, extremely well-connected, well-to-do people," Phillip rebuked her. "And as for Lord Carradice, my hosts *have* heard of him—and it's all to his discredit, believe you me! He is *notorious*, Prudence! He is a rake, a rogue, and a libertine—"

"Nonsense!" Prudence retorted. "He *was* a rake, I know, but to us he has been nothing but kind and generous and I will not have him slandered in this—"

"You cannot be expected to understand. No doubt he has exerted his fatal charm on your feminine sensibilities."

Prudence had had enough. "Well, yes, actually he has! So much so that I am going to marry him."

Phillip's jaw dropped. He rallied quickly. "So this is at the core of it. You poor, deluded creature! Rakes like Carradice don't marry girls, they seduce them and then abandon them."

His blatant hypocrisy took her breath away. Prudence raised her eyebrows and stared at him in silent indignation.

Phillip reddened as he made the connection. "That was different. I gave you a ring."

"That made it all right, did it? Well, now I'm giving the ring back."

"To marry Carradice?" he scoffed and put the ring on the table.

"Yes. As a matter of fact, he proposed to me not an hour ago, in this very room."

"Proposed or made you a proposition?"

"Proposed."

Phillip snorted. "I did not hear the thunderclaps announcing that the world had changed. Did he actually say it, in so many words?"

"What do you mean? Of course he said it."

"So he actually said, 'Will you marry me?' and used words like *marriage, settlements, wedding, church, banns, speak to your grandfather*."

Prudence tossed her head. "No, but—"

"What words did he use?"

Prudence did not want to share Gideon's tender words with Phillip, but she was determined to defend him, make Phillip understand. She said proudly, "He told me he wanted me. He begged me to let him take care of me, to protect me." Nobody in her life had ever spoken such words to her.

"Protect you!" Phillip scoffed. "You know what that means, don't you? To take a woman under your protection is another way of saying make her your mistress."

"No, that's not what he meant! He wants to marry me!"

"That's what you think. It's not what he said, though, is it?" Phillip shook his head. "You are such an innocent, Prue. How do you think rakes seduce good girls? By making them think a wedding is in the offing. Rake Carradice is too clever to say the words that will have him liable to a breach of promise case. If he did not say 'marriage' or 'wedding,' or discuss settlements, take it from me, he does not mean honestly by you."

"He does," Prudence argued. "He does mean honestly by me. I'm sure of it. You simply don't understand."

"I suppose you told him about the . . . the indiscretion."

He meant her baby. Prudence held her head high. "Yes, I did."

He nodded. "That explains it, then. Knows you're used goods. No need to treat you like a virtuous girl."

"That's not how it is!" Prudence's voice shook. "You don't understand."

"I understand, all right. Why buy the cow when you can get the milk for free?"

"You are vulgar and disgusting!" She stormed to the window and stared out, mastering her emotions. He was disgusting, of course. But his words shook her more than she wanted to admit. They echoed her earlier fears about Gideon's intentions.

Outside, mist was beginning to gather, seeping up from the cold valleys.

The unvarnished truth was that Gideon hadn't used the marriage words. He hadn't said, "Will you marry me?" He'd said, "Come live with me and be my love."

She pressed her hot cheek against the chilled glass of the window. Why had he put it that way? Why hadn't he used the simple age-old words, *I love you, will you marry me?*

Like acid, the questions slowly corroded away her earlier confidence.

She turned. Phillip sat, smug and righteous in his natty coat and over-ornate tie. Her self-confidence, never very high, plummeted. Here was a living example of her ability to judge men. It was very depressing.

All she could go on were her own feelings. She loved Gideon, she did. And he wanted her, she knew. But for what role?

Phillip had planted doubts deep enough to take root.

"This is what comes of running away from your grandfather. You should return there at once, where people respect you."

"People here respect me more than I've ever been respected! I will never go back to the Court!"

"That man is out to seduce you!"

Prudence shrugged. "I don't believe you." She had no intention of letting him see his doubts had affected her in any way.

Phillip, annoyed with her refusal to be persuaded, marched several paces back and forth across the room. His brow was furrowed as he considered the situation.

"So, you are determined to jilt me—and for a man who is a known rake!"

"Yes, I'm sorry. But I must."

"You realize it will make a total laughingstock of me?"

"I don't know why it should, since our betrothal has been secret to all but a few."

He paused, then shook his head. "I have my pride, Prudence. Besides, the people I am staying with must know there is some connection, since I have been making inquiries on your behalf."

"You had no need to make any inquiries."

"I disagree. Now, how to get through this mess with the least-possible unpleasantness? I have my pride to consider."

"Yes, so you said, but—"

"And since you have jilted me, I think it's only fair that you put my interests first in this. I don't wish to be embroiled in any awkwardness. I am to stay in Bath only another week. Would it be too much to ask if you stayed away from all public engagements for the next week, in order that we not meet in public and thus cause awkward questions to be asked?"

"I do not see why there need be any awkwardness. The betrothal was secret."

He waved her objection away. "Allow me to know what is best, Prudence. Besides, I have no wish to be associated in any way with the raffish and unsavory persons with whom you have become familiar. Even as neighbors from Norfolk, we would be forced into unwelcome contact, and I do not wish to embarrass my hosts with the connection."

"Raffish and unsavory? How dare you insult the kindest—"

He cut her off. "Carradice is a man not fit for you or your sisters to associate with. And neither, I'm sure, is this bogus duke and his opera-dancer aunt."

"Opera dancer, am I?" came a melodious voice from the doorway. "How delicious! I suspect I would have enjoyed being an opera dancer in my youth; they seem to have such fun." Lady August sailed into the room, amusement writ large on her face. "Only that sort of dancing is very strenuous and sometimes painful, I believe. After my first marriage I found a much more agreeable outlet for my energy." She smiled, her meaning as clear and shocking as it was unstated.

Phillip straightened, affronted. He took in the bright hair and the vivid face, which anyone could see was no stranger to the paint box. Manners got the better of him, however, and he gave a stiff little bow.

Lady Augusta looked him over, her gaze lingering on the complicated neckcloth, the extremely high, starched shirt points, the heavily embroidered waistcoat, and the tightly molded coat with its nipped-in waist. Her smile deepened, and she said, "I take it you are this Mr. Otterclogs we have heard so much about."

Phillip glared. "My name is Otterbury, madam. I believe you have the advantage of me."

"Oh, I'm certain I do," said Lady Augusta with a soft chuckle. She sank onto the sofa in a languid swish of purple silk. "Sit down, Mr. Otterbanks, sit down." She patted the sofa. "Miss Merridew's long-lost betrothed need stand on no ceremony here."

Clearly appalled by this friendly invitation, Phillip snapped at her, "As to that, madam, Miss Merridew and I have agreed to sever our erstwhile informal agreement."

Lady Augusta clapped her hands in delight. "Well done, Prudence, my dear. My felicitations!"

Phillip stiffened further. He turned to Prudence. "This is no fit company for you."

"I disagree," Prudence said frostily.

He said in a low, angry tone, "You have become very willful, Prudence. It is not seemly in a lady."

"Pshaw!" came a scornful voice from the sofa. "Absolute tosh, Mr. Otterbanks, and if this is the way you did your courting, I am not at all surprised that that you are still unwed."

To Prudence's amazement, a dull, red color flooded Phillip's cheeks. "My marital status is none of your business, madam," he snapped. "Be so good as to leave me alone with Miss Merridew, if you please."

"I do not please," Lady Augusta responded sweetly. "I am morally responsible for this young lady, and I can see it will do her no good at all to be alone in your company. In fact, Mr. Ottertosh"—she rose from the sofa—"I think it is high time you departed. Shoebridge shall show you the way out." She reached for the bellpull and yanked hard.

Phillip drew himself up stiffly. "I shall go, madam, since you demonstrate so little understanding of the ways of polite society. Not that it surprises me in the least! And my name is Otterbury, not Otterbanks or Ottertosh." He turned to Prudence and said in a low, angry voice, "Consider what you owe me. Your grandfather's good will is vital to my future. I *insist* you return to Dereham Court."

"Never!" Prudence grated through her teeth.

He set his jaw and considered her for a short moment. In a more conciliatory tone, he said, "Very well, I daresay you have your reasons. At the very least, will you refrain from making any public appearances in Bath?" He added in a low voice, "It can do you no good to be seen in public with this woman."

"I assure you, Lady Augusta is of the utmost—"

"We shall not argue," he interrupted. "Promise me not to attend any social events for the moment—your sisters, too. Will you make that small concession to me, at least? If you are determined to jilt me after all this time it is the least you can do."

Prudence regarded him a moment as she considered his request. Not to go to public balls and routs for a week; it was little enough to ask, and if his pride was truly lacerated by her betrayal, it might help him. Besides, they were in the throes of preparing for Charity's wedding. There would be little time for parties. She nodded. "Very well, I agree."

"You promise? No public appearances for the next week?"

She nodded again and Phillip heaved a sigh of relief.

"Good. Then in that case I will take my leave." He made a shallow, frosty bow in the direction of Lady August, "Good day to you, madam." Then he allowed the waiting butler to show him out.

Lady Augusta watched him leave, her eyes narrowed. The moment the door closed behind him she said, "That man is hiding something, mark my words. He has his own reasons for not wanting you to to be seen abroad—and they have nothing to do with his being jilted or my so-called past as an opera dancer."

Prudence picked up the ring Phillip had left behind. She was tempted to throw it out the window, but it was the traditional betrothal ring of the Otterbury brides. She might be furious with Phillip at the moment, but she had no quarrel with the women of his family. Mrs. Otterbury had once been very kind to Prudence and her sisters. She slipped the ring back on its chain and catching Lady Augusta's eyes, explained, "I'll give it back to him next time I see him. I've carried it like this all these years; a few more days won't matter."

Wednesday dawned fine and warm. Prudence woke early, having slept little through the night. She lay in bed, watching sun-kissed dust motes dancing in the air. The first Merridew girl would be wed this day. *Did Mama and Papa know?* she wondered.

"Prue, are you awake?" Charity pushed open the bedchamber door. She was barefoot and in her nightgown. "I'm too excited to sleep. Can I come in with you?"

"Of course, dearest."

With one bound, Charity jumped onto the bed and snuggled down into the bedclothes. She hugged her sister exuberantly. "I thought I would be nervous but I find I cannot wait. And yet I am a little sad, too. This is the last time we shall be sisters in quite this way. I am about to become a married lady . . . Prue, can you believe it?"

Prudence laughed. "Not only a married lady, you will be a duchess."

Charity pulled a wry face. "Now that part I am not at all sure of," she confessed. "I don't feel like a duchess."

"But you are sure about the duke, aren't you?"

"Oh yes," she said raptly. "He is so wonderful, Prue. So strong and kind and . . . he is such a dear, gentle, lovely man." She blinked suddenly as tears formed on her long lashes. "I cannot believe it. Prue. That such a man would care for me. I never thought . . . never believed I could be so happy." She hugged her sister convulsively. "Thank you, dearest Prue, thank you! If it had not been for your bravery, I don't know what would have become of us. And now, here we are, and the sun is shining, and I am so very much in love and happier than I could believe possible. You did it, Prue! You have brought me to that place you promised, and I thank you with all my heart."

Prudence felt tears prickle against her own lashes as she

hugged her sister to her. It was as if a load had been suddenly lifted off her shoulders. They had come through it. The grim days of Grandpapa were truly behind them. Charity was in love and about to be married. The Merridew girls were no longer alone and friendless. All would be well. It had to be.

Lady Augusta poked her bright head around the door. "Girls, girls, are you awake? Come, arise, there is so much to do. It is a perfect day for a wedding!"

Charity was radiant. Dressed in a celestial blue silk gown richly trimmed with blond lace, she was a vision to take one's breath away. It was as if she glowed from within. Her dress was the exact color of her eyes. *Mama's eyes*, thought Prudence. For a moment she wished she had not sold Mama's sapphires. They would have looked perfect on Charity but she dismissed the melancholy thought. This was not a day for regrets. And had they not sold the sapphires, they could not have reached this point . . .

They all looked beautiful, her sisters, like a bunch of perfect blooms; Faith and Hope in the palest of pale pink dresses, both with slightly scooped necklines and feeling very grown-up. Grace, like Prudence, was dressed in pale jonquil with knots of blue ribbon around the hem.

"Oh, what perfect visions you all are," exclaimed Lady Augusta, herself resplendent in a gown of rich maroon and aqua, which clashed brilliantly with her hair. "It is a crime, a positive crime to waste this sight on a bunch of Bath nobodies. Still, I comfort myself with the reflection that I shall attend to all your court presentations and preside over your coming-outs!"

Prudence glanced at her in surprise.

Lady Augusta caught her look. "You don't think I am letting you go now, do you, Prudence? I haven't had such fun in years. After this wedding I shall be Charity's aunt indeed, and therefore, you shall all be my nieces. I never had children, you see, was never blessed. And now . . . it's almost as good as having five daughters." She blinked rapidly and exclaimed crossly, "Dratted weddings! They always make me excessively sentimental, but I shall not cry! I vow it. If I do, this lampblack concoction will run, and then I shall look a sight!" She glanced at Prudence and winked. "Well, you don't think these dark lashes are natural, do you?"

Prudence laughed. "I never gave it any thought, ma'am."

Lady Augusta turned to Charity. "Now, my dear, here is your something old and something borrowed. I was married in it in Argentina, a gift from my husband. It was his mother's." She produced a magnificent handmade white-lace mantilla, laid it carefully over Charity's shining locks, and stood back. "Perfect, my dear, just perfect. You look like an angel. Oh dear, I should never have darkened my lashes." She pulled out a wisp of lace-edged cambric and carefully applied it to her eyes.

"Now, the something new is your gown, and I must say the dressmaker has done us proud, my dears. I hadn't dreamed we would find someone so capable in this town at such short notice."

"And it is also something blue," piped up Grace, "so that's everything."

"No, not quite, my dear. My nephew Carradice sent these around this morning. Said Miss Prudence would wish her sister to go to her bridal wearing these stones." And she drew from a box a sapphire necklace and matching earrings.

Prudence stared. "But they are . . . they are . . ." She was unable to speak for emotion. How had he known? How could he have guessed what this would mean to her, to all of them?

"Mama's sapphires," said Charity softly. She turned to her younger sisters and explained, "Mama was married in these. They were her wedding gift from Papa. Now we shall have Mama and Papa with us at my wedding. How kind of Lord Carradice to send for them. Did you ask him to, Prue?"

Prudence just shook her head, her heart too full to speak.

"Now, here are the carriages to take us to the abbey," said Lady Augusta briskly. "In you get, gels. Grace and the twins in the first one with me, and Prudence and the bride in the second one. Wait a few minutes before you set off, Prudence, the bride should always be a little late."

"Oh, but ma'am," Charity exclaimed.

"Nonsense. It is good for the groom to be made to wait.

Men need to be kept on their toes, ladies, remember that. Never let them take you for granted!"

Bath Abbey glowed in the sunshine. The bishop had agreed to perform the ceremony and stood at the altar, gorgeous in his embroidered vestments. Edward awaited the arrival of his bride, pale, neat, and anxious. Gideon lounged next to him.

The doors opened, the organ music swelled, filling the huge, vaulted abbey with magnificence. Neither Edward nor Gideon noticed. They each had eyes only for their beloved ones.

Prudence's eyes clung to Gideon. She wanted to thank him, to tell him what his gesture of the sapphires had meant to her, to them all. But the wedding began and the moment was lost.

The bishop began the service with a long and rambling sermon about the holy estate of matrimony and the solemn commitment it was. It seemed to go on forever. The attention of his small, captive congregation soon wandered.

In such a huge and venerable church Prudence felt small and insignificant in the scheme of things. Oddly enough, it was a comforting feeling. Her mind was filled with Gideon. His eyes caressed her; she tried to avoid his gaze. She needed to talk to him, to have it clear between them what he wanted of her, but she couldn't discuss such things at her sister's wedding.

She was aware of every slight shift and nuance in his posture.

Was Phillip right? Would this be the closest she would ever get to standing in front of the altar with Lord Carradice?

The bishop rambled on and on . . . and at one point surprised Prudence in a huge yawn. She'd hardly slept the night before. Embarrassed, she tried to pay better attention.

Finally, the bishop uttered the familiar words, "Who gives this woman to be married to this man?"

It was her cue. Prudence took a breath and stepped forward. As eldest sister, and in the absence of male relatives, she would give away the bride. "I—"

"I do." A ringing voice echoed from the back of the church.

With one accord, the entire wedding party swung around. "Great-uncle Oswald!"

And indeed it was Great-uncle Oswald himself, dressed in his finest morning suit, his hat tucked under his arm as he strode down the aisle, his face wreathed with smiles.

Great-uncle Oswald here in Bath? And how could he know to come here, to the abbey, at this time? Prudence swung around and met Lord Carradice's gaze with a silent question. Had he told Great-uncle Oswald? Lord Carradice shook his head. It seemed he was as surprised as anyone.

Had Grandpapa come, too? Prudence was filled with misgiving. Great-uncle Oswald was beaming, she told herself. Could she trust his smiles? He'd said "I do." It wouldn't be a trick, would it? Her anxious gaze swept the church behind him. Nobody followed him in.

"Grandpapa?" Prudence asked as he reached the small wedding party assembled at the altar.

Great-uncle Oswald shook his head and patted her shoulder. "Safely back at the Court," he said in a low voice. "Doesn't know anythin' about this little aff—" He stopped suddenly. "Good God! Is that Gussie Manningham? I thought she was in Argentina."

"Er, yes, I suppose it is, if you mean Edward and Gideon's aunt, Lady Augusta Montigua del Fuego," Prudence said, considerably surprised by the sudden change of subject.

"Where's her husband?" whispered Great-uncle Oswald.

"I believe she was widowed last year and returned to England some months ago," responded Prudence, distracted. "Great-uncle Oswald, how did you know about the wedding? How did you find us?"

"Widowed, eh?" muttered Great-uncle Oswald. He raised his voice. "Well, get on with it, Chuffy. I've already said I'd give this beautiful great-niece of mine in marriage, so let's finish this weddin'."

To everyone's amazement, the immensely dignified bishop responded mildly, "If you've finished nattering, Ozzie, I shall. Thought you'd never get here. Never bored a congregation so badly in my life." He winked at Prudence; then, returning to his usual sonorous tone, continued with the wedding service.

Prudence blinked. Chuffy and Ozzie? The bishop's sprawling speech had been a delaying tactic. He must have sent for Great-uncle Oswald. But how did he know they'd run away? And why send for Great-uncle Oswald and not Grandpapa? And why was Great-uncle Oswald suddenly more interested in Lady Augusta than in his great-niece's runaway wedding? It was all very confusing.

Chapter Eighteen

∞

"Now join your hands, and with your hands your hearts."
WILLIAM SHAKESPEARE

"GOOD-BYE, GOOD-BYE!"

The carriage rumbled away down the street, piled high with baggage, the Duke of Dinstable and his brand-new duchess waving from the windows. Prudence, the twins, and Grace spilled out into the street, calling farewells and exhortations to write. Lady Augusta and Great-uncle Oswald watched from the steps of the house. Lord Carradice leaned against the railings of his own house, watching the departure, an odd, twisted smile on his face. Prudence wondered for a fleeting moment what that look betokened, but the excitement of her sister's departure pushed it from her mind.

They watched until the coach swung out of sight. Feeling suddenly bereft, Prudence turned instinctively toward Gideon. She had barely spoken a word to him at the wedding, and Charity and the duke's decision to set out for Scotland immediately had meant an abbreviated wedding breakfast, much to Lady Augusta's frustration. It was the first real opportunity to speak to Lord Carradice.

But how did you ask a man whose wonderful gesture had brought magic to your sister's wedding day, if he wanted to make you his mistress? And if he did, what would she say?

She needed to repay him for the sapphires, too. She hoped she had enough money left.

Before she could speak to him, however, Great-uncle Oswald called her over. "Now young missy, I think you have some explainin' to do. Shall we step into the sittin' room and over a soothin' cup of tea you shall explain to me why the deuce you didn't tell me you'd run off from the Court in the first place!"

"Tea, Great-uncle Oswald?" Prudence asked in an effort to distract him. "I thought you didn't approve of tea."

"I've given Gussie's cook a packet of my best chamomile, so enough roundaboutation, miss, and into the house with you!"

Meekly, Prudence preceded him into Lady Augusta's house.

"You were protectin' *me?*" uttered Great-uncle Oswald in amazement. "You thought *I* was dependent on my brother?"

"Aren't you?" Prudence asked, puzzled. "He was always complaining of how much it cost to keep you."

"He what?" Great-uncle Oswald's eyebrows rose.

"And your extravagant ways."

He snorted. "Well, that I can believe. Always was the nipfarthingest fellow when it came to spendin' money on the good things in life. But when it came to business, now—"

"Business?" Prudence repeated. "I thought his business was hugely successful."

"Hah!" snorted Great-uncle Oswald. "Was until he and I parted ways more than ten years ago. Without me to prevent his wild schemes and mad speculation, the company went steadily downhill! No head for business at all, you know. Throws good money after bad on the most ludicrous ventures."

"But—"

He shook his head again in wonder. "Can't get over it— you were protectin' *me!* Five little gels, runnin' off to who knew where, exposin' yourselves to horrible danger, only to protect *me!*" He took out a large handkerchief and blew noisily into it.

Prudence was touched. "Of course we wanted to save you

from Grandpapa's wrath, Great-uncle Oswald. He was forever reading of your appearance at some society event, and he would invariably rant and rave and threaten to cut you off without a penny. And then when we came to you, you were so kind and generous toward us, taking us in without a murmur, and it can't have been easy for you."

"But it was delightful, m'dear," Great-uncle Oswald said, shocked. "Don't know when I've enjoyed so much excitement as I have since you gels came to enliven my home. M'life was dwindling into lonely old age before you arrived." He blew his nose again, a long, quavering trumpet of emotion.

Touched, Prudence prompted him into less emotional waters. "Er, the business, Great-uncle Oswald. You were saying it was failing . . ."

"Oh, couldn't let the family company fail—bad business for a start, even if it was nothing to do with me—bad for all of us! Employees who've been with us thirty years and more. Bought out your grandfather a few months back. Flatter myself it's on the up-and-up now."

Phillip had said much the same thing, Prudence recalled. Only he had not mentioned Great-uncle Oswald at all. "Do those employees know of your involvement in the company now?" she asked.

"No. No need to make a fuss o' things. Don't like it widely known I'm in trade at all, though it did get me my handle."

"Your handle?" Prudence was puzzled.

"Well, good gracious, gel, don't you remember anything from your schoolroom lessons? I'm *Sir* Oswald Merridew, ain't I? The younger son of a baron ain't usually a knight, is he?" He sat back in his chair with a satisfied air. "No, nothing of mine came to me from my father or my brother. Earned it all myself—includin' the knighthood." He noticed Prudence's confusion and explained, "Services to the Crown, say no more," and laid his finger along the side of his nose.

Prudence sat back in her chair, astounded. "So you do not depend on Grandpapa's charity?"

Great-uncle Oswald snorted. "I should say not! Boot's on

the other foot, if you want to know the truth. Old fool's speculations left him without a feather to fly with. Was in debt to his eyebrows until I towed him out of the River Tick."

"Grandpapa was in debt?" Prudence was stunned. "So you have supported us all along? Even before we came to London? We owe you so—"

"Nonsense, nonsense. Owe me nothin' at all! Such foolishness," he blustered in embarrassment. "What else am I going to do with my money, eh? Childless old widower like m'self. It'll all come to you gels in the end, so don't fret about anyone owin' anything, m'dear. But if anyone's a pensioner on somebody's charity, 'tis your grandfather, and so I told him when he arrived in London last week, blowin' sound and fury." He snorted again. "Sent him packin' back to Dereham with a flea in his ear and a warning that if he left the Court again without an invitation from me, I'd be cuttin' *him* off without a penny!" He glared at Prudence indignantly. "D' ye know, he was makin' threats against you that would make your hair curl! Has he done that before? Laid a finger on any of you gels?"

Prudence could not speak for the relief flowing through her. She jumped up and hugged Great-uncle Oswald fervently. She'd been half expecting Grandpapa to arrive at any minute; instead he was back at the Court to stay. She felt so much lighter and freer. Charity was married and happy, Grandpapa was no longer a threat to them, and their future, for the first time in years, looked rosy. She felt Great-uncle Oswald's hand patting her on the back, soothing, awkward, a little uncertain. She collected herself and stepped back.

"Well, missy? Did he mistreat you?" His kind, old face was crumpled with worry and not a little guilt.

She didn't want to lie anymore now that the need to lie had passed. On the other hand, to tell this sweet man how terribly Grandpapa had treated them would make him even more upset than he was. He would feel responsible and be racked with guilt. She could see no point in raking up old grievances. Better to let it go.

"He was a harsh disciplinarian," she said, recalling Phillip's view of the matter, "but then, having five young girls to deal with probably tried his patience severely. Let us talk of him no more, dear Great-uncle Oswald—or should I call you Great-uncle Ozzie? You are very sneaky, you know, turning up like that at the abbey."

He chuckled. "Surprised you, didn't I? Thing is, went to school with old Chuffy. Can't believe he's turned into a bishop, of all things. Was a shockin' loose screw at school. Anyway, when Dinstable and young Charity applied for the license, Chuffy smelled a rat. Recognized the name, of course. Knew I had my great-nieces staying with me in London, so wondered how one of them came to be in Bath applying for a weddin' license. Sent me a note, and I came posthaste. Can't have you gels getting married without me there to give you away, can I?" His smile died away, and he pursed his lips in a dissatisfied pout. "Didn't think much of the wedding itself, though, Prudence. The abbey is a fine big church, and good to have a bishop do the deed, but apart from that, bit of a hole-in-the-corner affair for a duke and a diamond like your sister, if you don't mind me sayin' so, m'dear."

"Oh, but it was exactly how Charity and Edward wanted it," Prudence assured him. "Small and private with only family present. I know Charity was thrilled you came. We all were." She rose from her chair and kissed him warmly on the cheek. "You are very dear to us all, you know."

He pulled out the handkerchief again and blew another long, emotional blast. "You're a dear good girl yourself, and when we fire you and Carradice off, we'll do it in grand style, what? St. George's, Hanover Square, and we'll get Chuffy down to officiate—he looks good in purple, have to say it—and then a ball to celebrate. And o'course, a ball beforehand to announce the engagement—when was it that the Welsh great-aunt died again? Carradice's mourning should be done by then, surely?"

Prudence swallowed. The time had come for her to confess the betrothal to Lord Carradice had been a stratagem. Not a very nice stratagem, she thought guiltily, looking at the beaming elderly man before her. He was such a dear. He would feel dreadful to discover his well-meaning effort to get her settled before letting her beautiful sisters loose on society had, in fact, been a source of much anxiety to them all.

She opened her mouth, but Great-uncle Oswald, clasping his damp handkerchief, smiled at her with such benevolent affection that she could not do it. And with her future relationship with Lord Carradice still unclear, she could not leave things as they were.

"Lord Carradice and I have quarreled," she blurted. "There will be no wedding in Hanover Square or anywhere else, I'm afraid." There, it was out. Not the whole truth, but enough.

To her amazement, Great-uncle Oswald only chuckled and tucked his handkerchief away. "Pooh! Lovers tiff," he said. "Happens to all newly betrothed couples, once the initial excitement wears off. What happened—Carradice balkin' at the prospect of parson's mousetrap? Shouldn't let it worry you—fellow was a rake. Bound to feel a few qualms about relinquishin' his freedom, but—"

Prudence shook her head. "No, it wasn't that."

"You, is it, gettin' cold feet? Now that *does* surprise me. A rake, now, that's understandable. But you . . ." He peered at her shrewdly. "Not gettin' missish on me, are you, Prudence? If it's . . . er . . . conjugal matters worryin' you, Gussie will set you right."

"No, no!" she assured him, embarrassed to find herself discussing such matters with an elderly male.

Great-uncle Oswald shook his head decisively. "In that case, just a tiff, mark my words. Boy was smitten. Swear to it on my life. And the glow in your face whenever Carradice walks in the door, m'dear —could light a candle with it."

Oh, dear Lord, had she been so obvious? That was what came of Gideon's way of looking at a girl as if . . . as if she were the only girl alive in the world. As if she were the only one he cared about . . . It was those velvet dark eyes of his that did it . . . made a girl feel . . . special, loved . . . cherished. *Wanted.*

Yes, but what did "wanted" *mean?* If Gideon didn't plan to marry her, she wouldn't allow him to be trapped into it by her own scheming and her well-meaning great-uncle's enthusiasm.

She bit her lip. "I'm sorry, Great-uncle Oswald, but our betrothal—Lord Carradice's and mine—is definitely off. And now I must . . . I must retire for a moment. Thank you for coming to the wedding. And you cannot know what a relief it is to me that you have dealt with Grandpapa for us, so thank you for that, as well." She kissed him on the cheek again and hurried from the room.

What a tangled web she had woven herself into. She had just severed two betrothals; no wonder her head ached.

She hesitated. Upstairs was her bed, narrow and cold and private. Lord Carradice would be with the others in the front parlor. She needed to talk to him but at the moment, there would be no chance to be private. There was a wedding to reminisce about and Great-uncle Oswald's arrival to exclaim over. She would have to sit there politely, as if the doubts were not burning her up inside, chatting of trifles, while his dark eyes caressed her and his honeyed tongue teased.

She turned toward the stairs. What she needed was a cup of hot chocolate and a good cry.

"We have been invited to a small party this evening by my old friend, Maud, Lady Gosforth," announced Lady Augusta, brandishing a note that had just arrived. It was the day after the wedding and they were all sitting in the parlor after tea. "I knew Maudie in the old days, before I left for Argentina. I haven't seen her for aeons. Her note says she arrived in Bath a day or two ago and and has just this minute learned I was here. She sent this around, urging me to come and saying if I had houseguests, to bring them, too." She set down the note on the mantelpiece. "How delightful. Maudie was always the one to know all the latest gossip! Oswald, you know Lady Gosforth, don't you?"

"Should say I do. All the world knows Maudie."

"It is exactly what we all need, a little entertainment to cheer us up, for there is nothing worse than a wedding without a proper party to make one feel sadly flat! Gels, you must come, too—not you, I'm sorry, Grace, dear, you are too young as yet. But Faith and Hope certainly, for though you are not yet out, a small, private party in Bath in the home of a family acquaintance is perfectly *comme il faut.*

Now hurry along, girls, we leave at eight. Oswald, may I request your escort?"

Great-uncle Oswald bowed. "Delighted to, Gussie, m'dear, delighted. I shall go next door and change immediately." The duke had given him the use of his house while he and Charity were away, so it was only natural that Lady Augusta had invited him in to tea. Lord Carradice, too, had been invited, but to Prudence's relief, some other engagement—or discretion—had kept him away.

She didn't know whether she wanted to see him or not. How could she keep him at arm's length to talk when all she wanted was to throw herself into his arms?

Faith and Hope followed Great-uncle Oswald from the room, excitedly discussing which dresses to wear. Prudence rose, uncertainly. She had promised Phillip she would not go about socially in Bath for a week and there were three more days to go.

Could a small, private party be called "in public"? No, Prudence decided, and Phillip's doubts about the respectability of Lady Augusta and the duke had always been nonsensical. In any case, she would have the escort of Great-uncle Oswald, and nothing could be more respectable than that.

Prudence went upstairs to change into a party dress.

"You look beautiful, my Prudence," a deep voice said as she came down the stairs a little before eight. "But then, you always do."

She looked down at him. Gideon. Lord Carradice. Gazing up at her, his dark hair gleaming, his eyes were dark and warm upon her. Her throat tightened, and she felt suddenly close to tears. Of course, it was just his way, but oh, when he looked at her like that, with that midnight gaze that caressed and heated her from within, she truly felt beautiful. And her dress really was beautiful, deep blue with a silver tissue overlay and silver trim. "Thank you," she murmured. "I didn't realize you were coming, too, Lord Carradice."

How did you ask a man, "Oh, by the way, did you ask me to marry you the other day or were you merely suggesting I become your mistress?" Formality was the key to surviving this, she hoped.

He stood at the foot of the stairs, smiling faintly, dressed in black satin knee breeches, striped stockings, a white waistcoat, and a black waisted coat with long tails, looking darkly elegant. He must have dispensed with the bandage, for nothing spoiled the line of that elegant coat. The thought gave her relief; he was healing from the injury she had done him.

Nobody else had yet come down. His long, angular face was freshly shaved but retained that dark tinge that she found so attractive in him. Her skin tingled with remembrance of the sensual abrasion of those dark bristles. A faint, pleasurable frisson passed through her. Holding the banister rail, she managed to resume her progress down the stairs, hoping the heat in her cheeks did not betoken that glow Great-uncle Oswald had spoken of.

"Yes, Aunt Gussie sent a note around informing me there was to be a small party and that I was required for escort duty. I did not dare refuse. A terrifying creature when crossed, my aunt."

"I've noticed," said Prudence dryly, even as a lump rose in her throat. He knew she was feeling awkward after their last encounter and was talking nonsense to spare her.

He strode forward as she reached the last few steps and took her hand, as if she were some fragile, delicate creature. Through her evening gloves, she felt his strength, his warmth. He took the silver tissue cloak that was draped across her arm, shook it out, and swung it around her, wrapping her in it, and him. His arms were around her and before she realized what he was about to do, he'd planted a soft kiss on the nape of her neck. A shiver passed through her entire body, and it was all Prudence could do not to lean back into his embrace.

She forced herself to resist, saying in a voice that squeaked with tension, "Could we talk privately tomorrow morning, please?"

"Of course." He added in a low, sincere voice, "Fear not, Imp. I'll importune you no more tonight. I did not mean to distress you just now, but you look so very lovely, like an angel in a silver cloud, I could not help myself. I apologize."

Prudence had no idea what to say. Just as the silence was

stretching to uncomfortable limits, she recalled she owed
him a debt of thanks. "I must thank you for sending us the
sapphire necklace. I don't know how you retrieved it, or how
you knew which one to retrieve, of all the jewelry I sold."
She gazed up at him, "It was the very sapphire set my
mother wore at her wedding, and it meant such a lot to Charity . . . and to me, for her to wear it. I will, of course,
repay—"

His face twisted. "Ah, don't, Imp. You know I don't
want—"

Just then, the twins clattered noisily down the stairs,
dressed in pale yellow muslin and calling for Lord Carradice
to admire them. This he did with alacrity, and her sisters
were delighted by his lavish and very silly compliments.
Grace hung over the banister, watching them a little wistfully.

Lord Carradice glanced up and noticed her. "Greetings,
young Limb," he called up to her. "I thought tomorrow afternoon we might visit a fair. There is one to be held in a village not far from here. Would you care to accompany me?"

Grace called down her assent, her eyes shining.

Prudence bit her lip. Of course he would offer her little
sister some sort of consolation for being left out of the party.
He was Gideon. How could anyone resist him?

Lady Augusta descended the stairs in a wonderfully low-
cut gown of emerald-shot satin and a black-and-gold shawl
draped in the Spanish manner. Around her neck was a necklace of gold and emeralds.

When Great-uncle Oswald arrived, he snatched off his
hat and gazed at her in stunned admiration, muttering,
"Magnificent, b'gad. Magnificent!"

Gideon nudged Prudence, and she followed his amused
gaze to where Lady Augusta was adjusting her shawl with a
vast deal of nonchalance and a satisfied little smile.

"Are we all ready to leave?" said Lady Augusta. "Then
let us do so at once."

Even though the evening was fine and Lady Gosforth's
home only a short walk away, Lady Augusta had ordered a
sedan chair to carry her. "I know they are a little passé," she
explained to the girls, "but I always loved the look of these

things when I was a gel. It looks so marvelous—a lady being carried along in a palanquin like an Oriental princess, with her cicisbei strolling along beside her, carrying her fan—drat it, forgot to bring a fan. Never mind. Oswald, you're my chief cicisbeo, pretend there is a fan, will you?"

To Prudence's astonishment, he chuckled coyly and pretended to carry an invisible fan. The twins exchanged glances and giggled. And indeed it was like an Oriental procession, with Lady Augusta reclining in the palanquin carried by four liveried servants, followed by Great-uncle Oswald, who was flanked on either side by a twin in yellow muslin, then Prudence on Lord Carradice's arm, and bringing up in the rear, James the footman.

They turned the corner. "I thought you said it was to be a small party, ma'am," exclaimed Prudence. Dozens of people milled in front of Lady Gosforth's house, some awaiting entry to the house, others simply there to watch.

Lady Gussie peered out of the palanquin. "Small by Maude's standards, I meant. You didn't think I would bring you to something insipid, did you?"

Prudence had to laugh, but it crossed her mind that this might indeed be what Phillip meant by "in public." It was too late now, however, for they had reached the front door.

Inside, despite the unfashionable early hour, it was a sad crush, by which Prudence was given to understand the party was already a success. The entry foyer and large withdrawing room were filled with people talking and laughing and exclaiming. Lady Gosforth, a tall, Roman-nosed matron, stood at the foot of the stairs, greeting her guests. Prudence thought she looked rather stern and intimidating. Then Lady Gosforth's gaze fell upon them.

"Gussie!" she shrieked.

"Maudie!" All formality disappeared as the two middle-aged ladies embraced like excited schoolgirls, chattering nineteen to the dozen. However, the press of new guests arriving soon forced Lady Gosforth to return to her duties. "But stay here with me, Gussie dearest, and I shall introduce you to everyone. It's been such an age since you were in England that you must be quite out of touch."

She glanced at Lord Carradice, who had reclaimed Prudence's hand and replaced it on his arm the moment she had completed her curtsy. Her shrewd blue eyes dwelt thoughtfully on Prudence, then traveled to her sisters. "I see you have lost no time in meeting the latest beauties on the scene, Carradice. Sir Oswald, my congratulations. These twin angels of yours will cause a sensation when they come out. Enjoy my little party, girls. Gussie, stay with me. I want to hear all about everything."

Gussie agreed enthusiastically and sent the girls and Gideon on ahead, promising to join them later.

It was very crowded in the front drawing room. As they shuffled their way forward, the crowd separated Great-uncle Oswald from them. Lord Carradice cupped Prudence's elbow in a protective grip and steered her through the crush, the twins following in their wake. He was greeted by dozens of people, most of them ladies. Numerous gentlemen, their eyes passing from Hope to Faith and back again, also pressed forward, recalling their acquaintanceship with Lord Carradice and demanding introductions to the new beauties. Eventually they reached a much less-crowded room with French doors standing open, leading out to the terrace and down to the garden. On either side was a shallow alcove, where a number of chairs had been placed.

"If you care to wait here," said Lord Carradice, "I shall procure refreshments. A glass of champagne, Miss Merridew? Ratafia for you, I'm afraid, Miss Hope and Miss Faith."

He had been on his best formal behavior. Prudence wondered why it made her feel so lonely. Given her doubts, formality was the safest, least-distressing path. But it made her feel a little melancholy all the same. She was not at all in the mood for a party. She watched as he disappeared into the crowd.

Instantly a small group of gentlemen surrounded them. They crowded around the twins, pelting them with questions, vying for the beauties' attention. Prudence was quickly relegated to the outer. She felt like the chaperone she had intended to be, but she had had a taste of being wooed, and returning to the role of the plain one was harder than she had expected. Not that she wanted any of these young men to court her.

There was only one man she wanted; she prayed he wanted her in the same way. Until that was resolved . . .

She moved aside and took pleasure in watching her young sisters enjoy their very first social success. Hope, in particular, had yearned for this for so long. She was no longer the clumsy, defiant girl of Dereham place. Now she was a beacon of loveliness and grace, growing in poise by the minute. Faith, too, was in her element, glowing with shy excitement.

Was it only a little over six weeks ago they'd been imprisoned at Dereham, subject to Grandpapa's harsh tyranny? An event such as tonight's had been but a hopeless dream then.

And in a matter of days, it would be Prudence's birthday.

"Prudence, what are you doing here?" It was Phillip, looking appalled.

Prudence offered him an apologetic smile and started to explain, but Phillip cut her off. "I thought I could rely on your promise, and look! You are here, when I specifically forbade it!"

"You do not have the power to forbid me anything," Prudence retorted. "I admit, I agreed to forgo public events for a week, but I understood this to be a small, private party—at least that's what Lady Augusta told me."

"Do you know the harm you have caused by coming here? You must leave immediately!"

"I will do no such thing! There is no harm, Phillip. You are overreacting. Nobody knows of our—our past."

He cast a hasty glance around the room. "You *must* leave. Trust me on this, Prudence. You have no idea how mortifying it would be for me if you are seen, here—with such a woman."

"Poppycock! She is an old friend of Lady Gosforth's. And I will not leave, particularly when the twins are having such a lovely time." Her voice softened. "Look, Phillip, see how happy they are? It is their first grown-up party—their first party of any sort, in fact, and I will not spoil it for them."

"Oh Lord, she cannot be a friend of Lady Gosforth's! You must leave now! If you do not, it will jeopardize everything I have worked for!"

Prudence clenched her fists. "I will not leave! You are too fearful of idle gossip. I assure you, Lady Augusta is of the utmost respectability."

Phillip glared at her in frustration and anger. Prudence glared back.

"Greetings, my bantams," said an amused voice at Prudence's elbow. "Your champagne, Miss Merridew." Lord Carradice handed her a tall glass, glanced from her to Phillip, and gave her a quizzical look. "Will you not introduce us, Miss Merridew?"

"Lord Carradice, Mr. Otterbury," Prudence said baldly.

Lord Carradice gave an affected start of surprise and seized Phillip's hand to shake it. "Let me be the first to congratulate you on your incredible escape, Mr. Ottershanks."

Prudence almost choked. Phillip's escape? From Prudence? But she hadn't yet told him she'd broken their betrothal. The devil was in his smile. She trusted him not an inch! She looked daggers at him.

Lord Carradice smiled blandly back at her.

Phillip bowed stiffly. "My name is Otterbury. Your servant, Lord Carradice." He glanced at Prudence, then added in a suspicious tone, "Escape from what, may I ask?"

"Why, from the tiger, of course." Lord Carradice took a leisurely sip of champagne.

Phillip stared. "I beg your pardon?"

Prudence suddenly realized what he was talking about. She pressed her lips together and tried to keep a straight face.

Lord Carradice frowned. "Or was it an elephant? That was it, yes—you were sat on by an elephant. I must say, you've recovered well—it hardly shows—of course, your head is rather an odd shape, but no one would ever suspect it was the elephant, I assure you."

A small snort of laughter escaped Prudence. She tried to turn it into a cough.

"Miss Merridew, you must be careful of the bubbles in champagne," Lord Carradice said solicitously.

Phillip stiffened even more. "I have no idea what you are talking about."

"I understood you'd been eaten by a tiger or squashed by an elephant. And yet here you are." Gideon smiled affably. "I don't suppose you'd care to tell us the tale of your escape?" He tucked Prudence's hand through his arm and regarded Phillip with every evidence of fascination.

Phillip focused on the hand and frowned. He glanced at the door again. "Miss Merridew, it is time you left. The company is"—he shot a significant glance at Lord Carradice— "inappropriate."

Prudence explained, "Mr. Otterbury wishes me to go home, Lord Carradice. He's afraid my presence here tonight with your aunt and yourself will reflect badly on him."

Lord Carradice turned to Phillip in mild surprise. "On you?"

"My . . . my hostess is a relative of Lady Gosforth," Phillip said stiffly, "and I was concerned her ladyship would be . . ." Unsettled by the look in Lord Carradice's eye, he faltered. "Lady Gosforth is the aunt of a duke, you know," he finished feebly.

"Yes, I know. She and Aunt Gussie have been friends for years," Gideon explained in a friendly fashion. He added, "Aunt Gussie is the aunt of a duke, too. And was once the sister-in-law of one."

"Ahh," Phillip said in a strangled tone.

"Mr. Otterbury suspects the Duke of Dinstable is an impostor," Prudence offered helpfully.

Phillip made faint noises of embarrassed denial.

"No! Is he? An impostor!" Lord Carradice was enchanted. "I shall tell Lady Gosforth at once. She is his godmother, you know. How exciting!"

Puce with mortification, Phillip ran a finger around his collar. "I must have been misinformed. I hope you haven't taken offense, my lord."

"Oh no, not at all, Ottershanks. Any friend of Miss Merridew is a friend of mine. She's the sister-in-law of a duke, you see."

"Otterbury," croaked Phillip.

"And I'm a duke's cousin and was once the nephew of a duke, before he died. Do dead dukes count?"

Phillip mumbled something and bowed again. Prudence buried her nose in champagne.

"There you are, Prudence, Carradice," a voice said from behind. "Wondered where you got to. Twins seem to be havin' a good time of it. There's dancin' in the back parlor, Prudence, if you and Carradice want to join in. I'll keep an eye on the gels here." He noticed Phillip edging inconspicuously away. "How d'ye do, sir."

Phillip bowed swiftly and turned to leave, so Prudence took great pleasure in calling him back and introducing him as a gentleman recently returned from India.

"India, eh? Have a few interests there, myself. And what were you doin' in India, young Otterbury? Ah, Maudie, Gussie, here you are," Great-uncle Oswald said. "Prudence and Carradice are off to dance."

"I suppose I should come with you, then," Lady Augusta said.

"No need for that, Gussie." Great-uncle Oswald stopped her. "Betrothed couple don't need chaperonin' at a private party."

"A betrothed couple!" Lady Gosforth exclaimed. "Carradice is betrothed?"

"Ha! Surprised you, did I, Maudie? Thought you was always ahead of the news, didn't you?"

"Betrothed!" Phillip sounded shocked.

"No, no," Prudence insisted. "It is a mistake! I am *not* betrothed to Lord Carradice."

"Yes, you are," Great-uncle Oswald contradicted her.

"No! I told you it was off." Prudence darted a guilty look at Lord Carradice. "I'm sorry."

"Nonsense," Great-uncle Oswald declared. "A tiff, that's all. Two of you were smellin' of April and May on the way here tonight."

"No, we were not!" Prudence said despairingly. "Truly we were not."

"Actually, I thought you smelled of gardenias," Lord Carradice said. "And I was wearing a cologne scented faintly with sandalwood. It may have worn off; it is very subtle. But you definitely smelled of gardenias. And moonlight."

She gave him a wrathful look, which he returned with a limpid smile. Prudence felt like shaking him. She was embroiled in a stew—of her own making, admittedly—and all he could do was say she smelled of gardenias and moonlight? The foolish man! Did he *want* to be trapped into having to marry her?

Phillip muttered so that only Prudence could hear him, "So your uncle forced his hand, eh, Prudence? Well done."

Prudence winced.

Instantly the humor left Lord Carradice's eyes. "Got something to say, Clotterbury? Spit it out. If you don't like Prudence being betrothed to me, tell it to my face."

"I am not betrothed to you," Prudence wailed.

" 'Course you are," Great-uncle Oswald contradicted her. "But what's it got to do with young Clotterbury here, eh? Clotterbury? Explain yourself."

Phillip's mouth opened and closed silently, like a codfish.

"When did this betrothal happen?" Lady Augusta demanded, distracting Great-uncle Oswald's attention from Otterbury, who heaved a sigh of relief.

"Several weeks back. Carradice came callin' on me in his courtin' clothes, asked my permission. I gave it. Betrothed, all right and tight. Not announced publicly yet because of his Welsh aunt, of course."

"Rake Carradice, caught at last," Lady Gosforth exclaimed with delight.

"Why didn't I know about this, Gideon?" Lady Augusta demanded, clearly aggrieved at not being first with the news. "And what Welsh aunt is this?"

"Auntie Angharad," Gideon informed her solemnly.

Lady Augusta thought for a moment and then declared, "You don't *have* an Auntie Angharad!"

"No," he agreed in a sorrowful voice. "She's dead."

Seeing that the conversation was heading down an impossible path, Prudence declared in a loud voice, "Lord Carradice and I are *not* betrothed and never were." She turned to him, her eyes beseeching him to rescue her. "It is all a misunderstanding, isn't it, Lord Carradice?"

He just looked at her, a small, odd smile on his face. His eyes were dark and suddenly serious. Then audience fell silent, awaiting his answer. Prudence suddenly realized he was not going to save her. He was going to be stupidly noble and confirm the betrothal story to protect her reputation.

But she couldn't allow him to become entrapped by a public declaration at a party held by one of the ton's biggest gossips. It was not fair. She had entangled him in so many lies of her making. It was time she set him free, set them all free, by telling the truth.

"The only man I have ever been betrothed to is Phillip Otterbury!" she announced loudly. Remembering she still carried his ring on a chain, she pulled it out of her bosom. "See? This is the ring he gave me."

There was a small, shocked silence. With one accord the group swung around to stare at Phillip, who looked as if he'd just swallowed a snail.

"Clotterbury?" Great-uncle Oswald exploded. "But you've only just met the fellow!"

"You can't possibly prefer him to Gideon," Lady Augusta exclaimed.

"Oh but this is delicious—" began Lady Gosforth.

"Be quiet, Maud!" snapped Great-uncle Oswald and Lady Augusta in unison.

Phillip gaped at this disrespect for the aunt of a duke, then shrank, realizing everyone was staring at him with varying degrees of hostility.

"Is this true, Clotterbury?"

He gave a sickly smile and hesitated, not knowing what to say.

"Yes, it's true." Prudence came forward and took his hand. He tried to pull away, but she wouldn't let him. She held up the ring. "See? This is the traditional betrothal ring of the Otterbury family."

Phillip swallowed. All eyes were upon him. He tried to speak, found no words came out, cleared his throat, and said finally, "Actually, it's not."

"Not?" Prudence stared at him in shock. "But . . . you told me it was. Handed down for generations."

Phillip shook his head, looking a little green. "It's not."

He swallowed. "It's a ring I got from a pawnbroker. Made of paste."

Prudence blinked, trying to take it in. "You cannot be serious. I've carried this ring for more than four years," she whispered. She looked at Phillip, but he wasn't looking at her. He was looking altogether green.

Paste! From a pawnbroker! Gideon met her stricken gaze, knowing what that ring had meant to her. She'd carried that blasted ugly thing on a chain for more than four years like a ball and chain, courted her grandfather's wrath by doing so, and had even risked her life with a highwayman over it—almost. A worthless old piece of trumpery from a pawnbroker. A symbol of love from a weasel. Damn Otterbury to hell and back!

Gideon strode forward, snatched the ring from Prudence's slackened grasp, gave it to Otterbury, and said, "That's enough, I think. A foolish charade, my Prudence, but that's enough. You and I are betrothed, and that's final." And in front of everyone, he planted a kiss, hard and possessive, on her mouth.

After a moment, Prudence struggled out of his embrace and stood there, staring at him.

"So here you are, Mr. Otterbury," an arch voice said into the silence. "I had quite given up on my ratafia. And now everyone has gone in to supper. Must I expire of hunger and thirst before you remember me?" A lady in a blue lutestring saque joined the group. She slipped her arm familiarly through Phillip's, nodded at Lady Gosforth, and smiled around the group with faint inquiry. "Gracious, how serious everyone looks. And I thought it such a lovely party." She seemed perfectly sure of her welcome.

Otterbury, doing his imitation of a fish, looked even greener than before.

Gideon noted Prudence's reaction; she had no idea who this young woman was. He wondered if Prudence realized the lady was increasing; the proud curve of her belly was not quite disguised by the folds of her gown.

"Er, yes, sorry, I shall take you in to supper immediately," Phillip muttered. "Come along." He began to hustle her away in a manner that had Gideon's suspicions bristling.

He blocked the lady's way. "Will you not introduce us, Clotterbury?"

The lady tittered gaily. "Otterbury, not Clotterbury. People do have trouble with the name, but that is the most amusing of mispronunciations I have yet encountered. And you are—?" She looked expectantly from Gideon to Phillip, who didn't utter a sound. His face was ashen.

"I am Carradice," Gideon bowed suavely. "And this is Miss Merridew; her great-uncle, Sir Oswald Merridew; my aunt, Lady Augusta Montigua del Fuego; and I gather you know Lady Gosforth."

The lady curtsied to each of them and then, since there was no introduction forthcoming from Phillip, she said with simple pride, "And I am Mrs. Otterbury." And as if there could be some doubt, she added, "Mrs. Phillip Otterbury."

Prudence went extremely still. Gideon wanted to wrap her in his arms so she could not be hurt any more by this stupid clod and his silly, vacuous wife. He took a cold, resistless little hand in his, tucked it under his arm, and then, to make sure, laid his hand over hers. "My felicitations, Otterbury, Mrs. Otterbury," he said coolly. "A secret wedding, was it, Otterbury?"

"Oh goodness me, no." Phillip's wife laughed. "Why ever would it be a secret?"

"I cannot imagine," Gideon said in a hard voice and looked at Otterbury. "I gather the marriage is of recent date?"

Mrs. Otterbury tittered again. "Heavens, no." She glanced coyly down at the bulge beneath her gown, smoothed it with a deliberate hand, and said, "We were married more than six months ago. In India."

With a sigh and a whisper of silk, Prudence fainted away.

Chapter Nineteen

∞

"Love can hope where reason would despair."
GEORGE LYTTELTON

GIDEON, WHO HAD BEEN WATCHING PRUDENCE LIKE A HAWK, READY to snatch her away at the first sign of distress, caught her in his arms. For a moment the idea crossed his mind that it might be like that other time, a faint to escape an uncomfortable situation, but the dead weight of her in his arms told him the truth. She had indeed fainted—and no wonder, he thought savagely.

She had produced that damned pawnbroker's ring with such innocent courage. He knew why she did it, too. That look she had given him after he'd claimed her with that kiss. The sort of look people gave when they were about to jump off a cliff or burn their bridges. She'd said she wouldn't entrap him. She had given her promise and meant to abide by it.

A testament to loyalty, and she'd been made to look a fool.

Bad enough for the swine to have married without telling her. Worse to reveal it in public, at a party, where Prudence was effectively pinned to a board like a butterfly, for all her feelings and thoughts to be displayed. Hard enough for anyone to have their declaration of faith and fidelity smacked in the face so brutally. But for his new wife to be presented in such glowing, smug fecundity,

There could be no crueler reminder of the babe Prudence had lost and still mourned.

She lay helpless, unconscious against his chest. He didn't want to put her down. He wanted to stride off with her to his home and care for her in privacy. He wanted to take her upstairs to his bed and simply hold her, let her weep and rail and grieve. He wanted her not to be alone. If any pillow was to be drenched with her tears, he wanted it to be his. He wanted to be the one to hold her, to dry her tears, to comfort and tend and love her.

"Put her down," said a voice beside him.

Never, thought Gideon.

"She needs air, boy, and my smelling salts. Lay her down on this sofa," Aunt Gussie instructed him. Reluctantly, he laid her on the sofa and held her hand, chafing it gently while Aunt Gussie administered the smelling salts.

Prudence came around in a moment. In two she'd repudiated his hand, thanked his aunt, and struggled to her feet. Alarmingly pale but very poised, she approached the faithless Otterbury and his bride, a brittle smile on her face.

"Please accept my felicitations," she said, "both for your marriage and for the forthcoming happy event. Phillip, I am sure your mother is delighted. Perhaps this explains why we have not heard from her in recent months."

Otterbury nodded vaguely, looking uncomfortable. *Another story there,* thought Gideon savagely.

Not for a moment did she betray the terrible blow she had just been dealt. No trace of bitterness escaped her. She was unique, Gideon thought proudly. He moved closer in case she needed a little support. His hand cupped her elbow. He could feel the tension in her, vibrating like a bowstring. She moved away, imperceptibly, deliberately breaking the fragile contact between them. Again. She did not want him.

"You will be wanting your supper, Mrs. Otterbury," she said with quiet grace.

"Yes, yes, so she is. Come, my dear." Hurriedly, Phillip escorted his wife from the room.

"Little weasel," said Aunt Gussie. "I knew he was hiding

something! Asking you to stay indoors for a week to save his pride at being jilted! Pretending it was me he didn't want you to be seen with, and all along he was trying to prevent his wife from meeting his fiancée. How did he think he could avoid it?"

"They planned to leave Bath tomorrow," Lady Gosforth said.

Aunt Gussie snorted. "That fits!"

Prudence shook her head. "It doesn't matter anymore," she said wearily. "I think I would like to leave now. I have a terrible headache. If you will excuse me, Lady Gosforth?"

"Yes of course, my dear."

"Great-uncle Oswald, Lady Augusta, may I leave the twins to you? They are having such a lovely time, and I would hate to ruin it for them."

"Yes, yes, m'dear," said Sir Oswald in a gruff voice. "Don't give 'em another thought."

"Shouldn't I come with you, Prue, dear?" asked Aunt Gussie.

Prudence shook her head. "No, no, I thank you. I really would prefer to be alone." Only her extreme pallor and the faint tremor in her voice revealed her distress.

"I shall escort you," Gideon announced.

"No!" Aware she had overreacted, Prudence moderated her tone. "Thank you, but no, Lord Carradice. I require no other escort than our footman, James. He is a stalwart fellow and will give me the support of his arm if I need it. Though I shan't need it, I'm sure."

Prudence just wanted to escape. Deeply embarrassed by her truly feeble response to Phillip's news, she needed to get away, to sort out her feelings. The last thing she wanted was to have to deal with Lord Carradice now, when she was in such a pathetically vaporish state. He would want to put his arms around her—he always did. She was just as likely to fall into his arms and sob out all her woes, and what an even more feeble creature she would be if she allowed it! She would not. She didn't want his pity. She didn't want anyone's pity.

"You must!" he insisted. "There is no question of it. I shall escort you."

"Thank you, but you shall not," she responded firmly. She was starting to get irritated now. Would no one let her make a graceful exit and escape from this dreadful scene?

"Take my palanquin," said Lady Gussie. "It is the perfect thing. Then, if you feel faint again—"

"No, thank you, dear Lady Augusta, but truly, I prefer to walk. I am quite steady on my feet now, I promise you, and will be all the better for a little exercise and some fresh air."

"But you cannot—" began Lord Carradice.

She held up a hand. "It is but a short step, and the night is warm. I shall be perfectly well, thank you." She stood and picked up her shawl, which had slipped to the floor. Lord Carradice took it from her and wrapped it around her. Prudence forced herself to resist the warm appeal of his protectiveness. She needed to think. And she could not do that while he was near.

Besides, for once in her life she wanted to be able to consider what she, Prudence Merridew, wanted, without having to take into account the desires, plans, or orders of a man. She was no longer bound to Phillip, she was about to turn one and twenty and would thus be free of Grandpapa. For the first time in her life she could be her own mistress and she needed to make a few decisions. Reasoned decisions, not those guided by emotion, not by fear, obligation, guilt, or love.

If Lord Carradice was with her, she knew what would happen to reason—it would fly out the window and be replaced by emotion.

"No, please," she entreated him. "But come and see me in the morning."

Finally, reluctantly he agreed, his eyes dark with emotion. And so Prudence had her way and left the party to walk home with only James the footman in attendance.

Prudence walked slowly along the pavement, caught up in her own thoughts. Beside her walked James, a silent shadow.

She tried to make sense of Phillip's situation. Why had he simply not written to her and told her he wished to marry another? She had given him repeated opportunities in her letters to speak up. She'd even assured him that if he wished to sever the connection, she would not reproach him.

Even if he felt awkward, he should still have written to her immediately on his marriage. Why had he not? When had he married? Six months ago, his wife had said. She worked it out. Six months ago . . . She walked along, head down, trying to recall letters she had received four or five months ago . . . but she could not recall any letters. He had stopped writing more than six months ago . . .

Suddenly she came to an abrupt halt. Words Phillip had spoken a few days before started to make sense. *It looked like your grandfather had lost his whole fortune.* She frowned, trying to recall his exact words. She had been thinking of other things at the time.

The company nearly went bankrupt, you know, and we all had an anxious time of it. Phillip had stopped writing during that anxious time, had stopped writing to his betrothed of four years, the heiress whose *grandfather had lost his whole fortune.*

And he had looked around and found himself another heiress. What had he said of his hosts? His in-laws, no doubt. *Extremely well off, extremely well connected.* Her mouth twisted wryly. Not to mention *related to a duke.* A far better bargain than Prudence of the bankrupt grandfather. Who was only a baron, after all.

Of course—money. It was Phillip's driving force. So stupid of him to lie, to pretend otherwise. He could not have hidden his wife from her forever. Surely it would have been both easier and simpler to have told Prudence he was married. The whole thing was a mystery.

It was also a relief. She needn't feel guilty about jilting him anymore. She was a different person, and not only because of the past four and a half years.

It was Gideon who'd changed her.

He'd ruined her for one such as Phillip. Gideon had taught her what a kiss could be. He'd shown her that love really could be joyful, and that life was for laughter as well as serious things.

She wanted him. Gideon. And in the morning they would speak and she would tell him what was in her heart.

She was so deep in thought that she did not hear the clip-clop of horses, nor the sound of wheels on the road behind her or if she did, she did not spare it a thought. Not until it was too late . . .

Gideon prowled around the party, brooding, scowling, and generally giving the lie to all those who thought a rake was supposed to be charming. It had gone against every instinct he had to let her leave with only a footman to accompany her.

He wanted to be with her. Dammit, he *needed* to be with her. He wanted to take her in his arms, to kiss away her distress, her feeling of betrayal. She would be home now, in bed, his little love, no doubt sobbing her eyes out over a cowardly, faithless, unworthy weasel and his stupid, pregnant wife.

Prudence should not be by herself at a time like this, no matter what she thought she needed. But she was stubborn, his lady. And he could hardly complain about her fiery streak of independence when it was one of the things he loved about her. Only he *did* want to complain of it. Right now, he didn't want her to be stubborn or independent or brave or self-bloody-sufficient; he wanted her in his arms, dammit, where she belonged.

A lady in a low-necked, bronze silk gown undulated toward him, a sultry smile of welcome on her face. Gideon glowered at her. How could he ever have thought this sort of empty dalliance had any appeal? She continued to flow toward him, open invitation in every movement of her luscious body, her smile deeper, more knowing.

Gideon bared his teeth at her, and she stopped, blinked, and hastily undulated away.

Dammit, he couldn't stay at this blasted party. Sir Oswald would take care of his aunt and the twins. He might just pop out and stroll along to his aunt's house—*to do what?* he thought savagely. Stare at Prudence's empty window? Well, it was better than being here, he decided, and began to thread his way toward the hall.

Hearing a sudden commotion at the front door, he quickened his pace and arrived just in time to see a man in livery stagger inside, blood pouring from his head. A lady screamed. Another fainted. There was a flurry of activity as a small knot of people gathered, then hung back uncertainly.

"Get a cloth, quickly," rapped Gideon as he lunged forward to catch the man, who was swaying on his feet. He carried him into the kitchen, out of the way of the guests. "You! Butler—send for a physician, fast, and you—fetch Sir Oswald Merridew here at once," he ordered, his heart racing, for he knew the injured man. It was the young footman, James. Last seen escorting Prudence home.

"What happened, man? Where is Miss Merridew?"

"Taken," gasped James. "Sorry, m'lord. They jumped me . . . from behind . . . Knocked me down . . ." He raised a hand to his wound and winced. "Took Miss Prue . . . carriage . . . black carriage . . . bay horses . . . one white foot."

Gideon swore. Sir Oswald arrived. "Prudence has been abducted." Gideon said tersely. "I'm going to follow them on horseback. You—" He snapped his finger at a nearby footman. "Fetch me a horse, the best in the stables!"

Sir Oswald, demonstrating the ability to take immediate action that had made him a rich man, turned to an onlooking servant. "Fellow—run around to my home and tell them to prepare my traveling chaise and fetch my pistols, too. And hop to it!"

The servant raced off.

"I'll be close behind you, Carradice, m'boy."

Gideon nodded and said urgently to the injured footman, "James, did you see which way they went?"

James frowned as he tried to gather his senses. "Toward . . . moonrise."

Gideon squeezed his shoulder in thanks. "Good man! Right, I'll be off. I'll get her back, don't worry." He stood and said, almost to himself, "Who the devil would snatch her off the street?"

James's hand shot out and grabbed his coat tail. "Thought you'd know, m'lord. 'Twas her granfer. The old lord . . . I saw him."

Gideon stared. "Why would her grandfather abduct her off the street?"

James fought for consciousness. "Hates her . . . hates

Miss Prue . . . You got to find 'er, m'lord. In one of his rages, 'e was . . ." His head fell back, and his eyes closed, but he managed to whisper, "Last time . . . old devil . . . nearly killed 'er . . ."

Gideon swore again as he raced from the house. A late guest was just dismounting from a fine-looking bay gelding. No other horse was to be seen. Gideon couldn't wait for the one to be brought from the stables. He strode forward and snatched the reins from the man's hand. "Need to borrow your horse, sir. Emergency. Lady Gosforth will vouch for me." And before the man could utter a protest, he'd leaped into the saddle and galloped off.

His mount thundered toward the rising moon as his gaze scoured the night for a black carriage pulled by four bay horses, one with one white foot.

Prudence lay huddled on the seat of the coach, numb with shock, fear, and confusion. One moment she'd been strolling along the street on a warm night, deep in thought, and then suddenly she'd been roughly seized and flung into a vehicle. She could see nothing. She was half smothered in some sort of thick cloth, like a cloak or a blanket. It was dusty, she knew that, as she could breathe only though her nose. A rag of some sort had been shoved into her mouth, and a gag tied over it, preventing her from screaming, or even breathing. Her hands were tied tight, with thick, rough twine that cut into her skin.

The carriage moved fast. It bounced over cobblestones, over drains and ruts, thudding into bone-jarring holes, swinging and swaying around corners at a fearsome pace. Prudence was tossed back and forth by the movement. Blind and bound as she was, it took all her concentration to remain on the seat. She was tossed to the floor several times. Hands grabbed her and hurled her back on the seat, not gently.

Finally, she managed to wedge herself into the corner of the vehicle and steady herself by bracing her feet against the floor and the side of the carriage. Only then was she able to consider her position.

For a few wild moments she'd imagined she'd been mistaken for someone else, kidnapped for profit. Or abducted for immoral purposes. There had been shouting when she was taken, but she'd been too occupied to notice, wholly occupied in fighting the rough hands that bound her. Hampered by the cloak over her head, she hadn't stood a chance. There were three men at least. Two had climbed on top of the carriage. One was the driver. She'd heard them.

Another man was in the carriage with her. The leader. He'd addressed not a word to her, but she'd heard his cane rap on the roof, and the carriage had lurched off. She could hear him breathing, wheezing stertorously.

He said not a word, but slowly, imperceptibly she realized who it was. And fear lodged like a knot in her chest, for even through the heavy blanket she could smell him, the fusty, goaty old-man smell of him. Grandpapa.

She tried to say something through the gag.

Thwack! The cane smashed across her shoulder and neck. Even through the blanket, it hurt. He had not spared his strength.

"Silence, bitch!"

Beneath the blanket, Prudence closed her eyes and braced her body. She knew he would not stop at a single blow. He never had before. Blind as she was, she would not know when the next one came, so she must be ready. She would survive this. She hunched her head into her shoulder. And waited . . . and waited.

Thwack! The cane smacked across her arm.

"Don't wriggle."

It would be a long night. She sent up a quick, silent prayer that she would live to see the dawn. And waited for the next blow. It was a long time coming, but then—

"Send me off on a wild-goose chase, would you, bitch? Down to London!" *Thwack!* "Then all the way to Derbyshire!" *Thwack!* "And then on to Scotland?" *Thwack!*

Prudence swallowed. She'd hoped the lie had bought them enough time, but . . .

Thwack! "Waste my blunt on expensive frippery!" The cane cut sharply across her legs, and her instant reflexive gasp of pain almost choked her because of the gag. The blanket did not reach to her legs, and the deep blue silk and the silver tissue overlay provided no protection at all. Her beautiful party dress.

Thwack! On her ankle bone. She heard the silver tissue rip, and he grunted with satisfaction. "Fine feathers do not make fine birds, missy."

Prudence could do nothing but endure. She braced herself for the next blow, but he seemed to have calmed a little. The silence stretched, the only sound the horses' hooves on the road and the creaking and groaning of the moving carriage.

"Wondering how I found you, eh?"

Surreptitiously, she flexed her toes. They moved. Her ankle throbbed but it wasn't broken. She sighed in relief. She might still be able to run, if she had the chance.

"Young Otterbury wrote. Letter waiting for me when I got back from Scotland. He let me know where you'd run off to. Hah! Currying favor. Used to work for me, did you know? Left the company some time ago. Been trying to get reinstated ever since. The fool! Do him no good, no good at all now . . ."

The last piece of the puzzle, Prudence thought wearily. Phillip had betrayed her at every turn, in every way.

The silence in the carriage stretched and stretched.

Thwack! "Damned if I'll be locked up for your interference, you doxy."

Locked up? What did he mean? This was not the frenzied attack of her youth, her grandfather in a spitting rage. There was something more . . . more leisured about it. Brooding. As if he had all the time in the world. And slowly building up to something. . . . She dared not think of what.

She did not know what was preferable: a burst of anger that was over in one violent outburst, or this waiting . . . not seeing . . . not knowing. Imagining all sorts of things. It was more horrifying, somehow. Long periods of silence and then, suddenly—

Thwack! "I am Dereham of Dereham Court . . . I'd see us both dead before I'd let myself be imprisoned."

Imprisoned for what? she wondered. *See us both dead?*

She huddled on the seat, choking for breath under the

blanket, swallowing convulsively on the gag. She had never felt so alone. This time, there was no one to help her; no sisters, no servants to interfere. She was alone with him, helpless, in the dark in a carriage. On the road to hell.

For the moment, the blows were intermittent. It was not so bad. It was frightening, cowering in the corner, never knowing when or where to expect them, but it was better than a frenzied attack. Less physically damaging, she hoped. It might be more endurable in the end. Whenever "the end" would be.

But she would not give up. She would not be defeated. She had seen the light of happiness, and it was within her grasp.

He muttered to himself from time to time. Sometimes she could hear the words; sometimes she could not. Sometimes they made sense to her, sometimes they did not. Sometimes whatever it was would enrage him, and he would lash out at her, the only warning the whistling of his cane through the air.

"Run off to your lover, would you?" *Thwack!* "Harlot! Faithless whore!"

Her ear rang with the blow, drowning out the ugly names he was calling her. Names did not hurt, anyway. He'd called her those before. Her lover? How had he discovered that? It did not matter. She did love Gideon. She did not care who knew it. She didn't have to hide it now, not even from herself.

She loved Gideon. She conjured up his face in the dark, clinging to the thought of him. Her beacon in the storm. Gideon. His dark eyes that teased her to laughter, and at the same time promised untold, wicked pleasures. *And we will all the pleasures prove.* Pleasures, not pain.

She kept that thought at the forefront of her mind.

The horses would need to be changed at some point. It was a long way from Bath to Norfolk. They'd have to get fresh horses soon, even though the early fast pace had steadied. There might be an opportunity for her to escape. She tried to flex her cramped limbs unobtrusively.

Thwack! Across her shin.

To block out the waves of hatred coming at her, she clung to thoughts of Gideon. Gideon, who made her feel beautiful. Gideon, whose kisses warmed her even now when she was trapped in Grandpapa's cold and bitter hell. Gideon, who'd grown up as a sad and lonely little boy, in a house without love. He needed so much to be loved, even if he didn't know it. And he'd said he wanted *her*, needed *her*, plain Prudence Merridew. He'd told her so with dark and potent heat in his eyes and poetry on his lips.

Come live with me and be my love, And we will all the pleasures prove.

And she'd let herself fall prey to doubts! Allowing the words of men like her grandfather and Phillip to influence her. Blind, foolish Prudence. Doubting the man who needed her so much, the man she loved with all her heart, only because he was a rake. So what if he had not used the right words? He had wanted to love her, and even if—

Thwack! What if she died tonight? What if she died without ever having the chance to tell him how much she loved him? Without ever knowing what it felt like to make love with him?

She would *not* die. She would survive this. She *had* to. She had to tell Gideon she loved him. She didn't care about the consequences. And she was going to make love with him at the very first opportunity.

Gideon arrowed his steed into the night. He'd gambled on his instincts, his instincts that said the old man would make for his lair, for Dereham Court. On the outskirts of Bath, he'd spotted an old chap on a bench by the main road, nursing a mug of ale in the warm evening. He wrenched his mount to a halt.

"Have you seen a black carriage pass by in the last half hour, drawn by four bay horses, one with a white foot?"

The old man considered a moment. "Dunno about a white foot, sorry, but there were a black carriage right enough, passed by here like the devil hisself were atop it. Sporting no lights they were, neither. Foolishness this late and when the moon's naught but a sliver."

"If you stay here another hour and tell a gentleman with

white hair what you told me, he will give you another of these." Gideon flipped him a guinea and raced on. He could make better speed than a carriage, but even so, he feared for Prudence.

James's words rang in his head. *Hates Miss Prue . . . Last time . . . old devil . . . nearly killed 'er.*

Nearly *killed* her? His mind was heavy with dread even as his body urged his mount to greater speed. Gideon recalled Hope's careless referral to the way he beat them all, but thrashed Prudence.

If he'd hurt Prudence, her grandfather was a dead man.

He raced headlong into the night, praying for Prudence's safety and wishing he'd worn spurs and boots to the party.

Rope burned into Prudence's wrists. She'd struggled surreptitiously for the last hour to loosen the knots and free herself, but her efforts were in vain. Almost. She had not managed to free herself, but she'd gripped the edge of the blanket covering her head. Inch by inch she gathered it, and it was now one big tug away from coming off her. She could run, and she could see. There would be a chance for her to try to escape. There must be.

She waited for her moment. Her arms cramped painfully. She flexed her fingers to get her circulation moving again.

Mercifully, Grandpapa seemed to have subsided. He had said nothing for many minutes now. Nor had the cane come whistling out of the darkness. She wondered if he had fallen asleep. She hoped so, but she dared not risk pulling the blanket off her in case he wasn't. She couldn't make a move yet, not until the carriage stopped. It would be madness to jump from a moving carriage in the dark, and she wasn't that desperate. Yet.

It seemed an age before the carriage finally slowed. The sound of the horses' hooves changed—the road surface was different. A town? A toll road? Would they be stopping for a change of horses, or to pay the toll? Inconspicuously she flexed what muscles she could, preparing for possible action.

It was a coaching inn. She heard the ostlers come hurrying out, heard the order for fresh horses. There was some slight argument about it, and she heard her grandfather slide across to the other side of the carriage to deal with the innkeeper's impertinence in delaying him.

With her bound hands she felt for the handle of the carriage door and twisted. It opened. In a flash she tugged the blanket from over her eyes and jumped out into the courtyard of the inn. Her knees buckled beneath her from the last hours of inactivity, and she staggered.

There was a shout behind her. Prudence stumbled doggedly forward, the blood rushing painfully back to her limbs with each step. A golden slab of light spilled across the cobblestones; the door of the inn stood ajar. Inside were people who might help her. Without hesitation she made for the light.

She burst through the door and looked wildly around her. The taproom was almost deserted. Two old men seated by the fire stared at her with mouths agape. A motherly looking woman was wiping down a table with a cloth. There was no one else. Prudence ran toward the woman, uttering noises of distress through her gag.

"Heavens to Betsy!" the woman exclaimed. "Whatever is going on? Look, Arthur, some villain's tied this poor lady's hands and stuffed a horrid rag in her mouth."

A middle-aged man, presumably Arthur, popped up from behind the bar and stared at her.

"'Ow d'ye know she's a lady?" one of the old men asked.

Prudence cast a frightened glance toward the door. She uttered urgent-sounding noises. Oh, why were these people so slow?

"Look at her clothes, gapeseed!" said the other. "Fine as fivepence she be—or *was,* until somebody ripped that silvery thing she's wearing. Cost a few quid, that would."

"Take no notice of these lummoxes, dearie," said the woman, "We'll look after you." She laid a comforting arm around Prudence. "Arthur, she's shaking like a leaf, poor little thing. I don't know what trouble you're in, miss, but you're safe now. My Arthur will protect you." She reached to unfasten the gag. "Who's done this terrible thing to you, dearie?"

Crack! It sounded like a gunshot in the small taproom. "I

forbid you to untie that woman!" Her grandfather's voice rang out, echoing with the authority and arrogance of generations. Leaning heavily on a silver-tipped ebony cane, he limped into the center of the small, low-ceilinged taproom as if he owned it. His cane was in his left hand, a horsewhip was in his right.

Despair flooded Prudence as she saw the effect of his bullying, aristocratic entrance on the villagers in the inn. They were frozen.

Crack! The occupants of the room jumped as one person when the whip cracked again. Her grandfather's two burly henchman stepped into the room after him, a silent message to any who might consider disobeying the man with the whip.

"She is a dangerous madwoman! Move away from her, alewife, for your own safety!" The lash of the horsewhip stirred and caressed his boot like a living thing as he flicked it back and forth.

Prudence shook her head vigorously in denial of her grandfather's charge. Her eyes beseeched the woman to give her the benefit of the doubt, to defy her grandfather and unfasten the gag. At least if her mouth were free, she could speak in her own defense.

The woman did not move. Nor did she move away from Prudence. A tiny spark of hope flared in Prudence's heart.

"I said move away from her!" He regarded the woman as if she were an insect. The lash stirred again.

"I don't take orders in my own inn," she responded boldly, giving him back look for look. "What have you to do with this young lady? How do I know you mean well by her?"

Prudence nodded frantically at the woman, to confirm her words. Grandpapa did not mean well by her at all.

"Insolent trollop! I am Lord Dereham of Dereham Court, Norfolk." He paused to let the words sink in. "And this is my runaway wife, who I am conducting to Bedlam. Now step aside and my men shall conduct her back to the carriage from which she escaped."

Runaway wife? Bedlam! The Bethlehem Royal Hospital, where lunatics were locked away. She felt sick, terrified.

Could he really mean to lock her up in Bedlam? Once she was shut away there, no one would ever believe her story, no one would ever release her. And in that hellish place, she would indeed go mad. She shook her head desperately at the woman.

"She doesn't look like a madwoman to me," the woman said slowly. "And she's awful young to be your wife. Let's see what she's got to say for herself." Again she reached for the gag.

"Don't touch her, you fat trollop!" The lash bit into the soft flesh of the woman's bare arm and as she cried out in anger and pain; he grabbed her and flung her roughly aside. She hit the bar hard.

"Oi! Leave my wife alone, you!" Arthur came forward, his fists bunched menacingly. "I don't 'old with toffs mishandling women, 'specially not my woman!"

Casually, Lord Dereham slashed him across the eyes with his whip. With a shriek of pain, Arthur fell back, clutching his eyes. His wife crawled forward to help him.

The whip writhed and flickered like a snake. "Anyone else?" The silky threat cowed the silent spectators. He didn't wait for a response. He grabbed Prudence by the hair and began to drag her toward the door. She kicked and struggled as hard as she could.

"Come quietly, you little bitch!" he roared and lifted the whip handle to clout her into insensibility.

"Touch her, and I'll kill you, Dereham!"

The whip handle stopped in midair. Prudence sagged in sudden thankfulness. She knew that voice. Gideon. Thank God, thank God.

Her grandfather turned and regarded the newcomer with outrage. "You'll *what?* How dare you bluster in here, making threats against me. Who the devil do you think you are?" The lash flickered out, like a striking snake.

Gideon stepped closer. "I am Carradice and I will not stand for violence against any woman, let alone this one."

"This woman has naught to do with you. She is evil and I—"

"She is my wife-to—"

Chapter Twenty

∞

"One word frees us of all the weight and pain of life:
That word is love."
SOPHOCLES

"*WIFE?*" LORD DEREHAM'S EYES ALMOST STARTED FROM THEIR SOCK-
ets. His face paled, then flushed suddenly with rage. He
shook Prudence like a dog shakes a rat. "You foul little slut,
I'll—" He raised the whip again.

"Let her go!" Gideon grabbed Lord Dereham's wrist,
squeezing it like a vise, harder and harder until the bones
threatened to crack. Her grandfather swore, and suddenly
Prudence was free. She staggered.

"Stand away, sweetheart," Gideon said gently, steadying
her on her feet with careful hands. All his attention was on
her.

She tried to warn him, but could only make a muffled
sound through the gag. Her grandfather's whip whistled
though the air and lashed Gideon across the back of the
head. He barely flinched, just pushed her gently toward the
corner of the room.

"Get him!" her grandfather roared, and the two burly
henchman leaped at Gideon. He ducked and swung a punch
that landed with a crunch on the shorter man. Blood spurted
from the man's nose, and he staggered back.

His partner struck Gideon a two-handed blow on the back

of the neck, and Prudence watched, horrified, as her beloved
staggered under the impact, then without turning, rammed
his elbow backward. It connected audibly with the man's
ribs. The man tried to grab his ear. Gideon responded with a
mighty punch to the stomach. The man grunted and kicked
out. Gideon slammed another punch to the head, then a third
to the jaw.

Prudence yelled helplessly through the gag as the second
man came rushing across the room, an iron poker raised. She
kicked a stool into his path, and the man went sprawling on
the flagstones. The poker clattered to the ground. She darted
forward and kicked it out of his reach. The man scrambled
to his feet just as Gideon felled his partner with one last,
frightful punch.

"Come on then, my bucko," Gideon beckoned him, his
fists raised. A faint smile lingered on his lips, and his eyes
were lit with a devilish glint. It looked almost as if he enjoyed this appalling brawl, she thought incredulously.

The man took one step forward, then hesitated.

"Go on, you filthy coward—get him!" roared Lord Dereham, spittle and rage dripping from his lips. He lashed at the
man with his whip.

The man stepped back, out of range. He glanced at Lord
Dereham, then at Gideon, then at his partner, sprawled
bloody and insensible on the taproom floor. He shook his
head. "Get 'im yerself, m'lord," he said. "I've 'ad enough o'
this business." And he left, ignoring Lord Dereham's shouts
of outrage.

Gideon, his chest heaving and blood welling from a cut
above his eye, stared across the room at Lord Dereham.
Slowly, the light of battle faded from his eyes. He lowered
his fists reluctantly.

"I cannot in all decency fight a man of your age, sir," he
said. "Let us agree that there has been enough violence
tonight. Admit defeat, and you may leave here unmolested,
though I would gladly see you hanged for what you have
done to Prudence." His fists clenched again, and he took
several deep breaths before he continued. "But I am young
and in my prime, and you are more than sixty and but recently recovered from injury." He glanced at Prudence and

added in a softer voice, "She has suffered enough distress this night. You are her grandfather, after all. We will be related."

Prudence felt unbearably moved by his gallantry. Oh, what a beautiful man he was!

"Will be related? You're not wed yet?"

"No, but we shall be as soon as possible. So, *pax*, Dereham?"

Prudence felt her eyes flood.

Lord Dereham shrugged and gave a grunt that seemed to indicate assent. He stumped toward the door, scowling but silent. Gideon watched for a moment, then reached for Prudence's gag. "I'm sorry I took so long, love. Are you all—"

Slash!

The whip cut across his hands, narrowly missing Prudence's face.

Gideon pushed her behind him and advanced on the old man, a murderous light in his eyes. He was pale, his mouth hard and unsmiling. His dark eyes glittered with a fierce and implacable rage. Prudence had never seen him like this. She wanted to call out to him, but the gag was still in place. She wanted to help, but her hands were still tied. She watched helplessly as her grandfather limped across the room in an insane rage, whip lashing furiously at the man she loved.

Crack! "Admit defeat, would I?"

Gideon ducked as the lash swung above his head but did not stop his advance.

Slash! "Give in to an insolent puppy?"

The lash cut his ear. Gideon moved forward.

Smash! The whip missed Gideon and sent a tankard of ale spinning across the room. *Slash!* At his face again. The old man was trying to blind him, he realized.

Nothing could blind him now, Gideon thought savagely. The old man had had his chance.

"Too *old* for a fight, am I?"

With a hiss, the lash snaked out at him again, and this time Gideon lifted his arm to receive the full brunt of it. He heard Prudence whimper as the lash slashed into him, but Gideon made not a sound. He bared his teeth in a grim smile, lowered his arm, and yanked hard. The whip flew out of the old man's hand. Behind him Prudence made a small, muffled sound.

Gideon calmly unwrapped the lash from his forearm and took the handle in his hand. "Fond of the whip, aren't you, Dereham? You're very skilled with it, we've all seen that." He cracked the whip an inch in front of the old man's nose. Lord Dereham stumbled backward.

"I admit, I haven't had the practice you have." *Snick!* A button flew off Lord Dereham's coat. "But then I haven't been practicing on women and little girls." *Snick!* Another button went rolling across the flagstones. The occupants of the room watched in silence.

Gideon's face hardened. He repeated, "Women. And. Little. Girls." He slashed at Lord Dereham with each word. By the end of the sentence, not a button remained on the coat.

"They are harlots, one and all!" shouted Lord Dereham, taking courage from the fact that so far he hadn't been touched by the lash. "The whip is all they understand! And as for you—I'll have you hanged for this!" Lord Dereham shook his fist at Gideon. The whip lashed, and a thin red line blossomed on the fist.

"How old was she when you first used your whip on her, eh? Eleven? Twelve? And what about Grace?" Gideon punctuated each word with the whip. "You are an obscenity! You should never have been allowed to rear young girls. It is a miracle they have emerged so sweet and pure."

"Pure?" Lord Dereham snorted. "What drivel has she been telling you? She is about as pure as—"

With a single enraged punch, Gideon knocked him out cold.

Ignoring the prone body on the floor, Gideon flung the whip into a corner and went instantly to Prudence. He took her into his arms, crooning and murmuring tender reassurances. He untied the gag, flung it in the fire, and called for a knife. It made short work of the ropes around her wrists. He swore when he saw how raw and chafed they were, and he hugged her gently to him, smoothing her hair, her cheek, checking to see if she was whole and unharmed.

Prudence kept saying, "It's all right, it's all right," over and over, as if he needed reassurance more than she did, and indeed, he blamed himself sorely.

"I'm sorry, love. I should have been there with you. I should have walked you home. I'll never—"

"Hush." She smoothed his hair back tenderly. "It was my choice, and they took us by surprise from behind. And I am all right. Grandpapa has done worse than this to me. But, you—your brow is bleeding. He nearly blinded you. And your injured shoulder, how is that?" she asked distressfully, and tried to examine his hurts.

"Faugh, makes me sick to my stomach!" Lord Dereham had come to and struggled to his feet. He observed them sourly.

"Get out, old man, if you value your life," Gideon said in a hard voice.

"She'll betray you. They all do. No concept of honor. She is already another man's leavings! Did you know that, hah?"

Gideon glared at him, but said calmly enough, "What do I care for that? Virginity can be given away, or lost, or wrested from a girl by force. It matters not to me. What matters is honor and a loving heart. My Prudence is the most honorable woman I've ever known. And she has the truest, most loving heart in all the world."

Prudence could not see for tears.

"Pah! Her fancy man! Wants you to marry her, does she? Is she carrying your bastard in her belly, eh? She did that once before, you know, but I beat it out of her."

"You beat it out—" Gideon could not finish the sentence. He felt sick with fury. "Her baby?"

The old man snorted righteously. "Thrashed her until she dropped the mongrel pup. There are no bastards in my family."

"I beg to differ," Gideon said coldly. He was gripped by a rage he had never before experienced. To have this evil old man boasting that he'd thrashed a young girl until she miscarried. He'd never heard of anything so barbaric. And it was Prudence, his sweet, loving Prudence who'd had this vile thing done to her.

"For that, you evil old man, I'm going to kill you." Gideon advanced, murder in his heart.

Crash! Lord Dereham sank slowly back to the floor in a welter of pottery shards, stale crusts, and vegetable peelings. Gideon blinked.

"Ahh, now that makes me feel a lot better!" The landlady stood over the prone body, grinning with satisfaction. "Call me a fat old trollop, would he? Try to blind my Alfred, the horrible old baskit!" She poked at the old man with her foot. He did not stir. She faced Gideon. "Now don't be angry with me, sir. I know you had every reason to want to kill him— the black-hearted old goat."

She glanced at Prudence and added in a lower voice, "I never heard anything so wicked and heartless in my life as what he done to miss here. But if you'da killed him you'd have to flee the country, and where would that leave your lady, eh?" She nodded. "Better I bash him over the noggin with the pigs' dinner." She glanced around the room and grinned. "And I can't say I didn't enjoy it! Fat old trollop, indeed!"

She was right, Gideon realized. In his rage he probably would have throttled the old man, and it would have been murder. He stared at the landlady, shaken, then collected himself.

"Madam," he said, "you have saved me from myself, and for that I humbly thank you." He bent and with all the grace he could muster, kissed her hand as if she were the grandest duchess in the land. "And as for his insults, I wouldn't let them rankle. The man obviously feared and hated women. There would be nothing so threatening to him as a magnificent woman in her prime." He kissed her hand again, this time as a man kisses the hand of a beauty and added mischievously, "With or without a bowl of pigs' slops in her hand."

She giggled and blushed, then bustled off to fetch them all a drink to settle their nerves.

"Hah! What's all this?" said a voice from the doorway. "Good God! Is that m'brother Theodore lyin' there on the floor? Why is he covered with vegetable peelin's and onion skins? Prudence, m'dear gel, there you are. Are you all right?" Great-uncle Oswald rushed across the room and embraced her heartily.

Prudence burst into tears. She tried to stop herself, but she couldn't. They just seemed to flow out of her. Though why she should turn into a watering pot now was a mystery to her. She hadn't cried when Phillip betrayed her. She refused utterly to cry when Grandpapa beat her, or when those men were fighting Gideon. So why she should cry when it was all over and a dear old man rushed up and hugged her, she could not say. She could only sob helplessly.

Great-uncle Oswald dabbed ineffectually on her shoulder murmuring such things as "There, there," and "Tut, tut," and after a few moments she heard him say, "Here, Carradice, this is more in your line than mine," and she was transferred to a much stronger, warmer embrace as Gideon wrapped her to him. The sobs came harder then. He swung her into his arms and carried her upstairs.

He found the inn's private sitting room, pushed the door open with his foot, and carried her to the settee, where he sat with Prudence cradled in his lap, held tenderly against his heart as she sobbed.

He held her in silence, stroking her hair as each sob reverberated through her body and his. There was little passion in the embrace, just warm, comforting strength and slowly the storm of weeping passed. A wood fire crackled in the grate. She lay against his chest, listening to the beat of his heart and the gentle hiss and pop of the flames, wishing the moment could last forever.

He shifted his arm slightly, awkwardly, and recollection flooded back to her. She sat up. "Your injured arm—did you hurt it again in the fight? Should you be holding me?"

He ignored her question, just hugged her tighter. "I'm sorry. I should have come with you, should have insisted on walking you home—"

"Hush." She laid a hand over his lips. "It's over now. Truly over."

"Yes. It is." Gently he tipped her face to his and possessed her in a long, tender kiss.

She must have made some small sound, for he instantly loosened his embrace. "Am I hurting you?"

"No," she murmured, winding her arms around his neck and pulling his mouth back down to hers. It was bliss being held like this, holding him. She'd wondered if it would even happen to her again, and now she just wanted to lie in his arms and kiss him, savoring the moment, planning nothing, thinking about nothing. Except Gideon. Reveling in his warmth and strength and tender protectiveness. And kisses.

"I should have protected you. I promised to keep you safe but—"

"Hush. It doesn't matter."

His face remained guilt-ridden, troubled. He stared at her left arm. "That old swine has bruised you."

"A hot bath will help, but truly it looks worse than they feel. I can scarcely feel any pain now that you are here."

"I've ordered a brandy to be brought up to you. It will help you sleep on the way home. Oh, I know how exhausted you are, with all that has happened this night, but a brandy will help you relax." His eyes were dark with concern. "For this to happen is bad enough, but on top of . . . I'm sorry about Otterbury, Prue."

"I'm not," she told him. "I'd already severed the betrothal."

He stared, uncomprehending.

"That day you called on me . . . and I said Phillip was coming at two o'clock. I was short with you, distracted because I was nerving myself to break the betrothal in a few moments' time."

"You broke the betrothal that day?"

"Yes. I told him I could not marry him. I cannot understand why I ever imagined I loved such a man. He didn't even care about the baby, Gideon." A quiver passed over her expressive features.

"Oh, love." He stroked her cheek. "To discover he had a wife who was increasing, too; it was a monstrous way to break the news to you."

"It was a shock, and yes, I cannot deny that for a moment I was hurt. I don't understand why Phillip didn't tell me straightaway." She shrugged. "I'd already told him I wouldn't marry him. I think he was worried his wife would find out about me." She sighed. "You were right. I imagined I was in love . . . but I was not yet seventeen, and so lonely. And I did not then know what love felt like, not truly."

"And you do now?"

She gave him a glowing look that took his breath away. "Oh, yes."

Gideon suddenly could not breathe.

"You told me you wanted me," she reminded him softly. He nodded.

"Well, I have wanted you almost from the moment we first met," she said. "I did my best to resist you for the sake of my promise to Phillip, but I could not. My will, no matter how much I tried to bolster it, could not override my heart. I think I was yours from that very first day."

He said nothing. Was frozen.

"You once asked me to come live with you and be your love. Is the offer still open?"

The obstruction in his throat moved. "You know it is," he croaked. "Prudence, you are my heart, my soul. I, too, never knew it could be like this." And he kissed her, kissed her as if she was rare and precious. Kissed her, mouth to mouth, man and woman, elemental, offering her his taste and his mouth and his body and his heart.

"A bad business! A very bad business!" Great-uncle Oswald entered the room. "I've brought you a possett."

Gideon and Prudence leaped apart. Then Gideon deliberately drew her back to his arms. "You are mine. We have nothing to hide." Prudence smiled and leaned against him. No, she could not hide how she felt if she tried.

Great-uncle Oswald set down the steaming possett and hurried across to the fire. "Cold to my bones, never mind it's a warm night. Whoever would have believed it? My own brother kidnappin' little Prue, here! And the way he's treated you m'dear, well, it's shocked me to my bones, I can tell you!"

The old man looked very worn and tired. "What did he think he was doin', I wonder? Did he think we wouldn't hunt him down and fetch you back?"

Prudence was silent. There was nothing to say.

He spread his hands to the fire and shook his head in bewilderment. "Must have bats in his belfry. As if we wouldn't stop scourin' the countryside till we found her, eh, Carradice? We love this little lass, don't we?" His voice broke, and he pulled out a large yellow handkerchief and blew his nose forcefully.

Gideon held Prudence tightly in wordless assent. Prudence could say not a word. Her heart was too full. No one in her life had stood up to Grandpapa for her, and now she had two champions, defending and protecting her. And saying they loved her. It was more than she'd ever dreamed of. Her eyes filled again. Truly, she was becoming the veriest watering pot.

Great-uncle Oswald stuffed the handkerchief back in his pocket. "Now, I'm sorry to have to tell you this, but I've had him tied up. Not what you'd expect for a baron, but he was utterin' the most frightful threats and carryin' on in an appallin' fashion. So he's tied up like a parcel, and I'll be away with him in the carriage back to the Court. Give him some time to cool down, and then I'll find out what the devil he imagined he was doin'. Not sure what the future will hold for him—he sounded barkin' ma—er, most peculiar—but whatever happens, he'll never harm you again, Prue, m'dear. That I promise you." He kissed Prudence on each cheek and gave her a big hug, then stumped to the door. "I'll be off then."

"But it's the middle of the night!" exclaimed Prudence.

"Best time for it. Travel at night. Don't want the whole world to see me transportin' my brother all trussed up like the Christmas goose. Best not be seen—or heard—in daylight." He patted her shoulder. "Besides, you'll sleep easier knowing I've got him locked up safe at Dereham Court. You've had a frightful ordeal, m'dear, but it's over now."

Prudence was obliged to own he was right. She would sleep better knowing Grandpapa was far away. But Great-uncle Oswald was an elderly man. He should not be racketing about the country in the middle of the night at his age.

She tried to be tactful. "But what about you. You must be tired, too. Do you not want to sleep?"

Great-uncle Oswald looked at her in amazement. "Of course I want to sleep."

"Well, then?"

"It's the coachman who has to stay awake, not me. I'll sleep like a babe in the carriage, never you fear. Can sleep anywhere, me. Comes of travelin' so much when I was younger." He patted her shoulder again, then turned and gave Gideon a straight look, man to man. "Carradice, I'll leave Prudence in your hands. Take good care of her, lad. She's a bonny, good gel—one of the best."

Gideon looked him in the eye. "I know, sir," he said. "I'll take care of her—my life on it."

He was getting the hang of this vow thing, he realized. It wasn't nearly as difficult as he'd imagined. Not when Prudence was involved.

"I'd like a bath now, before I go to bed," Prudence declared as Sir Oswald's carriage disappeared into the night.

Gideon stared. "Do you mean you wish to stay the night here, at this inn?"

"Yes."

"But don't you want to return to Bath? You have no chaperone, now that Sir Oswald has left with your grandfather."

"No," she agreed. "But I have done quite enough traveling for one day, so here I shall stay. You may arrange a bedchamber with the landlord while I arrange a bath." And off she went to find the landlady.

Shrugging, Gideon went downstairs to bespeak a couple of private bedchambers. Luckily there were two, one on either side of the private sitting room where the late events had taken place. He ordered fires be lit in both chambers and a brandy to be brought for himself and sat down to mull over the events of the night.

Some time later, Prudence appeared at the door. She was dressed in a garish, flowered dressing gown much too large for her. Her skin glowed from her bath, and her hair curled in damp, flame-colored corkscrews around her face. She looked fresh and wholesome, and when she smiled shyly at him, Gideon had never seen anything more beautiful in his life.

"I thought you would be in bed by now," he said. "How do you feel?"

She smiled. "Much better, thank you. The landlady had some herbal salve that was wonderfully efficacious. That, and the bath have made a new woman of me."

"Are you thirsty? Hungry? Shall I order—"

"No, thank you. All I need is to speak to you." She pulled a chair up opposite him and sat down. She folded her hands in her lap, wiped the palms, then folded them again. "When I was first tossed into the coach, I was very frightened and confused."

"I don't think I will ever forgive mys—"

"Please, just listen." He subsided, so she continued. "When I realized it was Grandpapa, and that he was in as black a mood as I'd ever experienced . . . well . . ." She took a breath and blurted it out. "I thought I might die before this night was through. He nearly killed me once before . . ."

The time she lost the baby, thought Gideon. "My poor—"

"No, please." She held up a hand to stop him. "I want to say this. I need to explain. At first, all I could think of was that I would die. And then I thought of you. My thoughts of you made me feel better. Stronger." Her eyes were misty as she said softly, "I know you blame yourself for not protecting me, Gideon, but no one is to blame except Grandpapa for the kidnapping. And you did protect me, in a way. I could have been lost in terror, but I wasn't. I knew you'd come. That gave me strength, and hope, and because of it, I was able to escape the coach and reach help in the inn."

Gideon felt immensely humbled. He would probably go to his grave regretting that he let her walk home alone, but her forgiveness touched him deeply.

"While I was trapped in the coach, I thought, what if I die without ever making love with him?"

He made a small, choked sound, but she continued. "What if I never get the chance to tell him how much I love him?" Her eyes were luminous with unshed tears. "I will waste no more of the time I have on this earth, and I want to tell you now that I love you with all my heart, and all my soul, and all my body. And tonight I want to lie in your arms. If you'll have me."

If he'd have her? Didn't she know he'd give his life for her?

He swallowed. "Are you sure of this?"

She nodded. "Quite, quite sure."

The look in her eyes drove every coherent thought from

his mind. He could say not a word, for fear that he would weep. It took him a moment to gather himself.

After all she had been through tonight— Otterbury's public betrayal and then her grandfather's violent kidnapping— she wanted him. Prudence wanted Gideon. Trusted *him* to love and comfort her. *Tonight I want to lie in your arms.*

Slowly, Gideon stood. He remained still and silent, looking down at her, this small, beautiful, gallant lady who had come to mean all the world to him. He could not speak, could only feel.

And slowly, slowly, he held out his hand to her in a gesture old as time. It trembled a little. Without hesitation she placed her hand in his, her smile unshadowed, trusting, full of more love than he had ever dreamed of, or deserved.

And so, his heart thick with love and pride and humility, Gideon led his Prudence to the bedchamber.

Chapter Twenty-one
∞

"And we shall all the pleasures prove."
ANDREW MARVELL

THE BEDCHAMBER WAS SMALL AND SPARE AND SIMPLE. THERE WAS one bed covered with a simple blue counterpane, a few rag rugs, a dresser, and a chair. There was a faint scent of camphor in the air. The room was spotlessly clean, and a fire crackled merrily in the grate. Two brass candlesticks gleamed in the firelight; one on the dresser, which had been lit, and one beside the bed, which had not.

Wind tossed the nearby trees about and rattled the panes of the small windows, but the candles in their room glowed with a sure and steady light, undisturbed by any draft. They were well protected from the world outside.

Prudence dropped his hand, hurried over, and turned back the bed in a housewifely manner. She took the unlit candles and carefully lit them from the ones on the dresser, then turned and looked at him, her eyes huge in a pale face. She smiled briefly, licked her lips, then tried it again, a brave little smile.

She was nervous. Of course she was. Despite Otterbury, despite the pregnancy, she was still very much an innocent. He tried to think of what he could say to reassure her. He could think of not a word.

"I'm not afraid," she said, though she was shaking like a

leaf. "Just a little bit cold." Her hands gripped the landlady's dressing gown convulsively, crushing it to her in bunches of anxiety.

"I know." He took her hand and untangled it from the bunch and drew her closer. The scent of camphor was all around him. His fingers were trembling, too, he noted wryly. He raised first one cold, little hand, then the other, and kissed each reverently. "Cold hands, warm heart," he said, aware even as he said it of the inanity. All his address had deserted him.

"I want this, I really do." She smiled tremulously, moved closer, and lifted her arms to wrap them around his neck.

"I know." And suddenly they were kissing, and all his hesitation dissolved. His mouth was gentle, teasing, coaxing, reassuring. She tasted of warmth and sweetness and Prudence, and he could not get enough of her. He had all the time in the world, he told himself, though his body was rigid with desire and trembling with want, but this night was for Prudence. Her satisfaction and pleasure were all he desired.

He reached for the tie on her dressing gown. He undid it, slid the sleeves down her arms, and tossed it over the chair. And one small mystery was solved.

Underneath the landlady's voluminous flowered dressing gown, Prudence was wearing the landlady's equally voluminous best linen nightgown. Gideon knew it was her best nightgown not only by the lace and satin ribbons that adorned it so lavishly, but by the faint odor of camphor that clung to the garment. This was a nightgown that had been put away for years, saved for a special occasion, and brought out now, very slightly yellowed but still perfect, starched and unworn.

A bridal nightgown.

He might wrinkle his nose at the scent, but he had no quarrel with the landlady's sense of occasion. This was the most important night of his life. His bridal night. Gideon swallowed thickly.

He undid the first button of the nightgown. The buttons were small, mother-of-pearl, and the buttonholes tight. His hands were clumsy and shaking, as if he had never unbuttoned a woman in his life. But this was Prudence.

He undid another button and something lodged in his chest as he saw the mark. A long, dark red blotch across her neck, marring the porcelain perfection of her skin.

He swore under his breath, leaned forward, and blew on it gently. "Poor little love. Is it very painful?"

She shook her head. "Don't worry about it." She reached for him again, but instead he caught her hands in his.

"A moment." Something else had caught his eye. He lifted a curl and found another dark mark beneath her left ear.

Gideon stared at the marks, appalled. Suddenly he was disgusted with himself. He should not for one moment have even thought about taking Prudence to bed. He had been selfish, thoughtless. His little love had been humiliated, kidnapped, jolted across the country in a carriage and beaten by a madman.

She must be utterly exhausted and in pain, yet all her thoughts were for him. He was not worthy of such a woman.

But he would learn to be.

They would not make love tonight. Not the way he'd so stupidly anticipated. She would be too sore, too tired. *Tonight I want to lie in your arms* took on new meaning. Protection, security, comfort. That's what she really wanted tonight, not a thoughtless, randy rake in her bed. She needed him to hold her gently and chastely while she slept. Enough men had made demands on his Prudence today. She needed Gideon's tender care and protection, and he vowed she would get it.

He looked at the dark bruises on her skin and tried to swallow his rage. "There are more of these?"

"A few," she admitted reluctantly. "Mostly on my left side. He was very angry. But truly, you need not worry, the herbal salve and the bath has made me forget my bruises."

"I let you down, Imp. I should have killed him."

"Hush! You did not let me down. You saved me. I was never so glad in all my life as when you walked in that door. As I knew you would." She kissed him, her mouth soft and sweet. "And I am glad you did not kill him." She stroked one finger down the line of his jaw in a loving gesture. "If you had, the shadow would have hung over us both forever.

Forget him, forget what has happened. It's in the past, and to rue the past is to dwell there in shadows." She cupped his face in soft palms. Her eyes implored him. "Right here, right now, you and I are alive in this room together. Let us celebrate that."

He took her hands in his, and lifted first one, then the other to his mouth and kissed them. "Wise as well as beautiful. How did I ever deserve to win you, Imp?"

She bit her lip, helplessly. Whenever he called her beautiful it robbed her mind of any semblance of sense. She knew it was not so, but when he said it, she felt beautiful.

He smoothed back her hair and traced her cheekbones with his thumbs. "You, my little love, are exhausted. I think you have been through quite enough this day. What you need now is not another man making demands on you, but a good, long sleep. Let us leave our celebration until tomorrow. You will feel better then. We have plenty of time, after all. Climb into bed and go to sleep. I will hold you, and keep you safe through the night." He bent and kissed her mouth softly. "I'll not leave you, Imp."

Prudence thought about it. Outside, the wind was picking up. Raindrops spattered in gusts against the windows. She was tired and her bruises ached. She did want to sleep, but more than that, more than anything, she wanted to lie with Gideon, to be possessed by him and to possess him back. Her world had been shaken to its foundations today and she needed to make it right again, to put an end to her old life and begin a new life now, with Gideon. That would heal her more than any amount of sleep. He started to withdraw his hands and she clutched them firmly.

"I know I am tired and I will sleep later. But I want you, Gideon. I need to lie with you. I don't mean just lie down on the bed. I need to *know* you." She shook her head in frustration. "Oh, I don't know the word for it! Why are girls kept so ignorant? It is positively gothic!"

She tried again to explain how she felt. "Everyone wants something of me but nobody ever asks me what I want. Well, I want you! Now, tonight! I want to give myself to you. I want you to possess me in the way a man possesses a woman. I want to take you into my body."

Her cheeks suddenly flamed and she looked away, flustered by the strength of her desire. "I'm sorry, that sounds completely shameless, I know." She looked back up at him. "But that's how I feel." The sudden burst of feminine self-confidence drained abruptly away. "If you would like to, that is," she added in a small voice.

His dark eyes devoured her. He said in a low, ragged voice, "Imp, you have unmanned me with such a declaration. *If I would like to?*" He tried to smile and failed. "I've never wanted anything more in my life. I've wanted to make love to you ever since I first met you. The hardest struggle of my existence has been to keep my hands off you."

"So you will lie with me tonight?"

"I will." His voice was husky with emotion. He cradled her in his arms, barely holding her, and yet she felt wrapped within his embrace. His body touched lightly against the full length of hers, hard, masculine, and gentle. She shivered in his arms and pressed closer, reveling in his heat, in his strength. This was what she'd promised herself in her darkest hour, this was what she needed now: Gideon.

He lowered his mouth to hers. His lips were so gentle. She marveled dazedly at his effect on her. That the touch, the caress of his mouth on hers could set other parts of her body to such aching . . . craving . . . yearning. She made a small sound deep in her throat, and he pulled back instantly until he barely touched her. His mouth gentled, and he covered her cheek, her jawbone, her eyelids with soft butterfly kisses.

He was being careful of her. She didn't want to be treated like an invalid. She wanted passion. Possession.

She reached up and wound her arms around his neck, pulling him closer, pressing herself against him, and immediately he deepened the kiss. She tasted him and gloried in the sensation. It was this she craved, the unique, intoxicating flavor of Gideon and desire.

His kiss was slow, intense, and drugging. It reached deep into her, body and soul.

His hands roamed over her, caressing, sending hot shivers in their wake. Sensations, needs she'd never before known, grew deep within her, quivering to life, spreading, rippling, building.

He returned to the buttons on her nightgown and continued undoing them. She jumped as his hands touched skin. She'd been so lost in the embrace that she'd almost forgotten what they were going to do. She knew what to expect next.

She braced herself.

He soothed her with soft kisses on her mouth, the hollow of her cheek, her jawline, and her neck. He undid another button, and she braced herself again.

He stilled and simply held her for a long moment, then reclaimed her mouth in an exquisitely tender kiss.

She reassured him. "I'm not . . . You don't have to worry. I've done this before." She tried to control her shaking. "I want you, Gideon. I truly do."

"I know, love." He gathered her closer and pressed tiny kisses across her eyelids. All the stiffness drained out of her.

Slowly, reluctantly, he relaxed his embrace. She floundered her way back to reality, feeling suddenly bereft. His gaze was dark and compelling in the shadows of the candlelight. Only a whisper of breath separated them. "Will you assist me to disrobe, love?"

Prudence blinked. She had expected him to want to keep unbuttoning her clothing—Philip had rip—No! She wasn't going to think of that time. This was too precious a moment to spoil with thoughts of the past.

Gideon wanted her to undo his buttons. Exactly what did he mean by "disrobe"? How much? She realized suddenly that he was waiting, a soft, unreadable look in his dark, dark eyes.

"Oh! Yes, of course!" she blurted and hurriedly started to undo the buttons of his waistcoat. Her fingers were all thumbs.

"Perhaps we should start with my coat. It's rather a close fit."

"Oh, very well!" She began to drag the coat off him. Her cheeks were hot. She had never done such a thing before. "It's a very nice coat, isn't it?"

"Yes, it is." He kissed her as she tugged at it.

"Very well cut. And the fabric is very fine." She draped the coat over the back of the chair and returned to his waistcoat. "This waistcoat is very nice, too. Quite elegant. Beautifully embroidered." What *did* you say to a man when you were taking his clothes off?

"Yes, it is a nice waistcoat." He smiled at her with such a tender look in his eyes that she blushed even more.

She removed it and surveyed his shirt. It was tucked into his breeches. *His breeches.* Oh heavens! She swallowed, then grabbed fistfuls of his shirt with determined hands and began to tug.

"It's a lovely shirt, too, isn't it?" he said conversationally. "Very fine linen."

There was a thread of amusement in his voice. She looked up at him. "Are you making fun of me?"

His eyes were dancing. "Never, my love. Never." He drew her close and kissed her thoroughly. "I love your conversation when you're nervous. But indeed, I promise you, there is nothing to be nervous about."

"I'm *not* nervous," she lied as she pulled his shirttails free.

He kissed her again. "I am."

She stared. "But you've done this hundreds of times!"

He smiled ruefully. "Not like this. And never with you, my love. With you, everything is different." And in case she doubted, he repeated it again.

"Everything." It almost sounded like a promise.

She could not quite catch her breath. Emotion filled her throat. He pulled the shirt over his head and tossed it carelessly aside. He was bared to her gaze, and she could not stop looking. His skin was golden in the candlelight, shadows and angles, the shift and curve of muscles as he moved.

He was beautiful.

She reached out and touched the skin of his chest, running her fingers over the warm planes, learning his texture. She had not known men could be beautiful. A hollow ache stirred deep within her.

He kissed her fingers, bent and swiftly removed his breeches. She averted her eyes hastily, shyly, but could not resist one quick glance. He was wearing drawers underneath.

He caught her glance. "Nice linen drawers?"

Her response was halfway between a laugh and a sob. His gentle teasing dissipated the raw tension inside her as nothing else could. She shook her head helplessly.

"Come here," he said softly, and she came to him in joy. He kissed her long and deep and she kissed him back with everything that was in her heart.

His hands roamed over her, creating the most spectacular sensations through the fine linen nightgown, leaving her hot, shaky, and breathless.

She pressed against him, wanting more. His chest was lightly furred, and the texture and feel of it enchanted her. She rubbed her hands through it, wanting to feel him against her, skin to skin. Yes, that was it, what she wanted, skin to skin. She began to drag impatiently at the buttons of her nightgown. His hands joined hers, and in seconds her nightgown, too, had joined the pile of discarded clothing.

He stared at her. Feeling suddenly self-conscious, she sucked in her stomach, and her hands moved to cover her nakedness. He reached out and stopped her, saying in a deep, husky voice, "You are beautiful, my Prudence."

She stood there, his gaze warming her, dissolving her doubts. She ought to feel ashamed, standing so immodestly naked before him. Yet she didn't. She felt . . . beautiful. Proud. Desired. And a little bit exposed.

She glanced at his drawers. In seconds he had removed them, and for a moment she could only look him in the chest. Slowly, slowly, her eyes dropped, and it was her turn to stare.

Not beautiful. Magnificent.

He lifted her and carried her to the bed. Effortlessly. She felt light, fragile, feminine in a way she'd only felt once before. He'd carried her then, too.

And then they were on the bed, in each others' arms again, touching, caressing, exploring. Loving.

He was so careful of her bruises she wanted to weep. With hands that shook slightly with fiercely reined-in need, he turned her gently onto her good side and, facing her, began to work his way down her body, kissing, stroking, licking. Everywhere he touched her she felt beautiful. She touched him wherever she could, kissing, stroking, wanting to return the pleasure but barely able to think.

His hands were slow, deliberate. They skimmed, pressed, stroked. She shivered, loving every new sensation. He lightly brushed the undersides of her breasts with his fingers, in slow, aching circles, and she moved against them, her eyes clenched shut against the waves of pleasure, as if they could somehow spill out and escape.

Her skin felt paper thin, tissue thin, aching with pleasurable sensitivity. The scrape of a bristle, the firm pressure of a mouth, the slow trail of a big, warm hand across her body.

He moved higher, brushing oh-so-lightly over the upper slopes of her breasts and she arched helplessly toward him. *More . . . more . . .*

He licked one tight, aching nipple, and it was like a warm, silken bath. He lifted his mouth and the cool night air pinched at her damp, deprived flesh, sending more ripples through her. Blindly, she clutched his head and brought it back to her.

More . . .

His mouth closed, a hot possession. *Yes!* She screamed and arched almost off the bed, then opened her eyes with sharp embarrassment.

He made a sound, deep and low in his throat, and took the other breast in his mouth. The hot, driving sensation swamped her before she could say anything.

Vaguely she felt his hands seeking between her legs, and she realized he was about to take her. She tried to brace herself for what she knew would follow, but he simply covered her with his hand, cupping her, warm and soothing, so she relaxed and gave herself up to the glories his mouth was performing on her breasts.

And then his hand began to move. He stroked her lightly, his fingers just skimming, circling, pressing gently, achingly slow. Shivers of pleasure followed his every movement. Gradually the rhythmic stroking increased, still too slow, too light, tantalizing. She pressed herself against him and a long, strong finger slipped inside her and the pace and pressure of his rhythmic stroking increased.

It built, a roiling, explosive pressure within her. She moved helplessly under his caresses, pushing herself at him, around him, against him. She wanted it to stop, she wanted it never to stop . . . she wanted . . . she wanted . . .

She did not know *what* she wanted and, oh, the frustration of it was eating her alive. Devouring her. Swamping her. She gripped him harder, her limbs moving restlessly, frenziedly.

She felt his hand shift, his fingers seek and find, and she half came off the bed in surprise as a shard of pleasure splintered her, over and over. She began shuddering uncontrollably. What was happening? She halfheartedly tried to push him away, but instead her body was pushing at him, demanding, seeking, wanting . . . It was as if some force, some power beyond her will, had taken over her body. She was a fallen leaf, swirling helplessly in a whirlpool, being swept along toward a waterfall.

Then his hands moved again, and all thought was driven from her mind.

Gideon's body was taut as an arrow, trembling like a bow about to snap. He could hold back no longer. In one smooth movement he entered her. Her muscles clamped around him, and she began to move with him in a hot, primeval rhythm. He felt her climax coming. She cried out in shock, a little panicky.

"I am here love, go with it, do not fight it."

She clung to him, and he held her tight and felt her shatter all around him. His own control splintered, and he let the dark waves take him, take them both. Deep within her he felt his body explode. And all he could do was hold her and keep her with him as he, too, shattered into blessed nothingness.

It was still dark outside but a few birds were chattering in the trees surrounding the inn. It would be dawn soon. The wind had dropped. A chill was in the air.

Gideon slipped from the bed and padded across to the fireplace. Embers were still glowing dully, so he stirred them up and added first some kindling, then coal until a warm, bright blaze gilded the room once more. He did not want this night to die, for who knew what the dawn would bring. He never trusted dawn.

He slipped back under the covers and watched her sleeping. God, she was beautiful. Her pale silken skin was flushed and dewy, her glorious hair a fiery tangle of curls clustered about her face. He touched a gleaming tendril. It curled possessively around his finger. He looked at her nose and smiled. Women were funny. She hated this nose of hers, the masterful little nose she'd looked down at him so often. He loved her nose. It was perfect. He bent over and kissed it lightly.

She stirred and muttered and vaguely swatted him away.

He lay there watching her, thinking about the night they'd passed. He'd thought he knew all there was to be known about the activities of the bedchamber. He had not known it could be like that.

Like this, he thought as he watched the rise and fall as she breathed. Who would have believed that simply watching her breathe could move him so deeply? She was more precious to him than life.

He was used to loving easily . . . but loving deeply . . .

She moved. The covers shifted. In the firelight she was all cream and gold and rose and flame.

Fresh need built in him.

Her shoulder was bared, hunched against the morning chill. A beautiful shoulder, marred by an ugly bruise. He kissed the shoulder. She sighed and smiled in her sleep. She was not in pain then. He kissed the shoulder again. She moved, shifting the covers.

Breasts. Creamy, rose-tipped, and more than beautiful. He tasted them lightly. Beautiful, but not his current goal. He slid lower, kissing and nibbling his way down her body, exploring and tasting each soft, delectable curve. Sleepily, luxuriously, she arched against him, and as she stirred, he reached his goal.

He tasted salt and heat and woman. His woman. The one he hadn't known, hadn't believed existed. Who had made a man out of a sham. His mouth claimed her.

"G-Gideon?" Her voice was hesitant, surprised. A little embarrassed.

"Morning, love," he said and continued with his task. She gasped but said no more. She communicated her pleasure in squeaks and gasps and silent tremors, and with small, convulsive clutches at his hair as she melted all around him. And as he took her to her climax, she cried out, shuddering against him. The words he had once dreaded . . . and now craved to hear.

"I love you."

Prudence sighed. It was a glorious sunny morning, one of those days where it seemed the whole of England smiled. She stared out of the carriage window, staring blankly at green fields, clean, prosperous villages, rolling hills.

Gideon and she would be married, she knew.

She ought to be over the moon with happiness. She was, almost. One tiny question niggled at the back of her mind, like a sore tooth.

Did he really *want* to marry her?

He desired and cared for her, she knew that now. How could she not, after that blissful night they'd spent together? And the blissful morning.

But did he truly desire to marry her, the way she wanted to marry him? And did he love her the way she loved him?

Because he hadn't yet said it. He hadn't said the simple little words, *I love you.*

He'd spoken of "want" and "need," not love. He'd called her "love" but endearments slipped easily off his tongue.

And he still hadn't uttered those simple little words, *Will you marry me?*

Was he being noble? Was his decision to marry her another kind of rescue, an apparently blithe acceptance of his fate?

If it was, he would be kind and try not to let her see it— he was gallant that way. But she would know, eventually. To have only kindness and gallantry and duty, and not his love . . . she would rather die.

He wanted her now, she knew, could feel his eyes on her. Her body still thrilled with secret knowledge of his wanting. But he hadn't indicated it was any more than that. Want and need were wonderful, she had to admit, but they were not enough for her.

True love grew and grew. To love and be loved like that was what she'd yearned for all her life.

She had to know. She would have to ask him. But it was so difficult to ask. She sighed again.

"That's the third time you've sighed in as many minutes. What is it, my Prudence?" His voice was tender, concerned.

"I need . . . I need to ask you something."

"Oh?"

She hurried on, "It is a little difficult to ask, after such a night of . . . of blissful splendor—"

"Blissful splendor, eh?"

She felt herself blushing. "Yes. But when you asked me the other day in Lady Augusta's parlor, to . . . to live with you and be your love, what exactly what did you mean?"

He was silent, so she hurried to explain. "Oh, I know you very kindly claimed me as your fiancée when Phillip let me down so publicly. And I know you told Grandpapa I was your wife-to-be, and so I know you are obliged to—um—because I know you are truly noble at heart and will marry me to protect me. So I am not doubting your intentions."

His eyes darkened.

"But back then, in Bath, in Lady Augusta's parlor, did you actually mean to invite me to be your mistress?"

He stared at her and she squirmed slightly in embarrassment. "I'm sorry, but I do need to know. It's all right if you did . . ." It wasn't really all right, but she desperately needed to know the truth. "I just . . . need to clarify matters. In my mind. I know it will not change anything. Just, please tell me." She found she was wringing her hands, quite painfully. She stopped, folding them in a ladylike fashion in her lap.

"Have you finished, Imp?"

She looked up from her folded hands. "Y-yes."

He reached out and took her hand in his. Prudence braced herself to accept an unpalatable truth with dignity.

"Firstly, let me make one thing quite clear. I did *not* ask you to become my mistress. Whatever gave you that idea?"

"Phillip said—"

He shook his head. "I might have known. I thought all that was the past."

She bit her lip and nodded. "I know. It is. I'm sorry. And at first I did believe that you had asked me—very indirectly—to marry you. But then he pointed out you'd only spoken of protection, and said, 'Come live with me and be my love and we shall all the pleasures prove.'" Her cheeks heated again as her body remembered the previous night when he had proved pleasures beyond any imagining. "Well, I wasn't sure anymore."

He closed his eyes, put his head in his hands, and made a sound halfway between a laugh and a moan. When he opened his eyes again, they were darkly rueful. "That piece of verse, my dearest love, was not a rake asking you to be his mistress but a poor, hopeless fool desperately in love for the first and last time in his life, and making a terrible mull of his first-ever marriage proposal."

Prudence could not breathe. *My dearest love? In love for the first and last time in his life? Desperately in love?*

He shook his head and smiled apologetically. "I am not very good at proposing, you see—haven't had a lot of practice. I was desperate to win you, but it wasn't going well. I thought poetry would help." He let go of her, and ran a hand through his hair. "God help me, I thought it was romantic!"

"Oh, but it was, it is!" Prudence clutched his hands again. "I'm sorry I doubted you. It was just—"

"My regrettable past, I know. I am not a rake anymore. There is only one woman in the world for me: my Prudence."

And there, in the jolting carriage, he knelt down at her feet, took her hand in his, and said, "My dearest love, will you please say you will marry me and make me the happiest man on earth?"

"Oh, yes," she breathed. She could not see him clearly for tears. "Yes, please. Oh, I am so glad! It was so distressing to find I still had doubts, even after we, we . . . um . . ." She paused, still not having a word for what they had done together.

"Had a moment of blissful splendor?" he prompted, rising, his eyes laughing, yet tender.

"Yes, that." Filled with feelings that had to burst from her or explode, she flung herself at his chest and they fell back on the seat. She wrapped her arms around him and kissed him hard. On the mouth. On the chin. On the jaw. On the mouth again.

"I love you, Gideon. I love you so much."

"Oh Prue," he groaned, "you are my life, my love, my heart."

Oh, but he tasted good. And he felt wonderful.

Her hands, her mouth, grew greedy with pleasure and desire. She wanted more of him. "May I open your shirt?"

He grinned. "You may open anything you wish."

"It is just that I wish to touch more of you; you feel so very nice," she explained as she tugged his shirt open.

"So do you, love." He reached for her but she stopped him.

"Not yet. This is my turn. Sit still, please."

He sat back, his eyes dancing. "Bossy little creature, aren't you?"

Her hands roamed over him, learning him, delighting in his differences, the hard angled muscles of his body, the rough friction of hair where she was smooth, the powerful strength of him where she was soft.

Remembering what he had done to her, she licked his skin, tentatively at first. She ran his taste around in her mouth, savoring it. So this was the taste of love. A little salty, a little tangy and dangerous, yet with an underlying rightness. His chest was all firm planes, lightly sprinkled with dark hair, wonderfully abrasive. She spotted a tiny disk of raised, dusky skin; like her in a way, and yet so very unlike. Remembering how exquisitely pleasurable it had been when he took her nipple into his mouth, she touched her tongue to it and licked. He moaned with pleasure.

It was a most satisfactory sound. She felt filled with feminine power. She moved to the other nipple and repeated the process, licking and sucking. Beneath her she felt his arousal thrusting against her. What a shame they would have to wait. She rubbed her body against him and he groaned again.

"You're killing me, Prue."

"Mmm," she purred against his chest. She licked his nipple once more, then bit him there lightly, experimentally. His body bucked beneath her, and all his restraint dissolved.

His mouth took hers, his hands caressed her feverishly, running down her back, her sides, her buttocks. Each time he shook and arched against her, an echoing response rippled through her, and a growing tension and a kind of aching hollowness intensified deep within her. And he had taught her last night, and again this morning, what that had meant. She felt her skirts being pushed higher.

"Gideon? In a carriage?"

"Yes, love, in a carriage."

Prudence smiled to herself. She had a lot to learn, she could see. She would not have to wait for the shift and glide of his body deep within hers. How quickly it had become familiar. No, not familiar—necessary. She craved it, craved his touch, craved their joining. With eager hands she unbuttoned his breeches. No nervous conversation this time. Softly, tentatively, she reached out to touch him. He groaned with pleasure and pushed against her hand. With growing confidence she explored him, explored his heat and power, silk over steel.

He moaned, and without warning lifted her to settle over his lap. He still amazed her with his ability to lift her as if she weighed nothing at all. But then she forgot to think anything at all, as gently, surely, he guided her to where she wanted him to be. He lowered her onto him and showed her how to move.

Rhythm. Power. Passion. Possession.

She flung back her head and let it engulf her . . .

"Dereham always was a dreary, joyless creature, but this is appalling, even for him." Lady Augusta hugged Prudence yet again. She'd done it frequently since Prudence and Gideon had arrived home several days before. "But you're safe and sound now with those who love you."

Prudence hugged her back, unable to say a word. She'd

come a long way since the gray days at Dereham Court. Her world was brimming with love. She was surrounded by it, filled with it, incandescent with it. In truth she had almost forgotten the terrible trip with Grandpapa. It was days ago now. Blissful days, awash with love and stolen moments of ecstasy. Gideon loved her. She was going to marry him.

"Bats in the belfry!" Great-uncle Oswald announced. He had arrived from Norfolk a few minutes before. They were all gathered in the front room at Lady Augusta's house. He shook his head. "Goes to show!"

Prudence and Gideon looked at each other blankly. "I don't follow you, Sir Oswald," Gideon said.

"Rats in the attic!" he explained. Then, when they still looked blank, he said, "My brother, Theodore. Talkin' all sorts o' rubbish. Ravin' on and on about Prudence and the others! Mixin' Prudence up with her mother." He shook his head again.

"He hated my mother," Prudence commented. "He blamed her for enticing my father away from Dereham Court, never to return."

Great-uncle Oswald snorted. "Your mother had nothin' to do with it. Your father left the Court for the same reason I did: because Theodore was such a demmed impossible swine to live with!"

There was a short silence.

"You're all thinkin' I should never have let him take charge of five little gels, and you're right." He mopped his forehead with a handkerchief. "Thing is, he was a difficult fellow to get along with then, but it was a natural difference of opinion. I couldn't stand havin' m'brother lordin' it over me as if he were my father. He got worse over time. Losin' your father—his sole heir—put him in a rage for years." He looked at them ruefully. "Maybe that's when he started to go peculiar. Maybe the rats have been gnawin' at his upper stories all this time."

"You mean you think he is insane?" asked Gideon bluntly.

Great-uncle Oswald nodded. "That's the word with no bark on it. Thought he was a little unbalanced when I saw him in London, but he's always hated being thwarted.

Now—" He grimaced. "Ravin' on about Prudence. Threatening to kill her. Swearin' about her breedin' bastards—forgive the language, m'dear." He turned to Gideon. "He's even carryin' on about Prudence putting him in debtors' prison, for heaven's sake, and if anyone's to blame for that, it's himself!"

"Yes, he mentioned debtors' prison," Prudence said. "I don't understand."

Great-uncle Oswald looked grave. "No easy way to put this, so I'll just spit it out. It seems he's embezzled your fortune, Prue—your sisters', too. That's why he kidnapped you. With your twenty-first birthday next week, and you assumin' guardianship of your sisters, Theodore thought if he locked you away, he'd get 'em all back and nobody would find out!"

Prudence started. "You mean we have no money? My sisters and I are—"

"Calm down, missy. You'll have your inheritance. I'll sort it all out and put everythin' back in place, never you fret. Everything invested in the funds, safe and sound, and a little more besides."

"Oh, but you cannot be expected to—"

"Pish, tosh!" He waved his hand in airy dismissal of her objections. "You gels will inherit my fortune when I pop off, so what's the difference? Besides, I've got a lot to make up for, leavin' you with Theodore all these years. I ought to have kept a closer eye on you, but I didn't, and I'll have to live with the guilt of that. I can't make it up to you, but I can do this, at least, so no argument, missy." He blew his nose again, a long, definitive blast.

Lady Augusta put the question in all their minds. "So what will happen now?"

Great-uncle Oswald sighed. "I'll not put my brother in Bedlam for all the world to gawk at, but I've got him safely locked away at Dereham. Get some reliable staff in to take care of him. A Dr. Gibson has agreed to oversee the matter." He looked around the small gathering and said, "Well, I can't have him wanderin' loose, the way he's behavin'. He'll kill someone! He's stark-starin' mad, m'dears." He paused, looked at his nails, and added casually, "Why, you wouldn't believe what Theodore did to young Clotterbury when he came callin'."

"Otterbury called on him!" exclaimed Gideon. "Whatever for?"

Great-uncle Oswald shrugged. "Seemed to think Theodore owed him somethin' for tellin' him that Prudence and the gels were in Bath."

There was an outbreak of indignation at this.

"I hope you showed the vile little tick the door," exclaimed Lady Augusta hotly.

"Oh, no," Great-uncle Oswald said innocently. "I agreed with him. He *was* owed somethin'."

"Oswald! How could you?" Lady Augusta exclaimed in disgust.

"So I showed him in to see Theodore." He buffed one nail carefully with a tiny chamois buffer and added, "And locked the door, of course. Can't let m'brother roam free, y'know."

"What happened?"

"Oh, well, there was a lot of shoutin' and bangin' and crashin' around, but I'm not the sort of fellow who listens at doors. Manners, you know. I came back, half an hour later, thinkin' they'd finished the interview, and when I opened the door—the most peculiar thing! Young Clotterbury had got himself all dirtied up. Shockin', the state he was in. Bleedin' from the nose—I fancy Theodore broke it for him—and one of his ears looked bitten. Most odd! He'd lost a tooth or two, and the rest of him was black and blue. His natty outfit was in shreds, too, positive shreds. And all the buttons ripped off." He shook his head in sorrow. "Beautiful clothes they were, too. Must have cost him a pretty penny. And Theodore ruined them. Clotterbury staggered out of there and scuttled off home, lookin like somethin' the cat coughed up." He gave them all a smile of wicked innocence. "Got his reward, didn't he? Never let it be said that a Merridew didn't pay his debts."

Gideon gave a crack of laughter and hugged Prudence.

Lady Augusta clapped her hands. "Excellent work, Oswald. I, too, have taken young Otterbury's future in hand. Maudie's friends are his employers, you know, and we've arranged a nice posting for him. A small island in the southern hemisphere, rather distant, but delightfully peaceful. Supervising sheep, I believe. Sadly, his wife and child-to-come won't be able to accompany him . . . I'm told the island is hideously wind-blasted . . ."

There was another outbreak of laughter.

Lady Augusta nodded in satisfaction. "Now, enough about those dreary men. Oswald, we have a wedding to plan!"

To Prudence's surprise, Great-uncle Oswald just stared at Lady Augusta and blushed. "Oh, Gussie."

To Gideon's amazement Aunt Gussie blushed, also. She said testily, "I meant these children here, Oswald! Prudence and Gideon! Their wedding, not . . . any other one."

"Oh, oh, yes, of course," Great-uncle Oswald agreed. But he did not stop gazing at Lady Augusta. And Lady Augusta's blush didn't go away for the longest time.

Prudence looked at Gideon, her eyes wide. Great-uncle Oswald and Lady Augusta? He grinned, winked, and lifted her hand to kiss it.

Sir Oswald cleared his throat. "St. George's, Hanover Square, I trust."

Gideon looked at Prudence, a question in his eyes. "Wherever you want, my love."

Prudence smiled back. "Bath Abbey, a week from today—if we can get word to Charity and Edward. I would like them there with us."

"Does nobody wish to get married in St. George's?" grumbled Sir Oswald. He darted a look at Lady Augusta.

She colored up again but addressed herself to Prudence and Gideon. "And where do you plan to take Prudence for her bride trip, nephew?"

Gideon looked down at his bride and grinned. "Into Italy, of course."

Prudence gasped. "Italy?" was all she could say. She hugged his arm and gave him a wavering, brilliant smile, knowing her eyes were filling again. "Italy."

"But why Italy?" asked Lady Augusta, amid general exclamations of excitement.

Gideon sighed, theatrically. "It seems I must instantly

flee the country. My tailor is pursuing me because of certain bills someone impetuously dashed into the fire."

Later that afternoon, Gideon and Prudence were ensconced in the cozy back parlor at Lady Augusta's. He was sprawled, loose-limbed, on the sofa; she was snuggled next to him. A fire crackled in the grate. Outside, wind and sleet pelted the windows.

Gideon said, "You know, Imp, looking back, I have idled away the years and wasted myself in folly. And all to no purpose."

"What do you mean no purpose? Can there be purpose to idleness and folly?"

"Oh, there can, indeed. In the shallow life I adopted, I was trying to avoid love. I thought it a weakness, you see, a point of extreme vulnerability. I thought love killed my father. But I was wrong. It wasn't love that caused him to kill himself—it was loss of love."

Prudence took his hands in hers and said passionately, "No, he was wrong. He may have lost your mother, but he had you, his son, to love and to love him back. If he had thought of you, instead of himself, he would have remembered that love. And it would have healed him. Even when no one loves you, there is *always* someone to love, someone who needs to be loved. Always. You just have to look outside yourself."

"As I did." He kissed her tenderly. "And I saw you, sitting on the edge of an Egyptian chair, scared stiff, clutching that ugly, great reticule, and I fell in love. And then you defended me from your great-uncle, and I fell even more deeply, in a way I never believed possible."

"I did, too, though I fought it for the longest time," she said shyly. "I thought it was your rakish wiles I couldn't resist, but it was you, just you. I love you, Gideon, more than even I believed possible."

His grip tightened around her. "And I love you. I'll never let you go, Prudence, never. If you ever run away from me, I'll want to come with you."

Nestled within his arms, she hugged him back. "Good, I would insist upon it, anyway. I never believed Mama's promise would come true for me, but it has. Sunshine and laughter and love and happiness." She laid her face against his throat. "And see, it has all come true."

"All of it? What about the sunshine?" Gideon looked out at the gray sleet still hammering against the windows as it had for the last hour and then down at the bright head of the woman in his arms. She looked up at him and smiled.

"Ah, yes," he said softly. "I can see the sunshine now."

Enter the rich world of *historical romance* with Berkley Books.

Lynn Kurland

Patricia Potter

Betina Krahn

Jodi Thomas

Anne Gracie

Love is timeless.

penguin.com

M9G0907